A LAND WITHOUT SIN

A LAND WITHOUT SIN

A NOVEL

Paula Huston

SLANT

A LAND WITHOUT SIN
A Novel

Slant
An Imprint of Wipf and Stock Publishers
199 W. 8th Ave., Suite 3
Eugene, OR 97401

www.wipfandstock.com

ISBN 13: 978-1-62032-658-9

Cataloging-in-Publication data:

Huston, Paula.

A land without sin : a novel / Paula Huston.

vi + 306 p.; 23 cm.

ISBN 13: 978-1-62032-658-9

1. Mexico — Fiction. 2. Clergy — Fiction. 3. Catholics — Fiction. I. Title.

PZ3 2013

Manufactured in the USA.

Though many of the historical events described in this story actually happened, I have used this history for my own fictional purposes. When episodes in this book do not match up with historical fact, that is the reason. At times I have taken novelistic liberties with real historical figures. The main characters in this novel are all fictitious, however, and any resemblance to persons living or dead is purely coincidental and most definitely unintended.

This novel is dedicated to Mike, beloved husband,
best friend, and fellow pilgrim.

Chapter One

Tikal, Guatemala, 1993

I was looking for my brother. Whether or not Stefan even wanted to be found, I did not know. By now he could be the neo-Che of the Lacandon jungle, or lying in his own filth in a Chiapan jail, or even dead. Because of the way our family is, we'd only been in the same country at the same time on a very sporadic basis for the past sixteen years, the most recent occasion being his priestly ordination, so it was hard to say what was going on with him. But I was ready for anything.

In my clothes were sewn a false passport bearing a two-year-old photo of him, the best I could do, and a one-way ticket out of Mexico, in case we had to scramble. And because I didn't know whose list he might be on, I had a fake passport of my own, one of several made for me when I dated a USIA man stationed in Burma. This USIA man's theory was that no American female could be overly prepared for extended stays in international hotspots, and since it looked like that's where I would be spending most of my time, I took him up on his offer. A helpful fellow indeed, he also taught me how to throw a knife, a handy trick he no doubt picked up in CIA school, even though he would never admit he'd been.

Besides the false passport, I had a false job, thanks to a fellow freelancer I first met back when I was still schlepping my cameras through war zones on behalf of the Associated Press. I bumped into Dirk a month ago in Burundi right about the time I heard about Stefan's disappearance. Dirk told me that a Mayanist named Bource was looking for a good photographer who was used to roughing it and used to the jungle and didn't care about making campesino wages for the next couple of months. Given the annual income of most freelancers, this could have been almost anyone—under normal circumstances, it would have certainly been Dirk, who would go anywhere, anytime, as long as there was a good chance of dying in a heroic manner and/or securing himself a book contract with a major publisher. But Dirk was getting married, a recent trend among my footloose cronies. "I'm thirty-eight," he said, as though that would explain it. However, thanks to Dirk's new direction in life, I now had my cover and an airtight excuse for snooping around in Central America, where I had not been for nearly ten years and which I had not missed in the slightest.

My false boss for the false job, Bource, turned out to be a bespectacled, formerly-handsome Dutchman in a red baseball cap who asked me, in a gloomy, preoccupied way, to please call him Jan. He, of course, did not know he was helping me in my scam, and clearly was not the kind of man who would understand the need for duplicity. He'd told me to meet him in Guatemala, in the island town of Flores, which was not exactly where I needed to be. But we were at least pointed in the right direction, and I could afford to be patient.

Jan's son Rikki, a mere sixteen but already, I noticed, a stunning young pre-man, was extremely efficient and not at all gloomy, and the family truck, as his father had requested, was loaded and ready to roll at 3:30 that afternoon. We were headed for Tikal, perhaps the only Maya site in Guatemala with 100 percent name recognition, though I myself, being more focused on current events than dead civilizations, had always vaguely supposed it to be in Honduras. I'd been set straight on this by my Aviateca Airlines seatmate, a bearded Berkeley rainforest savior headed for the Biosphere Reserve, and his lecture pretty much covered my knowledge of the Mayas.

I spent the hour before we left doing a final check on all my photography equipment. Though I still had only the haziest notion of what my new job would entail—Jan had been stubbornly close-lipped about it—over the years, I'd learned what you should haul into the jungle if you were going to be there for a while. For instance, you never foray into boonies of any kind without your spare camera; in my case, that means hauling a second Canon EOS-1. Besides the two cameras, I had packed a tripod and a tiny can of WD-40, plus silica gel to protect the film from jungle rot.

Next, I pulled out my lenses. For an unsentimental person, I have a strangely passionate relationship with my lenses. First, there's my workhorse, the 50mm macro for up-close work. Some of my best photographs over the years have been headshots, particularly of children, particularly in dire circumstances. I'm drawn to those faces. Somehow we click, those skinny kids with the big, sad eyes and me. Which is maybe why my one and only award of any consequence was for a shot of a baffled Afghan toddler—two, maybe?—standing in front of a just-bombed, still-burning house.

But I don't confine myself to close-ups. There's also my beloved f2.8 Ultrasonic, a slick 300mm lens for distance work, at which I'm not bad. I've found that if you're willing to plant yourself in front of a scene, foregoing any fussy instincts to "arrange" the elements to suit yourself or other people, things turn up in the darkroom later you could swear weren't there during the shoot.

Last, I dragged out my two trusty zooms, the 28-105 and the 100-300 Ultrasonic, which is great for daytime photography. Based on the infinitesimal amount of information gleaned from my taciturn boss, I didn't know how much of that there would be—outside daytime work—but the circular polarizing filter went into the pack anyway. Taking photographs at the equator is tricky business. The humidity level is so high that you might as well be shooting through fog, and that problem gets amplified by a persistent, jungly sun-glare that turns the sky silver; the polarizing filter is just about your only recourse here. Another reason to add my Minolta 4F strobe meter to the pack, which is good, I've found through years of jerry-rigging in the jungle, for measuring ambient light.

Light was actually going to be the biggest problem. One of the few things Jan let slip was that a lot of the shooting would be in the dark, either night shots of carved inscriptions, where raking lights could be used to bring the glyphs into sharper relief, or inside the pyramids themselves. I'd done some of this during a project involving Thai temples, my one major credit and a plum that would probably not fall out of the tree again, thanks to the precipitous end of my relationship with Robert, professional adventurer, poetic genius, photographer extraordinaire, and, as it turned out, major jerk.

One thing was clear: this gig with Jan and company was not going to be a big *National Geographic*–style operation like only Robert or someone of his ilk has the clout to command, with porters along to carry light stands and strobe lights and generators. We couldn't even take Jan's truck all the way in to where we were going. Three big packs was all we could handle. For a minute, I allowed myself to muse wistfully: a Norman 200 strobe setup would be just about perfect—we'd used them in Thailand—but then we'd have to have electricity, which last time I checked, didn't exist inside most crumbling Guatemalan temples. Instead, Jan could provide me with a single rickety light stand, some quantum battery packs for off-camera flashes, and a couple of big lanterns. That would have to do.

In my obsessive little way, I also checked over my art supplies, though it was doubtful they could be replenished in Flores or even in nearby San Benito if something were missing. There were plenty of good drawing pencils, a graphite stick, and fine-tip pens, plus extra ink. Hauling loose drawing paper in a backpack is a recipe for disaster; I had found that out the hard way years ago. So I'd decided on a couple of ringed sketchbooks with 90 lb paper in them, which I put inside plastic bags to protect them from molding. On a whim, I'd also brought along rice paper and Conté crayons, though rubbings would no doubt be tough, given the depth of the carvings.

At 3:30 sharp, we drove the loaded truck off the island and onto the earthen causeway that crosses the lapping lake water, bouncing past the Santa Elena airport and onto the highway to Tikal, the only asphalt, Rikki informed me, in the whole Petén. I'd already noticed that Rikki did at least 85 percent of the talking.

Riding around in remote places with strange men was something I was used to, and in spite of the big question mark concerning my brother, I could feel myself getting primed for a new adventure. I knew a dog once who ran like a racehorse, tongue streaming back, black ears flying, and could run like that for hours and then go unconscious for half a day in the sun, twitching and dreaming, and wake up and start running again. There was nothing this dog was running toward, nothing it was trying to catch. Running was it, pure and simple. That was me at the start of something new.

We drove for perhaps an hour. A big stretch of scenery was taken up by a sluggish-looking military outpost, the jumping-off point, Rikki said, for raids against Tikal-based guerrillas during the eighties. My ears pricked up. Though I'd been in Guatemala during those days, I hadn't been in this part of the country. Guerrillas were of vital importance to the Stefan question. I wanted to ask Rikki more, specifically if he knew what was happening on the Chiapan guerrilla front, but thought it prudent to shelve the interrogation about southern Mexico until his father was out of earshot. In fact, Jan was probably an empty well anyway. Men like him tended to avoid politics completely. In every messed-up country I've ever been there are the Jans—foreigners not connected with the government or business or humanitarian projects, scholarly oddballs who meander right through the middle of battle-fields and whose sole reason for being is tied up in what has become of the pink river dolphins or whether Australopithecines ate more meat or vegetables.

We stopped briefly at the entrance to the park while Jan checked in at a guardhouse, then took a narrow dirt road that veered away from the groups of straggling tourists heading toward the Great Plaza of Ti-kal and went straight into heavy forest where we clattered along for some time seeing nothing but trees. Rikki explained that this was a guard road that would get us a couple of miles closer to where we were going, but that the last part would be a hike. Ahead on both sides was nothing but green.

After a while, the ribbon of brown ahead of us began to narrow and

then, abruptly, vanished. Jan nosed the truck between two magnificent
ceiba trees and turned off the engine. The windows of the truck were
open to the screechings and strange cries and hollow boomings of the
jungle, noises that reminded me of lush and deadly Burundi. Above
everything else was the crashing in the trees that signaled monkeys were
moving in. Something orange and yellow flashed in front of the windshield and landed on a branch not far off the ground—a black toucan
with his brilliant beak. Jan opened the truck door.

The pack was heavy but all right. Once upon a time, I'd been lost
in a rainforest and was not hot to repeat the experience, so on the trail
I stuck close to Rikki. It was strange to think that several hundred
tourists were climbing pyramids only a mile or two away and we could
neither hear nor see them. In spite of the weird airlessness you get in
jungles, the climate wasn't so bad. I'd expected to sweat—I remembered sweating a lot when I'd been in Guatemala before, though maybe
that had just been nerves—but instead there was a pleasant balminess
I was immediately grateful for. Jan handed me a water bottle. As I was
upending it into my mouth, it began to rain, just a dripping at first, as
though it were coming straight from the trees, and then a more serious
thrumming that signaled a downpour on its way. He motioned, and
the three of us huddled together beneath a tall shrub with six-foot brilliant green leaves that ended in fringes.

"Look," said Rikki, crouching. I squatted beside him and in the
dim, rainy light saw a weaving line of leaves marching steadily off into
the forest. Leafcutter ants, large but dwarfed by the pieces of leaves they
carried, which were at least five times their size.

Jan was not interested in the ants. He said in his prim Nederlander
way, "There is a small temple where we are going. If it keeps raining,
we can sleep inside."

"So put on the ponchos?" said Rikki.

"Yes."

We each dug into our packs and draped ourselves in khaki rain gear,
then hoisted everything back on our shoulders and went out onto the
trail. Ten minutes later the sun broke through and steam began rising

from the forest floor, and after another ten minutes Rikki said, "Can we stop? I'm dying inside this poncho," which of course I was also, but not about to admit it. Jan looked back at the two of us and just then a shaft of weak sunlight caught him right across his Dutch face, and I saw him old in the way you sometimes see people on film when you are developing it and realize you have seen the future. There's an age one has to be for this to happen and it's not my age, not yet, but sometime within the next six years.

In spite of what my extensive preparations for this trip might suggest, I was not actually terribly worried about Stefan yet. We'd been out of touch more than we'd been in it—my fault, mostly—and for a long time, if we communicated at all, we went through Jonah. Jonah, no doubt voted "least likely to become a monk" in his high school yearbook, was indeed a monk, based at a Camaldolese Benedictine hermitage in California ("Camaldolese" equaling "reasonable hermits who live under a rule," he once told me, laughing). This was where Stefan in his late twenties, no longer seeking enlightenment in Nepal, no longer hammering away in grad school, spent three apparently fruitful Big Sur years. Fruitful, in the sense that he seemed to have finally figured out what he was going to do with his life and why he was going to do it, though I couldn't in a million years grasp his logic. As a monk, Jonah was unable to change addresses whenever he felt like it. Thus, he provided us a convenient mailbox.

Over the past several years Stefan had sent a series of slightly disturbing letters to Jonah, intermixed with a couple of red herring versions of the same thing to me, then several somewhat more disturbing ones to Jonah, and then silence. This silence had gone on for only eleven weeks so far and probably meant nothing, given the fact that Stefan and I share the same penchant for secrecy and independence, not to mention how long the gaps between letters usually were. But Jonah, who for a monk is quite the worrywart, was by definition trapped and helpless to go check things out on his own. He had put a call through to the diocese in southern Mexico where Stefan was stationed, only to discover that no one had anything to say about my brother's whereabouts. Stefan was not there, but as far as they were concerned, he was not missing either. When I made my own call, I ran into the same stone wall. This, I found irritating. Though as I say, I wasn't yet particularly worried about Stefan, I didn't like their attitude, and told Jonah I'd make the trip if I could set it up.

Now I was here, or at least in the country next door, and it came to mind that there was a fairly major difference between my brother and me that might be important to consider. This was Stefan's rather weak attachment to earthly life. He liked it well enough, but didn't cling, not enough to make him a fighter, anyway. He was much more passive in that way than I was, which used to drive me crazy when we were kids and probably explains why, for his own good, I was always trying to boss him around even though he was four years older than me.

For passive, I am not. Soon after the Thai temple project, when Robert and I still liked each other well enough to sign on for another joint adventure, he convinced me to go to Cambodia to help him snoop around the former killing fields. Something he needed for a new book project, he said, and I, with all my vaccinations up to date and realizing I'd grown a lot fonder of him than I'd been of anybody in a long time, said sure. We had the teamwork thing down cold. We understood each other's vision, which meant we could help each other take better pictures. And he was bright and sexy and made me laugh. So Cambodia felt like an investment, the kind I'd never been willing to make before.

Not for long, though. We spent a couple of nights in town prior to heading for the refugee camps, just to plan things out, and somewhere in the middle of that, Robert showed his cards. Our hotel was your typical tiny equatorial affair, heavily reliant on bamboo. I remember there was an enormous spider plastered to the outside of the window screen. Robert, wearing nothing but his boxers and his handsome skin, was propped up in bed on one elbow observing me with his connoisseur's eye, which had put me into full basking mode. And then he said, apropos of nothing, "If you had a knife and you woke up and some guy was in your sleeping bag with you, would you stick him?"

"This person isn't you?" I asked, still clueless.

He shook his head. "Some guy. You don't know him."

"Well, sure," I said. "Of course."

He shook his head and gave me his famous wry smile. "Wow."

"Wouldn't you?"

"No guy's going to crawl in with me, baby. How about this? You've got a gun and you're out in the boonies and some guy is stealing your pack with all your food and chances are good you won't get out alive without it. But you know he's hungry and he's got a family to feed."

"But I'll die if he takes my food?"

"Right."

"I'd shoot him."

He stared at me admiringly and shook his head again. "If he's begging for mercy?"

"If he gives the food back, okay. Otherwise, it's him or me."

"This is so wild. This is exactly what I thought you'd say."

"Really." I was beginning to pick up the tone here, one I recognized through hard experience, though this was the first time I'd ever heard it coming out of Robert.

"How about if the guy who's taking your food is me? We've been lost for three weeks and we're out of everything except toothpaste and four crackers and suddenly I snap and grab for the pack and you've got a gun . . ."

"What's going on here?"

"Just wondering, is all."

"What do you think I'd do?"

"I hate to say, really." He peered into my face. He was still grinning, but I was not. "Oh, come on now, Eva, lighten up. This is just a . . . what do you call it? Party game? Something to pass the time."

I stared back at him. "I wasn't bored. Were you? Is this relationship starting to bore you?"

His eyes shifted then, and he reeled in the little cruel streak I hadn't known was there. Until, of course, we got safely out of the country and then it was, as I already figured it would be, goodbye dear Eva and best of luck and it's been truly grand and I'll never forget you, which naturally he did the second the next decent-looking female dove into view. But I'd told him the truth. I'd shoot. Because obviously—he'd just proved it—if I didn't take care of myself, who would?

I could not, however, say what Stefan would do if his life were similarly threatened, and that made everything more uncertain. If he were being held captive, for example, would he even try to make a break for it? Or, good Catholic boy that he was, would he be unable to resist the call to martyrdom?

Chapter Two

Jan and Rikki and I had come upon something that looked like a small hill covered in shrubs and tree roots but that turned out to be a temple in disguise and the apparent object of our soggy hike. Rikki and I set up camp while our leader went somewhere with his high-powered battery lantern and didn't come back for nearly an hour. "What's he doing?" I asked Rikki, who said, "He's checking things out inside the temple."

"So we'll be at it tonight already?"

He nodded. "My dad has been planning this for a long time."

"What's he up to? Do you know?"

He started to say something, then stopped. He didn't shake his head, didn't lie, just stopped.

"Sorry," I said. "I forgot it was a big secret."

"Not really a big secret," he said. "But he can't take a chance of it getting out there. He's got his reputation to protect."

That sounded like a direct quote. In fact, Jan had been quite adamant about the conditions of my employment. I was hired for three months, no more, and this was a private project, paid for out of his own pocket. I must agree not to discuss our work with anyone, nor could I sell any of my photographs or drawings afterward. My glum boss was up to something potentially ludicrous, it sounded like, or maybe even illegal. And I was making almost nothing in the way of quetzales for the privilege of sharing this adventure. "Are there snakes in that temple?"

"Víboras. Sí. Maybe."

I saw a porter get bitten once, by some kind of viper. We had been in a place where there were no doctors for two hundred miles and only one functioning jeep. I don't like snakes.

Pretty soon Jan came back, silent as ever but with a hot little glow behind his glasses, and I could tell that whatever he was hoping to get on film was still there exactly as he remembered it, and tonight I would find out what it was. But first there was dinner to cook—a pot of beans and rice—and some fluffing up of the nest (I like a cozy tent) and then sitting by the cook fire for a bit while the sun started its long slide into the trees.

An hour later, Rikki and I were standing in front of the passageway, loaded up like pack mules with my equipment, waiting for Jan to set up a light inside the chamber. This was not one of those strange steep Tikal pyramids like the ones in the rainforest savior's guidebook, but something much smaller and flatter that we were able to enter near ground level through a stone doorway that looked like an open mouth. "It *is* a mouth," Rikki explained when I asked. "The mouth of a Witz monster. It takes you into what they called Xibalba, the Underworld."

I raised my eyebrows.

"The land of the dead," he added helpfully.

"Why is the temple so small? Aren't they usually much bigger?" Straight out of the guidebook, but Rikki didn't know the difference.

"This is an older section of the city," he said. "It was probably built around 50 B.C., seven hundred years or so before the big pyramids were put up. Lots of times, they just built right over the old ones, but this one must have been in the wrong spot."

Just then Jan called out that we should come in, and we shuffle-crouched down a long passageway filled with rubble, a perfect hideout for víboras, to a tiny room with a low stone bench at the back. Beneath the bench was an open shallow pit. Even in the dubious light from the big battery-powered lanterns, traces of red on the walls made it clear that this room had once been plastered and painted.

Jan seemed to know exactly what he wanted to do, though I could not figure out what he thought was worth photographing. The room seemed entirely empty except for the bench. He spent some time arranging the two lights in different ways, then beckoned. I went and stood beside him. He pointed to the faintest traces of something black on the wall behind the bench. If this keeps up, I thought, we might actually get through the entire three months in sign language. I moved closer, squinting, and made out what looked like a hieroglyph, the merest squiggle.

"Can you photograph this?" he asked me.

"I don't know if I can pick anything up." I hated saying that—photographers never admit defeat—but it was true. The lines of the glyph were so faded I could hardly see them with my eyes.

"Try," he said. "Take as many photographs as you need. Try everything you can think of." He was leaning in close to the wall beside me and his arm brushed mine. I remembered that sensation—someone's tensed muscles coming into sudden contact with my skin—from sitting on the couch beside Bruno, aka my father, watching boxing when I was a kid. Bruno looked upon boxing as a blood sport, especially when it pitted a noble white guy—i.e., Rocky Marciano, Ingemar Johansson—against one of those "black kopiles," as he called them, sad that I'd been born too late to witness Marciano's glory days. My father was not exactly with the times, especially when it came to race relations in our fair city of Chicago. Back then, he had the massive forearms of the steelworker he was, and when, at six, seven, eight years old, I felt one of them brush up against mine, I always got a disorienting jolt.

No jolt this time, however, or at least not a nasty one. Jan's forearm was tense but radiated a pleasant warmth, the likes of which I had not experienced since abandoning co-ed tent life after Cambodia. Well, well, I thought, glancing down at the corded muscles, the bone-deep jungle tan under its gray pelt. Then I went back to squinting at my hieroglyphic quarry. Without actually touching the wall, I ran my fingers lightly above the painted area. Sure enough, there was a slight bulge in the plaster, just enough to bring out the glyph a little, which meant a light held to one side would cast a bit of a shadow, which we didn't need.

"Rikki, come here," I said. "Try holding your light this way." Rikki trotted over and I stood him behind me and made him hold the light square on the glyph in a line directly above my head. Since height-wise he had me by at least six inches, the plan worked out nicely. "Okay," I said. "Can you steady that without the light stand? If you can, I'm going to use the stand for an off-camera flash."

Jan said, "Rikki can balance the lantern against my shoulder." So that was how we did it: the tripod up as high as it would go, me on tiptoe sighting, Jan breathing down my neck, and Rikki pressed up against his father, stabilizing the light.

After a while, I switched over to pencil and sketchbook and attempted to draw what I could hardly see, though once I began, the shape unfolded fairly naturally. It was a single glyph, quite simple, that looked like a four-petaled flower inside of a squarish double oval. At the bottom, below the oval, was a group of painted streamers, blown sideways. I made four different drawings, a close-up of the glyph on its own and then in context, holding them up silently for Jan's approval and getting a thumbs-up each time.

It was clear that this particular tomb had already been stripped, either by robbers or archeologists. My boss himself was the most likely candidate—how else would he know about the glyph? Then I felt someone watching me and turned to meet Jan's blue stare. He'd noticed me speculating away, exactly what he'd hired me not to do. "Quite a place," I said. "Never been in one of these before." I shook my head like an admiring tourist and added a heartfelt "wow." He narrowed his gaze, then turned abruptly toward the passageway. Rikki and I fell in line like two ducks behind him.

Night in the jungle is like nothing else on earth. The darkness is absolute and has an underwater texture to it, as though you are flutter-kicking through it in a wetsuit, with limited air. The forest sways—a moving kelp bed of trees, insects, nocturnal creatures hunting for food—and the ground swells and sinks, an oceanic illusion of tides and the rising backs of whales. I lay awake in my sleeping bag, listening to the sea-surge of the jungle, and thought about Stefan.

Before I got on the plane to Guatemala, Jonah gave me all his letters, hoping they would help me contact the people I needed to find in Chiapas. It was strange to read the words my brother had written to someone else, someone who not only understood his singular worldview but shared it. I knew the child version of Stefan well, better than I've ever known another living being. We were best friends back then, true compadres, the only people either of us could trust. But since we'd grown up and became who we were, we had found ourselves on totally different roads, and I could no longer predict what he would do or why.

In the morning, after café and scrambled huevos, Rikki and I were told we had the day off. After all the hustling, this was a surprise. "I need some time to plan," Jan explained. These were the first words of the day for him, except for whatever he had muttered when the spatula turned up missing. The repressed intensity he'd revealed inside the tomb was gone; once again, he was sunk in contemplation.

"When do you want us back?" asked Rikki.

"Four," he said. "We'll be hiking in to the North Acropolis after dark."

"I didn't know. . ." Rikki began, then snapped shut. They certainly weren't very subtle about hiding things. He gave me an apologetic look and said, "Would you like to see the park?"

An hour later, Rikki and I were standing in the Great Plaza of Tikal. I'd seen pictures, but nothing one-dimensional could come close. The limestone pyramids, black with mold and scraped-off jungle, were so steep their faces looked vertical. Their crumbled roof combs, like broken molars, jutted into the sky high above the trees. Straight up the front of each were wide stairways made of slick and dangerous-looking steps. Rikki gestured toward the only one not swarming with people. "That's Temple I," he said. "The tomb of Ah-Cacaw. They've had it blocked off since the early eighties when a tourist fell a hundred fifty feet and killed himself."

"Who was Ah-Cacaw?"

"You've never heard of Ah-Cacaw?" He sounded amazed.

"Obviously not."

"Sorry." He really was sorry, his face flushed with pity for my igno-rance. "He was the king who brought the city back to life when it had been under the thumb of Caracol for over six k'atuns." He checked my face, and added humbly, "That's a hundred and twenty years. Caracol was a rival lowland kingdom like Uaxactún. You do know about the Maya wars?"

"Not really. I knew they were good at math. And I vaguely remem-ber from fourth grade that they were supposed to be the peaceful ones as opposed to the bloody Aztecs."

"That's what everybody thought for a long time, until they started translating the inscriptions. Now we know they were a major warrior society and fought each other all the time, at first to get sacrifice vic-tims, and then to build empires." He pointed at a complex of smaller pyramids, some of them encased in scaffolding. "That's the North Acropolis, where we'll be working tonight. It's got layers of older stuff under it. Along with building these two big central pyramids, Ah-Ca-caw reworked the whole Acropolis after it had been damaged by Lord Water, the king of Caracol, in the siege of the 500s."

Just then the sun, which had been hiding most of the morning be-hind a cottony sky made up of jungle steam and carbon dioxide, broke through, and the grass that stretched between the facing pyramids of the Great Plaza came to green life. I could imagine the view from up top. "Hey," I said. "I want to climb one of those."

Rikki seemed pleased. The best one, he informed me, sounding more like an adolescent tour guide every minute, was the 230-foot-high Temple IV, the tallest pyramid in the Petén, "except of course for the one at El Mirador." I nodded sagely. Of course. I knew that. Didn't everyone? "But," he added, "only if you're willing to hike some more to get there."

A group of Italians in expensive leather hiking boots must have had the same idea. Clogging the Temple IV trail entirely, they looked like a family reunion where everyone had actually shown up, even the grandmother in her widow's weeds. She was steadying herself on the arm of a magnetic, blue-jawed Romeo somewhat older than Rikki but definitely younger than thirty-four, which is code for "younger than me." This did not matter; the sight of that glossy black hair combed back along the sides of his sleek head put me in mind of my first love, Peter, the stormy, self-absorbed film student I lived with during photography school, or maybe even of Robert, though neither of them, as far as I knew, had a drop of Italian blood. But they shared with him that restless, seeking quality that women, like stampeding buffalo, rush toward headlong. I like to think of myself as immune to the buffalo syndrome, but maybe not. Somehow, I'm always getting involved with guys who make me even more cynical than I already am.

After a minute, as though he could feel my eyes on him, he turned and gave me a long-lashed Italian stare over his shoulder. Now, I'm no great beauty—I've got the deep-set brown eyes, thick wren-brown braid, and long runner's legs of a million other people from my ancestors' part of the globe—but I'm slender and makeup free and come across as calm and non-neurotic, and I think that men, or a certain kind of man, must be drawn to that. This one seemed to be. I sent him back enough of a glance to let him know that if he could manage to park Grandma somewhere, I might be interested, and it was the old thing all over again. He began to slow, pointing out interesting shrubbery to the dour little widow and keeping an eye on me. This was my cue—and then I remembered Rikki. It was a damn shame, but there it was. "We'd better get in the passing lane," I said, "or we'll never make it to your precious temple." His cheeks heated up—he'd apparently seen the whole pregnant interchange—but he took me by the upper arm and towed me around the group of chattering relatives. I felt the Italian shrug as we passed him on the left.

Temple IV was a slog indeed, most of it on a steep trail through cleared but unleveled earth with a number of immense tree roots acting as foot and handholds. The highest section of the climb involved a vertical ladder that seemed to lean out backward over the jungle below. At the top of the ladder, there was a bit of a scramble to get safely parked on the flat limestone slabs at the summit of the pyramid, and then we were sitting together, our backs against what was left of the roof comb, staring out over one of the last real rainforests in the world.

"People sneak sleeping bags up here sometimes," Rikki said. "That's the thing—to watch the sun come up from the top of Temple IV. The guards usually chase them out, though."

"Have you done it?"

"My mom and I, when I was eight. Totally cool."

It crossed my mind, then, that there was no woman in the picture, no wife of Jan or mother of Rikki. Now Rikki spoke of her as though eulogizing a dear departed. Poor kid. I knew enough not to ask, I wasn't *going* to ask, and then he said, almost offhandedly, "When we're done here, we're heading up to Palenque for a while, so you'll get to meet her."

"I will?"

"You'll like her. She's great."

I turned back toward the panoramic jungle scene and said, carefully, "Will your dad be with us?" which was code for "So they're still married?" and he winced and said, "Of course."

"Rikki," I said, deliberately changing the subject after an appropriately long pause. "What's up tonight? What am I shooting?"

"A tomb in North Acropolis. He doesn't want to do it until all the tourists are out."

"Is it going to be as exciting as last night?"

That got a smile out of him. "Better," he said.

"Something to do with the famous Ah-Cacaw?"

He turned to look me in the face. We were sitting two feet apart in the shade of the roof comb, with the sun, just behind the massive blocks, backlighting his head. One of his ears, the one closest to the sunlight, looked translucent, like a baby's ear or the ear of a very young animal. His lashes were thick as fronds. But he'd be grown up soon enough, out in the world like all the beautiful ones, playing the same game as the Italian on the trail. "You really don't care about this stuff, do you?" he said.

"You mean about your precious Mayas?"

Silently, in the way his father might have done it, he put his arm out flat, palm down, and ran it over the scene below us.

I pushed him harder, payback for them keeping me in the dark. "This is all life and death to you two, right? Figuring out what happened here, why they abandoned their big cities? But hey, they're all dead and gone now, so what's the big deal?"

"I know," he said. "I know." But for a moment he looked startled, as though this were the first time the thought had ever crossed his mind. And I thought, poor kid. Sixteen, and still totally enslaved to his parents. For all our differences, Stefan and I were completely on the same page with the whole filial devotion thing. We'd both blown the family nest at the soonest possible opportunity.

Chapter Three

Weirdly enough, Stefan was not the first of my relatives to disappear. And in neither previous case was the outcome good. For a long time I assumed that my family was just unlucky, that we walked around under a curse, like the Kennedys, another tragic Catholic clan, if not nearly so rich and famous. My pregnant grandmother, for example, went missing a week before her thirty-second birthday. She'd gone to visit a friend in another village, which required a strenuous walk through a gloomy forest—this was Croatia in the early thirties, and being the peasant she was, she would have been walking—and just by chance or maybe through divine intervention (what Stefan would say), she had left my dad at home with my grandfather that morning. Bruno was eight. The Serbian king over Croatia had been assassinated six days before, allegedly by the Croatian Ustaše, hardcore nationalist militants who were willing to wreak any amount of havoc for the sake of independence, and in the usual Balkan way, the reaction was immediate and murderous.

Apparently, she walked straight into a village marked for retaliation. Nobody knows for sure what happened, just that the twenty-five or so people in town that day, mostly the usual collection of old men, women, and children, were marched deeper into the mountains and shot at the edge of a gorge. My grandfather never got over it. Neither did Bruno, who knows, if ever a man did, how to hate with a passion.

Though all I have to go on is Bruno's version of the story, Milo, my grandfather, did a good job of raising his motherless son. Several years later, when Germany invaded and the Nazis struck their famous bargain with the founder of the Ustaše and then-ruler of newly independent Croatia, Milo did what he needed to do, choosing to help run a camp for kids to keep young Bruno by his side rather than volunteering for the front lines as he so mightily desired.

When the war ended in 1945, Milo and Bruno, with the help of some friendly Franciscans in Rome, escaped the general massacre at the hands of Tito's "godless Communist Partisans," as my mother so affectionately refers to them, and wound up at St. Silvan's in Chicago. There, they found a community of true believers. Not, I have to say, in God—though of course they didn't not believe in him—but rather in the superiority of the Croatian culture, which, at least in a certain percentage of Croats, is marked by its intense and self-sacrificial loyalty to the Catholic Church. Milo ate it up. Bruno, with his immense capacity for hate, loathed everything about it. Both of them got jobs in the steel mills, wherein they found a lot of second-generation Croatian immigrants, virtually all of them as starry-eyed as Milo about the beauty, truth, and goodness of the "old country," which none of them would ever see again.

Milo told Bruno to find a wife. St. Silvan's had plenty of candidates. So he married Hana, daughter of one of those immigrants, in 1954. Stefan was born a year later. I showed up in 1959. And that, despite Hana's absolute devotion to the Church (which meant no artificial birth control), was all they wrote in terms of kids.

Here's what I remember. Stefan, who looks exactly like me only taller, skinnier, and with big horn-rimmed glasses, is eight. I am a self-satisfied four. We are marching in the Velika Gospa procession in honor, as the priest keeps reminding us, of "Our Lady," as we do every year in August, as Croatians have done since who knows when. Despite the fact that Stefan and I live in America and have always lived in America, he is dressed like a nineteenth-century peasant boy, and I am wearing a traditional old-country village costume, which at this age looks mighty cute on me: big, poofy white sleeves, a long white skirt, a multicolored apron, a funny little embroidered headdress, all assembled by that eminently loyal Croat, Hana. Afterward, we'll glut ourselves on barbecued lamb, mostaccioli, rizot, sarma, strudels, povitica, fritula, the whole while being serenaded by an endless string of old men playing the tamburitza. I know these guys, if vaguely, from all the time I've spent in the local tamburitza bar with my tata and my djed, Bruno and Milo.

They take me to the bar with them at the end of their long work weeks because I tend to ham it up in front of an audience, plus I like to sing and dance. They lift me to the shiny top of the bar counter. My shoes are shiny too—Hana polishes them as if they were the nonexistent family silver—and I like to fling myself around in time to the peppy folk dance music, all of which seems to please the heavy-lidded men. Most of them look like my tata and my djed: serious, even tragic, with their high cheekbones and abundant hair combed straight back, and their eyes that tell you almost nothing, except when they weep, which they often do while they are drinking their šljivovica, their powerful plum brandy. Hoping to cheer them up, I sing a bird-like, four-year-old's version of the Croatian national anthem, "Our Beautiful Homeland," and, with a tremendous snuffling and clearing of throats, they all join in.

I love these sad-eyed men, their cigarettes and their šljivovica and their impassive, male faces. I love their smells, which are exactly like the male smells of my tata and my djed, and I feel safe and whole with them. But where is Stefan? Why isn't Stefan ever along? Even at four, I know they have rejected him, Bruno and Milo. They have cast him out of the family, or would if only Hana let them.

Here's what else I remember. I am seven and my brother is eleven and we are taking a bus by ourselves to some place in the city I've never been, which is really most of Chicago since our family rarely strays from the neighborhood around St. Silvan's. It's late in the day and we are both wearing our gray and blue Catholic school uniforms. Stefan seems nervous, probably because I'm along. For several years now, ever since he got his paper route, he's been making private excursions to who knows where, and I've been bugging him for quite some time to take me too so I don't have to rattle around the house alone with Hana. Which is what happens on most weekdays after school since Tata and Djed only take me to the bar on Friday nights and Saturday afternoons. Hana, who is always messing with my hair and giving me lectures about being more ladylike, drives me nuts, so I'm in constant trouble with her these days, a thorn in her otherwise impervious flesh, which makes Bruno appreciate me all the more.

Stefan has finally succumbed to my pleadings, no doubt with trepidation; if anything happens to me while we're out and about, he knows what our father will do. Hana thinks I'm spoiled (of course I am), but my beef with her is nothing like Stefan's with his tata. Bruno can barely stand to look at him, except when he's got an excuse to take off his belt. Stefan has learned to stay out of his way, which means out of Milo's way too. The two of them are like peas in a pod, Milo simply a smaller, older, and somehow more ominous version of Bruno, though with a lot less English at his disposal. I, who am still so full of charm, so childishly untroubled by any notion of justice, remain perfectly at ease with all three of them.

But more than anything, I love being alone with Stefan, whom I call "Brat," which means brother in Croatian, a term I think completely hilarious. I give him a complacent glance and pipe, "Brat, where are we going?"

Sunk in his own worried thoughts, he's been staring out the bus window, but now he looks down at me in his kindly, abstracted way. No matter how hard I push him, no matter how I swashbuckle around the house when Bruno and Milo are there to watch my back, Stefan loves me like nobody else does or ever will. Even at seven, I recognize this. He sees something in me that's not simply funny or cute or entertaining, but instead hidden and valuable and mysterious, something that even now, at thirty-four, I've never yet had a single glimpse of no matter how hard I've hunted.

He slings an arm around my narrow little shoulders. "I'm taking you to the art museum," he says. We spend the next two hours in the Art Institute's photography collection, and when we emerge into a chill wind off the lake, I am in a state. I have never seen anything so glorious, not in church, not in the interminable Croatian festivals we go to, not in books. Riding the buses home in the dark, suddenly understanding what a price Stefan's going to pay for this adventure of ours, still and all, I am happy. Silent, entranced with what I've seen, I cling to my brother's hand.

Here's what I remember. It's my birthday, I am eight, and for once, everybody seems relaxed. I have agreed without a battle to wear the frilly dress that Hana sewed for me, have even allowed her to put ribbons in my hair. Bruno and Milo are smoking celebratory cigars, a practice normally forbidden within the confines of my mother's domain. Stefan's hanging around in the background, looking bashfully pleased with himself. I open my gifts—a light-up Virgin Mary from that eminently predictable Catholic amongst us, a chocolate bar from my silent grandfather, a little green jackknife with a satisfyingly sharp blade from my abnormally boisterous tata. Then Stefan's, which to my joyous surprise turns out to be a camera, my very first, a Brownie 127 bought with his hard-earned paper route money.

Here's what else I remember. Milo, my taciturn djed with the give-away-nothing eyes, becoming fixated overnight on fourteen-year-old Stefan. Suddenly wanting to talk with my brat, the same sweet and skinny boy he's always been, though much taller now, taller even than Bruno. My grandfather standing guard on the porch until my brother appears at the end of the block in his too-short Catholic school uniform, then shepherding him into his room and closing the door behind them, shutting me out entirely. I resent this, but not as much as Bruno does when he finally figures out what's going on. It's not just that he's been replaced as the long-time apple of his tata's eye. It's a whole lot more than this, though I can't figure out what. Silent Milo wants to talk, the silence of years is sloughing off like dead skin, and Bruno is half-frantic about . . . what? What is driving him so crazy all of a sudden?

And why has Milo zeroed in on Stefan this way? Is it because he's become, at fourteen, the star pupil at St. Silvan's? Or that he's rapidly morphing into a long-legged young man with hints of incipient handsomeness about him, who clearly has a future? Whatever's going on, Milo is determined to harness something in Stefan for his own purposes. And weirdly enough, Hana, normally so suspicious, so resentful of being left out of things, is fine with this. She's immensely proud of her boy, who is not only the valedictorian of our school but also head altar server. It's only Bruno who can't handle the new family dynamic. Only Bruno, and of course, sweet little me.

I try to worm my way in, but Stefan's having none of it. For the first time in his life, the family patriarch is taking him seriously. And after years of brutal rejection, he's totally vulnerable, swept entirely off his feet by the attention. I lurk sullenly around, trying to make him feel guilty, and when that doesn't work, I wait till he's off delivering papers, then sneak into his room with my Brownie. What's Djed been giving him? Because I've seen Brat carrying things when he leaves my grandfather's room.

Nothing is hidden very well. Stefan is too trusting for that. I find a faded watch cap, a small bag of medals that look to me like something you'd buy in the St. Silvan's Catholic gift shop, a red-and-white checkered scarf. I find some old papers, written in Croatian, which I can't read, and a handful of black-and-white photos, one of which may actually be of my dead grandmother. I study this for a while. She's pretty, I decide, though definitely looks exhausted. And then I find the box. It's under Stefan's bed, pushed to the back corner, up against the wall. It's scuffed and stained, and at first I think it's an old cigar box except there's a lock on it with no attached key. I hold it sideways next to my ear and shake it. Something—it sounds heavy—shifts inside. I pick at the lock with my fingernail. Nothing. I find all of this highly irritating, Brat hiding something important from me, so I set the box in the middle of the bed, hold up my Brownie, and snap a photo. I snap photos of everything, and to make sure Stefan knows I'm onto him, leave all of it spread out across the bedspread, then flounce out of the room, slamming the door behind me. There.

This is what I remember. Out of the blue, Milo vanishing. One afternoon closeted in the bedroom with Stefan, the next, gone without a trace. Bruno going berserk, brandishing a pistol I've never seen before—even at ten, this concerns me—vowing vengeance against the kopiles, whoever they may be, who've kidnapped his dad. Hana, on the other hand, noticing out loud that Milo has not been himself these days (look at all the hours he's been spending with Stefan, though she doesn't say a word about this to the cops and neither do the rest of us, nor do we mention the murderous kopile theory). She surmises that perhaps he's just getting old-people crazy and has wandered off and will show up soon.

Neither of these conjectures strike anywhere near the truth, which is that Milo is hanging in a tree in a big park on the other side of town. Eventually, he is discovered by some hapless homeless guy. His death is ruled a suicide. Though of course, confides one of the detectives to Bruno with the rest of us standing, wide-eyed, behind him in the living room, you never know for sure.

"My brother's a police captain in Iowa," says the detective, "and he thinks at least 60 percent of all suicides are actually murders in disguise."

Bruno makes a strangled sound—of *course*, his father did not kill himself; of *course* he was murdered—but remains mute. Why? I've wondered this for years. All that foamy-lipped rage, bottled up tight in front of the cops, then spewed out so viciously on the three of us—day after endless day of fountaining bile—that for the first time I am sure Hana will finally leave him. Which, being the exemplary Catholic she is, she won't even consider.

And Stefan? What you would expect. His grades go to hell, he can't eat, can't sleep, walks around like a zombie. Later I'll see the same look on kids' faces in war zones, the look of being pushed too far, of being shocked out of their real selves with nobody around to help them figure out what happened. This is what's happening to Stefan, because Hana and Bruno, neither of whom believe in psychology, much less in something so completely nonproductive as clinical depression, are worthless at this point. As for me, as long as I stay angry enough at

Djed for killing himself, I don't have to feel sad.

In another year—by now it is 1970—Stefan is well over six feet tall with hair the same color and length as mine. His horn-rims have given way to hip-looking gold granny glasses, and he is about an inch away from getting booted out of St. Silvan's. Bruno gets livid just looking at him, has endless theories about drug-dealing, needle-sharing, war-protesting faggotry. I'm only eleven, but even to someone as clueless as me this sounds like an exaggeration. Not that I come to his defense. Most of Stefan's time, as far as I can tell, is spent lounging in the park with a couple of bell-bottomed, dope-smoking losers from the public high school down the road, neither of whom wants a kid sister around. So the day Bruno uncovers a stash of pot in Stefan's room and officially throws him out, I am momentarily, perversely glad. I haven't had a brother since Milo died, not really, and whose fault it that? Not mine, that's for sure.

The next day, before Bruno gets home from work, Stefan makes a quick, quiet visit to the house. I am brooding in my room with music blaring and do not hear him enter. But then there is a knock at my door, and when I shut off the radio and open it, my brat is standing there with a brown paper shopping bag in his arms, looking uncomfortable and ashamed, as though he might be trying and failing to come up with an explanation I can understand. I stare back at him defiantly, daring him to try and make me feel better.

Finally, as though giving up the ill-advised effort at reconciliation, he shrugs. "My clothes," he says, "and some other stuff I'm going to need." And then, watching my face, which must have revealed right then what I was desperately trying to hide, he sets the bag carefully on the floor and takes me into his arms. Instantly, the waterworks come on, a flood of them down the front of his old green T-shirt. "Oh, Eva," he murmurs into my hair, "don't worry about me, okay? It's not as bad as you think. Okay?" And after I finish with the snorting and the gulping and the pathetic little moans of sorrow and despair, he adds, "Be strong, little sister. And get the hell out of here as soon as you can."

Afterward, I take myself and my grief-swollen eyes into his

abandoned bedroom and make my search. He's taken some of his underwear, a couple of shirts, some jeans, his tennis shoes. A few books are missing from the shelf. On the bedspread is a neat stack of Milo's crap: the red-and-white checkered scarf, the cluster of old papers in Croatian, the watch cap, the bag of cheap religious medals. The black-and-white photos, including the one of my massacred grandmother.

When I peer under the bed, I see that the locked box is gone.

Much as I hate to admit it, Robert was probably right about me. There's a coldness inside that can scare people—men—while attracting them in ways that must feel vaguely uncomfortable to them, no doubt what eventually kills each of these relationships. I'm not the kind of woman who's going to cling. They don't have to worry about being guilt-tripped or grasped at with desperate female fingers should they decide to head on down the road. I got cured of all that when I was eleven. You can only feel devastated for so long—especially when you are a kid, especially when you are that self-centered—and then you start to harden up.

Bruno was actually my biggest help here. On the rare occasions he mentioned his exiled son, it was with loud, scornful assertions that Stefan was fine, no doubt making more money as a drug dealer than he himself was making at the steel plant, no doubt living it up and laughing through his cocaine-stuffed nose at the rest of us. Sometimes, when I was at my most self-pitying, I almost believed him. Mostly, though, I simply adopted what looked to me like strength, working furiously to make my tata's legendary toughness my own.

As for Stefan, I thought about him almost every day for months and months, and then, finally, hardly at all. As though he'd died and been buried after a big Croatian funeral Mass—the kind of no-holds-barred ethnic mourning-fest St. Silvan's had refused to put on for Djed—and now it was time to get over it.

Chapter Four

Jan and Rikki and I were headed for the North Acropolis. I wasn't
wild about hiking in the jungle at night. You never know what's prowl-
ing behind you, and it's easy to get disoriented by the intensity of the
blackness. Sounds are distorted and you're always brushing up against
something you don't want to touch. However, we really didn't have far
to go—while it was still twilight, we'd hauled the equipment up our
private trail as close as we could get while steering clear of tourists—so
after dark, when the last voices faded away down the long trail that led
to the park entrance, we were within a quarter mile of the Great Plaza.
"There will be guards," Jan said over his shoulder. "So don't jump out
of your skin when one comes up behind us."

A few minutes later I was glad for the warning, for a hand suddenly
came out of nowhere and touched my arm. I didn't scream, but I did
turn and raise my knee, and whoever it was took a step back. "Buenas
noches," said Jan invisibly.

"Ah, señor," said someone off to my left. Apparently, we were surrounded. "Lo siento—we could not see you well in the dark."

"No hay problema."

"Y quién es esa señora?"

"My photographer."

"Ah." The owner of the hand stepped forward again. "Do you need
guides?"

"Gracias," said Jan, "pero no."

"Muy bien. Entonces buena suerte, señor. Que le vaya bien."

I was embarrassed at the way my heart was slamming around. I hadn't heard a single footfall—nothing. They'd surrounded us like a pack of ghosts, and then vanished just as silently. I thought of the Chiapan rebels Stefan talked about in his letters to Jonah, not to mention the ones I'd photographed in Nicaragua and El Salvador the last time I was in Central America.

Jan said, "Are you all right?"

"Si." It came out more gruffly than intended, but I'd found over the years that the minute you started admitting to men that you were a little shaken up, they went into their hero mode and forced you to consult them about every step you took thereafter.

Just then a roaring began almost directly overhead, and it took every ounce of grit I had not to hit the deck and cover my head. Because of course it was howler monkeys, not jaguars at all, and the funniest thing you can do in the Guatemalan jungle is fall for their mimicry. I wasn't up for being the butt of anybody's joke. The roaring went on for minutes, then died away. We stood there in silence in the pitch black. Then Jan moved off and I hurried to catch up.

In ten minutes we broke out from under the canopy to the open grass of the Great Plaza, and suddenly the darkness lightened a bit because we were under the stars instead of the ceiba trees. Jan snapped off his flashlight. The pyramids, enormous black mountains, rose up against the faint glow of the star-spattered sky, and behind them was the black wall of the jungle. Frogs throbbed like drums; a maddened cicada went on and on, but otherwise it was quiet. Rikki and I came to a dead halt, and Jan stopped too and stepped back toward us but did not speak. Gradually, the jungle, which had hushed at our passing, began to tune.

The North Acropolis by day is a maze of tunnels that go nowhere and crumbling rooms and enormous masks under sunshades of palm fronds. Rikki and I had explored it earlier. Five hundred years of building, some of it ritually "terminated," as Rikki called it, by deliberately filling in the structures with rubble or through a ceremony that involved smashing pots and burning incense. "Because they had to contain the power," he said, "and redirect it into the new temples. There've been all kinds of things found under the North Acropolis. It goes back a long way—the Mayas lived here starting about 800 B.C., and they used to dump all their trash here and bury their dead."

Jan, ignoring his son's lecture, trained his flashlight on the outer wall of the complex, and I found myself staring into the face of an enormous monster, one of the stucco masks protected by a palm frond shelter that we had seen earlier in the day. Then he pointed the light to the right of the mask and down. We went carefully over broken blocks, around a couple of sharp corners, and down again, and finally came upon the opening of a passageway less than a meter wide, hidden by a clumsy screen of more palm fronds, which Jan lifted aside. One by one, we entered.

It wasn't too bad, as passageways go. Narrow, but the ceiling was plenty high, the floor was clear, and there were no major twists or turns. After a while we came to a dead end. While I was looking around to see what happened next, Rikki vanished. One moment he was there, and the next he was gone, though his pack was lying on the floor in front of me.

"Jan?"

"Put your equipment down. We will have to come back for it," he said, moving to the left into what looked like the juncture of two blank walls but was not. The edges of the limestone blocks that formed the corner were slightly ajar, leaving just enough room for a man's body to slip through. Inside the new, much smaller passageway, Rikki was crouched, waiting for us. The light played over the tiny corridor, slanting downward and covered with jagged rock chips, and which from this angle looked impassable. Jan said, "It gets better after thirty yards or so." Thirty yards. It didn't look like we could get thirty feet, especially if we were carrying the packs. But Jan was already pushing ahead, scrambling over broken chunks of cut stone and shining his light backward so we could see.

It was like being in a cave. The air was perfectly still except for the rock dust we were stirring up, and it had a dead, unhealthy quality to it. Even víboras, I thought, would not be brave enough to live this far in. So I put them out of my mind as I crawled on all fours over the broken stones. And then there was the silence, which, without our grunting and breathing, would have been absolute. Once again, we were entering Xibalba, realm of the dead.

I'd been in old jungle temples before, with Robert in Thailand. But that was a wetter, hotter jungle, and the vines had woven their way into every crack, and with the vines came the forest creatures. Those temples were like decaying trees. As they crumbled, they fed new life. And in the midst of the decay were incense pots, still smoking, and bits of food left in sacrifice, and scraps of bright cloth tied to twigs, so you knew nothing had been truly finished in these places and the cycle was still going on.

This was different. The full weight of the pyramid sat directly above the four-foot ceiling. And we were crawling deeper and deeper, on a long descent, into the center of it. Suddenly, though I was not afraid, I did not want to go on. I inched along a few more feet, fighting the urge to stop, wiggle around, and make my way back up to the mask that guarded the entrance of this little hellhole. Jan, however, was moving steadily forward, his light bobbing ahead of and behind him, and Rikki was breathing hard behind me. This was crazy; we didn't even have the cameras. Someone was going to have to run back and get them after we got where we were going. But at last Jan stopped and waited till I had come up almost to his back, with Rikki on my tail, before he silently pointed the light forward.

At first, all I could see was another apparent dead end. A three-and-a-half-foot block sat directly in front of us, sealing off the way. Jan edged up to it and shouldered his way into the corner, again to the left, and the light was suddenly gone. "In here," he called back, and his voice sounded odd, as though he were speaking into a conch shell. A thin wedge of light appeared on the floor in front of the block, and I crawled toward it and squeezed through, with little bits of rock rattling down around me and my braid getting caught on the edge of the slab. The stones were cold. Jan had the light trained through the crack for Rikki, so wherever we were was not yet visible, but I could sense we were in a bigger space. I could stand up, for one thing, and Jan, beside me, was standing at his full height too. For some no doubt deeply psychological reason, it was easier to breathe.

After we were all inside, Jan snapped off the light for a moment, and we stood there close together in the thickest darkness I've ever experienced. No sound, no light, no up or down. If there were eyes that could pierce the blackness, then we were at their mercy, because we were helpless as cave fish. I briefly wondered if death might be like a cave. My greater impulse, however, was to not think at all but find the nearest human being, which is what I did. As it turned out, I had snuggled up to Jan, who almost dropped the flashlight in his effort to get away.

"Look," he said, sounding flustered, and clicked on the light. In less than three seconds, he'd managed to put half the chamber between us. I gave a mental shrug. He was either a lot more married than he looked, or there was something a wee bit off here. I'd met guys like him before. They were only dangerous if you were the kind of woman who engaged in a lot of self-doubt.

We were in some kind of vault, not large but much roomier than the passage. The walls, white stucco, were covered in glyphs painted in black, some of them as large as a man's head. One group of them, in long vertical rows, looked calligraphic, as though they had been done by a professional; others were more like children's drawings—simple, animal-like shapes with teddy bear ears and large noses. The number and complexity of the professional-looking glyphs meant that someone had spent a long time decorating this little chamber cut deep into the bedrock below the pyramid. My guess was that this was not art for art's sake.

"Who was buried here?" I asked.

"A king and two sacrifice victims," said Jan as he ran the light over the amateur side of the wall. He still sounded a little stiff, but that was his problem, not mine.

One by one, the simple shapes with their rounded ears and goggly eyes came into view. I saw that some of them had little arms, turned up at the ends where hands should be. "Did the Mayas have a thing about sacrificing kids?" I asked.

"These sacrifices were adolescents, maybe sixteen or so."

"That means kids."

He shrugged. I looked over at his son, who was studying one of the vertical lines of the glyphs, and remembered the way the sunlight had caught the edge of his ear on top of Temple IV. "His age," I added, nodding toward Rikki.

Jan looked at his son, then at me. "So what is your point?" he said bluntly.

This time it was my turn to back off. Why was I even bringing this stuff up? It was not like I hadn't seen much worse. I'd been in hospital camps in Darfur where the kids who were still alive looked like they were made out of pencils. I'd been in Iraq after the Kurdish genocide. So where did I get off begrudging Jan his two teenaged sacrifice victims? "Nothing," I said. "What do you want me to shoot in here?"

He studied me for another long moment and I realized that I'd not yet seen him smile. He was a genuinely somber man, but I was actually starting to get used to him. You could count on him. Always preoccupied, unless you deliberately woke him up, as I had without meaning to when I leaned into him in the dark. He didn't chat for the sake of chatting, or tell stories about his own exploits around the campfire at night, a habit endemic among the crowd I usually ran with. He didn't joke. And most of the time, except when he was deep in thought or angry, he treated Rikki and me with old-time courtesy. A serious man. Aside from Stefan, who was lighter about it, I'd never met one before. I began to wish I hadn't startled him so badly.

"Over here," he said finally, and put his hand toward a glyph that had been partially obliterated by the crumbling of the stucco but was unmistakably a version of the same one I'd photographed in the first temple, back at camp. The four-petaled flower inside the squarish oval, but this time with no streamers attached. Once it had been pointed out to me, I couldn't see how I'd overlooked it the first time. It stood out among the teddy bears, and it did not fit with the other glyphs either, almost as though a third artist had been at work. Too bad we didn't have those cameras.

"There's an easier way in," said Jan, reading my mind, "but almost impossible to find from the outside at night. We will go out that way, leave Rikki to mark the entrance, and you and I will get the equipment." He glanced at me. "If you don't mind."

Truce. I nodded.

At the other end of the vault was a small opening that looked completely blocked and was, indeed, a tight squeeze for Jan, who was not a large man, but then it quickly turned into a steep but spacious passageway made out of earth instead of rock, like a mine shaft. We climbed for fifteen minutes, the light bouncing ahead of us, and as we approached the end of the tunnel, it began to close around us once again until we came to another tight squeeze.

Though we were still inside, I could taste the first breath of night air and hear the faint throb of the frogs. Suddenly, I could hardly wait to leave the Underworld. "I'm smallest," I said. "I'll go through first."

Jan hesitated, then handed me his flashlight, and I scrambled up into Rikki and Jan's cupped hands and used their shoulders to lever myself out into the world. Tired as I already was, for a moment I thought about heading back to camp and leaving the two of them to their mysterious underground enterprise. Instead, I dutifully aimed the flashlight at the entrance so they could see their way out.

Naturally, the minute Jan and I had loaded ourselves up with the camera equipment, it began to rain. We were just stepping out of the shorter passageway for the hike back to where Rikki was waiting for us at the mouth of the shaft with only a penlight for company when the sky came bucketing down. You couldn't see through it and of course we hadn't brought the ponchos. And I wasn't about to risk my cameras if I didn't have to. I made eye contact with Jan, and he motioned with his drenched head for us to get back inside the passageway.

"What'll we do?" I asked once we were out of the thunder of the rain. You could hear it, but it was muffled, like stones being shaken in a far-off box.

"Wait it out," he said. "It will slow down soon—this is not the rainy season."

So we spread out the wet packs and made ourselves comfortable on the floor against the wall. Then Jan turned off the light to save the battery. Silence, except for the hollow racketing outside. After a while I cleared my throat and said, "Rikki will crawl back inside the tunnel, won't he?" It wasn't actually meant to be a question—Rikki was a big boy, he could take care of himself—but it came out that way.

"Oh, yes," said Jan out of the dark. I heard the snick of a match and the sound of him drawing on a pipe. I hadn't known he smoked a pipe. I love pipes, don't ask me why. Nobody at the tamburitza bar smoked them. Neither Milo nor Bruno smoked them. But somewhere in my misty infant days, I must have had a happy pipe experience with a person I've by now forgotten, somebody I trusted, whose fragrant pipe smoke was burned into my memory.

A little rosy glow lit up the bottom part of Jan's face and the sweet aroma of burning tobacco rolled my way. I closed my eyes and took it in through my nostrils. Neither of us made any effort to talk. We were too tired after the long crawl, and there was too much left to do. Jan puffed away and I took surreptitious sips of his smoke and thought about my adventurous pal Dirk settling down and getting married.

Sometime during Jan's second pipe, I closed my eyes and must have dropped off for a bit, long enough to have a dream, anyway. In the middle of it, I heard my name—Eva, Eva—being repeated softly, and at first I thought Stefan was calling me, the timbre was so close, and then I realized it was Jan, who was trying to wake me without startling me. "Look," he said. "Down by your feet." He had the flashlight on, but shielded by his jacket so the light was very dim. I could just make out something moving around in the passageway on four legs, not large but definitely alive. It was sniffing the air and its eyes shone wildly green. It turned, and I saw the sweep of a long tail.

"A coati snooping around to see what we might have in our packs," he said. "I did not want it to frighten you."

Half-asleep as I was, the coati looked like an emissary from another world. "Oh, wow," I whispered.

The creature seemed more interested in me now that it had heard my voice and came closer, bobbing its small nose toward my boots. Sometimes on trips like these, I'll find myself in a situation that is so un-Chicagolike that I start thinking about what it would have been like to stay there. But when I try to imagine Chicago, it is as weird as the place I'm in. So over the years, I've stopped trying to figure out why I've chosen the life I have. In spite of occasional bouts of homesickness for a home that doesn't exist, it's been a good way to handle things. Except that this unexpectedly trusting animal was all of a sudden making me feel wistful. Or maybe it was the pipe, still lingering in the air.

"Still raining?"

He nodded.

"You must know this place pretty well. Rikki said you were here for six years."

He cleared his throat, nervous, probably, about talking so much. "There is no place like Tikal, that is certainly true."

"What do you mean?"

He readjusted the flashlight so we could see each other's faces. The coati was speculatively circling around us. "This is where the Classic Maya culture probably got started. If you are an archeologist, it is like getting to work at the junction of the Tigris and the Euphrates."

I nodded. I may be ignorant, but I can recognize the seat of Western civilization when I hear it.

"My training was all in Asia Minor. But years ago I met a Mayanist at a conference in England and he convinced me that the most exciting digs in the world were taking place here in Central America and Mexico."

"Why?"

"The breakthroughs in glyph translation. It was finally starting to open up after centuries of false starts. It was the linguists and ethnographers who were responsible, not so much the archeologists. But I wanted to be here so that when they started to put together the written history of this culture and they needed people who knew the sites and where the inscriptions were, I could help." He stopped abruptly, as though he'd just inadvertently dominated an entire dinner table conversation.

"Go on," I said. "Please. I don't know much about all this."

But he'd withdrawn again. "Not much to tell. I was lucky enough to be here for some interesting burial discoveries, and my wife . . . well, being here for six years, you get to know a place because each site is different. You will see what I am talking about when we get to Palenque. To be here when the dynasties were being compiled was a rare privilege. I am glad Rikki could be in on part of it, even if he was just a child."

"You have an outstanding son, by the way."

In spite of the pipe, he looked as somber as ever. "How so?"

I didn't much want to get into the details—I don't like revealing my soft spots—but I did say that Rikki had an ability to relate to adults in a way that was almost unnerving, and that he was one of the most courteous teenagers I'd ever met. Also impressively intelligent.

Jan seemed pleased. "If things had gone better, he would have been a good epigrapher by the time he was twenty. He was taking what his mother taught him and training himself. I will never catch up with him as it is. I am better in the dirt."

"So his . . . mother was a Mayanist too?"

I felt him pull away, as he'd done in the dark tomb when I leaned against him. I thought he might not answer at all. After a moment, however, he said, "Considering she was self-trained, quite a good one. She is gifted in languages, but took a degree in art history. It was a good combination for work in Central America."

I was trying to decipher the tenses. I took another stab at it. "Rikki said I might be meeting her soon. In Palenque."

He nodded.

"Well," I said, "I'm looking forward to meeting Rikki's mother."

I thought this was subtle, but apparently not. He made a little motion with his hands, as though to brush away my words. Then he got to his feet and walked quickly toward the door of the passageway and stood there for a few minutes. When he came back, he said, "We can go now."

I got the message. We gathered up our packs, re-strapped everything, and headed back out into the jungle. I looked behind me just as we went out into the night. The coati had vanished.

Poor Rikki was waiting for us, wet and shivering but loyally marking out the spot. It can't have been any fun hanging around alone that way, especially with the deluge going on and only a pocket-size penlight for a weapon. "You're some guy," I said and patted him on the shoulder.

Back in the death chamber, we set up the tripod and lanterns and off-camera flashes, just like the night before. The first glyph I'd photographed and drawn had been so faint that I hadn't really had a chance to absorb it, except as a technician. This one was quite clear, however, and I spent some time just looking at it before going to work. I'm no handwriting expert, but I was positive my first impression was right— neither the professional scribe nor the amateur cartoonist had done this particular glyph. It seemed to be in another hand entirely; the brush lines were thinner, and the proportions were different. It was larger, for example, than the official glyphs, but smaller than the teddy bears. And it seemed to have been placed to catch the eye, as though all the other painting had been done first and this one was added as an afterthought.

"Jan," I asked casually, "is this one of the glyphs that has been translated?"

He paused over the tripod, as though considering whether or not this information might ruin me as an accomplice, then said, "It has."

"What does it mean?"

He paused again, this time looking at Rikki, who was clearly dying for me to know, then gave an exasperated sigh. "It has several meanings.

It is a very common glyph—you find it almost everywhere, including in some month names, some god names, and in a lot of the iconography. Nothing mysterious."

I waited.

"The most common meaning seems to be k'in, which refers to the sun," he added reluctantly. "Also, time in general. And k'in is the name for day. So you can see this is a very mundane sort of glyph, really."

Which is why, I thought, we just army-crawled thirty yards to get to this chamber. Which is why we are hiking around in the middle of the jungle at night and poor Rikki is probably going to die of pneumonia.

"I see," I said. "Thank you, Jan."

I went back to my camera. He went back to his light stand.

In less than two hours I was done. I'd taken another two rolls of film, one up close and one with the glyph in context, and at the end of the evening, I handed Jan the sketchbook with six new drawings in it, one of them pretty damn good. He seemed pleased with the night's work, though I was suddenly exhausted. We hadn't had a shower for two days, and our tents were going to be soaked. It was close to 11:00 p.m., and we still had the hike up the shaft and the long trudge back to our camp. This was nothing new in my line of work, but I'd been spoiled, maybe, by the rest in the passageway with Jan's cozy pipe. I could hardly stagger around.

Jan caught it. "Steady on," he said, more kindly than I'd ever heard him. Maybe he was starting to get used to me.

Chapter Five

It took me six days to figure out an interesting fact, which was that not every photograph I took was equally important to my boss. In fact, three-quarters of my work seemed entirely extraneous. After a while, I could tell pretty easily when we were just shooting and when it was a very big deal. The same old glyph—the four-petaled k'in symbol—night after night, but never the same reaction out of our leader.

I also noticed another thing. He spent a lot of time writing things down, usually in the morning before Rikki and I crawled out of our tents to cook breakfast. He wrote in a large, bound journal, often with an open book beside him, which he would study from time to time before writing some more. I know this because I was studying *him* through the open flap of my tent as I lay in my sleeping sheet with one arm crooked behind my head.

It was the strange similarity between him and Stefan that fascinated me. Once I made the connection, I could not shake the thought that there was something I could learn about my brother if I just watched Jan long enough. Jan was older, of course, and weighted down by cares probably having to do with his mysterious marriage and who knows what else, while Stefan was, in contrast, less burdened by worldly matters, or at least less burdened than he'd been for so many years after Djed died, finally letting that grief slip from him. They also did not resemble each other physically. Stefan looked like a male version of me, tall and slenderly built, his prodigious nervous energy masked, like mine, beneath an air of studious calm, while Jan came across as the Dutchman he was, slow-moving and rock solid. In spite of his old demons, Stefan had managed to retain his sweet, abstracted smile—at least he still had it the last time I saw him—while Jan seemed sunk beyond where happiness could reach. But in some important way—maybe in the focused way they tackled life, or how they were both at home with silence—they shared some common ground that, on first blush, you wouldn't think to look for.

As it turned out, Bruno was dead wrong about Stefan's drug dealing, or, for that matter, all other aspects of his alleged debauchery. I was wrong, too. I figured my brother must have found shelter in one of his pothead friend's garages when he got kicked out. Instead, he was quietly taken in by one of the priests at St. Silvan's, Fr. Anthony, yet another postwar immigrant, the very guy who'd baptized both of us and who apparently understood everything there was to know about our family without having to be told. Priest or not, he was streetwise enough not to flaunt what he was doing in front of my parents. He made sure Stefan ate, slept in an actual bed, found a night-shift job at a grocery store stocking shelves, and got enrolled at the local public high school, from which, by some miracle, he actually graduated on time.

I learned all this when I caught up with Stefan a few years later in Nepal. My leaving Chicago was preordained. Not only had my brother advised me to get the hell out as soon as I possibly could, I'd also managed to embroil myself in an increasingly dicey liaison, my first venture into the dangerous thickets of erotic love, during my senior year at St. Silvan's. Alexander was his name. Urgent were his hands. Perilous was my lot. It was time to flee.

Over the years, I'd gotten sporadic postcards from Stefan, sent not to the house but directly to St. Silvan's and mysteriously passed on to me, who never figured out the identity of our cagey postman, Fr. Anthony. I knew that for the past three years, Stefan had been living in Kathmandu, but I assumed—thanks in part to Bruno's self-confident, made-up accounts of what Stefan was up to—that he'd probably been hanging out somewhere my tata had never heard of: on the infamous Jochen Tole, aka Freak Street, just another pilgrim on the long and winding hippie trail. As it turned out, he was taking care of terminal TB patients at a hospice run by—you guessed it—Catholics. Or one Catholic, at least: a Yoda-like priest from India called Fr. John.

At first, though Stefan seemed happily shocked to see me, we were a little shy with one another. It had been so ridiculously long. And we had both changed. I was no longer the little girl who'd sobbed into his T-shirt during that final, agonizing farewell. And after years of nothing but dal bhat and endless cups of chai, he himself was almost unrecognizable. Clothed in your typical Newari villager garb—loose white pants, loose white shirt, woven skull cap, and Goodrich tire sandals—he didn't even look American anymore. But slowly, in the warm glow of Fr. John's benevolent presence, we started to relax. At Fr. John's insistence, Stefan took a few days off to show me the countryside.

And this is where, in the car-less streets of medieval Bhaktapur, in the shadow of the Himalaya, I caught a glimpse of the future, which was that I would be a photojournalist. I'd go to crazy places and meet people I'd never meet except in the boonies. Life would be a thrill instead of the boring grind my parents had inflicted on themselves. And I would *do* something with it, though it was hard to say, even to myself, what that meant. I tried to explain all this to Stefan, who nodded wisely (all that time with Yoda) and said he could see it. That I was brave and tough and willing and smart—I took this with a large grain of salt—and already a good photographer. That all I needed to do was take myself seriously.

Then we indulged in some tender reminiscing about our long-ago visit to the Art Institute. He'd known right then, he told me, which was why he bought me the Brownie 127.

"I'm sorry," I said, "that I broke into your room that day. I was so jealous of you and Djed . . ."

He waved me off, and I could see he was not yet ready to talk about our grandfather. So I held myself back from quizzing him about the mysterious locked box.

After we parted with a vow to stay in better touch, I kicked around on my own for a bit, testing out my wee new wings. Riding third-class buses into the mountains, venturing down into the Terai, the grasslands and jungles of southernmost Nepal, then taking the trains to South India, everywhere snapping pictures like a madwoman. When I finally ran out of money and it was time to catch a flight back home, I could not bring myself to do it. So I headed to London instead, got myself a job at the front desk of a twee hotel, and on my days off, started hanging around the Magnum office, hoping to meet a world-class photographer or two. Not only did I meet one, I got offered six unpaid hours a week as a volunteer file clerk, the official start of my brand-new life.

For Stefan's part, three years with Fr. John at the hospice must have taught him whatever it was he needed to know, because shortly after I headed for London, he flew to California, enrolled himself in college, and, smarty-pants that he always was, set out to earn himself degrees in philosophy and theology. Back in London, I was grappling with an unwelcome revelation: not everything gets learned through osmosis. Like the celebrity photographers among whom I so diligently filed, if I were serious about the craft, I needed to hie me to photography school. And the only good one I could afford was in Southern California, which turned out to be a mere six-hour drive from where my brat was beavering away at the university.

I glanced through the tent flap. Jan was still frowningly absorbed, and Rikki slumbered on in his happy teenaged coma. I pulled out the packet of letters Jonah had given me before I flew to Guatemala. Though I'd skimmed them on the plane, understanding very little, it was time to read them again, slowly.

The first one, dated November 7, 1990, was inscribed on yellow legal paper in my brother's backward slanting hand and mailed from his new post in Chiapas, where he'd been sent, at his own request, as soon as he was ordained. I held the sheet in my hand for a moment, thinking that Stefan had written this. I was surprised at what the thought of him sitting at some dusty desk in southern Mexico did to the back of my throat.

Dear Jonah,

I'm not sure whether I should say thanks or not for the date nut cake, which was waiting for me at the rectory of Iglesia de Guadalupe when I arrived last Tuesday. It was smashed flat. But it reminded me of you and the kitchen and the barrel of brandy, and how hard I used to work at pulling bookstore duty so I didn't have to chop dates anymore.

Knowing you, you're waiting for a rundown on my new home, so I'll start with the city itself, which is famous in the guidebooks as the jewel of los altos, the highlands. Downtown, where all the tourists go, it's still sixteenth-century Colonial. The first impression you get is that you've arrived in a Europe transplanted to the mountains of Mexico—all those monumental old Spanish edifices, like the Cathedral and the governmental palace. But woven in and around the relics of Castilian Spain are the colors of los indigenas, the vibrant blues and purples and yellows and oranges of the Tzeltales, Tzotziles, Zoque, Tojolabales. You see them in the huipiles, on sale everywhere, and in the flowerpots and on the painted wooden doors. They remind me of Sherpa women's dresses in Nepal.

My church was built in the 1830s on top of a steep hill overlooking the city. You have to hike up seventy-nine steep steps to get to it, but the view from the top is worth it. I stay in a small house in one of the neighborhoods below. Everybody here let me know right off the bat that I'm filling some pretty big shoes and not doing a very hot job of it. The last priest, Fr. Carlos, keeled over with a heart attack at fifty-one, and nobody's gotten over it yet. I sleep in his bed.

Jorge is the deacon here. He's local, grew up in Barrio el Cerrillo, a neighborhood built in the mid-1500s to house the Indian ex-slaves of the Spanish. He speaks all three of the

Mayan dialects you hear most often in San Cristóbal, even though after four hundred years there are probably more ladinos on the family tree than pure indigenas anymore. His father was shot by robbers when Jorge was five; his mother died of pneumonia when he was sixteen. Since he'd been an altar boy for years at one of the biggest churches in town, the congregation there split the kids up between them. He was allowed to live in the rectory with the priests and eventually got a couple years of seminary under his belt. In spite of the Dickens story line, he's your basic, normal guy.

The head priest is Fr. Martin, sixty or so, a sad survivor of the Salvadoran nightmare. He hasn't talked to me about it yet. Jorge filled me in the day after I arrived. He was a friend of Rutilio Grande. I'm sure you've read about all that. Another priest friend, one of his closest, was tortured for days. And three of his own catechists were run off a mountain road. He was supposed to be with them. The congregation here, almost all indigenas, seem very protective of him. Some of them know firsthand what he's been through, and not because they're Salvadorans or Guatemalans. I'm talking about right here in Chiapas.

So, I promised you an explanation. And now it's been almost six years since I left the Hermitage and went gallivanting off to seminary, not to mention Mexico, and I still haven't given you one. So I'm going to try.

All my life I've been a coward. Or maybe that's not right. All my life I've been afraid. It started when I was a little kid, this weird blank nothingness interposing itself between me and everything else, and it hasn't fully lifted off since, though I've gotten used to it. When I was fourteen, my grandfather died under somewhat strange circumstances, you could say, and things got a lot worse. As in, I started obsessing about getting rid of myself. But that was probably just teenage drama—who knows? Pot helped, at least for a while.

Actually, there's a lot more to this story—a lot—but I've

never told a soul and I can't tell you yet either. Not till I tell it to Eva. It's our family, hers and mine, and I owe it to her, even though I can't imagine when she's going to hear it. Sorry, Jonah. Nothing to do with you.

I don't know when I figured out what I was really dealing with. For a long time I thought this death cloud was my own creation, that it was coming from some putrid place inside me, and that what I needed to do was get strong enough to push it back. But then I got to be friends with that priest in Chicago I told you about, Fr. Anthony, and somehow he knew what was going on with me. He's the one who put me in touch with Fr. John in Nepal. Said I needed to be in a place where I could learn about love. In a "school of the Lord's service," as Benedict would say. So I went. And three years of tending the dying made the blankness lift a little. Enough, anyway, to get me past the crisis point. Enough to get me into college, to begin tackling this thing as a philosophical or religious question rather than as my own personal problem—i.e., what is the nature of evil?

I'm out of time. I'll keep this going in the next one. But that's why I'm here. Because of evil and because I've been so afraid of it.

Sorry to make this so heavy, but you asked.

Yours,

Stefan

Evil. Yes, I'd read that on the plane, but impatiently, trying to get to the facts, and the term hadn't really registered. Not, at least, like it was registering now. My brother, my brat, that sweet kid with the big horn-rims, had been obsessed with evil, had thought that he himself was some festering source of it, had even thought about offing himself. While I was busy feeling slighted. While I was passing judgment, Bruno-style.

And what was he talking about, the family secret I didn't know? Had Djed been murdered after all? It was not beyond the realm of possibility.

I swallowed, then looked up. Jan was still frowning at his journal, Rikki still asleep. I pulled out Letter #2, written April 1, 1991.

Dear Jonah,

Hello, and hope you are well. Life goes on at Iglesia de Guadalupe. Every morning I get up for Vigil with Jorge and Martin. We don't hold it in the church, but in a small back room of our house. It's a good time: dawn just breaking, a chill in the air, the town still asleep. I started it; they'd never done it before, but when I described our schedule at the Hermitage, both of them thought it would be good. Sometimes we have to wait ten minutes for Martin. He seems to have lost a lot of sleep over the years.

At 7:00 I celebrate Mass in the church, and there's usually a crowd. You would like our altar. It would appeal to the snob in you that secretly prefers Florentine architecture to the 1950s stucco at the Hermitage. Guadalupe is your standard old Mexican iglesia, complete with fully decked-out statues and a murky oil of Our Lady on the wall. Tourists love it, but little do they know. This place—really, most of the San Cristóbal diocese—is up to its eyeballs in controversy, which is exactly (I know this will surprise you) why I requested placement here.

Basically, it's the old story: a few rich latifundistas (large landholders) hoarding all the wealth, while the peasants (mostly Maya subsistence farmers clustered in small villages throughout the mountains) live in crushing poverty. It's feudal, and the colonial mind-set that still reigns here requires that the power remain in the hands of the landholders. Any protest on the part of the indigenas is automatically labeled Marxist and brutally suppressed. But it's not just the official cops and army at work. Many of the latifundistas fund their own private police (they call them the Guardia Blanca here) who specialize in terror tactics—kidnappings, torture, beheadings, massacres.

Our bishop, Samuel Ruiz García, is the bane of their existence. He's a powerful force here, and not afraid to mix it up with the PRI-istas who run the country. His friends call him one of the best advertisements for liberation theology in Central America. His enemies, including Televisa, the media network that dominates Mexico, refer to him as the "Red Bishop." Two years ago he established a non-denominational, ecumenical human rights center here in San Cristóbal called Frayba, after Fray Bartolomé de las Casas, a sixteenth-century friar who became the first bishop of Chiapas. There's a lot of similarity between Ruiz and de las Casas, who spent fifty years trying to overthrow the colonial encomienda system that kept the Mayas and other indigenous people enslaved.

But the Church is in a very tricky situation here. Political developments over the past few years have been devastating for the subsistence farmers. The twentieth-century reestablishment of their right to commonly owned village land (the ejido system) is currently under attack, and everyone's convinced that soon there will be a constitutional amendment in favor of the big private landholders and/or foreign investors. Plus the forces arrayed against small farmers are not just local but international—the new NAFTA treaty spearheaded by the U.S., if and when it goes into effect, will flood the Mexican market with cheap corn, essentially wiping them out.

So as you would expect, guerrilla movements are afoot. There's one located in the Lacandon Selva nearby that everybody seems to know about and nobody's mentioning. From the perspective of the powers that be, anything that looks like it's raising the political consciousness of the indigenas, including the Christian base communities (small family or village Bible studies and worship groups) that have any ties to our diocese, should be scrutinized with great suspicion. Over and over, the bishop and even the Vatican are having to emphasize the firm dividing lines between these small Christian communities and de facto political organizations, especially armed groups. But the situation is volatile.

So what am I, a would-be monk, a lover of the desert fathers and contemplative prayer, doing in the middle of this hotbed? Good question. But once again I'm out of time. Just know that it's got to do with the same old issue and my inability to let it go till I work it out.

Stefan

A rabble-rousing bishop. A guerrilla group parked in a nearby jungle. Private police forces roving around looking to behead people. None of this sounded promising concerning Stefan's disappearance. He could have run afoul of any variety of thugs, including the Catholic ones, though I had to admit that this Ruiz character did not sound like your typical episcopal spin doctor. And my sense was that if Ruiz even remotely suspected Stefan had been kidnapped by the bad guys, he'd be raising all kinds of hell about it. Yet the diocese had been almost totally silent on the subject of Stefan's vanishing and professed to have no idea whatsoever where he might be.

That seemed extremely weird to me. Stefan worked for them. He had a superior. Somebody must be reporting to somebody on this, or at the very least the Church rumor mill had to be operating overtime. Nothing, however, was leaking out. The official word was that they did not consider him to be a missing person, though they did not know his whereabouts at the present time. This part had Jonah truly rattled, because according to him, it could only mean one thing: Stefan had gone off on his own. For whatever reason, whether to protect the hierarchy or to defy it, he'd cut himself out of the group and headed off on his own personal mission. And Jonah and I both knew that nothing in Stefan's personality would give him one ounce of real help if he had launched out on some such heroic, harebrained venture.

Musing hard, I cast another fierce glance out the tent flap, only to meet the cold blue stare of my boss, who'd clearly been watching me for a while. Quietly, without dropping my eyes, I folded up the letters and slipped them under my sleeping sheet. But I could tell by the look on his face that his naturally suspicious nature, at least when it came to me, had been stirred back to life.

Chapter Six

A week later we were done in Tikal, and Jan gave us a couple of days of R and R in Flores before we started the next leg of the journey. Though I'd only spent half a day on the island before heading out to the field, I was happy to return to the sinking town in the middle of Lake Petén Itzá. The house, which was not their house, Rikki explained, but a kind of way station for traveling archeologists and anthropologists, was on the high side of one of the flooded streets. My upstairs bedroom with its woven bedspread and green-shuttered window looked out across the shifting silver water, dotted with small wooden cayucos, toward San Benito.

It wasn't just the view that made me happy. I like living in tents, but after ten days in the jungle, I was covered with bites and needed to wash my clothes in something besides cold water and camp suds. At least here we could heat well water on the stove.

We could also cook. And I was a pretty good cook. Peter, my first official boyfriend, passed on some culinary skills during the couple of years we lived together. Peter was in film school, I was in photography school, and what kind of creative geniuses would we have been without knowing how to braise, sauté, and whisk? Plus, he informed me early on, he liked to be surprised by food, and he couldn't very well surprise him*self*, could he? So I learned, though I rarely demonstrated my talents these days because it was the kind of thing men were tempted to manipulate for their own ends. Now, however, with access to an oven for twenty-four more hours before we headed out, I decided to cook for the three of us, a real dinner that would take half a day to prepare.

I unhooked the two woven bags from the kitchen wall, stuffed a handful of quetzales in my skirt pocket, and went out into the street. The houses across from us sat in at least a foot of lake water, so the electricity had long ago been shut off, but there were still families in them, using candles, I suppose, and cooking over fires. A group of schoolgirls with tight, patent-leather braids skipped along, holding hands, and I watched as a cloud of white butterflies coming the other way dipped down toward their black heads. Christmas was only two weeks away, and Flores was ready for it. Colored lights were strung across the small open-front stores that sold baskets and weavings and leather belts and clusters of purses. Bells hung from the ceilings. People had set out crèches and candles in their window sills.

The air in the mercado was thick with incense and spices. I found pollo, pescado, pan, banana empanadas, cerveza. Fruit was piled in yellow, green, pink, and maroon heaps on brilliant Maya blankets, encased in thorny shells or tough husks, fruit that grew on trees in the jungle or swelled on vines. I bought too much food, more than we'd ever eat, but who cared? Some completely atypical domestic urge was apparently running the show here.

Rikki and Jan were out when I got back. One of them had left the radio on, and a Mexican tenor complained to me of his love wounds. A kingfisher sat on a post across the street by a tied-up boat that banged against the sides of the underwater house. I chopped onions and chilies, then stirred them around in the snapping grease of the frying pan, stopping halfway through to crack an icy beer for company while I cooked. As dinnertime approached, I found myself listening for the door and thinking about how I was going to surprise everybody.

When they finally arrived, though, taller Rikki behind his father in the doorway, both of them observing the set table, the candles, all the food, I could see that once again I'd made some kind of mistake, at least as far as Jan was concerned. Rikki was just Rikki, a perpetually starving sixteen-year-old. He couldn't have been more delighted at the prospect of a feast. But something went over Jan's face as he stared at my day's work, the edge of a shadow, and after one piercing look at me, he wouldn't meet my eyes. Somehow, as in the North Acropolis tomb when I had startled him so badly, I'd wandered into territory I didn't belong.

This ruined the meal, in spite of Rikki's stuffing himself. This, and what Jan said at the end of it, which was, "You could leave if you want."

It took a moment to digest this. "I don't understand," I said. "Leave?"

"When I hired you, I did not think the project would be so rugged."

"It's not rugged."

"I did not think you would get so interested."

"Interested in what?"

"Has Rikki been teaching you how to read the glyphs?"

Actually, sometimes on those long, lazy jungle days when Rikki and I had nothing to do but wait for night to fall, he had indeed taught me some things. I knew, for example, about Glyph G, the nine Lords of the Night who each ruled their own hour of darkness. There was my favorite, monkey-faced G1. And then, probably more to the point in Jan's paranoid mind, G3, which had our old friend the k'in sign buried right in the middle of it. My noticing this had led to a discussion, not Rikki's fault, about the fact that k'in showed up practically everywhere, as common as a stop sign or an exit marker. I asked him why on earth we were recording something so mundane. He had gotten wound up and blurted out what he probably wasn't supposed to: that it was this very quality, the fact that you could find it everywhere, that made it such a perfect code sign. Then he'd blushed like crazy and snapped his mouth shut, and I hadn't gotten another peep out of him for an hour. Now, with Jan's brooding gaze on him, he hung his head like a bad dog.

That made me mad. "What's wrong with me learning a few basic facts?" I said.

"Our agreement was that you would never publish any of your photographs or drawings, and that you would keep whatever you are doing for me to yourself."

"Who says I'm not?"

He was looking uncomfortable. "One morning I saw you going

through a lot of paperwork in your tent. I cannot keep you on if you are working for somebody else."

"Look, what are you thinking?" I demanded. "That I'm some kind of spy for the Maya Hunting Club, or whatever it is you people belong to? I don't care if we shoot that damn glyph every night for another year as long as you get me to Chiapas."

If there'd been a reverse button, I would have hit it, but the words were already out, filling the air like the lingering odor of frying onions.

"Why Chiapas?"

And suddenly, though still angry, I was tempted to spill it. The case of the unofficially missing priest. But that was impossible, so instead I mutely lowered my head.

"Do you need help of some kind?" he said quietly.

Again I shook my head no.

He frowned. "But you are happy with this job?"

"Very."

I could see him thinking all this over. Then he put his hands on his knees and stood up. "All right then. We leave in the morning for Palenque. It is a two-day trip, a long two days. We will take the truck as far as the Usumacinta River. You two had better pack."

Rikki offered to do the dishes, and I went upstairs. Palenque. Where the wife was. I took off my skirt and sandals and crawled into bed in my black T-shirt, where I lay staring at the ceiling. A dim light from the street undulated across it like water. For a couple of long moments, I felt strangely queasy, as though the dinner had suddenly turned against me, which, in a sense, it had. I found myself thinking of Chicago again and, much to my surprise, whether or not I was living the way I should. Whether I should have just married some Italian or Pole or maybe even Alexander, straight out of high school, and settled down in a Polish or Italian neighborhood a few miles from Hana and Bruno and given that sad pair a couple of grandkids to distract them. Whether, if I'd kept on going to Mass, Stefan wouldn't have gone searching all over the world for someone he could talk to. We'd had a family, I thought, screwed up as it was. I had always assumed Stefan was the one who broke it to pieces, but maybe not.

Drowsing, I tried to imagine myself married, but couldn't. So I thought about the secret thing I'd purchased today, along with all that gorgeous fruit, at the downtown Flores market. A lovely boot knife, just like the one the USIA man had taught me to throw. Because you never knew what would happen next, especially in places like the Petén, across which we would be driving, or Chiapas, where guerrillas and the Guardia Blanca roamed like antelope across the plains.

The other, the bit about my wasted life, was just the kind of sentimental schlock you think about alone in bed in strange countries. And I realized a long time ago that it's not some weird bug from Africa that finishes off people like me. It's self-pity. But just to make myself feel better, I crawled back out of the sheets and rooted through my camera packs, supposedly double-checking, but really to feel the familiar shape of them against my fingers. Then I got back under the woven blanket, turned over and went to sleep, which is what I should have done in the first place.

Jan was not kidding about the length of a single day when you are crossing the Petén. It might have been even longer, but luckily we were waved on through the military checkpoint at La Libertad where a guy with a .38 in his hand was directing a bus search that looked like it was going to take a while. After La Libertad, we rocked west for hours through long stretches of open savannah, ragged with burnt tree stumps, what was left of the rainforest after three decades of civil war and thousands of highland Maya refugees streaming north into the jungle, burning trees to plant their little cornfields, and right behind them, the loggers and the oilmen and the cattlemen.

Occasionally, the forest reappeared, and a group of men would emerge from a muddy track through the trees, feet bare, machetes slung across their backs. They would stare at us patiently as we rolled by until Jan stopped and motioned toward the bed of the truck. Then we would jounce along with our new passengers for a few kilometers until they knocked on the back window. Jan would stop, they would leap down, duck their heads and murmur "Gracias," and once again vanish into the trees.

Rubber tappers, maybe. Strong, undernourished little men with broken teeth and dirt ingrained in patterns like tattoos. I'd seen the same kind of men in El Salvador, Nicaragua, Afghanistan, Thailand, Burundi. It didn't matter what forest or desert they were in. Each of them had eight to ten kids and half of those would die, especially if yet another war between this big man and that big man broke out. It was okay with me that Jan kept picking them up, but I hoped nobody tried to make off with our stuff.

Hours later, we pulled into Bethel. Even in the dark, you could see that it was a mean, unfriendly little hole dominated by young, drunk soldiers, some without their shirts on but none without their Uzis or AK-47s. They ambled around town in groups, swinging their complicated guns as though they were plastic toys and staring at us imposingly, as they had been taught to do. The trick was to ignore them without displaying overt disrespect.

Immigration was housed inside a concertina-laced military compound. The officer was in army uniform and asked for double the going visa fee. We handed over our papers, and I held my breath as he glanced down at my name, Eva Kovic, hoping the "Kovic," shared by Stefan, wouldn't ring any bells for him. Though I had the phony passports tucked away if I needed them, I was saving those for a last-ditch escape. The guy seemed more interested in my legs than in my passport, however, and I threw in an extra five bucks just get out of there.

After we found a boatman willing to do a night run to Corozal, we unloaded the truck and carried the gear down the steepest and muddiest excuse for a landing I've ever seen. But across the river was Mexico, and in Mexico was Chiapas, and in Chiapas was San Cristóbal de las Casas, the last place anyone had seen my brother, so what choice did I have? Then we were on the water and it was slipping by us, glimmering with starlight, and the familiar night noises of the jungle were drifting out of the mist. I found a spot in the middle of the boat under a palm roof and tried to put myself in order.

If Stefan were in a place like Bethel, a Mexican version of it, then he was in the hands of bullies and sharks. And when the bullies had you, it usually meant torture. The least creative of them tended to rely on cigarette burns, but there were fancier methods—forcing a mixture of chili piquín and bubbly water into the nasal cavities, for example, and then attaching electric wires to the genitals.

I couldn't think about that. I had to stick with my first hunch: that the Red Bishop would have gone to war over Stefan's disappearance if he thought it were a political kidnapping. I had to stick with Jonah's growing conviction—mine too—that my brother had gone off on his own to accomplish some secret purpose entirely unrelated to the obvious issues of church and politics. Thankfully, in less than forty minutes, we saw the first lights on the Mexican side of the river.

Compared to the immigration station at Bethel, Corozal's was a palace, a Spanish adobe with a tile roof and a long veranda. Jan left us with the luggage and went off to get the lay of the land. After a murmured conversation at the door with someone I could not see, he came back and told us we could put up our tents on the lawn. Pathetically thankful to finally be in Mexico, I fell asleep the minute my head hit the pillow, only to bounce back out of bed when the roosters began to crow. From the veranda steps, I had a ringside seat on Stefan's world. Smoke from breakfast fires drifted in the air. Women with enormous striped jars on their heads made their way toward the river across a field of stubble. Three barking dogs chased each other around the comedor beside the dock where we had come off the boat the night before. Far off, in the opposite direction from the rest of town, lay an acre or so of palm frond shelters, most of them collapsed, and part of a surrounding wire fence that was still standing.

The immigration officer-in-residence, still damp from shaving and looking very spruce in his green uniform, came out to sit beside me on the steps. He could have been an older brother of the Italian at Tikal. I had my automatic thoughts, especially about how long it had been. He asked me in Spanish how I had slept. I told him wonderfully well. He asked where we had been. I was not sure what to say, so I pretended not to understand. He asked how I liked Corozal. I said it was delightful to be in Corozal.

We were getting along just fine.

I pointed to the ruined encampment up the road and asked him what it might be. Refugees from across the river, he said. But they are no longer here. He shook his handsome head. The Guatemalan army kept violating the border to get at them.

"That is very sad," I said.

We sat watching the women go by with their striped jugs. "Did you grow up in this town?" I asked.

"No, no," he told me. "I am from Tuxtla Guittérez, do you know that place?"

I shook my head.

"That is where my wife and son are," he said, giving me a regretful look.

"I see," I told him, equally regretfully.

Jan chose this special moment to come crawling out of his tent, yawning and stretching and looking like a rumpled Dutchman, with Rikki following in short order, checking his watch. The bus was supposed to leave for Palenque at 8:00, but who knew when it would really go, since we could see it parked behind the comedor minus its driver, who was presumably inside enjoying his beans and rice and tortillas. We went down to join him, accompanied by our friendly officer, and by the time everyone finished breakfast and wandered out to our ride, it was nearly 9:00. The officer stood with us in the crowd and the rumble and the black fumes while a couple of nimble guys tied boxes and satchels to the roof. When it was time, he helped me up, his brown hand big and warm under mine, and we gave each other one last regretful look.

Our bus pulled into town ten hours after leaving Corozal, and the young bucks climbed back on the roof to unload our packs, which I could not stop myself from immediately checking after a long day of secret fretting. No matter how often I sally forth in this vagabond life of mine, I am constantly plagued by worry about my equipment. Not only do I have thousands of dollars invested in all this gear by now, it's what allows me to live the life I live. Losing a camera would be like losing an arm.

She—the wife—wasn't at the bus stop to meet us, so we took a taxi, which ferried us through the hotel district and past the zócalo in front of the church, then north to a residential district on the outskirts of town. The neighborhood surprised me. I hadn't let myself think much about the wife or where she—they—would live, but this collection of small farmsteads was not the kind of barrio in which you'd expect a gringa to take up residence. We passed fenced yards with chickens scratching in them, some with pigs and burros. At one place, a good-sized Brahma cow hung her mournful head over the gate.

The taxi stopped in front of one of the poorer-looking places, a cheap box of cracked yellow stucco with a burro tied up in the front yard and an old red jeep parked in the driveway. Puzzled, I looked at Jan. He was gazing intently out the window as though this were not his house and his wife were not inside it. Rikki, on the other hand, was already climbing out of the car, dragging his hand over one long ear of the donkey as he passed it on his way to the porch. "Mom," he called, "we're here. Merry Christmas!" And then went in and closed the door behind him.

Jan sat for another couple of moments, and I wondered if the two of us were going to wind up going off somewhere to rent a hotel room together. Finally, he sighed and slowly got out of the taxi, giving me a sad, abstracted look as though he'd forgotten I was there. Together we unloaded the trunk and the backseat, and he paid the driver. Then he turned toward the house. "Six months ago," he said, as though I'd know what he was talking about, "she would have at least been out on the porch." I had no idea what to say. "Well, come on in, then," he said. "She will be dying of curiosity by now." That didn't sound so good either, and I thought about climbing back in the taxi and taking off for San Cristóbal, where at least I had something important to do.

Chapter Seven

Jan scraped his feet on the straw porch mat a couple of times, still stalling, then opened the door and went inside. I hung back as long as I could, until Rikki came back out. "Eva," he said, "what are you doing?"

I followed him obediently, through the empty living room decorated with a small Christmas tree and down a hall to what, it suddenly occurred to me, could only be a bedroom. Oh, God, I thought, she's sick. *That's* the deal here. And then Rikki stepped aside and gently pushed me into the room, and I saw for myself: a bed with a thin woman in it, her eyes as brown as the immigration officer's, and classic cheekbones, too sharp, as though she never ate enough. She was wearing a white T-shirt and a dark blue Indian skirt and sandals, and was propped up against pillows. She didn't move, except to turn her head, and the curious limpness of her arms and hands made me think for a moment that she was paralyzed. But then she brought one hand up and extended it out toward me, and I saw the way that it wavered in the air like kelp shifting in the tide. She couldn't even shape a symmetrical smile.

"This is my mom, Anne," said Rikki.

I stepped forward and took her limp hand. Her skin was smooth and cold, and I could feel the bones inside.

"Eva," she said slowly in a slight but unmistakable British accent. "How nice to meet you."

I was still holding her hand and not sure what to do next.

"I am so sorry not to be up when you arrived. Felice went off to the market to get the things for dinner, and it's hard to make it into the chair on my own these days."

The accent, also a surprise, added a note of class to a scene that seemed to be drifting dangerously close to the rocky shoals of melodrama, but then I made the mistake of glancing around at the rest of the room. Sure enough, there sat a serious-looking wheelchair, the kind used by people who are never going to walk again. I set her hand back on the bedspread and tried not to look at the chair. I felt clammy, as though I'd breathed too many diesel fumes or drunk bad water.

She was still smiling, difficult though it must have been, and I thought, she's smiled more in ten minutes than Jan has the whole time I've known him. I tried to fix my eyes on hers so that it didn't appear that I was avoiding looking at her, but it was hard. Despite my prize-winning headshots of bewildered two-year-olds in war zones, weakness is a kind of horror to me, and once I smell it, I keep as much distance as I can. A strange form of cowardice on my part, but there it is. I looked at Jan for the first time, who was not showing much but not hiding anything either. Somber, dependable Jan, who liked to smoke his pipe in the evenings. Good old Jan with his red driving cap and his hands easy on the wheel.

"How about," I said, "if I start things going in the kitchen? You know, whatever Felice—that's her name?—was thinking of making for dinner."

Anne started to shake her head no, a slow, painful-to-watch motion, but I cut her off before she could say it. "I like to cook," I said. "Ask these guys if I like to cook." I wanted to be out of the room. I could feel my hands fidgeting.

"She does, Mom," said Rikki. "She makes great arroz con pollo."

"It's no problem, really," I said, "and I need to stretch after sitting all day on that bus." Then I came to a belated halt, realizing how this must sound.

She'd stopped trying to say no and simply watched my face with a faint, uncertain smile. I backed out of the room and fled down the hall to the living room before I made it worse. There, I sank down on the sofa and sat for a minute, getting my breath. This was impossible.

I could not deal with handicapped people. Dead people, fine. I'd photographed my share. People scarred and scalded and shot, all right, as long as it was clear they were either going to die or get better. But the long, drawn-out, permanent stuff was beyond me.

Pretty soon Rikki came down the hall. He stood in front of the sofa looking down, not saying anything. Looking at my face, he must have been able to see what was there—that his mother revolted me. He got pale, then flushed, then went pale again. Then he gave me what on anyone else would have been a hard look and went to the kitchen. I sat there for a few minutes longer. When I finally went in, he was dragging things out of the cupboard and didn't turn around.

"Look, Rikki," I began.

He waved me off.

"You don't even know what I'm going to say."

"Never mind."

I put my hand on his arm, which was shaking a little, he was so upset with me. I could see that for years his job had been to defend her against the cruel world and its cruel remarks. This was the way he judged people: by how they reacted to her. "Nobody told me," I said. "Neither of you. You shied away from it every time I brought her up. So I built a different picture of her in my mind and it was a shock, that's all. I didn't figure on her being sick. You could have said."

"My dad doesn't like to talk about it," he said, still not looking at me or down at my hand on his arm. "He said it's better that way. It's nobody's business but ours. He doesn't like people gossiping about her, he says."

"But Rikki. I'm not just anybody. I'm living here for the next two weeks, or at least I'm supposed to. And it's Christmas. That's not somebody who's going to gossip, that's somebody who needs to know ahead of time."

"You think she's ugly."

"No." I shook my head and I shook his arm. "That's not fair."

"You looked sick to your stomach when you saw her."

"Well, okay," I said. "I admit it. I'm not good around sick people.

I'd make a bad nurse. I get the willies when I see people hurting like that."

"She's not hurting."

"What's wrong with her? You still haven't said."

He shrugged. "She's got MS. Multiple sclerosis. She got it when I was six, when we were first at Tikal. It wasn't that bad for a long time. But now. . ." He shrugged again.

"What's going to happen to her?" I still had my hand on his arm, but now I was giving it a little squeeze.

He finally looked down at me, sighing. "What do you think?"

"She's going to die."

He nodded. We looked at each other.

"They don't know how long," he said, "but when they get to this stage, sometimes it speeds up. First she won't be able to get up at all anymore, then she won't be able to talk or see."

"She'll have to go to a hospital."

"Somewhere. We don't know where yet. But for now she wants to stay in the house and do her usual stuff until she can't anymore."

"What stuff?"

"She's been teaching since a couple of years after she got sick, after she couldn't keep her balance enough to be out in the field with Dad anymore."

I thought about Jan in the early morning, sitting by the campfire with his big bound journal. "What does she teach?" I asked.

"She teaches people how to read. She always used to have classes at the church, but now it's too hard for her to get there, even with Felice. So they come here, and Felice writes on the board for her because she can't hold onto the chalk anymore. But I don't know how much longer she can do it." He stopped.

We stood there in the kitchen for long moment while the light died outside. It was a nice little kitchen without any charm. Functional, like the monastery buildings at the Hermitage. I could see modifications here and there, like the chopping block on cut-down legs at wheelchair height. I gave his arm a final pat and let it go.

"Have you always lived in this house?"

He nodded. "My dad's tried to move her out of here. He says it's embarrassing how rundown the place is getting, but she won't leave. He wants her closer to the doctors, maybe in Tuxtla or Villahermosa, but she feels at home here, and she's got her students."

"It must be tough on you."

"It's harder on my dad." He stopped, as though he were edging into indiscretion.

"I don't think she's ugly, Rikki. Just give me a chance to get used to the idea, okay?"

"Okay," he said in a muffled voice.

"I like you, Rikki. I don't say that to many people. And she's your mom, so I'm guessing I'll like her too. When I get used to everything."

"Well," he said. "At least you're honest about it. Some people just pretend, but she's too smart for that. She picks right up on it. So just ask her things, if you want to know something. It's better than faking that you don't mind what she looks like."

Somebody came through the back door without knocking. "In here," called Rikki, and a young girl, nineteen or twenty, poked her head into the kitchen. She had big eyes pulled down sweetly at the outer corners and glossy hair in a horse tail down her back. "Felice," he said, brightening, and then, "This is Felice, Eva. The person who helps out my mom."

"Hello," she said shyly. "I'm glad to meet you." Her English was very good. She motioned with her head toward the hallway, where Anne's bedroom was. "Did she sleep? She has been sleeping a lot in the afternoon these days."

"We woke her up when we came in. She was embarrassed about not being up."

Felice shook her head and the glossy tail shifted like prairie grass. "She says naps are for babies. But they help, you know? She is refreshed."

Rikki said to me, "The thing about her disease is that you need a lot of rest. You can't push yourself too hard or you get worse faster. And she was so active—she'd want to scramble all over the pyramids, even after she couldn't hold her balance. But the heat in the jungle wore her out."

"And she was sick already when you spent the night on Temple IV?"

"That's what I mean. Dad could have killed us. Her right leg was all goofed up by then, and she was always losing her grip on things, dropping coffee cups and forks. And there she was, going up that crazy ladder. Luckily, I was too young to realize how nuts we were. I just thought it was the coolest thing any kid ever did with his mom, especially since they never caught us."

"She had her ladies this morning," said Felice. "There are twelve of them in that group now, and five in the men's, but she does the men's at night because of their jobs."

Rikki said, "So she hasn't cut back any yet."

"Not yet," said Felice cheerfully. "Not Señora Anne."

Meanwhile, the two of them were laying out queso and chilies and fresh tortillas, and Felice took a big bowl covered with plastic wrap out of the refrigerator and poured it into a pan on the stove. "Mole," said Rikki. "How'd you know I was dying for mole?"

"You are always dying for mole, muchacho."

I watched them working together at the chopping block, the tall young Dutchman and the Mexican girl with her sad eyes and sweet smile. They bantered like siblings. The affection clearly went both ways, but without any apparent sparks. That's nice, I thought, that brotherly, sisterly stuff—and of course thought immediately of Stefan.

"Felice," I said. "Señora Anne—she used to teach her classes at the Catholic church?"

"Yes. But it is very hard for her to go out now. So her students on their own say no, they will come here instead, she can teach them in her house."

"But you know the priest at the church?"

"Oh, yes, si. Padre Miguel. He is not the real priest, but he is here for a while so that Padre Gilberto can travel to la Ciudad."

"If I want to go to Mass, what time would that be?"

"You are Catholic," said Felice happily.

"Well, not really. Well, I am but I haven't been for a while. But I

might want to go while we're here. You know. Christmas and everything." Rikki was giving me an odd look, and Felice was trying her best
to comprehend. Nominal Catholics, I took it, were rare in these parts;
you either were or you weren't. "Anyway, Fr. Miguel, right?"

She nodded.

"Okay. Maybe tomorrow, if we're not out at the ruins." I glanced
at Rikki.

"Not tomorrow. We've got the day off, Dad said."

"Early Mass is at seven in the morning," said Felice, "and another
one at nine."

Jan came down the hall and into the kitchen. He looked old. "Felice," he said, "good to see you. How have you been?"

"She looks fine, doesn't she, Señor? Good spirits."

"Oh, yes," he said. "She seems in very good spirits. Has she been
sleeping more? It seems to me she has been sleeping more, and not up
so much."

"Not so much," said Felice. "But her spirits are good."

"You are doing a fine job, Felice. I am grateful to you." He had
not yet looked in my direction. I felt like the only person in the room
without a reason for being there. Here they were, all united in their
common cause, Señora Anne, and I couldn't even look her in the face.
This was a test and I wasn't passing.

"Is there anything she needs right now?" I said. "Something to
drink, maybe? Water? I'll just trot it down the hall, if you want."

All three of them turned and stared at me.

"No problem," I said. "You all need to catch up with each other. So
I'll just . . . go check up on her or something."

"She's sleeping now," said Jan.

"Oh."

"But after she wakes up," he said very slowly, "it might be a good
idea for you to chat with her for a few minutes."

"Okay," I said. "After she wakes up. No problem."

"She doesn't see many American women. She was looking forward
to this."

"Well, then, that's what we'll do. A little chat."

"Eva," he said, right in front of everybody. "Don't patronize my wife."

A cold knife slipped between my ribs. It was the first time I could see how angry he was, much angrier than Rikki had been after I went plunging out of the room. Rikki was transparent. Jan could hold it in, but it was in his voice. And I knew I would not be forgiven soon.

"All right," I said, putting my chin up, which was what I always did when I was caught out. "I wouldn't do that, though. I might not be great in the sickroom, but at least I don't put on some act. If you knew me, you'd know I wouldn't do that." And then I turned and went out the front door and took a long walk through streets that were filled with the clamor of barnyard animals. All I could think of was that Stefan would have handled everything differently. He wouldn't have been thinking of himself, for starters, and he wouldn't have let the hospital atmosphere get to him. He would have walked right by the wheelchair like he never even noticed it and sat down beside her and taken her bony hand in his. And then he would have listened to her for as long as she wanted to talk.

But it was no good comparing us. It never had been. I was no more like my brother than Bruno was like Jesus Christ.

I didn't sleep much that night even though I was plenty tired. It was raining hard, for one thing, and the wind was blowing in gusts around the stucco house. I was on the sofa in my sleeping sheet with an extra blanket on top, feeling just about as blue as I ever had. It wasn't loneliness, exactly, though if you'd asked me right then, I would have said that the one thing I could take to the bank was that I was all by myself in this world, even before Stefan disappeared. Whatever it was, it had started in Flores, and Palenque was making it worse.

I must have finally dropped off about 3:30 and was awakened after an hour or so by the clacking of the wheelchair rolling down the hall. Jan, helping his wife to the bathroom. They said a few words I couldn't hear, the light went on briefly, the door closed, and he waited in there with her until she was done. What a life, I thought. Did they actually sleep in that sickbed together? Did he ever feel like touching her, except in the way a caregiver would? And yet he'd bitten off my head to defend her honor.

I knew I wouldn't get back to sleep. I waited until he had rolled her back down the hall, and then I got up and turned on the living room light. My pack was propped against the wall, and I sat down on the floor in front of it in my black T-shirt and underwear and white socks and dug around until I found the packet of Stefan's letters. Then I began to read from where I'd left off in Tikal. Letter #3 was dated February 16, 1992.

> Dear Jonah,
>
>   Sorry about yet another long silence. I don't mean to leave you hanging between letters. But I'm pretty much up to the eyeballs all the time, and when I do get a minute to myself, I try my best to hide out somewhere, even if it's only for a couple of hours. Next time you're tempted to gnash your teeth about the rigors of the hermit life (i.e., your *New York Times* is a day or so late), try to spare me a thought. Right now, I'd give my left arm to be sitting on that redwood bench outside my cell, watching the whales go by.
>
>   But I chose this, right?
>
>   There's a young man here I'm asking you to pray for. Mat—a Maya name—has only been in San Cristóbal for three years. Before that he lived in the Ejido Morelia, a Tzeltal community outside of Altamirano, where his family grew corn and coffee. It's an independent-minded ejido, and for a number of years has resisted the overtures of the PRI's official campesino federation (which is more about keeping the campesinos in line than it is about helping them), despite having to face even worse neglect by the government as a result. Morelia has no doctor, no potable water, no full-time teacher, no priest.

Three years ago, Mat's father drew down the wrath of a powerful local latifundista, Donaldo Aguilar, whose plantation runs along the ejido boundaries, and who's had his eye on Morelia's land for years. Mat's father made it his business to keep track of Aguilar's plans, and spoke out against them once too often. So Aguilar called out his private little police squad, which, like most of these mercenary gangs, is primarily made up of disgruntled ladino ex-cowboys.

Mat's father was kidnapped on the road to Belisario Dominguez. Witnesses, a ten-year-old girl and her eight-year-old brother, recognized at least two of the men, rough types from Altamirano they often saw lounging around town when they went to the market. They were in a new blue Ford pickup without any license plates, and there were six of them, four riding in the bed. The little girl said they beat Mat's father with the butts of their guns, then slung him in the back. Six days later, he reappeared on the track to Belisario Dominguez in almost the same place, this time propped against a rock, with his severed head in his lap. Based on the burns on him, he'd been put through hell.

Mat was old enough to be next, so the community smuggled him out of Morelia, and he resurfaced in San Cristóbal, living at first in La Hormiga slum with a group of expulsados. Did I mention the expulsado thing in my last letter? How Maya converts to evangelicalism, or else what's known as "Word of God" Catholicism, are being driven out of their ancestral villages? The charge is that they no longer recognize the authority of the caciques (local chiefs), but the real issue is that they've started thinking for themselves, which power brokers like Aguilar and company, who more often than not have the caciques in their back pockets, refuse to countenance. Sadly, the villages themselves are no help, only too happy to drive out those who they feel are passing moral judgment by swearing off drinking, wife beating, and polygamy. Homeless and landless, the exiles head for the towns and cities where they are making up an increasingly large portion of the slum populations.

Mat was lucky. He found his way into the Guadalupe barrio, a community founded by former expulsados, where he lives with a Tzeltal family from the congregation. In three years he's learned Spanish, and in the few months I've known him a fair amount of English besides. He has the idea that when he learns enough, he will bring his father's killers to justice. What I can't help hoping is that when he learns enough, he'll want to become a priest instead. He's got it in him, Jonah. I can see it from a hundred miles away.

And why, you are no doubt asking, is someone like me, a confessed coward, getting so wrapped up in this kid's situation? Lots of reasons, but here's the most direct. When I was in Nepal, probably nineteen or so, young enough to have not yet personally witnessed a purely evil act, I was dragged to a festival at a little village called Khokana at the far end of the Kathmandu Valley. A normal little town, mostly known for its mustard seed industry. Nobody would tell me what was going to happen, only that I was about to see one of the old, authentic rituals tourists are not invited to.

There's a temple there, the Rudrayani, and nearby is a walled pond. At a certain point, people started gathering on the ledge above this pond, jocular but intent, and you could feel the excitement level starting to rise. The next thing I know, someone tosses in a young goat. This poor creature is terrified and bleating and trying its best to swim, and I'm already getting sick to my stomach at the callousness of what's going on here. Then nine guys leap in after it like they are going to save it, and I breathe a sigh of relief.

But instead, they drag it to a pole rising up out of the water, brace themselves, and start biting and grabbing various body parts—the tail, a back leg, an ear—and the goat is thrashing like a heron who's gotten its wing tip caught in the mouth of a crocodile and, even though it's going to die, is trying its best to catapult itself into the air, and above all the splashing and yelling and lunging there's this unearthly crying going on, like a child who's being beaten by somebody it loves. In no time at all, they've torn the thing from limb to limb. The water turns a muddy pink. They toss the carcass and its several pieces up on the wall. The guy who gets credit for the kill is dubbed hero-of-the-day and leads the big dance afterward.

I go back to the hospice and have a long talk with Fr. John, who grew up in India and saw versions of this kind of stuff throughout his childhood, pretty much always the same scenario. He pointed out that animal sacrifice was a step up from what no doubt preceded it, and the real question, the question I should focus on, was what prompted these bloody sacrifices at all? And more importantly, what did it all mean in light of the Christian story? Because for him, the cross was the great historical wedge, the event that finally began to de-mystify eons of bloodletting in the name of the divine and render it all absurd.

As usual, I've got to quit before I'm finished here, but now you know what launched me out of the death cloud, where I might have twisted in the wind for the rest of my days, and into a serious study of evil.

Your compadre,
Stefan

Not exactly a great way to cheer myself up, I thought. And then, surprisingly, I felt myself getting angry. My brother seemed to believe he was the one and only person in the world who'd noticed just how shitty it can get. The goat story was troubling, sure, but what about some of the things *I'd* seen? And unlike Stefan, who was determined to wallow in it, I'd learned early on that you can't be an eyewitness to brutality, you can't zero in on it with your cool camera lens, unless you figure out how to shield yourself against it. I've known war correspondents who never got there, and before you knew it, they were limping off in various states of trauma. What a waste of talent and hard work.

What a cop-out.

Because if nobody records this stuff, how does anyone know it really happened?

That's my standard response, anyway, to anyone who asks how I can stand to do what I do. I've told myself that, given a choice, I would have long ago focused my talents on nature scenes or fashion design or artsy-fartsy portraits of eccentric people, the kind that get exhibited at the Art Institute of Chicago. That's not true, though. Because I *had* a choice, and what I chose were war zones and refugee camps, and not for the reason I so piously serve up when anybody questions me. People believe what they want to believe happened or didn't happen, and it doesn't matter how much evidence there is to the contrary. Pictures don't make a damn bit of difference there. All the Nazi death camp photos in the world aren't going to convince die-hard conspiracy theorists that the Holocaust wasn't Allied propaganda.

Truth be known, I choose to work in war zones because they are the realest places I've ever been. It doesn't matter what anybody does with the raw facts of war—they can spin them from here to eternity—but when you're there in the middle of the bullets and the bombs, and people are wailing and bleeding and dying, nobody can tell you what you are seeing and not seeing. Nobody can run any bullshit by you. You are there, and you know what's going on. You know what the world's like after all. You know what to expect out of it. You're not sitting around telling yourself stories about giving peace a chance or the power of love. Your feet are on the ground and nobody can shake you out of that place, as long as you've got the guts to stay put.

So why was I suddenly so miffed at Stefan? Maybe because he couldn't let it be. He had to keep poking at it, trying to figure it out, what to do with it, how to make it into something else. *Evil*, he called it, as though it had a personality, as though that term weren't just jargon for the clean, cold reality religious people couldn't tolerate. As though nosing around the way he was, refusing to let up, wouldn't eventually get you killed. Or worse.

Eventually, I roused myself and dragged out Letter #4, dated December 9, 1992.

Dear Jonah,

I'm going to try this one backwards, or at least backwards from the way I usually write these. Instead of starting with the local news, I'm going to dive in where I left off: the aftermath of the goat ritual and what it did to me.

In a way, it was so horrific it was cathartic. It shocked me out of the vaguer, spookier, spiderweb of fear I'd been tangled in for so long. The experience jolted me alive, flooded me with righteous anger, put some fire in my belly. Up till then, I'd been flirting with Tibetan Buddhism (drawn, as you can imagine, to the concept of no-self, which seemed like a welcome break from my-self), but suddenly that felt like your typical stoic's dodge. I needed a philosophy that saw evil as real, even if it had no being. A no-thing, a lacuna, a parasite. Too much of Eastern philosophy calls evil an illusion or assumes it's well-deserved punishment for crimes committed in a previous life. After the goat, I couldn't buy it.

So within a couple of years I was back in the States with my nose in a book, making my way through your typical undergraduate reading list for philosophy majors. The one who really got my attention was Nietzsche, the way he grudgingly admired Christ while despising Christianity as "life-denying." Life-denying? As though the old sacrificial cults were somehow more respectful of human dignity, or for that matter, the life of poor dumb beasts? I thought to myself as I was reading him (me all of twenty-one, but still), now *here* is a philosophy begging to be taken up for evil purposes, as it clearly was by the Nazis. You can't go on rhapsodizing about the noble aristocratic values of the Übermensch and how the weak need to clear out of his mighty way without some would-be superman taking you up on it.

I guess what I'm saying here is that I finally started getting a feel for the shape and personality of evil. Yes, I know that sounds paradoxical—how can evil have a shape and personality if it has no being? What I mean is, I started to sense how people behave and think when they're trying to live out of that absence. I started to see how years of floating in the death cloud had nearly shut me down, and I realized that I hadn't necessarily been a coward or a fool to fear evil the way I had. On my own, I found Unamuno ("always it comes about that the beginning of wisdom is a fear"), then René Girard, which was life-changing for me. Have you read him, Jonah? If not, you should, though I would say that unless you've personally witnessed something like what I saw in that pond, he may not immediately snap into focus for you. He doesn't for a lot of modern Western readers.

Here's what I think he'd say about the goat: sometime in the misty past, a little clan of primitive folk, dependent on each other but also competitive with each other in the way that humans are, began to get dangerously stressed. Too many people were wanting what the other guy had, an ancient version of "the grass is always greener." Why is the grass always greener? Because that's the way we are—we can't help thinking our neighbor always gets the better deal.

How does our little clan defuse all this building turmoil? The only way is to find a safe outlet, one that won't harm anyone in the group but still allows all the pent-up violence to be discharged. A victim is needed, somebody on the outside, or even somebody on the inside who is too poor or crippled or impaired or ugly to matter. And when that person gets singled out and somebody raises the first stone and shouts the first accusation, the scapegoat process erupts. All the stored-up rage of our small community is loaded onto the shoulders of the hapless victim, and he or she is destroyed, murdered for the sake of the group. Relief. Not only has our clan undergone catharsis, it has been cleansed of all guilt. It can start over on a new footing, and it is thankful.

But of course all this is temporary. Soon the rivalries are back, the tension builds, the survival of the community is in danger once again. And then somebody remembers how good it felt to get rid of all of that with the first murder. So they do it again, in exactly the same way, using another stand-in. And it works. It always works. Gradually it becomes an established practice, something sacred. I have no doubt that the goat in the pond was once a human being, and that the victim, human or animal, has been slaughtered through ritual dismemberment by killers in a state of Dionysian frenzy year after year since time began.

Girard believes that the sacrificial rituals that characterize every culture we know about, even if by now they are only faint remnants of what they once were, have their beginnings in a primal need for group catharsis. We can't bear the burden of our own evil. We've got to load it onto someone else's shoulders and then destroy it. Even the rational Greeks had their Thargelia with the pharmakos, the one who "cures" through his own death by stoning. Though the modern tendency is to dismiss all of this as archaic barbarism, it's more complicated than it looks—take those rituals away without providing some kind of cathartic substitute, and soon enough you'll have cultural self-destruction.

Girard made me think of Fr. John and his conviction that the cross became the great historical wedge, the event that put an end to the sacrifice cycle once and for all. It's difficult to see it that way. On the surface, Christ is just another ancient scapegoat and the crucifixion/resurrection story is just another myth. I wrote to Fr. John about that, but he didn't have a lot to say, just that he knew in his bones it was true. That's how he knows things—in his bones.

So I went back to the Gospels and reread the account, over and over again, and I came to know it in my bones, too. Even though the goat in the pond and Jesus are both innocent victims, and even though their murders accomplish pretty much the same thing—relief for a riled-up group—something else is going on in the Jesus story that I'm guessing never happened during the eons of ritual sacrifice that preceded it. I wish I could tell you what it was, but I haven't figured it out yet. All I know (in my bones) is that the crucifixion somehow redeems innocent suffering.

As for how all this is playing out here in San Cristóbal, that will have to wait. But tensions are building, and I do wonder what will save us from ourselves.

Stefan

Exhausted and discouraged, I shoved away the packet. There were a couple of letters left, but my memory was that they were a lot like this last one: endless theological theorizing. I turned off the lamp and sat on the floor for a long time. Then I realized that the wind had stopped and it was getting light outside. I took off my white socks, pulled on my skirt and sandals, and rummaged around in my pack until I found some pesos. Then I smoothed my braid, scrubbed my teeth with one finger, and tucked my T-shirt into my skirt. When I slipped out the front door, the sun was just hitting the horizon and the high clouds were tinged a brilliant salmon.

Everywhere, the roosters were starting up.

Chapter Eight

The church was maybe a mile and a half from Anne's house, almost all downhill and then up again at the end. I didn't know exactly how to get there, but after a few blocks I could see it sitting right above the lower part of town. Whenever a street seemed to be headed in the right direction, I took it. Partway there, I realized how hungry I was after being up all night. I wondered if this qualified as fasting. If so, maybe it would help me get something out of the priest.

The morning air was candy soft. I turned down a street that led past a small tortilla factory where three women were flattening handfuls of dough and flipping the tortillas onto a rickety conveyor belt for frying. Women carrying net bags, some holding little children by the hand, were lined up at the open door, chatting with one another while they waited. A huge black-and-white pig snuffled among the discards that had been tossed out into the yard. I was feeling low, but the walk and the aroma of frying corn—hot, the way it was best—was good.

When I got to the long narrow plaza in front of the stucco church, I checked my watch: 6:45. People were already streaming up the steps through the open front doors, so I followed them inside and found myself a spot halfway down the aisle from the altar, automatically genuflecting as I entered the pew. It's a weird thing about being raised Catholic—you might not go inside a church for ten years, but the minute you do, everything comes back to you. Which is doubly true when you spent your childhood at a place like St. Silvan's.

It was a cheap church, both inside and out. The floor was un-smoothed concrete that had dried into sharp ridges, the railing moved when you put your hand on it, the pews were straight benches with a slat between two posts for a back. There weren't any kneelers. Up front, amongst the altar and the old wooden podium that served as a pulpit, was a fantasia of a manger scene, with life-size plastic wise men and the Blessed Virgin and Baby Jesus himself, all perched in straw scattered halfway down the center aisle. Christmas lights snaked up around the tricolored plastic window panes. Potted shrubs stood in for barn walls. People were filing past the scene, crossing themselves when they got to the manger itself and laying gifts in the straw around the Holy Family.

The pews were filling: bent old ladies in black shoes clutching big colored-glass rosaries, young wives with basketball-sized bellies pushing out their dresses and a toddler hooked to each hand, barefoot farmers carrying their straw cowboy hats against their thighs, tiny Maya women in their electric-blue embroidered huipiles. Pretty soon, they were pushing right up beside me in the pew, giving me shy looks. I tried to put a name to how all this was making me feel. Maybe deja vu was it, the eerie recognition that you've been here and done this before, only I hadn't, not here, though I'd spent plenty of pew time with the Chicago Croatians.

The bells, as cheap as the rest of the church, went crazy. Up the aisle came the usual procession of altar boys, one carrying the crucifix on a long wooden pole, and a young friar swinging the censor all over the place. Behind them, hands folded and aimed skyward, trudged Padre Miguel, a middle-aged man with a dark brown Indian-looking face and copious salt-and-pepper hair.

The altar boys took their chairs in the front row, the young friar censed everyone within twenty feet of the manger scene, and Fr. Miguel turned to face the crowd. "En el nombre del Padre, y del Hijo, y del Espíritu Santo," he began in that familiar, chanting priest voice. Everyone made the sign of the cross again, some of them thumping their chests two or three times and kissing their fists at the end of it.

I could follow most of the Spanish, but what I couldn't follow, I could guess at. The Mass is the same, no matter what language it's in. The only difference between this service and the one Hana was no doubt attending at St. Silvan's that very day was the rough concrete and what it did to your knees when you had to kneel on it. Also the singing, even less coordinated than at home, which was saying a lot.

Finally it was over. Fr. Mike drew an enormous cross in the air and admonished the crowd to go in peace and to love and serve the Lord, thanks be to God. People around me were dipping and crossing and shuffling their way out, and I was caught up in the flood, a gringa infidel in a linen skirt, as they poured slowly outside and down the steps of the church to engulf their priest. I waited off to the side for a long time before he was done with them. Then, as he stuffed both hands into the sleeves of his cassock and turned to go back inside, I made my move.

"Padre Miguel," I said quietly, so as not to startle him with my foreign accent. He looked up, and I could see that he had already forgotten about his parishioners, that he was thinking of something else entirely, maybe breakfast, maybe the newspaper, and I had interrupted the natural course of his morning. "Tienes momento?" I asked.

"You are an American," he said. His English was slow but good, better than my Spanish for sure.

I nodded. "Could we talk?"

"Of course. Come to the sacristy where it is quieter."

I followed him back up the aisle of the cheap church, past the manger scene, and around the altar to a door in the back, which he unlocked and held open for me. Here there was a small room with a couple of cupboards in it, some shelves containing the usual paraphernalia—candles, candle holders, censers, a spare crucifix—and a closet with three albs and a couple of chasubles inside. Cinctures and stoles hung from a hook. "Pardon me," he said, and rooted around behind the albs until he found two folding chairs. "Here we are. It is easier to talk this way."

We sat. We studied each other. He had a kind, even welcoming, face, but now that I was here, I didn't have the slightest idea of what to say. Somehow, I'd never imagined just going up to somebody and asking outright about my brother. I'd been thinking in terms of surreptitious researching, sly prodding, disguises. But Fr. Miguel's honest face precluded all that. "I have a problem," I said.

He nodded. What else could it be, after all? How many American women showed up at his 7:00 a.m. Mass in Palenque and asked for a private audience?

I stared at him helplessly. He smiled, as if to encourage me. "It's my brother," I said. "You may have met him. Stefan Kovic?"

He looked puzzled.

"An American priest in San Cristóbal de las Casas?"

The light was dawning. Fr. Miguel drew back a little, and then leaned forward and stared into my eyes with sudden intensity. "Ah," he said, slipping into Spanish, "I am so sorry. Of course I have heard of your brother, though I have never met him. Has he been found?"

It was the way he put it, "been found," as though Stefan could not possibly be anything more than a decomposing body at this point, that made the blood rush from my head. I had to close my eyes for a moment. "No," I managed finally. "Still missing."

"Ah," said the priest. He swung his head back and forth and made the kind of tsk-ing sound Hana might have made. "A bad thing. Very bad."

"I'm trying to find him," I said, "and I thought you might . . . "

"You are here by yourself?" Once again he seemed stunned.

"Yes."

"Listen," he said, this time in English as though to make sure I really got it. "You must be extremely careful, do you understand?"

"What are people saying about my brother? What do the priests say? Nobody's able to get anything out of the Church."

He shook his head again. "I know nothing."

"But you must have heard rumors. He's in Bishop Ruiz's diocese. Doesn't that make any difference? Why aren't they looking for him? Why won't they say anything?"

"San Cristóbal has a very good bishop, a brave man. But you do not understand Mexico. After the Revolution, priests were declared the enemy of the people. For a long time, you risked death if you served the Mass. Up until very recently, we could not vote or even wear our clerical collars in public when we traveled. Our power to change things here is limited."

"But how can the Church just abandon him like this?"

"They have not abandoned him. But until they know what has happened, they cannot say anything, do you understand? If he is alive, that would only put him in more danger. After El Salvador, Nicaragua, Guatemala, any bishop or priest who becomes too involved with the indigenas is branded a Marxist and blamed for whatever political trouble follows. Which means he becomes a target for the military or the police or the Guardia Blanca. "

"Is that what my brother did? Speak up for the Indians?"

Padre Miguel put his fingertips together and dropped his head so that his lips were touching them. "I did not know your brother," he said at last, "but it seems that he made several visits to Las Cañadas in the Lacandon, which is known as guerrillero territory." He glanced up at me when he said this as if he believed I would be shocked.

But I was already thinking in this direction. Mat, the guy with the beheaded dad, seemed like a shoo-in for guerrilla recruitment. And Stefan had clearly been getting wrapped up in his situation. I could see my brother, easily see him in fact, following this kid out into the jungle in a vain attempt to keep him from picking up a gun. But I tried to keep any sign of recognition off my face. I wanted to see what else I could get out of this priest, who thought I was the typical ignorant norteamericano. "And so now he's a Marxist? Is that it?"

"Marxist," he said. "So simple. In this country, it is not so simple, however. The left in this country is not just one group. Leftists become enemies of leftists. Everyone has a new idea about the indios. Everyone is going to save them—the campesino organizations, the guerrilleros, the evangelicos, the priests. While they are fighting among themselves, the government is getting richer and more powerful. The drug lords are gaining more territory. The Guardia Blanca is killing the peasants. What good are all these ideas of the left? Your brother was no doubt a good man, but naive. He should have never become involved with the guerrilleros."

Perhaps pleading would help. I pulled my chair closer and leaned toward him. "Look," I said with all the drama of a distraught sister in my voice, "he's my only brother. My parents' only son. If you know anything, you *must* tell me what you know."

He ran the palm of his hand from his cheekbone to his chin, then turned his head and gazed up at the small window. The breakfast light came through it and struck low on the opposite wall. His thick hair caught some of the gleam. Up close, you could see he was indeed a ladino with a healthy dose of indigena in him. Why was he holding out on me? After a moment, he raised his shoulders and let them fall. "Even if I did know, which I do not, I could not speak about it to you. It is very dangerous to become involved in affairs like these."

So that was it. Kind he might be, but also spineless. My temples began to pound. There was not, however, a lot I could do about it. I tried one last tack. "At least tell me this. Do you think he was taken by the government? Or do you think he is with the guerrillas?"

"Señorita," he said. "Do not ask me to speculate. All I know is that your brother put himself in grave danger by going to the jungle that way. He may have done it out of ignorance, but you cannot afford to be ignorant in Mexico. You yourself are naive. You show this by coming here and asking questions about things you do not understand. All everyone in your country is talking about right now is NAFTA. Nobody there wants to think about the poverty in Chiapas. And nobody here, except the naive idealists, wants to talk seriously about latifundismo and the stealing of peasant land. In Mexico, it is the powerful, not the naive, who rule. If you come here asking your questions without realizing that, then you are a fool." He stopped and looked at me as if to see whether I finally understood. Then he added, "Go back to the United States. This is my very best advice to you. If you see your brother again, it will be because God decided to perform a miracle."

"So everyone thinks he's dead, that's what you're telling me?"

"Go back to the United States."

I stood up. If I told him what I thought of cowards, I'd never get in the door of this place again, something I might need to do. "Thank you," I said instead. "I am staying with Anne Bource for two weeks, if you think of anything else that might be useful."

"Señora Anne?"

I nodded.

For the third time, he seemed genuinely startled. "You are a friend of Señora Anne's?"

"I am working for her husband. I've only just met her. Neither of them knows I am here."

His discomfort had turned to distress. "I must ask you not to talk to people in this town about your brother, do you understand? Not when you are staying with Señora Anne. She is alone most of the time and helpless in her wheelchair. She is a good woman, but she has attracted attention in the past, do you know what I am saying? Her classes are a source of suspicion for some people. She is helping the indios, no? And some of them are expulsados. You could put her in great danger."

I was halfway home before I calmed down enough to think about what I'd just experienced. A kindhearted coward, but that shouldn't have been so surprising. People were never just one thing.

When I got back to the house, the red jeep was gone and nobody answered the door when I knocked, so I went in. My rolled-up sleeping bag and my pack sat in one corner of the living room where I'd left them, and my boots were by the front door, though Jan's and Rikki's were not. I went into the kitchen and drank a tall glass of water, then scanned the refrigerator shelves for food.

I was busy frying myself some eggs when the wheelchair came squeaking down the hall, the sound releasing a shower of ice crystals down the back of my neck. Anne. She was coming very slowly, I could hear each turn of the wheels, and it was creepy beyond anything I'd experienced before, even the night I once spent without a tent in the Thai jungle, where you knew a hand-sized spider might be poised above you in the dark, ready to lower itself onto your face. She stopped just before the doorway, getting ready to make her turn. I could see the front edge of the chair and her narrow feet in big white socks, the thin legs beneath the same blue Indian skirt, the knees jutting out in two sharp knobs. I could have gone forward to help her turn the chair into the kitchen. I could have said something, but I didn't. I just stood there by the stove with the ice slipping down my neck and the eggs starting to smoke.

She rested for a few seconds, then the little clattering squeak began again as she slowly maneuvered back a few inches and forward a few, and finally swung herself into view. "Good morning," she said breathlessly. "Did you sleep well?"

"Great," I lied, striving for hearty and welcoming. "It was a little windy, though."

"I didn't wake you up in the night?"

I wasn't about to admit I'd eavesdropped on her trip to the bathroom. Instead I said, "Eggs?"

"No, thanks. I was after some juice. You have to drink a lot with this. Gallons. I'm always forgetting."

I looked over at the refrigerator and then back at her in her chair. It was going to be a twenty-minute operation unless I helped her. I went to the cupboard and got down a glass. When I handed it to her, filled with orange juice, she took it in her thin hand, and I could see by the way that the juice sloshed around that her fingers didn't work in concert. She managed a couple of long sips, closing her eyes as she drank, and then she looked up at me with that same puzzled expression from the day before. I realized I was hovering over her chair like someone waiting to snag a fly ball, which would have made me feel like hell if I'd been her, so I took a couple of obvious backward steps, which no doubt only made it worse.

"Your eggs," she said. "They don't smell very good."

I grabbed the spatula and scooped them onto the plate, and could see that they weren't going to be my best eggs ever. "They're fine," I informed her. "Just the way I like them." I tried to think of how to be more solicitous without being obnoxious. "You're sure you won't have any?"

"Oh no, thank you. Rikki was the cook this morning. He's always stuffing me with food."

"He's a great kid," I said, and it was a relief to say something honest.

"He's a blessing," she said in a matter-of-fact way.

This was a favorite platitude among a particular brand of Catholics. Everything good was a blessing and everything bad was the will of God. Uttered by certain people, it turned my stomach. Yet coming from Anne, it sounded weirdly fresh, like it actually meant something. Curious, I allowed myself to look directly at her for the first time, which confirmed what I'd already suspected: there was no earthly reason for her to sound so pleased with life. The slanting, dramatic morning light was starting to flatten into the boring afternoon now, but in any light you could see she was a human wreck, rotted from the inside out. If you shook her, she'd come apart right there in the chair.

Terrible. Yet at the same time, which maybe made it sadder, there were still traces of beauty there. In the eyes, the thick sleepy lashes, the cheekbones, the line of the jaw. I could see what I'd focus on if I were hired to make a portrait of her, where I'd seat her (not in the wheelchair) and in what kind of setting, to bring all that out.

"Eat," she said. "Your eggs are getting cold."

I pulled out a chair from the table and sat down with my plate of charred scramble. She rolled herself into the empty space opposite me, her very own parking spot they kept free for the chair. There was some adjusting, more of the backing and forthing she'd gone through in the hallway, and then she looked over at me. Out of the blue, I realized that even though her condition repelled me, I respected her for the way she made her way around the place and didn't try to fight off your help when you offered it.

"Jan tells me you're doing a marvelous job with the photography and drawing," she said.

I checked for nuances, but there were none. "Those two characters are easy to be around," I answered.

"They are, aren't they?" She smiled again, and again I could detect no hidden meanings. "I hope you don't mind, but I'm so curious about your work. There can't be many women your age who have already won a major press award."

People, usually men, had said things like this before, usually with something ulterior in mind. But what could *she* possibly want out of me? I found myself slipping into an aw-shucks mode, the kind where you lead someone into increasingly flattering statements while pretending that praise makes you uncomfortable. The thing was, I wasn't leading her—she was leading me, a fact I was aware of even as I was letting her do it. I can't say how she pulled it off, except that maybe because I'd had no admirers for a while, I was temporarily praise-starved. She asked questions, I answered, and pretty soon she was scratching me behind my ears and I was licking her hand. Eventually, I got up and poured us both more orange juice and then abandoned myself entirely and made a full pot of coffee.

By the time Jan and Rikki came home, we had drunk most of it. There they stood in the doorway, shuffling their feet in surprise at the sight of us, and I started to feel defensive and charged up again at the sight of Jan's face, but Anne reached out and tapped the back of my hand with one finger right then, like she knew, and I calmed down. Instantly. Like a high-strung dog who quiets down in two seconds if you just stroke it the right way along the bottom of the chin.

As it turned out, I had plenty of time to get to know Anne better. Jan suddenly decided he had to get up to Mexico City for a few days to see somebody named Guillermo, a decision that did not seem to bother Anne, but transformed Rikki from a happy-go-lucky kid into a resentful teenager. "I don't see why he had to go right now," he complained to his mother after the jeep had pulled out of the driveway the next morning. "We just got here. It's almost Christmas."

"Guillermo is going to Germany soon. This is the only time."

"Who cares? It's not fair."

She cast her big eyes in my direction, a gesture he obviously caught because he dropped the subject, at least for then. I had no idea who

Guillermo might be, but it didn't really matter. The issue was Jan's going off. This apparently wasn't a new thing, the anger between Jan and Rikki that had shown its teeth all of a sudden, and I filed it away for future reference.

In the meantime, I was free for seventy-two hours, and the first thing that came to mind was that I should call Jonah to see if anything had changed since I left the States. The question was, where to call. There was a phone at the house, but I didn't want anyone to overhear me. A public phone, even if I could find one, would be too public. But Padre Miguel no doubt had a desk with a phone on it. I set off once again for the church.

The sacristy door, when I tried it, was locked, so I went back outside, past three women in black veils praying in a row in front of a hokey little grotto constructed mostly out of plastic flowers. I made my way along the side of the church to the back, where there was an office door with a small inset window. Through this I could see Padre Miguel with his black shoes on the floor beside him and his feet propped up on the desk. He was reading a newspaper. I tapped on the glass.

I saw him sigh when he realized who it was, then lay the newspaper face down on the desk. He came to the door. Without his shoes on, he was only a few inches taller than I was.

"Hello again," I said when he'd opened up. "I need to make a call to the States and I can't find a phone." This was not strictly true; I had not looked for one.

"To the States," he said, as though I'd told him I needed to fly to the moon but would be back shortly.

"I've got a calling card. The bill will go to me."

He made an eloquent gesture, which I interpreted to mean that money was not the issue, something far more weighty was at stake. Then he held the door wider, though reluctantly, for me to come in. I didn't see any phone on the desk, but it could have been hidden under the newspaper. I went over and sat down in his chair. I was trying his Christian patience. Humbly, he took the paper, folded it, and tucked it under his arm, like a man about to go on a journey. The phone, which had indeed been under the paper, turned out to be an old black rotary. He bent and picked up his shoes. "Your Spanish is adequate to make this call?" he asked.

I wasn't sure if he meant this to be offensive, but probably not. I nodded at him.

The international calling process was complicated, and I wasn't entirely sure about the time difference. However, by some miracle, I actually got through, though of course not to Jonah immediately. One of the young monks had to run from the bookstore all the way to Jonah's cell to fetch him to the phone.

"Eva?" he kept calling into the receiver "Eva?" The connection was bad, a fierce roar punctuated by sharp clicks every so often, and I supposed he interpreted this to mean an emergency. "Have you found him? Is it bad news?"

At the sound of his voice, I began, unexpectedly, to cry. "No, no," I got out. I rubbed my nose hard against my shoulder. "I just wanted to check in with you to see if you'd heard anything I didn't know about. I'm not even in San Cristóbal yet."

"Not a thing," he said loudly. I could hear him better than he could hear me. "The biggest blank you can imagine. For some reason nobody in Mexico seems to want to say a word. And here I am in this Eden making date nut cakes while you're there all by yourself slogging through guerrilla-infested jungles. I'm just so damn disgusted right now. I feel paralyzed."

"Not exactly guerrilla *infested*." He was making me smile in spite of my wet face. "Jonah, I'll be in San Cristóbal right after Christmas."

"You're a brave girl. Your brother was always saying that."

The connective roar suddenly got louder, and I had to struggle to follow what came next, which had to do with, I thought he said, the Jesuit Refugee Service center and dire predictions of imminent revolution in southern Mexico. He was talking about the guerrillas again. It crossed my mind that we shouldn't be talking about guerrillas over the phone line like this. "Jonah," I tried to get in, but he was saying, "It's the worst sort of problem for a priest, though the public always thinks that priests have a harder time with lust."

Lust?

"It's this business of outright oppression," he said, "and how you deal with it. It's not a question of whether the rebels' cause is just or not. It's clear he thinks it is. It's what you should advise your own parishioners to do. Or for that matter, what you should do yourself."

Something that sounded like a jungle cicada had taken over the line. "What are you talking about?" I shouted into the receiver.

"Priests taking up arms," he shouted back.

I was dumbfounded. The static cleared for a minute, like the eerie break you sometimes get in the middle of a storm. I asked if he was kidding, if he really thought that Stefan in a million years would do something as nuts as joining the guerrillas.

"Possibly. God knows there are famous precedents in the rest of Central America."

I could not see my brother toting a gun, no way, and I said so. Bringing them food, maybe, treating their wounds. But not killing people.

"Well, I won't argue with you, Eva, but I'd far rather believe he's gone off voluntarily than the other prospect."

"But what do you *think* he did? Honestly."

It was that "honestly" I'd tacked on. He couldn't not say it now, though I could tell he would have preferred to pass. "I think," he said finally, "that he's gone off on some mission of his own, and he's deliberately bypassed the Church so it can't be blamed for whatever disaster ensues. From what he's been saying in his letters, the Chiapas diocese has already gotten itself totally sideways with the state, and it can't afford to be connected in any way with the guerrillas. But I'm guessing that one of his church folk, maybe this kid Mat, has gotten involved with them, and Stefan's set off to bring him back."

"I thought of that, too. God, sometimes he's his own worst enemy. With all the crazies running around down here, just waiting for an excuse to bag a 'Marxist' priest."

Before he could respond, the phone began to roar again, then went dead. "Jonah?" I said, but it was just me talking to myself. I could have called him back, but what was the point? All at once, the abrupt severing of the conversation made me cry again, a short fierce bout that left my nose swollen and my braid twisted into a corkscrew. When it was over, I laid the receiver back in its cradle and stared at the wall for half a minute, thinking, before I went off to find the long-suffering Fr. Mike to let him know he could have his desk back.

Chapter Nine

There wasn't much else I could do for the present, so when Rikki, still subdued but starting to come out of it, wanted to show me the ruins, I said sure I'd go, if only as a distraction. The ruins of Palenque are like something you've seen in a childhood dream: white limestone buildings that look more Greek than Mayan, floating halfway up a green hillside over the Rio Otolum. Rikki, having cut his epigraphic teeth on the famous inscriptions there, was as usual a wonderful guide, and though he couldn't accomplish the impossible (take my mind off Jonah's theory about Stefan), we had a good day scrambling around in the hot sun, especially with the lunch of cold tamales and green tea Felice had packed for us. Green tea was a favorite of Anne's, Felice informed me, and of herself also. Felice, in fact, seemed to have colonized most of Señora Anne's little quirks and habits and added them in modified form to her own character, which seemed odd to me. Felice was a healthy nineteen and Anne was dying. On the other hand, dying or not, Anne had her effect on people. I was feeling it myself, a silent pull, an anticipation.

While we ate our tamales, I asked Rikki whether there would be as much photography in Palenque as there had been in Tikal. This was an idle question, meant to pass the time, but he was pleased, as though I'd been given clues in a treasure hunt and had just moved considerably closer to the treasure. "Not as much," he said, "but that's because Pacal died only a year after Ah-Cacaw became king of Tikal," as if this explained everything. I asked him who Pacal was, which was apparently like asking who George Washington might be, but Rikki, after failing to conceal his fresh shock at my ignorance, simply said, "He ruled here for sixty-eight years. He built almost all of this." "This" included a four-story tower with a stone hat of a roof, a sprawl of connected rooms that Rikki called the Palace, and a pyramid much more graceful than the ones at Tikal. "He's buried at the base of that," added Rikki. "You'll be working inside."

I asked him why it mattered to our photography project when Pacal died, and he said that it had to do with his dad's idea about why the lowland Classic kingdoms so suddenly collapsed. Then he clammed up. But this was interesting, and I thought I now knew why Jan was so touchy about his project: I may not be up on Maya history, but I've watched a late-night show or two. Every crackpot has an explanation for what happened, including the one that insists ancient astronauts visited Central America a couple of millennia ago and then whizzed back into space. I wondered what Jan's theory was.

Rikki, though still upset with his father, was too loyal to tell me, though he was willing to talk about everything else. He told me about the discovery of Pacal's tomb in the late forties, the Mexican archeologist who'd noticed a double row of holes with stone stoppers in them in the floor at the top of the pyramid and pried up the slab to find the secret stairway. It took the man four years to clear out all the rubble, but when they got to the bottom of the passageway, the payoff was big, according to Rikki, and included the remains of Pacal himself under a five-ton carved sarcophagus lid. Better yet, he'd left huge king lists behind, a family tree that allowed the ethnographers to finally crack the Maya code.

That night at dinner, Anne asked what I'd thought of the ruins, and which set of them, Palenque or Tikal, had appealed more to my photographer's eye. While I was deciding about this, she brought her napkin up to her mouth to dab at it, only she missed it because her hands were out of control again. "Señora Anne," said Felice, and gently took the cloth away from her and patted her all over her face with it as though she were a baby or an Alzheimer's patient. Then she spread the napkin across her patient's lap to catch the food that wobbled off her fork.

This would have driven me nuts, but Anne thanked her.

I said, "Tikal, I think. It's so barbaric." I don't know why I said this. Maybe her unquenchable niceness was starting to get on my nerves.

"That's interesting," she said, "though there was not a lot of difference between the two in terms of what we'd call barbarism." She set her elbow on the table and cupped her hand in her chin, pondering, and I could tell she had taken me seriously. She seemed to have an impenetrable screen when it came to nastiness, which cranked me up another notch.

"I can't imagine spending a lifetime studying people who stuck stingray barbs through their penises," I said cruelly. Rikki, blushing, had told me all about this one day at Tikal, the Maya ritual carried out by the kings to open the portal to the Underworld. Their wives were equally masochistic; they pierced their tongues and then pulled thorn-encrusted ropes through the holes to make them bleed more.

"Oh, yes," she said. "Isn't that amazing? A particularly graphic form of self-sacrifice."

"If they'd been Catholic, they would have made them saints."

She finally caught the tone and fell silent. Of course I felt bad then, but what could I do? I don't trust niceness in either sex. It can mask the real agenda, only revealed after you've invested yourself. I was in the habit of nipping it in the bud.

Then I noticed her mashed potatoes. She had only taken two bites, though mashed potatoes, according to Felice, were her main source of nutrition, being easiest to swallow. I immediately went into my nagging Hana imitation, an aspect of myself that I usually try to hide. "You should eat," I told her gruffly. "You need to keep up your strength."

She started to shake her head, but in that moment something in her changed. She was still sitting at the table, upright, with a fork in her hand, but she'd gone dead white, as if someone had pulled a plug or she'd shorted out. We all sat there looking at her. "Time for bed, Mom?" Rikki said at last. "I'll push you down the hall if you're ready."

You could see her trying to focus on his face when he said this, but instead her eyes went sideways and then back, and her head fell forward and hung there, swaying on the end of her flower-stem neck. Her fingers on the wheelchair arms clutched and splayed. Rikki jumped up and went to her, saying, "Mom, Mom," crouching beside the chair to get a better look, but there was nothing to see, just blank eyes and a mouth hanging open. He shot me a terrified glance, then fell to stroking her brown hair, his fingers pattering against her skull, crooning words you could tell she didn't even hear. I'd never felt like such a bitch, not even with Robert.

"Let's get her in bed," I said. "Wouldn't she be better in bed?"

"I wish Dad was here," he said, agonized. "Felice, has she done this before?"

"Oh, yes, she does this now. But it passes."

It was already passing, in fact. We watched the current switch back on, first her head lifting, then her eyes coming back into focus, and then her body unfolding in the chair, like a collapsed puppet being pulled upright by its strings. She gazed at us for thirty seconds or so with bewildered baby's eyes.

Felice moved calmly to the back of the wheelchair and rolled it away from the table. As she and Anne made the turn into the hallway, I found myself engaged in an unexpected struggle. Should I go with her? Was there something I could do to help? Probably not. What could I possibly do that wasn't already being done? "Goodnight, Señora Anne," I could hear Felice saying kindly as they headed for the bedroom. "You'll be better in the morning, won't you?"

Later, Rikki and I did the dishes together and then went and sat in the living room where we didn't say anything for a long time. It was clear to me that Anne was out of everybody's hands, like one of those unfolding disasters I would get sent to photograph. A little country obliterated by a bigger one, or the aftermath of an earthquake in a place with no building codes. Hers was the kind of case that made me sure there was no God. Maybe an evil demon, the kind of malevolent force Pacal and the rest of them thought they could propitiate with enough blood. But surely not the God of love my brother was staking his life on.

I tried to think of something to say to Rikki, but what could I? I would have hated it if someone who didn't know my mother and hadn't been around for most of the trauma decided it was all right to push advice at me. Outside, the night wind was picking up in the ravine, clattering through the banana leaves and whirling around the grape stake backyard fence where Felice kept her red chickens. Finally Rikki got up and went to the window, even though it was full dark beyond it with nothing to see. He really was a beautiful boy. People would no doubt try to manipulate him because of that, or maybe he'd learn to manipulate them. Right now, though, he was still beautiful, without any garbage over the top of it. It made me angry that he had to go through this.

Gazing out at the night, he said, "My dad should be here."

This was so.

"What is she supposed to *think*? He's never here, and then we come home for Christmas and he takes off again." His voice was low but passionate. He looked rigid with embarrassment.

"So she's mostly alone with Felice?"

"Always. That was their agreement. She didn't want him to give up his work to take care of her." He had one elbow resting high on the wall with his hand hooked over the top of the window sill. He was tall enough that he had to bend over to see out.

"But now she's going down," I said. This was blunt, but true.

"Yes, and she needs us to be with her now. But he won't admit it. He's always got excuses, like Guillermo, so how do you think she feels?"

I had a possible answer for this, but decided not to say. Instead, I pried the story from him, the kind of self-sacrificial tale you might get on the soaps but would normally never buy in real life. She'd been sick for ten years. Not bad at the beginning, but knowing what lay ahead, she'd taken her stand early and given it some punch by threatening divorce if Jan wouldn't comply. Nobody was foregoing any careers. She'd work as part of their team as long as she could, then she'd find something else to occupy her. Rikki would go to school in Palenque unless his father needed him in the field, in which case she'd tutor him until he caught up again. She'd stay in the yellow house until there was no other choice. Her husband could come home when he liked, but not to be her nurse. That would all be handled by someone like Felice. Otherwise, she told them both, something good would turn to bitterness, maybe even hatred.

"He was mad at her at first," said Rikki, "but he got used to it. Now you can hardly get him in the house."

"Why, do you think?"

He pushed off from the wall and turned toward me with his hands shoved down in his pockets. I could see the thoughts tumbling around inside his blond head, one of them being whether or not he should say any of this out loud. He was a good kid, after all, courteous and kindhearted, not to mention loyal. But some of this business needed to come out. Not that I'm any kind of therapist—far from it. In spite of my occasional maternal streak, I am low on sympathy and hate confessions, especially when they are about messes people have created for themselves. But I liked Rikki, who didn't deserve any of this, and besides, I knew what it was like to be stuck between miserable parents. I smiled, hoping to knock over his defenses.

He looked down at his tennis shoes and said, almost inaudibly, "He doesn't love her anymore."

I thought about this. Of course it was a possibility. It had crossed my own mind the night I heard him wheeling her to the bathroom, whether a man could continue to love someone he could no longer sleep with. Not that I'd had any experience with marriage, but it had always seemed to me that if you took sex out of it, what was left? Memory lane?

Worse, she'd gotten to the point of physical degradation. It was hard to look at her: her head bobbed, sometimes her mouth needed wiping, she couldn't make a move without fumbling or dropping or bumping. What was left to love? Yet I didn't think Rikki was right.

"Then what about the first day we were here?" I asked him. "Your dad almost canning me for being rude to her?"

"I don't know. He doesn't let people say anything about her, that's for sure. But that could be, I don't know, pride or something, couldn't it? She's still his wife."

"Maybe."

He kicked at the rug with the toe of his shoe. "Well, whatever he thinks, he should let her know. This way, it looks like he's just waiting."

"You mean, for her to die?" I put it this way deliberately, knowing it rang harsh. But nobody else, it seemed, was being straight with this kid.

"Yes," he said simply, sounding relieved. "He's been waiting a long time, but he can't say it to anyone. So he pretends he still cares about her, and then he goes off to Mexico City."

This did not seem to be an exaggerated or hysterical conjecture on Rikki's part. A bleak one, yes, but not beyond imagining. And in all fairness to Jan, I'd probably be up the same creek if I were shackled to a dying spouse. I asked Rikki what he thought his father should do.

"Stay home," he said. "She's too sick now to say no. It's time for us to be with her."

At 10:00 the next morning, Anne's twelve students began to arrive at the house for their lesson. Felice was still helping her dress, so Rikki and I answered the door for the flock of murmuring, nodding women. I looked at them curiously. Some of them, according to Padre Miguel, were expulsados, farmers without land, villagers without a village, just as Stefan had described in his letter. But these were the lucky ones. They'd found a way to make a living as weavers in a women's cooperative run by Quakers based in Mexico City. Expulsado husbands were not usually as fortunate, Felice had told me. They worked as temporary day laborers, picking up jobs whenever they could, selling popsicles on the street, or going off for months to labor on the fincas.

The women arranged themselves on the sofa and chairs and floor of the small living room, talking among themselves and with Rikki and casting shy glances at the strange gringa in their midst, so I slipped off to the kitchen, thinking I'd help pull together some refreshments. A lame attempt to make up for my mean-spirited behavior to Anne the night before. Lame, because nobody in the house was apparently holding anything against me. What was this nasty thing that came over me sometimes? Stefan had triggered it every so often when we were kids and he was being particularly long-suffering. Maybe there was a competitive element to it. I knew that good was something I could never be, so I had an urge to stifle it when I saw it. In more ways than I cared to admit, I was an awful lot like Bruno.

Just then Anne rode by the open kitchen door, wearing a yellow blouse and a denim skirt and the usual white fluffy socks with her sandals, though it was not cold. Felice, who was pushing her chair, had brushed her dark hair into a ponytail. Going by in profile that way, ponytail swinging, Anne did not look sick, but like a girl just growing up, someone who'd not yet experienced much of life and was eager to get out there and meet it, a thought that squelched my self-absorbed musings.

The cooing sounds died away the moment she greeted them, and even though I was in another room, I could feel the anticipatory silence filling the house. She was their maestra, and it was clear that they respected her and were grateful to her. Illiterate and without even much spoken Spanish at their disposal, they were helpless to defend themselves against the system. Even a little English would help. Someday, maybe, they might be able to deal directly with their buyers in the States, independence that the Quakers in Mexico City endorsed.

Poking her head in and seeing that I was willing to make the coffee and set out the cups and cookies, Felice returned to the living room to take up her duties as Anne's scribe at the chalkboard. It crossed my mind that *I* had some unexpected duties now: serving refreshments at expulsado language classes had not been in my job description. But then neither had counseling troubled teenagers or visiting the handicapped. Stefan, if he could see me, would no doubt be pleased at the points I was racking up on the great scorecard in the sky. He never said anything, but I knew he was always alert for promising signs. I wondered how he'd explain the occasional barbs I threw just for the hell of throwing them. His religion ought to have something to say about that.

I was thinking all this as I bustled around the kitchen, listening with one ear as Anne put the class through their paces, when I heard her switch from her British-accented Spanish to English. "The verse for today," she said, "is from Matthew 7. Repeat it after me: 'Do not judge, or you too will be judged.'" The class, with varying degrees of success, struggled with this series of "j's." "What," she asked them, switching back to Spanish, "do you think Christ meant here? Elisandra, do you have an idea?"

A Bible verse, right in the middle of an alleged English lesson. Right then I abandoned my duties, poured myself a cup of coffee and took it to the kitchen table to work through this unanticipated and unwelcome eureka moment. The first thing I saw was what a fool I'd been, how I'd managed somehow to miss the most obvious clues. Her unrelenting niceness and good cheer, her ignoring my bad behavior, her husband's disenchantment with her—it was all adding up. She was, as they like to call themselves, a believer. I couldn't believe how disappointed this made me.

Because I am not fond of martyrs, which, as far as I was concerned, was the only possible term for an uncomplaining Christian in a wheel-chair. Though, to be fair, what I remembered of martyrs, their visions and their disguised erotic relationships with Jesus, didn't seem to fit the woman I knew. And I didn't think she was Catholic. I was pretty sure you had to be a Catholic to be an official martyr—at least I'd never heard of Methodists getting burned at the stake. Still, it would explain a lot. Oh God, I thought. It was hard enough to have a priest for a brother. All of this meant our long talk over coffee that first day wasn't going to lead anywhere after all, wherever I'd been hoping it would lead—maybe to an actual friendship with a woman.

What a strange, enormous letdown.

When it was time to bring in the coffee, I played it straight, as though I'd never heard a thing, even though part of me was already planning to shake the dust of this house off my feet. Yes, I'd need the cover of the job when I got to San Cristóbal, but nothing in my implied contract with Jan said I had to live with his family in the meantime. I could tell him I needed some space, go to a cheap hotel. He'd no doubt be offended, but what was he going to do about it? Fire me, after all the photos I'd already taken, all the drawings I'd made?

I tried not to meet Anne's eyes when I handed her the cup—if I were really leaving, it was better to break the attachment right away— but she was smiling up at me the way she smiled at Felice when she scrubbed Anne's face with a napkin. Gratefully, as though she loved everything anyone was willing to do for her. I thought about my talk with Rikki, how Jan stayed away because he couldn't deal with things, and how she must feel about that. This was not my usual way of thinking. I felt an odd twinge.

She reached up and took the cup from me like it was welcome medicine, and you could see by the lack of color in her face that a half hour of teaching had already worn her out. The class members watched me with interest, wondering, no doubt, what a gringa my age was doing single and running around Mexico when I should be home having babies. I wondered what they thought of Anne and her Bible verses, especially since Bible verses were what had gotten them thrown out of their villages in the first place. But they all seemed happy about the class, Anne, me, and the coffee and cookies I was serving them.

Do not judge, or you too will be judged, I thought. Except that her teaching them Bible verses in English truly did give me the willies. Too much like the missionaries in the movie *Hawaii*, maybe, who forced the natives to learn the Lord's Prayer and then made them wear flour sacks when they'd always been naked and happy before. For a moment, I longed for my brother's good sense, his way of laughing me out of things.

After the class, I went for a long walk and a long, unproductive think. When I finally got back to the house, I made more coffee and sat drinking it at the kitchen table by myself. The red jeep wasn't due for another day, but twice I caught myself listening for it. Even Jan and his gray moods would be better than this.

Chapter Ten

Jan returned to Palenque at 3:30 the next afternoon, and just before nightfall he and I left alone for the ruins because, at the last moment, Rikki opted to stay at home with Anne. The sun was just setting when Jan parked the jeep at the bottom of the hill, and we sat for a while in the cab between two smoky, idling buses, watching the tourists come down from different parts of the park and waiting for them to leave. He was brooding again, and I could think of nothing to say—certainly not that I had actually missed him while he was in Mexico City. Especially since, now that he was back, I couldn't imagine missing him at all.

It had been a warm day and was going to be a warm evening. The canvas top of the jeep was up, but he had the window down with his elbow sticking out. I thought that I'd never met somebody who could sit so still or look so down. He was wearing his red cap, and the little lines that fanned out from the corners of his eyes were extra deep, as they got when he'd been thinking too much.

A group of schoolchildren went skipping by our jeep, shepherded by a young woman in a narrow black skirt and a white blouse with the collar turned up in the back like a movie star from the fifties. She looked much too elegant to be teaching third graders, and as I watched I saw that her attention was not being held by the kids after all but by an equally sophisticated young man, no doubt her boyfriend, who was coming down the hill behind the group, a small boy clinging to each of his hands.

She was my age, maybe younger, but around the same time in life.

I watched the man help the last child onto the bus, and then he took her fingers and held them for a moment, and they gave each other a long, unsmiling, but highly charged look. I was suddenly aware of the old urgency at the base of my belly that meant it was time to find a man with a warm tent. This had never been a problem before—there were always men around when you needed them. But here I was, stuck in the middle of a complicated family mess while seeking my celibate brother, unable, for the first time in my adult life, to simply do as I wished. And this was a state of affairs that made me both restless and resentful.

The bus shifted painfully into first gear, and Jan roused himself and glanced over at me, a quick blue flash in the dropping light that, in his usual sign language, meant it was time to get going.

It's a long climb to the top of Pacal's pyramid during the day, even without a pack. At twilight, with pounds of camera equipment on your back, you have to go slowly. The stone stairs are wider and friendlier than those at Tikal, but the evening dampness was already making them slick. Around us the night sounds of the jungle were beginning: peepers singing in the stone reservoirs, some animal crying hoarsely for its mate. A flock of large birds, black against the twilit sky, wheeled above us over the big temple, their wings creaking.

The guard at the top greeted Jan like an old friend, helping us down into the passage and agreeing to leave the metal grate above us un-locked until we were done. As soon as we were inside, Jan turned on his big flashlight and showed me the way ahead, a long incline of stone stairs, which he warned me were both steep and slippery. I tightened a pack strap and fell into place behind him, mentioning, as we descended into the pyramid, Rikki's story about the four years it had taken to clear the passageway of rubble.

This was a deliberate conversational ploy. I was tired of working in silence. After a moment, he said grudgingly, "If it had not been such a job, robbers would have stripped the place long ago."

"Robbers are still a big problem?"

"The more sites we open up, the worse it gets. In Colombia, grave robbing is so much a part of the national economy that the robbers tried to start a union."

I asked a question I'd been saving up.

"Why do we have such easy access to, say, Pacal's tomb when robbers are all over the place? You would think there'd be armed guards everywhere."

"There is not enough money for that," he explained. "Instead, the government made it much harder to get permits to excavate, especially in Mexico if you are not Mexican."

This was good; I'd gotten him talking. I asked why he was an exception.

He looked over his shoulder at me. He'd taken off his cap, and I could see the ridges in his hair where it had been. Without the shadow of the brim across his eyes, he had "insomniac" stamped all over him. But at least he was starting to relax.

"I am cashing in on some chits from long ago. People are looking the other way, but that is because this is not a dig, just a quick look around at places I have already been. But we are doing nothing illegal, if that is what you mean."

We made a turn down into a steeper part of the passageway. He glanced over his shoulder again and said, as though it were an afterthought, "By the way, I apologize for the other day."

This took me by surprise, and at first I wasn't sure what he meant. Then I realized he was talking about the way he'd jumped down my throat over Anne. "No problem," I said. "I'd forgotten all about it, actually." I hated going back over embarrassing moments.

"Sometimes I expect too much of people."

By this time we were stopped, him standing one step below me looking up, me with a hand against the damp wall to steady myself. This seemed to be an invitation to respond, and I could either keep my mouth shut or say it. If I kept my mouth shut, we'd go back to being boss and temporary employee. In fact, the distance between us, which I was pretty sure I wanted, would increase. I'd take his pictures, draw his drawings, and in a month or so, I'd be on my way and never see him or Rikki or Anne again. Given what I'd figured out the day before, this was fine with me.

Instead, I took a big breath, thinking I should be keeping what I was about to say to myself. "Maybe you expect too much out of your son."

This brought him up. But I couldn't tell if he was angry or simply surprised.

"What exactly," he said, "are you talking about?"

There was ice in his voice, as though I were either crazy or crude beyond belief to have crossed the line this way. That made *me* angry, especially when I thought of Rikki standing alone and confused by the window, gazing out at the dark.

"I mean," I said equally coldly, "that your son thinks you don't love his mother anymore."

Even in the dim light I could see his face change, a vivid transformation that for a moment made him seem like another person altogether. He put his head down and his hand to his forehead as though it hurt. Then he looked back up at me. "That is what he thinks?"

"I'm sorry."

He stood there for another moment, looking stunned, then turned away abruptly and hurried down the wet stairs, faster than was safe. The conversation, it was clear, was over. He was furious at me, maybe at Rikki too, and I'd betrayed Rikki's trust besides. This is what people get for interfering, I thought bitterly, so why the hell did I do it?

When we finally reached ground level, both of us breathless with indignation and the plunging descent, we found ourselves in a short corridor with three steps leading up to a triangular opening carved into solid rock. This was the tomb chamber door, blocked by a closed but unlocked iron gate. The gate swung open with a metallic whine, and he motioned for me to follow him inside. Still in tight-lipped silence, he went down another short flight of stairs to set up the two big battery-powered lanterns, leaving me at the top.

Then he hit the lights, and there, spread out in front of us, was Pacal's splendid five-ton stone sarcophagus. Though Rikki had shown me pictures, the effect of the real thing was overwhelming. I went down the steps to stand beside him on the platform, and ruffled as we were, we stood side by side staring at the white banquet table–sized slab, covered in intricate carvings. In the middle of the scene depicted on the top, Pacal fell through space, his body cupped, his knees bent, his two bare feet spread out like wings. His arms were locked around something I couldn't identify. He did not look frightened. Above him rose an elaborate structure. I recognized the quetzal in its divine Celestial Bird form on the top. Pacal himself was falling through the World Tree toward Xibalba, the Underworld, to do battle with the Lords of Death. Rikki had explained the myth to me. If Pacal were successful in outwitting them, he would appear on earth once again in regenerated form.

"One of the world's great works of art," Jan said, and I could see how we were going to weather this crisis, by pretending my words had never been said. He was leaning over the lid, holding his big flashlight above us for extra light, his other hand resting on the stone next to mine. The light picked out the corded veins running down his arm and along the backs of his fingers, and the slow pulse of blood going through them. He shifted the light to the upper right quadrant of the lid, to a hanging face, contorted, with three feathers fanning out from the severed neck, and I thought of what Anne had said, that there was little difference between the barbarism of Tikal and the barbarism of Palenque, and how Rikki had set me straight about the Mayas being just as violent as the Aztecs, both of them using obsidian knives to carve out the beating hearts of living human victims. And I thought of Stefan's long and irritating treatise on why cultures need ritual murder in order to keep from imploding. Jan probably would have been interested, though there was no way I was going to bring it up. Even if I understood it. Especially given his current mood.

The ancient obsession with ritual killing. I thought of a detail Rikki had dropped: that when the archeologists had finally gotten into the pyramid, the first grave they opened was not the sarcophagus of the mighty Pacal, but a sealed box with five tangled skeletons inside. War captives from another kingdom. Yet how many times had I photographed some version of that during my stint with the Associated Press? It seemed to me that ritualized murder was just as common in lots of supposedly modern cultures. Look at twentieth-century Yugoslavia, birthplace of my progenitors. Look at my grandmother, put out of her peasant misery at the ripe old age of thirty-two. Look at what that did to Djed.

Jan wanted me to photograph the death date carved on the south edge of the five-ton lid. When I'd gotten myself and my Canon into position, a tight squeeze, he got down next to me, so close I could smell his blue work shirt, and explained that these particular carvings were quite sloppy compared to the elegant ones on the top surface of the lid, as though they'd been done by an amateur or in a rush at the last minute. I could see this. I took my shots, and then he had me stand up again, this time to zero in on the several k'in signs I'd already noticed on the top. The first, lying beside Pacal's elaborate hair knot, was one of a magnificent line of glyphs that marched along the outer edge of the top of the lid. He let me study this for a moment, then put the light up near the top right corner of the immense carving again. The same sign, only cut in half. Silently, he moved the flashlight right below the lowest point of the falling body, directly above a skull motif. Another version of k'in, this time elongated.

"What do you think?" he asked. "Did the same sculptor do all three of these?"

"So now I'm a graphologist?"

"I do not have the eye. You do."

It took me nearly fifteen minutes, but when I was done, I was positive. The glyphs on the top corner and right edge had been carved by the same hand; the glyph in the center had not, or if it had, it had been carved in haste. The lines were not so deep and sure, and the emphasis was different.

"So which one would you choose?" he asked when I told him. "Two separate sculptors, or a single person under different circumstances?"

"Two, I think."

"And the death date you just photographed?"

I thought back to the image I'd seen through my lens, the multiple shots I'd taken. Of course, the glyphs were entirely different, which didn't help. But I thought I saw more similarity in one than in the other. "If I had to say, I think they were done by this guy." I pointed to the central glyph.

"Not a third person?"

"I don't think so." I leaned in close and traced the elongated k'in with my finger. "See here, this little ridge? It's not in those more precise ones along the side. But something like it is in the death date, as though he were holding his tool at a slightly different angle. Or maybe he was left-handed instead of right."

Jan was staring at me. "You think these glyphs could have been carved by two people with different handedness?"

"You see it in drawing classes sometimes. A whole different orientation to the paper. You emphasize different lines because of the angle."

"You are right-handed."

I nodded.

"I want to show you something," he said abruptly.

The something turned out to be at the back corner of the chamber, under the lip of the lid, which required my climbing down from the platform onto a cold stone floor where the huge limestone block that held the body rested on piers. The only way to get where he wanted me to go was to lay on my back and inch slowly, using my feet and hips, until my head was positioned under the edge. He'd given me the light, but it was a problem. When I shone it directly above me, I was blinded. I experimented until I got a good angle, and then looked up. At first, nothing, but then, out of the corner of my eye, the sign, small but unmistakable, and all on its own.

"Is it there?"

It was the way he put the question—is it there?—that clued me in to just how long he'd been working on this problem and how many times he'd doubted it along the way. "It's there," I assured him. "Big as life."

"Does it look like something that was carved by either of the sculptors on the top of the lid?" His voice was muffled by the stone chamber.

I studied the sign. It didn't belong where it was, that was easy to see. Whoever carved it must have done it on his own, perhaps secretly. If so, he would have had to do it in the same position I was lying, which would have distorted the image, unless he were left-handed and able to brace the back of his curved wrist against the stone edge of the sarcophagus itself while he worked. I put my own left hand up into the spot, and sure enough, the sign sat just above where I would have positioned a stylus. This was odd, however, since presumably the sculptor was a man. His hand should have been larger than mine. "Were they small?" I asked.

"Very small. The men were about five feet tall."

"Okay, then, that would work."

I studied the sign for another few moments, memorizing it carefully, then slid out and sat up next to Jan, who'd dropped down to his knees beside me. "What do you mean, Eva?"

"I mean I think the artist who did the death date and the k'in sign in the center of the lid was left-handed. And I think whoever did the one underneath was left-handed too."

By the time we got back up top, it was nearly 10:00 on a moonless night, almost as black outside as it was down in the tomb. Jan closed the grate over the entryway and then, by mutual silent agreement, we slipped off our packs and sat down together at the top of the steps that went down the front face of the pyramid. It was still balmy out, with a damp smell like mulch in the warm currents of air that swirled up the sides of the temple. Somewhere below us, the guard was no doubt patrolling the ruins, but wherever he was, we couldn't see him.

I didn't think Jan was angry anymore. He was a cheerless man, but he had his good qualities, one of them being honesty, and when I gave it some thought, I couldn't imagine him holding a grudge against me for telling him the truth. What emanated from him as we sat together under the velvety tropical sky was a sense of absolute loneliness, unrelieved by any hope of rescue. Some women specialize in this kind of man, engulfing him in warm flesh and imagining they are his savior.

But who are they kidding? That's like rubbing ointment on the back of somebody's hand when his liver is degenerating.

Thus, in spite of my sharp hunger for the basic, sweaty pleasures of life, and despite the flat sun-warmed stones beneath us, I wasn't tempted to seduce my boss. It wasn't that I didn't find him sufficiently attractive. In my present state, he'd have had to have been a genuine gargoyle for me to pass him up, and Jan was no gargoyle. As I'd realized when he took off for Mexico City, there was something about him that hung around in his wake, like a tune you kept humming.

But I wasn't thinking of Anne or Rikki, either. I've never been a virtuous person. Why should I start on top of Pacal's Temple of the Inscriptions on a balmy Mexican evening? I simply didn't want to take it on, that black ocean where he drifted. Maybe if there'd been alcohol, enough to loosen limbs and tongues, enough to . . . but there wasn't. By the time I'd figured all this out, that it wasn't going to happen despite the splendid darkness and the warm air and the golden opportunity, I was even glummer than he was. So we sat on and on in our mutual loneliness, thinking our private thoughts beneath the jungle sky and not starting back toward the yellow house until almost midnight simply because neither of us, for our own reasons, could bear the thought of Anne right then.

In the morning I woke to a headache that felt like six kids banging on a trash can lid. Sexual frustration coupled with disappointment coupled with worry—I'd never had to deal with that trio all at once before. It felt like the hangover I might have gotten if there had been booze on top of that pyramid. I rolled over on the sofa and swung my feet to the floor, but gingerly, because it felt like my skull was going to drop off the end of my neck, and then got up and carefully glided down the hall to the bathroom where I assumed there would be some aspirin. There was. I took three, just to make sure, and Anne must have heard me because suddenly she called from her bedroom, "Eva? Could you come in here for a moment, please?"

I froze, then sang out, "Just a minute," while I scrambled into my skirt. I wasn't ready to see her yet for a lot of reasons, but no matter. When someone in a wheelchair calls you, you don't have a choice.

She was sitting near the open door of her closet, peering in. She turned and smiled at me, and the smile was her usual one, entirely unaltered regardless of how late Jan and I had gotten in the night before. "Good morning," she said. "How did it go last night?"

Her unnatural lack of jealousy had its usual paradoxical effect on me. I immediately wanted to punish her for being good. I thought of several things I could mention, one of them being Rikki's theory about the sorry state of her marriage. Your son, I could say to her, doesn't think his father loves you anymore. What would happen to that sunny smile of hers then? Instead I said, "Fine. I spent some time on my back studying a k'in sign under the edge of the lid."

"*Did* you," she said delightedly. "I wouldn't want to be down there."

"Jan was pretty wound up about what we found."

"I can imagine. You're a great help to him, Eva."

This, from any other woman, would have been hissed.

"You know," she said, "I admire you. I've been in some exotic places, but I was there with my husband. You're here on your own. And you've been everywhere else on your own, too. You're very brave, I think."

She was like water: transparent, but able to cut through rock. If I didn't watch out, she'd wear me down. "No," I said, "it's more like I'm blind. I don't even see the danger half the time. As for traveling alone, I am alone. That's my life. So if I'm ever going to see anything, I don't have much of a choice, do I?"

"I suppose not. However, most women wouldn't do it. They wouldn't leave their comforts behind. I don't think I would have done it on my own. But I was given the opportunity, and I'm very glad I was."

Oh, really. My head was still pounding. I didn't want to be standing there.

"It's fascinating work, especially for an artist, I imagine." She looked entirely serene when she said this, as though it were not her but somebody else who climbed Temple IV with a bum leg and the shakes just to make sure her eight-year-old kid had the experience before she was permanently sidelined. I stared at her with a stiff, evil-tasting smile on my face. What did she think? That if she taught enough Bible verses to her Indians God would raise her up out of that chair?

"Eva, I was wondering if you would do me an enormous favor."

So here it came after all. The point of her relentless cheerfulness. "Sure thing," I said ungraciously. "What do you need?"

She gave me an apologetic look. "We have a tradition of big Christmas dinners in this family, but I'm afraid I'm not up to cooking this year. Felice said she would do it, but I told her to take the week between Christmas and New Year's to be with her family in Ocosingo."

"And you need someone to do the turkey."

She flushed, and I could tell it hurt her to have to ask, that it must be something she was doing for her son and husband, not herself, otherwise her impeccable British manners would have stopped her. "Rikki tells me you're a wonderful cook."

I shrugged, knowing I wasn't making it any easier for her.

"Just say if you don't want to," she said softly, her big eyes suddenly brilliant with shame. Just like that, I'd reduced her to beggar status, which made me, in another paradoxical shift, into a magnanimous human being.

"Okay," I said, with a fine, careless generosity. "No problem."

She didn't say anything, not even thank you, but clasped her hands together in her lap, and I thought, Don't pray. Do not, I repeat, pray. No Bible verses, no prayers, or I'm out of here and you'll never even see that damn turkey. "But where am I going to get the stuff?" I said.

"You can start up there," she said, unclasping her hands and pointing to the top shelf in the closet. "I had my mum send a box from home—some tins of cranberries and a big bag of walnuts in the shell. And Rikki will help you with the rest of the shopping and the cooking, too. You can't imagine how much he loves Christmas."

A week later, after finishing up a couple more photo sessions in the ruins, I saw for myself what she meant. Rikki, padding around the kitchen barefoot in baggy shorts and a T-shirt streaked with flour, looked happier than he had since before Jan took off for Mexico City. In his father, melancholy was the norm, but in him, at sixteen, with his bright hair, it was unhealthy. Even his golden skin had gone sallow over the past week and a half. You wanted to put him in bed and bring him eggnog. Making Christmas dinner was like a fast-acting antibiotic, and I understood why it had been so important to Anne that we do it.

Now that I saw Rikki's rejuvenation, I was ashamed of myself. Long ago, when Stefan and I were both still in school in different parts of California and I was living with Peter, my stormy film student, I'd had plenty of time to study the effects of selfish pettiness. All I had to do then was look in the mirror: the circles under my eyes, the twitchy smile, the hollow cheeks. Peter and his endless string of tiny but inflexible demands, all in service of keeping him in charge. I'd hated that. But I was infected by him like you are by a slow-acting virus that years later releases its armies inside you. From Peter, I'd learned to be petty; from Robert, to be cruel. The USIA man had taught me never to let down my guard, and even my platonic pal Dirk had soured me on sentiment. And the parade of strangers in between? They'd shown me how to leave.

The turkey ("kutz" in Yucatec Maya, the kid informed me), now roasting to a glazed amber color, was stuffed with water chestnuts and cornbread crumbs and onions. The rich smell of it reminded me of Hana and her endless cooking for those Croatian festivals nobody at St. Silvan's ever dreamed of skipping. A big pot of potatoes, peeled by Rikki, waited on the back burner, and beside it, lemon sauce bubbling in a small pan, which would go over the orange persimmon pudding. I'd made two pecan pies (easy) and cloverleaf rolls (harder) so, like some TV family celebrating a Hallmark moment, we also had the sweet, warm, yeasty scent of rising bread to keep us jovial and full of love.

Which might explain what came over me when Anne rolled herself to the kitchen door. Felice, before she went off to Ocosingo, had helped her dress for the day: a long black skirt, a blouse of green silk, a red poinsettia pin at her collar. Her brown hair had been brushed into a

French twist, and that, plus her extreme slenderness, gave her a weird, high-fashion look, like a supermodel coming down the runway in a wheelchair. With her hair up that way, the cheekbones came into their own, and the shadows beneath her brows and large eyes looked more like a sophisticated makeup job than a disease. The moment I saw her that way, I went to the faucet and washed my hands, then got one of the Canons out of my pack and took a whole series of pictures of her sitting by the living room window. She was terribly embarrassed, but Rikki loved it. I had no idea what had kicked me into gear this way, except that if I waited, the light, which was perfect, would go, and maybe whatever was in her right then would go too.

The strangest thing of all was that she was as excited about Christmas as Rikki. There I stood, wearing her apron, rolling out pie dough at her table, chatting with her son, and, for all she knew, having an affair with the husband who didn't love her anymore. But she was happy, and it wasn't faked. She kept out of our way, but every so often, she'd push herself forward to check on something. One time, I straightened up from a peek in the oven to find the wheelchair right at my elbow and her peering intently over the open door as though she were looking for her lost life.

Halfway through the cooking, Rikki skipped off to the living room and the next thing I knew, "White Christmas" came sliding down the hallway. I hate Bing Crosby. He reminds me of Chicago, which on Christmas is a prison of wind and snow, and he reminds me of Hana and her aged cronies at St. Silvan's and their annual white elephant party, complete with hot toddies. Yet trapped as I was in southern Mexico on the biggest holiday of the year, it was actually comforting to hear Bing's mellow voice, and I found myself humming along as I washed pots and pans in the sink. Rikki didn't hum, he sang, which didn't do anything to improve Bing, but almost made me laugh. The day was turning into something like that afternoon in Flores, when I'd fried chilies and onions and watched the kingfisher watching me from the sinking side of the street.

An odd thought came to me then: these people are getting under my skin. I was starting to care about their moods, their struggles with one another, their secrets. Yes, Jan was about as vibrant as a boarded-up business. And yes, Rikki asked me for advice I couldn't give. But lately, as I lay on the sofa at night listening to the wind in the ravine, I'd catch myself trying to rig a solution for them. Rikki could stay here, I thought, and Jan could hire a kid right out of grad school, some eager beaver with a brand-new PhD in linguistics whom he could train himself. They could set up a visiting schedule, once a month, say, so Anne could count on her husband sticking around for a few days. This wouldn't be that hard for him, and it would give her something to look forward to without feeling like she was disrupting his career. And Jan wouldn't hate himself so much. Because that was the conclusion I'd come to: in spite of his pipe-smoking reserve, Jan was a man at war.

By the time Andy Williams began "Silver Bells," everything on the menu was either cooked or cooking, and Rikki pushed Anne down the hall for her nap. I sat down at the kitchen table with a cup of café con leche between my hands, thinking of my brother and whether anyone would feed him Christmas dinner tonight. I doubted that. If I'd been able to sit on Santa's lap right then, or if I believed, like Anne and Stefan did, in the power of prayer, I would have asked for that one thing. To load up a plate of turkey and all the trimmings for my brother who never ate enough.

Chapter Eleven

Anne was still napping, Rikki had gone to visit a friend, Jan wasn't due back until right before we served dinner, and all the food was covered and keeping warm on the top of the stove while the kutz finished browning in the oven. I decided to slip out for a walk. My field body was going. Soft beds and plenty of food never did me any good. I needed a stretch. I laced up my boots and had actually gotten through the front door when something turned me around. Nothing conscious, just a strong feeling that I should go down the hallway and take a peek at Anne.

By the time I got to her bedroom door, I already felt awkward. What if she were awake and fine and there I was, gawking at her like I expected to find a corpse under the sheets? What if she were asleep and I woke her up, like you can when you stare hard enough at someone who's snoozing away?

It turned out that she was neither: not asleep, not fine. I found her sitting up against her pillows, still decked out in her Christmas blouse with the poinsettia pin, but with the French twist starting to list to one side. When she turned her head in her slow way to look at me in the doorway, there was a gap of thirty seconds or so when it was clear she didn't know who she was looking at. It was a baby's gaze, steady and uncomprehending, and I held my breath, waiting for her to return.

Finally, she blinked at me, as though startled, but before she could recover enough to start her usual sweetness and light routine, I said a thing that stopped her. What I said was this: her name—Anne—out loud. I said it without emphasis or any kind of special tone, but it arrested her, as though nobody had said it for a long, long time. Rikki called her "Mom," Felice always "Señora," and who knew how Jan, in the dark sadness of their bedroom, addressed his wife. It was something to see, the way she took it. A wince, as though it hurt, and then the eyes closing, and then a long sigh that she had been hanging onto for years, maybe.

I stood watching her for a few moments, and then, when I saw tears sliding out from under her closed lids, went into the room and took a seat in the chair beside the bed. I had no idea why I was there or what I was supposed to do next. But I couldn't have walked out on her if I'd tried.

The tears kept coming, absolutely silent, with an occasional long breathy sigh thrown in, and she didn't try to stop herself, nor did she wipe them away. Her hands lay open, palms down, on the bony thighs beneath the Christmas skirt. I thought about taking one of her hands and just holding it. But that sort of thing had never been my style. So instead I sat beside her, not moving, not speaking, while the silent weeping went on.

Pretty soon I heard Rikki come in and walk down the hall to the kitchen, where I'd left him a note: Gone walking. I could hear him checking the turkey, and the oven door making its usual pinging sound when he closed it. The water went on in the sink, and then he set his water glass on the counter and walked across the room. In two seconds, I thought, he'll come down the hallway and find me here and then what am I going to say?

But he didn't come down the hallway. He went back out the front door instead, maybe to catch up with me wherever I was on my walk. We were alone, Anne and me. The last two women in the world you'd ever think would be sitting there sharing a serious cry.

I'm not much of a crier myself, so I understood what was going on with her. She'd been saving it up too long, just like I found out I'd been doing the morning I talked to Jonah on the phone. I figure it's like a flood control system, crying. Most of the time people are fine and there shouldn't be any reason to open the gates. But then some major storm comes along and water starts to rise behind the dam and you either turn on the release valves or it all starts coming over the top. And when that happens, you're in danger of the whole thing breaking apart. Of course, there are people who think they ought to send some spill down the creek every week or so. They cry at movies, in front of paintings, every time their kid gives them a kiss. But these are not my kind of folks.

After a while she stopped, though she kept her eyes closed. If it were me, I would have been embarrassed, so I kept my mouth shut and pretended this was something I would have done today anyway—sit in her room and watch the dust motes spin. There was a damp smell coming from her, a whelping box smell, and I figured this was the smell of effort. She hadn't wanted to do this in front of me. I looked around at her walls, which I'd never been in her room long enough to notice. They were bare and white except for an old sepia photo of a rustic-looking farm. I got up from my chair and leaned closer to it, which put me closer to Anne, too, though I figured this was all right since I wasn't looking at her but at it.

"My great grandmother's place," she said, eyes still closed. "In Devonshire." Her voice was still a tad off-key.

"Nice photo. Eighteen-eighty or so?"

"Yes," she said, shifting a little. I could tell she was now looking up at me.

"Old photos are great," I said. "They had unbelievable equipment, wet plates, the whole works. You needed a cart to haul all your stuff. But they got amazingly good shots."

"My mum inherited a whole trunk load. She wanted me to take one for here."

I leaned in closer to the photograph. Sure enough, tiny women in long dresses sat on chairs on the front porch, one of them no doubt the great grandmother. "Her name was Elsie," Anne said. "She lived in the United States for a few years, but when her husband died, she took her three children and went back home. I was only eight when she passed on, but I remember her very well."

Still looking hard at the picture, I said, "I couldn't do what you do."
She didn't answer.

I said, "You were like me. You were healthy and active and loved it out there in the jungle. And now you're stuck in that chair. I could never do it, Anne. I'd be the biggest drama queen you ever saw." These were probably the truest words I'd yet spoken to her, but I had to force myself to say them.

She gave a quiet laugh with a lot of pain in it. "You wouldn't."

"It's true. I know myself. I'm like a child when I can't do what I want."

"We all are."

"No. Not you."

"I am. I'm no different than anyone else. This is *hard* sometimes, Eva. Sometimes I don't think I can bear it."

I sat back down in the chair, but I didn't think it would be wise to look at her. For one thing, my throat was aching like mad and I was afraid my own release valves might open if I wasn't careful. There she was, no more than forty, probably, a truly striking human being, even with her evangelical tendencies, with a great kid and a good, if gloomy, man. And all of it was crashing down around her ears. I said, "It isn't fair."

She gave that quiet little laugh again, as if this were something she'd had plenty of time to think about. "Fair? What's fair, Eva?"

"It shouldn't be this way."

"What? Life? Whoever said life was supposed to be fair?"

I had to think about that. Because somewhere during my formative years I'd learned to be fiercely aggrieved when things didn't turn out the way I thought they should. From Bruno, maybe? Whose defining characteristic was a steaming, habitual rage? I'd never given this much thought, the question of what was fueling my father's disgust with the world, not to mention my own. I took it as a given that his view was the accurate one, that most people, if you gave them half an excuse, would turn on you. That you had to fend for yourself or die a hapless fool.

All at once, I had a clear flash of Bruno's face as he stared down at my skinny, four-eyed brother, who was probably eight at the time. It was a look that said that Stefan was doomed to be one of the fools, and right there, you could see my father mentally washing his hands of him. Exiling my brother. I wondered whether Stefan ever understood for himself why. Probably not. Stefan had his own demons, but they weren't Bruno's. Or mine. I don't think he could bend his mind around what was happening.

I risked a glance in Anne's direction. Her face was still wet, but otherwise she seemed normal. "It must have been my dad," I said. "It wasn't like he went around expecting things to be fair, though. Just the opposite. He constantly assumed the worst. His philosophy was, if you let down your guard for a second, life will screw you."

"What was his name?"

"Is. Bruno. He lives in Chicago."

The left corner of her mouth wavered. I'd noticed that lately, the wavering. Rikki explained that when you started getting involuntary muscle movements, things were speeding up. There was a small struggle, and then she finally got it out: "Your mother?"

"Hana. Her philosophy is different. Life may not be fair, but at the end of it, you always get what you've got coming. If you scorn the Church like my father does, you're going hell. If you follow The Rules as interpreted by St. Silvan's Catholic Church, you're going straight to heaven."

Anne smiled. I was cheering her up. "So you're Catholic," she said.

"Not me. Not anymore." Then I remembered having gone to Mass. "Well, you know, sometimes. You can't ever really get out of it, actually. It's like you're sentenced for life."

"Oh, Eva," she said. She tried to shake her head at me, but it was more like a bobble, like one of those baseball players people set in the back window of their cars.

"I know," I said. "I'm terrible."

"No, I don't think you are."

There was something in her voice that made me nervous. I stared at the photograph of the farm so she couldn't catch my eye. I wasn't up for any pronouncements about my character or having blind spots or latent potential pointed out. But instead she said, "Did those two— Bruno and Hana, did you say?—have any other children besides you?"

I flashed to her face. Fr. Miguel? Someone who'd overheard me talking to Jonah? But there was nothing in her eyes to indicate she knew about Stefan. A random question, meant to put me at ease. "One," I said neutrally. "A brother. He . . . died a while ago."

"Oh, I'm so sorry," she said, and it was clear she felt terrible about bringing it up. I, of course, was feeling equally bad about lying, but what could I do? I couldn't tell her. Fr. Mike, in fact, had expressly warned me about involving Señora Anne, that it might put her in danger.

"I know a little bit about it," she said. "My own brother died when I was fourteen. We were close. You don't ever let that go completely."

I started to say something, but she stopped me by raising a hand. "No, it happened a long time ago. Thirty years, almost. And I know he's all right."

All right? Okay. I knew where this was going if I didn't watch out.

"But I feel for you, Eva. That's hard. Especially when it's your only sibling."

I was mute. Here we were, talking about Stefan as though he were buried already. Everything in me wanted to rise up in protest, yet maybe she was right without knowing it. Maybe he'd been dead for weeks, tortured by bullies or tossed out of a truck somewhere with a bullet in his head. Maybe he was halfway to the sea by now, floating on his back in the yellow Usumacinta. And me: it could be that I was a fool who should be crying my eyes out in her lap right now.

But I couldn't let all that in. If I did, I'd give up. I'd leave these people and all their problems, and I'd say the hell with Chiapas, and I'd get on a plane and go back to Africa or Thailand or someplace where there were young, good-looking journalists who liked to sleep in tents as much as I did. I'd go back to my life, or that series of events I called my life. I'd give up all this thinking and go back to being myself, whoever that was. She who was always game for anything.

Anne was beginning to nod. She'd had a big afternoon with all those tears. She was trying to stay awake for my sake, in case I wanted to talk about my poor dead brother, but I could tell she was about to crash. "Go to sleep," I told her. "Jan will be pulling in soon, and the turkey's just about done. Catch up while you can. There are big doings tonight."

She gave me one last smile, the left side of it in a goofy droop, and then she was out. I pulled the afghan from the end of the bed over her legs and tiptoed out and shut the door behind me. This, hands down, was the most responsibility I'd ever had in my life. I didn't know how much longer I could take it.

It wasn't until later that it occurred to me: she'd never mentioned God once, not today, not during the entire time I'd been in her house. She'd never quoted a single line of Scripture at me. Which meant one of two things. Either she was afraid to say what she thought, which I didn't believe for a minute, or she understood where I was and had too much class to foist something on me I didn't want. Which, if true, shot to hell my theories about her holier-than-thou attempts at martyrdom and her unethical use of Bible verses.

By the time Jan came through the door at five, Rikki and I had dragged the kitchen table out to its holiday location beside the Christmas tree in the living room. We'd also done the full decoration routine: green tablecloth, green candles, green bananas, and ruby pomegranates for a centerpiece. Anne had six china place settings from England, which she kept on the top shelf in the hallway linen closet. Rikki carefully handed them down to me and we rinsed off the dust and polished them until they hurt our eyes. It kept surprising me how much I was enjoying myself in this unfamiliar domestic role. When Stefan and I were kids, Hana invariably wanted this kind of thing on holidays, and maybe because I knew ahead of time what a disaster it was bound to become—Milo grumpy, Bruno obnoxious, everybody miserable—I'd always resisted. Now here I was, bustling around like Betty Crocker.

Jan caught me in the act. As he came through the front door, I was shaving the bottoms of the candles so they would fit inside the holders. It was a precision job, easily botched, so I hardly glanced at him when he came in, or as he came over to the festive-looking table with its unripe banana and pomegranate arrangement and stood beside me, surveying what we'd created.

"You have been busy," he said, sounding uncharacteristically humble.

"Rikki helped." I went on with my candle job.

"It is very nice."

"Thanks."

"Is there anything I can do?"

"Too late. Except you might want to look in on your wife." I said this deliberately and looked over at him for the first time. He didn't look so hot already, and that line made him blanch.

"Is there anything wrong?" he said, still humble. "Is she okay?"

I could see what he was thinking. Every time you came home, you'd have to be wondering: did she have some kind of spell? Did she die in your absence?

"She's okay," I said.

He gave a billowing sigh, and I saw his shoulders slump.

"We're eating pretty soon," I said.

"Right. I will go change now, and then peek in on her."

"Good deal."

Rikki must have heard us chatting away, but he hadn't even poked his head out of the kitchen yet. It was a message, though I wondered whether his father had caught it. I wished I could just pick a side and stick with it, but somehow all three of them had their hooks in me. I'd watched Anne cry, I knew how upset Rikki was at his dad's taking off again on Christmas Day, and now I was talking to the culprit himself and couldn't seem to work up much indignation.

This last thought was significant, and I looked up from my candle. Sure enough, Jan was still there, staring at me, and not in his usual way—not as a man interrupted from some really important work, trying to orient himself in space and time. He was watching me in a way he never had before, unsmiling as ever, but alert, for the first time, to my presence. Maybe it was his wife's apron, tied around my waist, or the moment of truth inside Pacal's tomb, or the long celibate sit on top of the pyramid together. But suddenly I was within his ken, as they say, when I hadn't been before. Suddenly, he was taking my measure.

Naturally, he didn't say a word. His eyes simply got, for a moment, bluer and narrower. Then he turned and went slumping down the hallway, and before he was even at her door, I was switching over to Anne's perspective. You *bastard*, I thought. *She's* the one who's been stuck all day waiting for you. *She's* the one who can't get out of that damn wheelchair. Where do *you* get off walking around like a storm cloud all the time?

I jammed the candle back into its holder, and of course I'd shaved off too much, and now it wanted to gyrate a little, which only added to my frustration. And besides, it was Christmas. Christmas. And I was fewer than three hours from where my brother, my only family, was supposed to be but wasn't, and I'd have given most of the rest of my life to have been able to sit across the table from him at this stillborn Christmas dinner we were about to have.

I didn't want to be doing the Betty Crocker thing anymore. I took off Anne's apron and laid it over the back of the chair and went to the front door, where I stood for a long time with my hand on the knob, wanting to turn it, wanting to go out, wanting to walk away from this and never come back. I stood and stood, frozen in place, though my heart was banging around inside like a bird flying into walls. After a while, I realized I wasn't going to turn the knob no matter how long I stood there. I couldn't do it. I was caught. Whether Stefan was alive or dead, he wasn't where I could get to him. Hana and Bruno, shivering up north in that freezing wind off the lake, might as well be dead for all the feeling that existed between us and how rarely I ever saw them. And the men I'd been with over the years—Peter, Robert, all the others—where were they? This—green bananas and red pomegranates, a blond sixteen-year-old boy, a weeping woman in a wheelchair—might be the closest I would ever get to a genuine family Christmas dinner. And if you were going to wear the apron, you had to pay the price.

It was an elevating experience in a weird kind of way. Finding out I couldn't leave. I turned around, embarrassed that maybe Rikki had come in or Jan was back down the hall watching me, but I was alone. Just me and the pathetic Christmas tree, the boxy little living room with its sparse furniture and noisy wall heater, the table with its Carmen Miranda centerpiece. Well, Merry Christmas, I thought. And Merry Christmas to you, Stefan. I wish you were here, damn it. I wish you were.

A few moments later, Jan came back down the hallway pushing Anne, and I could tell he'd done something to her hair because the French twist was back in place. Besides that, they'd talked. Or maybe they hadn't. But something had changed, if only for the evening. His shoulders were straight again and she was smiling, and when he got her to the hallway door and she saw our table, she half rose out of the chair, she was so excited. "It's great," she said. "It's gorgeous. You did a gorgeous job. Look at those bananas."

Instead, I was looking at the two of them. His hands were still resting on the handles of the wheelchair and he was watching, half smiling, his wife in her excitement. They were handsome together. If you took the wheelchair away, they could have been any couple in graceful middle age. But in a single day I'd watched her heart breaking in the bedroom and seen the plea on his face for salvation from this hell. "Wait," I said. I went to my pack and got out my Canon.

"Eva," she said, "not again. You're wasting your film."

"Not a waste. Jan, move her over by the tree, all right? Let's do something wildly untraditional here."

He raised an eyebrow at me but did as I asked.

"Rikki," I called. "Get yourself in here pronto, boy."

He appeared in the doorway with his hands in his pockets, as though reluctant, now that it was actually here, to begin the event. He'd showered and changed into a midnight blue dress shirt with a gray tie and gray pants, and his hair, still wet, was combed slickly back.

"What's up?" he said.

"You look like a gangster," I told him. "A handsome movie gangster. But I didn't bring you out here to admire you. Go pose with your family. A Christmas photo."

Rikki shot Jan a sheepish look, and in that look I could read the last two weeks of silent tension between them. Jan said, "If I have to do it, so do you."

"Okay, all right," Rikki said, and went and stood beside his father.

I got them in my viewer, a boy's youthful lankiness, his mother's disintegrating beauty, his father's steel blue eyes. "Queso," I said. "Cheese."

"Wait," said Rikki, and we waited as he put in a new cassette tape. Emmylou Harris singing country western carols. "All right," he said, and took his place at his mother's left.

"Smile," I ordered, and used up half a roll on them.

The ice successfully broken, dinner went fine. Jan proposed a toast to the cooks, then to Anne, who blushed at being the center of attention, and then to the absent Felice. The kutz was perfect, flaky and tender, and the water chestnut dressing had soaked up all the juices. Rikki fell into an eating trance and got gravy on his tie. Anne reminisced about their days at Cerros, El Mirador, Tikal, filling me in on the various people they'd worked with over the years. My candles, even the wobbly ones, cast a misleading, holy-looking glow over people's faces. We weren't holy. Well, maybe Anne. Not the rest of us. But it didn't matter to me right then—the falseness of our beauty.

After dinner came the surprise: Jan had brought presents. For Anne, a stunning pair of woven slippers made in Zinacantán, and for Rikki, a green backpack with a ton of special compartments. He'd even bought a gift for me: a new canteen. When I tried to protest—I'd never even thought of buying them presents—he said, "Who made this dinner?"

Anne had gotten me something too, after a weeklong search by Rikki. She watched my face like a pleased child as I opened the small red box, as though she could hardly wait to see my reaction. This was one of the things that made her Anne, this odd innocence of hers. In the box was a tiny silver water lily on a chain. "A Classic Maya symbol," she said, leaning toward me. "Very special. Water trapped in canals was their source of life. They planted their crops on raised beds alongside them. Where the water lilies grew, the fish lived also, so there was food for them and fertilizer for their maize crops, all in one place." She glanced over at Rikki, as though he'd learned all this at her knee, which he probably had. "Right before summer, before the rains began, some of the canals dried up. Then the trees looked like ghosts and the leaves were white and dusty. The season of death. If it was dry enough, or if there was a drought, the water lilies vanished. But when the rains came, they came back too, along with the fish and the streams in the jungle. The Mayas loved the plants so much they even called their nobles Ah Nab: the 'Water Lily People.'"

I ran the thin chain through my fingers, then held the lily up, swinging, to the light so that everyone could see it. They were all looking at me with their different thoughts running behind their eyes, but I couldn't tell what they were, or even what I was thinking myself. Besides the Brownie 127, I'd never gotten a present like this before, not even as a kid. Saints' medals and glow-in-the-dark Virgins weren't the same. "I like it," I said lamely. "Thanks a lot."

It's true that I'm not a person who wears jewelry. Anne, who saw more clearly than most, had probably seen that. But she'd gotten it for me anyway, as though she knew something about me that I didn't.

"Rikki," I said, "could you help me hook this thing in the back?" He got up obediently and came and stood behind my chair, and I handed him both ends of the chain and then lifted my braid out of the way. I could feel his fingers against the indented place in the back of my neck as he fumbled around with the clasp, and I sat there feeling foolish and trustful and sentimental, listening to Emmylou Harris and thinking about my water lily and wishing, as much as I needed to get to San Cristóbal de las Casas, that Christmas wasn't already over.

Jan was sitting back in his chair, watching us.

Anne said, "They believed the world floats on water. Some people think that Xibalba itself was underwater. You can see it in some of the iconography—water welling up out of the portal that leads to the spirit world. But when the sun goes into Xibalba at the end of the day, the whole Underworld rotates in a huge circle and becomes the night sky. As if, every night, the sea becomes the sky." She had those hands of her clasped together once again. "A beautiful idea, don't you think?"

Tomorrow, I thought, this moment will be over. Jan and I will pack the red jeep and take off for San Cristóbal, back in our roles of boss and employee. Rikki will stay here with Anne until Felice comes. And I'll take up my search for Stefan again. Everything back to normal.

So what was new? You can't hang on to the happy times. I'd found that out years ago.

Chapter Twelve

Jan and Rikki and I got up the next morning before dawn to pack and load the jeep. San Cristóbal de las Casas was not far compared to the distances we'd traveled across the Petén or from Corozal to Palenque, but Jan liked to get on the road early. Rikki was to come down by bus five days later, when Felice returned. I was already missing him.

Anne insisted that we wake her to say goodbye. The farewell turned out to be harder than I'd expected. In spite of my revelation at the doorknob the night before, I wasn't sure what would happen after I got to my brother's city, whether if I found some clues I'd have to ask Jan for leave or put in my resignation. Maybe there wouldn't even be time for that much formality. And if I did abandon him in the middle of his top secret project, I didn't know whether I'd be giving up all claims of friendship. I didn't know, in other words, if I'd see Anne again or not.

Jan and Rikki were outside in the sleepy pearl light, working on the jeep. I pulled open Anne's curtains so she could see them from the bed, and so she could see the donkey at the end of his tether, cropping the grass around his post. Animals were up—chickens, ducks, sheep—but most of the human population of Palenque was still under the covers.

She hadn't slept. You could see it in the shadows under her eyes, the tangled hair where she'd been turning against her pillows. Yet she was half propped up, and I was sitting beside her on the edge of the bed. By her slow, easy conversation, you would have thought we were two friends having coffee at a café instead of what we were doing, which was maybe saying goodbye forever. Although she didn't know that.

"I've loved having you here, Eva," she said. "You don't know how much."

"You've been good to me."

She smiled and raised her hand to her hair. "Look at this mess. You've definitely seen me in all my stages."

"You're a gladiator, Anne."

"Oh, come on now."

"I mean it. I've worked with some tough people. They don't compare."

"I'm not tough. That's my problem."

"You're better than tough."

She blinked at me. "I've told Jan," she said, "that he should share with you what he's doing. That maybe you could help."

"I have no training."

"But you're intelligent. And you remember things."

"I told him that Rikki is his man, as far as epigraphy goes. He knows a lot for his age."

She nodded slowly. "I think you're right. But they're a little rocky together right now."

"I know. But I think if . . . "

"What?"

"Well, if Jan would just focus a little, he'd see it. How much Rikki wants to do it, and how good he'd be."

"Will you tell him that again? Because you're right."

"That would be a first."

She laughed a little. The afghan had slipped off one leg. I pulled it back over her. "Anne," I said, "could I ask you a question?"

"Anything." She looked at me expectantly.

"That women's cooperative in Mexico City. They're Quaker, right?"

She nodded, looking surprised.

"Does that mean you're a Quaker too?"

She cocked her head. I could see her thinking. Then she said, "May I ask you a question first?"

"Shoot."

"Why do you want to know?"

This was unexpected. I thought about it for a moment. Why *did* I want to know? Something, probably, about wanting to lay my fears about her to rest. To settle in my mind that she was not a fanatic in disguise, waiting to convert me. Quakers, as far as I knew, didn't do much proselytizing. They let you be. I thought I might even be all right about the Bible verses in class if she were a Quaker, though I wasn't sure why.

"I'm just curious, I guess. I know Catholics cold, but I've never had any experience with Quakers. What do they do?"

She looked away from me, out the window. In spite of the clear signs of exhaustion on her face, and her husband loading up to leave her again, she looked fairly serene. Not how I would have been, that was for sure. "They're no great mystery," she said finally. "Maybe quieter than most denominations. Depending on the group, there's usually no singing, no preaching, no ritual of any kind. You simply sit together, all thinking of God at the same time. Like a meditation. Sometimes people are moved to say something. Mostly, it's silence."

A roomful of people sitting together with their eyes closed. "That's it?" I said.

"That's it. Their hallmark is simplicity."

"So what happens? When you're doing all this sitting around not talking?"

She turned her eyes back on me and studied my face. "Well, sometimes it's just a big bore. You're too distracted with your own thoughts to focus in. Or your body is too restless and you can't sit still."

"That would be me," I said. "I can't sit still for ten minutes."

She smiled. "That's everyone, when they first start. It's like any other discipline—you've got to practice for quite a while, sometimes years, before you get any good at it."

"But what's the point?"

"The point is learning how to concentrate the gaze. Zen practitioners say that you have to focus on something for at least twenty minutes before you really begin to see it. But most of us rush around too fast to spend that kind of time. So the practice of stillness and silence is really just about developing a new way of interacting with the world."

"I don't get it."

She smiled. "I know—it sounds very esoteric, but it's not, really. It's more about developing a few new habits. Maybe we Quakers are more apt to try to control life than other people—I don't know—but the way we deal with that tendency is to practice being still and silent and alert to what we are usually missing. To begin seeing things as they really are instead of through the lens of the ego. It's about finding our real place in the scheme of things."

I thought about this, the notion that sitting in silence with a group of other silent people could be a kind of discipline that you had to practice for a long time before you reaped the benefit of being at peace with yourself. I, for one, would be grateful for a cease-fire. If Quaker silence could do that for a person, I'd be up for a try. Especially since no one would take me by the shoulder halfway through and tell me why I really needed to be reading the Bible or suffering through Mass instead. But the only thing I'd ever been disciplined about in my life was photography, and I'd been at it for enough years that I knew how long it took to become decent, much less adept, at anything. If I took up meditation tomorrow, it could be a couple of decades before there was an ounce of payoff.

"So," I said carefully, still nervous about triggering a latent urge in Anne to evangelize me, "what was the biggest change for you personally?"

She thought about that one. "That's a good question," she said. "I don't know if I've ever tried to put it in words before. It's always been such a private thing for me." There was a delicate pause as we both digested the implications of this statement—i.e., Jan was not remotely interested in this Quaker business and likely never would be.

Then, still thoughtful, she said, "I think the biggest effect on me was a major drop in my anxiety level. When I was younger, I used to fret and stew about everything. Marriage, motherhood, my career. But somehow, you can't sit in the Quaker meetinghouse week after week, contemplating God, without everything else sort of fading in importance. Especially your own needs and wants and desires. You're just . . . more at peace. Somehow you know that it's all going to work out in a way you could have never imagined if you were in charge of it." She shifted her gaze from the wall to me. "Does that make any sense?"

Considering what she was dealing with, it made no sense at all, but what could I say? "Sure," I told her. "And thanks. You know, for the explanation."

But inside, where she couldn't see, I could feel myself curling up and beginning to die. Because now that I'd gotten her on the subject of God, she was sounding just like Stefan, like someone standing on one side of a giant chasm, waving a confident, friendly wave, not realizing that you, stuck on the other side, have no way of crossing over. That even if you wanted to join her, you know enough to understand that the gulf is permanent. That there are things you can never believe in, even with the best will in the world, which, naturally, you don't have.

I gave Anne what must have been a fairly miserable look, for suddenly she straightened up against the pillows and put a hand on my arm. "Did I say something?" she asked. "If I did, I'm sorry, Eva."

I shook my head no, but my eyes were starting to burn. What was I going to do if I finally got to San Cristóbal and found out Stefan was dead after all? Because even though we'd spent most of our lives on separate sides of that chasm, at least I always knew he was there, waving across at me. At least I could count on that.

Her hand still on my arm, Anne was speaking again. "I will be thinking of you, Eva. Whatever it is you are seeking, I hope you find it."

All of a sudden, I knew I was in imminent danger of blubbering. All systems were go, the release valves were opening. But I couldn't let loose. Not now. Not when I was going out the door and leaving her to sort through the debris. So instead I said in a nasally stopped voice, "Take care of yourself, Anne," which was pretty much the limit of my linguistic capabilities right then. She nodded, though she was still looking up at me with concern. A hug of some kind seemed appropriate, even though I'm normally not a hugger, especially of women. The angle, however, was completely wrong. I reached out and put my palm against her cheek and held it there for a few seconds. Her skin was cool and very smooth. I could feel a faint pulse beneath it.

Then I took my hand away and got out of there before I did anything else to make myself blush.

Jan and I left Santo Domingo de Palenque just as the sun was coming up. I gazed at the church on the hill, thinking of Padre Miguel and the men filing into Mass with their straw hats against their thighs. We drove past the municipal building, the courthouse, the army barracks, the place where the buses picked up tourists headed for the ruins. Finally we came to the Carretera Ocosingo, a good road that eventually winds its way up into the mountains to San Cristóbal. There were farmers switching their zebu cows along the road already, but no cars, and pretty soon we had left the outskirts of town behind us. Near the turnoff to the ruins, I saw two barefoot, long-haired men in white shifts with quivers of arrows on their backs heading up into the mist that surrounded the site. Lacandon Mayas come to sell their souvenirs.

Jan didn't talk. Both of us, I think, were feeling somewhat mopey after the goodbyes. But we were going to see Rikki soon. It was Anne I couldn't stop thinking about. I wondered whether Rikki would remember to check the turkey carcass, boiling away in a soup pot on the stove. Turkey soup would be good for her, easy to get down and jammed with protein. That, and some of those leftover yams. I hoped he would remember and not just let things sit in the refrigerator the way most kids would.

I began to notice that every time I thought of something else that might go wrong, I got sadder. It was probably better not to think of the little yellow stucco house at all.

After we had been driving for almost an hour, Jan pulled onto a side road with a sign on it that said Agua Azul Crucero. We rattled along on the dirt for four kilometers or so and came out into a parking area. There was an admission booth with nobody in it. "Come on," he said, getting out. "You have to see this."

I looked around, frowning. My camera gear was in the jeep, and the jeep couldn't be locked. "How far?" I said.

"Ten minutes?"

"Hold on." I was already rifling through the packs. "Can't leave the equipment unguarded, Jan."

"Okay," he said. "Even though there is nobody around."

"Still." I got everything on my back and followed him along a trail into heavy rainforest. Somewhere was the steady roar of water, which got louder and more deafening as we walked. Then we came out of the trees onto the bank of a big river fed by hundreds of cascades, some small as water pouring out of spouts, and some powerful waterfalls. Cold spray rose all around us, weighting down my eyelashes and clouding our view of the ceiba trees that overhung the banks. The water tumbled into limestone pools, which were a brilliant azure that didn't look real. I knelt and put my hand into the river. It was cool and felt very clean.

"Agua Azul," he said. "More than five hundred falls in this one area, the most popular swimming in Chiapas. By noon today, you would find hundreds of people here, lots of them from Tuxtla or even Villahermosa."

I was thinking that this was possibly the first time I'd ever been alone in such an exotic environment with someone of the male persuasion and not had the obvious in mind. Though with that thought, perhaps I just had. Eva, I said to myself with enormous disgust, you are truly a hopeless person.

Jan said, "I used to come here with Anne and Rikki on weekends when he was small. He would spend the whole day on his own making friends at one pool or another."

"I can picture him."

Jan squatted down on the bank beside me and stared at the falls. He was wearing his usual cap, and his work shirt was rolled up at the elbows. Back on the road again. Nothing had changed. The water thundered all around us, and he stood up and put his arms over his head and stretched, then stuck out his legs, one at a time, stretching them too. Dumping tension, I thought. And then another thought, not so euphemistic: he could hardly wait to get away from there. From her. What a life for them.

We sat there watching the boiling water, our faces bathed in mist, and I tried to look at it in a Quakerish sort of way, the way Anne had described. Really look at it. Try to see it. But pretty soon, I couldn't stand being still anymore and had to get up and move around, so I dug out my camera and wandered off, letting Jan be, framing exquisite water scenes in the viewfinder instead. Not exactly *looking*, the way Anne did, but maybe my version of it. Maybe photography was a kind of practice run for that. At one point I got Jan in my frame, brooding and alone at the edge of the cataracts like some hoary Dutch river god. Then we trudged back along the rainforest trail to the truck.

In another hour, we were passing through Ocosingo, home of Felice and 20,000 Tzeltal Mayas. Encircling the town were deep green mountains with clouds hanging from the peaks, a kind of paradise. But the town itself was plain and poor. Small crumbling houses, a beef-processing plant, a Pemex oil drilling operation, a jail, two large establishments that were pretty obviously brothels. A big army barracks sprawled out behind them.

We pulled over to let a huge Pemex truck rumble by. "They are pumping a lot of oil out of Chiapas these days," Jan remarked, surprising me. Normally he didn't comment on contemporary matters. I sneaked a look at him, trying to gauge what had prompted this departure from the status quo, and whether I might milk the opportunity for my own purposes.

"Who's they?" I asked casually.

"The usual. Those who control the land and the resources. Those with the connections to foreign markets." A barefoot family, three kids and a mother with a baby in a brilliant shawl on her back, went by us, none of them looking at the jeep. One of the little boys was dragging a net bag along the ground. His legs curved out and then in, as though he'd spent his life on horseback, which of course he hadn't.

"Jan," I said carefully, not wanting to push it but wanting to find out what he knew. "What's going to happen here?"

"In Ocosingo?"

"Chiapas in general. It seems like things are building."

He glanced over at me from under his cap. I could see that in his aggravating way he was pondering my motivation for asking, like I might be taking the long way around to quizzing him about his mysterious quest. I gave him an innocent look—no hidden agendas here, Jan!—and added, "Something one of the priests in Palenque said. And I have kind of a sixth sense about this stuff, after some of the places I've worked. You can smell it coming."

He sighed, but I didn't think it had anything to do with me and my questions. Maybe he was just feeling troubled about a place where he'd spent so much of his life. Maybe he was worried about what would happen to Anne and Rikki and him, their life together in Palenque, if revolution broke out. Finally he said, almost reluctantly, "If armed conflict does occur, I believe it will be here in Chiapas."

I leaned forward, staring out the windshield as though fascinated by the winding mountain road ahead. Trying not to look overly interested in what he'd just said. But here was a guy who'd spent years in the area, who personally knew the guards at ruin sites and had border patrol officers willing to guard an itinerate archeologist's truck. Who spoke a couple of Mayan dialects. "Why?" I asked.

He sighed again. "Because the inequities are so extreme here. The poverty and the wealth. And the government is so obviously on the side of the wealthy. You can see it in the propaganda put out by the media, and the racist policies of the state. Plus, it has gone on for so long by now and it is only getting worse. The sense of betrayal is deep. These are the basic ingredients in any revolution. All it takes is someone to fire the first shot."

I nodded. I'd seen it myself. A pretty simple formula.

"But there is a unique factor here," he added.

"What's that?"

"The Mayas themselves."

"What do you mean?"

"They tend to be a closed culture. The Tzotziles, Tzeltales, Zoque, and Choles around San Cristóbal can get really fierce about protecting their privacy. I know ethnographers who have worked in the highlands, and they say that even somebody who has dealt with these communities for years can experience severe penalties for taking pictures without permission. In Zinacantán and San Juan Chamula, you are not allowed to stay overnight if you are a ladino or a foreigner. If you try to film a religious ceremony or a church, you could end up in jail, or worse."

"Worse?"

"Mostly just rumors. But I cannot imagine anyone coming in from the outside to start a revolution. That person would have to have strong roots in the culture here."

I thought about this. Stefan was not just an outsider, he was a norteamericano. I said, "That priest in Palenque? He also told me that people disappear around here. They turn up dead in the forest or by the side of the road. Is that true?"

"You will not see it in the papers," Jan said.

"But it's true?"

He nodded. "The latifundistas do not like it when the campesinos agitate for higher wages. And they hate it when an Indian tries to reclaim land. So they hire pistoleros, private armies of thugs, to put the fear of God in people. Terror tactics. Here, they are called the Guardia Blanca. Legal private police."

I knew this from Stefan's letter. "So torture and all of that?"

"All of that."

I went back to staring at the road. This was the most information Jan had offered the whole time I'd been riding around with him in the jungle. I wanted to glean more if I could.

"What about guerrillas? I mean, guerrilla organizations made up of the indigenous themselves?" I knew there were, but I wanted to see what Jan had to say.

He was glancing my way, I could feel it. "What about them?" he said.

"Are they part of the mix?"

He was quiet. Then, "For the past few years, there has been a group training in the Lacandon Selva. They call themselves the EZLN, the Zapatista army, after the original revolutionaries of 1910. According to the government, they are a rural arm of the National Liberation Forces, who have been around for years. That they are a Marxist group based in Mexico City. Or that's what the official word is, anyway. But again, I do not believe the Mayas will take orders from an outsider. They are too independent. I doubt they can be intimidated or seduced."

"Which means?"

"Whatever is going on in the jungle, however it started, is now homegrown. But that is only my opinion."

We both digested this for a moment.

And then he added, "Your priest in Palenque? He was probably hinting at something he had heard from Don Samuel, the bishop of San Cristóbal. Ruiz—the indios call him 'Tatic'—has been a trusted advocate for the campesinos in his diocese, mostly Mayas, since he took office in 1960. So if he put out a word of warning, there is probably something to it. Though I hope not."

Don Samuel. Stefan's boss. Or, if Jonah was right, possibly his former boss.

"If the local Mayas *are* embracing guerrilla tactics," Jan added, "Ruiz is in a tight position. Like I said, most of the Catholics in his diocese are Maya, and so are many of his catechists and deacons. A few years ago he helped start a group that calls itself Las Abejas, The Bees, a religious community trying to change the system without violence. They have been harassed by the government, and even put in jail, in spite of being strictly pacifist, just because they dare to protest the injustice. For years he has been attacked by the press as a Marxist revolutionary in disguise, and the state is just waiting for an excuse to go after him and the Church. Which is why he has been extremely careful all along to keep the Church's work with the poor completely separate from whatever it is the guerrillas are up to. Even though he and Las Abejas support some of the Zapatista demands, he cannot afford even a hint of a relationship with them."

"But what if an individual priest, on his own . . . " I began, then stopped cold.

Jan gave me a quizzical look. I realized that if I didn't watch myself very carefully when we got to San Cristóbal, I could easily spill the whole thing to him. Even though I thought he was clueless when it came to his own wife, I trusted him. Or at least I trusted his judgment and his years of experience in southern Mexico. He would give me good advice, I was sure of it. But I couldn't do it. In some ways, his position working in Mexico with the permission of the government was just as tricky as Ruiz's. In order to be left alone, he could not afford to make any waves. And given his responsibility to Anne and Rikki, he had enough on his plate.

I was on my own.

San Cristóbal, which gets tons of tourists every year, was like Stefan's letters had described it. It had that dignified, colonial, we-have-a-history look in a spectacular mountain setting that outsiders can't resist. Pleased with the scenery in spite of myself, I gazed around, wondering if it was time to start bugging travel editors for assignments instead of racing off to war zones all the time.

Big, white cathedral-like churches rose gracefully from the valley floor. As we came down into the city, you could see that these weren't just churches but genuine monuments like you'd find in Florence or Paris, covered with master baroque carvings, dark with age. The city knew it was a knockout; everything that wasn't a church was painted in vibrant yellows and blues and greens set off by clay urns of flowers. The kind of place that inspires women to shop. "Hotels here must be a fortune," I said, wondering where in the world we could afford to stay.

Jan was negotiating a narrow intersection, cobblestone streets jammed with small cars, but he gave his faint grin, just about as big a smile as I ever got out of him. "They are."

"So I suppose we're putting up the tents in the central zócalo or something?"

"You may be very impressed with where you are staying."

"Really?"

"Really."

And then, in his usual way, he clammed up entirely, though I could tell by the depth of the lines around his eyes that he was enjoying himself and that somehow things were different between us than they'd been before. I went back to reading street signs, trying to figure out where Stefan's district might be. Iglesia de Guadalupe. The Church of Our Lady of Guadalupe. There must be a million of them in Mexico. I rolled down my window to see an upcoming sign. The cold took my breath away, so I rolled it back up again. "It's winter out there."

"We are in the highlands now. Seven thousand feet. Sometimes there is snow on those mountains at this time of year."

"Have you heard of a church called Guadalupe?"

He gave me a look. "It is in the Barrio de Guadalupe, I assume?"

"Probably."

"Then it is on the other side of town. Near where we are headed."

"Which is?"

He was turning down a street called Insurgentes. "I am going to take you on a tour first, since we are right in the heart of the city. This is la Plaza Mayor, built by the Spanish in the 1500s." He drove slowly so I could see. Tourists thronged the narrow streets, wending their way past Indians huddled on the pavement, whole families sometimes, dressed in hot pinks and oranges and purples, sitting beside blankets covered in trinkets. In spite of the cold, I rolled down the window again to get a better view. The smell of wood fires came into the car, and the strange plaintive sound of what Jan told me was called Chol, spoken not by the vendors but the beggars wandering among the crowds. Someone was playing an instrument that sounded like pieces of metal chinking together. I looked at Jan.

"Mostly expulsados," he said. "Converts exiled from the mountain villages." Like Anne's students, I thought but didn't add. We drove on slowly past the crowds. An exotic-looking young man in spotless white pants strolled along with an old woman in black on his arm, and for a moment I thought I was looking at the handsome young Italian from

Tikal. The thought made me go hot with embarrassment, and I glanced at Jan to see if he'd noticed, though he hadn't even been with Rikki and me that day. I couldn't remember details at this point, just the look in those limpid eyes, the silent bargain we'd proposed and then abandoned, and Rikki noticing the whole interchange. Somehow, all that was beginning to seem like another life.

"There," said Jan. "I cannot park here, but you must come back on your own and see the inside of this church, Santo Domingo. A combination of Spanish gold and Maya copal incense. Supposedly, Ikal Ahau, the 'Black Lord,' haunts the towers of the church. The death god of the Tzotziles of Larráinzar, a fierce little creature who wanders around at night attacking people and eating human flesh."

"Lovely."

"He is black because he was burned up four hundred years ago. Orders of the Spanish bishop, who did not approve of idols. They had to spit on him before they put him in the fire. But apparently he is alive and well, though now with a genuine chip on his shoulder."

I thought I detected in his voice a tone I had heard in my own. "You're not fond of the Church, are you?"

"Which one?"

"Any of them."

He got quiet. Then he said, "Not particularly."

I knew I was starting to sound nosy, but today we'd had the longest conversation we'd ever had, so I risked it. "Did you know Anne was Quaker when you married her?"

I saw his lips tighten, which should have warned me. "Of course I knew. What on earth are you talking about?"

"I mean, doesn't it ever bother you that she preaches that way to her students?"

He drove past an enormous warren of seller's booths, some under bright fluttering canopies beneath which tourists elbowed Indians and shawl-wrapped babies cried. "Central market. All the live chickens you would ever want. Sacks of pine needles. Flowers. Love potions. Domination powder. Potatoes. And what," he said, turning to look directly at me, "gives you the right to ask me something like that? She's dying. She can do what she wants. She can *believe* what she wants."

I looked down at my braid, which had fallen over my shoulder and was lying across my chest like a sleepy animal. The cold mountain air with its wood fire smell was pouring in the window, but I was burning with a peculiarly painful humiliation, the humiliation of being misunderstood. I wasn't good with words. I hadn't said it right. He had no idea about Stefan and the gulf that lay between us. That's what I'd been trying to find out. How, when you loved someone, you made a life with each other in spite of the gulf. Instead, I'd outraged him, which in the past would have made me flare defensively, but now, for some reason, reduced me to the child who'd been smacked in the face by Hana for speaking out of line. Tears sprang to my eyes, and I turned my face to the window, blinking hard.

He pulled over to the curb and stopped. "Eva," he said. I blinked harder, then rearranged my expression and turned to him. His face had that set, white look it sometimes got; his eyes were like blue points. "I'm sorry," he said. "Damn it anyway."

This somehow made it worse. I squirmed, flushing, wanting to fling open the door and vanish into the market crowds.

"This thing," he said, "is doing something to me. I don't seem to have a lot of control over it. Can you understand that?" He stared at me with his set face.

For just a moment I wondered if he were making a bid for sympathy. Even though I'd always liked men better than I did women, I'd found out the hard way that some of them had this unappealing side to them, seeking female sympathy as assiduously as they sought sex. Sometimes it was even hard to tell the difference. Sex, for these men, becoming a bizarre form of therapy freeing them to indulge themselves in all the emotional turmoil they'd been so manfully suppressing. I didn't think, however, that Jan was looking for sympathy. He wasn't like that. Maybe he just wanted someone to tell him what to do next. But despite the plan I'd come up with in Palenque—his hiring a grad student so Rikki could stay home, his visiting Anne once a month—I had nothing to say to him. What he was talking about was marrow-deep, the likes of which I'd never experienced.

Our eyes locked, helpless, and it was not so much a moment of profundity as it was like animals meeting face-to-face on a jungle path. The first thing they need to know is whether the other one is going to go for them. The basic question: am I safe? And then one of them lowers its head, slowly, keeping its ears flicked forward and watching out of the corner of its eye, and starts cropping around, pretending it isn't afraid. And after a while, the other one does it too, and pretty soon you've got the two of them heading the same way down the trail, still wary, still keeping a close eye on each other, but together, the beginnings of a herd.

Jan and I had ridden for miles in the same beat-up truck, crawled into pyramids one in front of the other, slept in adjoining tents. He'd gotten me a canteen and given me that long speculative stare last night before Christmas dinner. I'd touched his wife's smooth cheek. But this was something new between us.

"I believe you," I said. "Even though I don't know for myself how it would be."

He closed his eyes for a moment, then turned them back on my face. "There used to be a certain kind of man I thought I was. Or if I wasn't yet, I would be."

"Sometimes," I said, "I feel like a case of arrested development."

He gave a half nod.

"Usually when I'm letting someone down," I added.

I saw him flinch at that, and then he looked ahead and touched his fingers to his brow, the way he had that night in Pacal's tomb, as though his head were killing him. "I am hurting my boy."

I had to agree with him there. Rikki had said it himself, and there didn't seem to be any reason to soft-pedal since things were finally opening up. "You are," I said, "but you can probably fix that. I have no idea how, but I think you probably can."

Jan rubbed the bridge of his nose and let out a long breath he'd been holding. More was coming, and mentally I assumed my stance. "I am a bloody coward," he said. His voice was actually hoarse with the effort of getting that one out. You could tell he didn't even want to think it, but again, it was true. I nodded at him, understanding. "I am a coward about my wife," he added, as if I didn't know what he meant.

I thought about describing the crying scene in Anne's bedroom, but couldn't see how that would change what he'd already figured out.

So I said, "I've always told myself that even if I'm not good at a lot of things, I've got guts. But lately, since I met Anne, I've been wondering if I'm kidding myself. I could never handle it like she does."

"Nor I."

"Look at us—pathetic. And we're not even the sick ones."

"Oh, yes we are," he said, looking over at me again. "Or I am. Self-pity can ruin you just as fast as any sickness."

He let go of my eyes. He was right, and we both knew it. Suddenly I could see it, though I never would have figured it to be the thing we had in common. Self-pity. People who felt sorry for themselves filled me with dread. I'd rather fight than start crying the blues. But maybe that was it—it was just what I was trying to get away from, too: a big ache we both carried around with nobody to tell us to get over ourselves.

We sat there in silence for a couple of minutes, and for the first time, I looked around the neighborhood. He'd parked us away from the central market on a narrow street lined with Colonial-style houses. Both of us stared out the windshield at a man opening a wrought iron courtyard gate and then getting into a green car parked at the curb.

"Thank you," he said, still looking out the front window.

I was feeling a tad unsettled. "I'm not that good at this," I told him.

The lines around his eyes were starting to relax a little. "At what?"

"People. Their innermost . . . shit."

"Me either."

"This kind of stuff has always been out of my territory."

"The same."

"I'm probably not a lot of help."

"Well, not much, actually," he said, with a small smile, "but then

I am a tough case, as they say." The color was back in his face, and his eyes looked human again. He took in a big breath, then turned back to the wheel and set both his hands on top of it. His usual position, the hat down low, eyes on the road, hands ready to drive. "What do you say we get where we are going?"

Sometimes he said things that sounded so California, I could almost forget he was Dutch.

Chapter Thirteen

Our destination turned out to be Casa Na Bolom, House of the Jaguar, a place I'd actually heard of before, probably from thumbing through the rainforest savior's guidebook on that flight from Guatemala City. We parked on the street a half block from a big traditional-looking estate house painted the intense gold yellow I was beginning to associate with the highlands. After I rescued my camera equipment from the unlocked jeep, we made our way through enormous old wooden doors and into a large flagstone courtyard of shade trees and potted red geraniums. The arched, covered walkway, under which I could see rows of deep-set mullioned windows and wooden doors, ran cloister-style along the four sides of the courtyard, giving off a vaguely monastic vibe. Stefan, I thought, would love this place. Everything was wet and green and misty cold, and the tang of burning logs was still in the air.

I looked at Jan. "We're staying *here*?" What I meant was, this is fabulous, I can't get enough of this place, but it's obviously way too expensive.

"Well, I hope so, though I am not too sure what is going on just now. You see, Trudi died in Mexico City just last week. Her funeral was here in San Cristóbal only two days ago. Obviously, it was impossible for me to come."

Trudi. Trudi. I had read about her too, no doubt in the same guidebook, though I could not for the life of me remember her last name. One of those intrepid old European ladies who spent their lives tramping through jungles and exploring ancient ruins. "So she died," I said, trying to sound like I was in the know. "That's a shame. She sounded like a real character."

"She was," he said. "And she was also a good friend to Anne and me. For many years, until she got too old to run things anymore, this was her home, and the door was always open to us. I wish you could have met her. You had some things in common."

"How so?"

"She was a photographer as well, though never professionally trained. She used her camera to document the culture of the Lacandon Maya, who became her dear friends. Later in life she worked hard to keep the jungle from being destroyed by lumber companies." He smiled slightly. "Trudi Blom was a real fighter. Perhaps that is something else you shared."

I gave him an astonished look. Was this the Jan I knew, ever the laconic Dutchman? Was he actually complimenting me?

Then he said something equally surprising, something with a self-accusatory edge to it—perhaps the aftereffect of his earlier confession. "I wish I had made the attempt to see her when I was in the city meeting with Guillermo. But no, I was so very busy with my important work." This was followed by a painful pause. "Maybe I could have said goodbye for Anne."

No doubt true, but I let that one pass. He'd been through enough soul-searching for one day.

We started down one arm of the long cloister-like walkway and stopped in front of a closed glass door. He knocked, and when no one answered, peered inside, then turned and looked across the big court-yard as though the office clerk might suddenly materialize. "Maybe they are closed up in her honor," he said. "Even though she turned over the reins some years ago, she still had a lot of influence here at Na Bolom and over the whole region. For years she and her husband, Frans, who was one of the first archeologists to excavate Palenque, have provided rooms for visiting scholars and students, not to mention the Lacandones themselves when they are in San Cristóbal. Her death, I am afraid, will open up another wound here."

"Wound?" I asked, following along as he headed further down the walkway.

"For years there has been a big struggle going on in the Lacandon Selva between a couple of different clans," he said. "In the past, over religion, but also the cutting of the mahoganies. Trudi's group, Chan K'in's group, was the traditional one. They managed to escape the Christianizers after the Conquest and were not about to take it up in the twentieth century. They still wear the white garments and long hair and hunt with bows and arrows on occasion, though they are also becoming quite worldly-wise." He stopped to look inside another room whose door was cracked open. Nada.

"You saw a couple of them at the Palenque ruins," he added, setting off again. "They have probably become the most photographed, filmed, and scrutinized 'lost tribe' that ever was. And Chan K'in, who is a shrewd, intelligent person, a man Trudi considered to be her best friend, used that to great political advantage. Though in the end the two of them could not win. There was too much money in the lumber interests."

As we walked, I was taking in quick glimpses of the black-and-white jungle photographs lining the walls, most of them from the forties and fifties. I would have to come back and give these a proper look. "A photographer, you said?"

"She was. Supposedly, there are some fifty thousand of her prints and negatives stored here. But she never thought of herself as a real photojournalist. She took the pictures to document what she was seeing, not for the images themselves." He opened a third door and poked his head in. "Hello?"

Someone sang out in a throaty female voice, "Come in."

Inside, we found an earnest young woman, a gringa, who was sitting behind a desk filing negatives. "Sorry," she said. "Everybody went to the, uh, event Friday and nobody was in the mood to come to work this morning. I wasn't scheduled for the front desk, but I can help you."

"No problem," said Jan. "Might you have a couple of rooms available for the next few days? The name is Bource."

"Dr. Bource, *welcome*. Of *course* we've got rooms for you. I'm so glad to finally *meet* you." She leaned forward, compressing her earnest American breasts into an eye-stopping vee.

I looked at Jan, impressed. Apparently, in this part of the world he was some kind of archeological rock star.

"Anyone else in town?" he asked her.

"Not really," she said. "Nobody, you know, in *your* class. The ones who were here left after the . . . you know." For some reason, she seemed incapable of saying the word "funeral." The vee writhed a little as she shifted ruefully in her chair. I wondered how many anthropology credits she was getting for filing slides at Na Bolom. Also, if she were ever going to acknowledge my existence.

Jan had noticed. "This," he said, clearly amused, "is my colleague. She will need a room too."

"Oh, of *course*. No problem." She scribbled things on cards, then had us wait while she went and fetched the room keys for us. I was tempted to say something rude in her absence, but for once managed to hold it in. And then she was back, bustling and self-important. "If you need anything else, Dr. Bource, please don't hesitate to let me know."

"Dinner at the same time?"

"Oh, *yes*. You'll be joining us? That's so wonderful—I'll let the others know. It's been, you know, awfully quiet here since . . ." She trailed off significantly.

"Chan K'in isn't in town by any chance?"

"He was," she said. "You know, yesterday, because of everything."

"Never mind," said Jan. "We are going to be working quite a bit in the library and the museum, doing some photography, if that is all right."

"Oh, of course. I'll let Bill know."

"Thanks," said Jan. "See you at dinner."

"God," I said, as we walked through the front courtyard toward the back section of the property, a small jungle of graceful trees and flower beds with winding dirt paths lined with upended wine bottles. "Does this happen to you a lot?"

He gave me a preoccupied look over his shoulder. "We are in these two," he said, and put his key in the lock. "You get settled and I will knock in a couple of hours."

My room was fine, not self-consciously Mexican in the way that tourist hotels sometimes are, but old and quiet, with small-paned windows that looked out onto the back part of the courtyard, Maya weavings on the walls, and rugs on the tile floor. There was a white-plastered fireplace in one corner, near a lovely old hardwood desk, no doubt mahogany, and a wooden bookshelf by the bed with pieces of pottery and an Indian doll on the top shelf. Best of all, a few of Trudi's framed black-and-white photographs were hung on the walls, and I spent some time studying them before I sat down on the edge of the bed and put my mind to work on the problem at hand: how I was going to pull off getting to Iglesia de Guadalupe.

The hard part was keeping myself from walking out those big front doors that very minute. Jan had given me two hours on my own, after all. But I knew that if I were able to connect with anyone—Jorge or that Fr. Martin person Stefan talked about in his letters—I couldn't be worrying about having to get back to Na Bolom by a certain time. And if I wasn't here when Jan came looking for me, he'd not only be pissed off, he'd be concerned and suspicious. So it would have to be tonight, sometime after I was officially off duty.

Meanwhile, I could finish rereading Stefan's last letters, to see if anything new jumped out. I pulled out the one dated May 25, 1993.

> Dear Jonah,
>
> Sorry not to write for a while. I figured you could use a break from these treatises of mine. But I've been glad for the chance to get some of this down. And you've been a good listener. Though I wrote a lot of papers in grad school, they weren't about me and what's driving me. I hope you don't mind a little more.
>
> As I said in the last one, finding Girard and his work precipitated a real breakthrough for me. I finally had a shape

and a personality for this thing I understood as "evil." But I needed to fit his theory into a larger picture, one I'd started to glimpse the outlines of when I was still in Nepal with Fr. John and the TB patients. If I had to characterize Fr. John's spirituality, it would be very much like the Camaldolese. He'd be right at home at the Hermitage, in fact, which is why it was inevitable that I would eventually arrive on your doorstep. Living in the presence of an urban desert father for three years did its work on me, I guess.

But he wasn't all that good at putting things into words. What I learned from him, I learned through watching. And it was the way he interacted with the world, especially the dying people we cared for every day, that gave me the original notion that I wound up pursuing in grad school. He lived as though constantly aware of a great mystery. He took nothing for granted. He did not believe that he understood things or had any real knowledge. His only compass was his heart, and even that he doubted. But holiness shone out of him.

So it was this experience with Fr. John that spurred my intellectual quest later on. Because by then I'd already been on intimate terms with evil and its effects—how it sucks the life right out of you—and I'd gotten a lot better at spotting it when I saw it, especially after the goat episode. But what that experience opened up in me, besides righteous anger, was a great hunger for the opposite. If evil was rooted in a lie, as Girard said, then goodness must be rooted in truth. But what was that truth and where could I find it?

It was Fr. Anthony, back in Chicago, who wrote to me that I should read the nouvelle theologians. You know who I'm talking about. De Lubac and Daniélou, von Balthasar and Chenu, Congar—those guys. And so I started immersing myself in sacramental ontology, the ancient Platonist-Christian synthesis we've long since abandoned, and for the first time, things began to light up for me. I don't mean intellectually, though that too, but spiritually. If the entire cosmos is an outward and visible sign of God's love, then evil, no matter how destructive, does not win out in the end. It can't.

For the first time, I started to feel genuine joy in being alive. How could you not when everything around you, every rock and tree and human being, is in some way participating in a heavenly reality? Everything thrumming with the echoes of its own original name, the name by which God spoke it into existence? The mystery of the world had always frightened me, but now I began to see this mystery as marvelously beautiful, even more beautiful than the loveliness of the created realm. I understood that the mystery of the world was connected to the invisible reality of which it was a sign.

As you can imagine, I'd spent so many years in the death cloud that this great realization propelled me straight into an extended spell of spiritual ecstasy. I showed up at the Hermitage in this state. All I wanted to do was sit on my bench and contemplate the sea, or spend hours on my knees in the adoration chapel. I was higher than a kite. I felt like a man who'd just been reprieved from a bloody execution he fully deserved, only now I was convinced that whatever was bad in me, that sense of putridness and pollution I'd been oppressed by for so many years, could be redeemed too. That all evil can be redeemed in Christ.

Something I've been carrying around since I was a kid, part of the sad family tale I'm not at liberty to tell, has forced me to think this intuition through. I had always believed that this thing, a legacy from my grandfather, was the ultimate sign of evil. And it is that, there's no doubt about it. But what I now realize is that evil cannot ultimately trump good, which in Christianity means evil cannot win out over love. That this thing I hold in my hand, a sacrament of evil, if you will, is fully and completely redeemable through the power of the love of Christ. And that it has been given into my hands so that I could be part of its transformation.

I cannot tell you, Jonah, how grateful I am for those three years with you and the guys. For those hours of silence and solitude and prayer. For the sheer natural beauty of the place and the loving-kindness I experienced there. Sorry. It's gotten tough here these days and I'm in a self-pitying mode right now, as you can see. But I wanted to say all this, just in case.

Things are heating up. Earlier this month, the army got nervous and moved a lot more troops into the area. Several days ago, a group of soldiers ran into some guerrilleros at a place called Las Calabazas and there was a daylong firefight that killed a few people. The next morning, as the army tried to follow the guerrilleros into the jungle, they came upon a training camp: four caves and six huts jammed with food and guns and ammo. So they began retaliating, including bombing near Morelia, where Mat is from. This was all in the Tuxtla papers this morning.

Some of the young guys in my Wednesday night group are very keyed up. These are young men who've been working off and on with Las Abejas, which is strictly committed to pacifist resistance. But now they've got the seductive whiff of impending violence in their nostrils. Mat has taken off, and his friends won't say where. My guess is that he's gone to the jungle to join up with the guerrilleros. They call themselves the EZLN, or Ejército Zapatista de Liberación Nacional. Keep us both in your prayers.

Your brother,

Stefan

Okay, so maybe I'd been so impatient to get through the letters the first time around that I'd totally missed it, but I did not remember the bit about my grandfather and whatever he'd left Stefan. The evil thing. I ran down a mental list of all the stuff I'd uncovered in Stefan's bedroom. The red-and-white scarf. The religious medals. The watch cap. The scuffed up, locked box.

It had to be the box. I'd looked at everything else.

The rest of the letter made him sound like a religious loony. I was completely out of my depth with this stuff. But I had to try to understand, since this ecstasy business presumably had something to do with where he was now. I wished I could show it to Anne, who would no doubt totally get it. I only hoped that if I ever got to the Guadalupe church, there'd be a priest who could translate.

Meanwhile, I had another letter to tackle. This one was dated a month later.

> Dear Jonah,
>
> Things are unfolding here in a way that seems both in-exorable and, at the same time, absolutely unnecessary. It's frustrating to have to stand by and watch it happen, and I'm starting to question whether that's what I am supposed to do. Mat stayed away for three weeks, then slipped into the rectory one night to let us know he was okay. He's been with them in the jungle, training. He's come to believe that revolution is not only nigh, but just. I told him Christ would never pick up a gun. He quoted Hebrews at me: "'Consider how he endured such opposition from sinners, in order that you may not grow weary and lose heart. In your struggle against sin you have not yet resisted to the point of shedding blood.'" He said, "The men who killed my father were sinners. Donaldo Aguilar is a sinner."
>
> Which is always how the logic goes. Sin must be avenged. Sinners must be punished.
>
> Fr. Anthony sent me a book last month, another bomb-shell from Girard. I've been reading and rereading it, not like I read his work before, out of curiosity or the need to understand, but as a guidebook for what to do next. Fr. Anthony, too, has had Fr. John's revelation, which is that the cross broke apart that endless cycle of sin and blood sacrifice. The crucifixion pulled the curtain back on what has always been covered up, revealed the sacrificial mechanism for what it really is, and showed us why we are doomed to keep repeat-ing and repeating it unless we finally see it as the great lie. As Satanic. The intoxicating, unifying effect of mob violence is always bought with the blood of an innocent victim. And once we become aware that the victim truly is innocent, we

are no longer purified by his sacrificial death. Indeed, we must now convict ourselves of murderous self-deception.

Once we see this, the old mystique that has always hovered around ritual sacrifice begins to dissipate. Because unlike the great pagan myths, which valorize the mechanism at the same time they work to conceal it, the Gospels are written from the perspective of the victim himself. Which is why as we have slowly absorbed the Christ event into Western culture, we've become more and more invested in the plight of scapegoats, those sacrificed on the altar of other people's self-worship. So invested that we now engage in a different self-deception—that it is our God-given duty to avenge the suffering of innocents. We call this just retribution, and it underlies the modern rationale for state-administered violence. Not to mention ideologies of revolution.

If this sounds garbled, don't blame Girard. I'm running on two cylinders right now, and I'm trying to sum up in a paragraph what it took him an entire book to lay out. I'm also shamelessly piggybacking and making conjectures he'd probably never make. But there's one he does make that truly has me reeling, which is that Christians have misread the crucifixion story for 2,000 years now. We have taught that Christ paid the price for human sin through his "sacrifice." But how can that be, if the whole event was meant to reveal the hidden evil, the lie, that undergirds sacrificial ritual itself?

A god who would demand his own son's death as "payment" for human sin is, it has always seemed to me, a hateful being. A god who demands that his honor be avenged through blood sacrifice is equally hateful. And that picture of God has never squared, for me, with the loving, merciful abba that Jesus describes. The one I see when I am truly seeing. When I am paying attention to what is really there. When I am not caught up in my own fear and self-drama and rage.

All of this has implications for what I do or don't do next. Pray for me, Jonah.

Stefan

Wearily, for I knew the conclusion to all this, I picked up the last letter, written September 9, 1993.

> Dear Jonah,
>
> I can't say much but I've got to say something in case it all comes out wrong. I've been there myself. I don't know how Mat got me inside, but he did. It's easy to see that his star is rising. None of the rest of them liked it much, my being there, but they put up with it because of him and the visit was short.
>
> But here's the thing, Jonah. I'm starting to see how evil fits into a sacramental ontology, that cosmos in love with God and God in love with it. If at the heart of evil lies the urge to foist my sin upon my brother's back and then eliminate him, then at the heart of evil indeed lurks a lie. And lies distort my view of reality. I can't see anything through them, much less glimpse the Presence that glimmers in nature. That gleams in my brother's face. Instead, I focus on myself, and the more I do that, the more I feel cheated, and the more I feel cheated, the angrier I get. Life is unjust, the world is out to get me, I can only count on myself. And none of this is my fault. It's his, always his, that terrible brother of mine.
>
> What's next? Violent retribution against him, he who reminds me of my own sin. He who reflects it back at me. How can it be stopped? Only by someone who can still see clearly enough to hold up a hand. Not to act, not to be a hero—that's what I've finally seen—but simply to *be* while everything else is going nuts around him.
>
> Whatever happens down here, Jonah, you know how grateful I am. And not just to all of you. God's finally giving me my chance, and I don't want to miss it.
> Much love,
> Stefan

And that was it. I bundled it all back together and slipped it in with my camera gear, which I would take with me tonight, just in case there was anything to document. Then I lay down on the pretty Mexican coverlet and stared beadily at the ceiling until Jan collected me an hour later.

The library turned out to be a two-story room where books lined every wall as far up as the high windows where the late afternoon sun came in. In one corner was an immense fireplace with a chair beside it, which Jan told me had belonged to the long-dead Frans Blom. Near the door, a young man with an incredibly wiry black beard and a sun-burned bald spot sat behind another of those fine hardwood desks, reading. No doubt this was the Bill the woman who'd checked us in had mentioned.

"One of the finest collections in the world," said Jan. "Over eleven thousand books on the Maya alone, and in all the major languages. You can see why everybody in the field eventually winds up at Trudi's place."

Bill glanced up from his book, then half rose. "Dr. Bource?" he said.

Jan gave a sheepish nod, as though his renown were a tad embarrass-ing to him, and went over to the desk and put out his hand. Bill, still in a half crouch, clasped it, looking a little awed, and then straightened up to his full height, which turned out to be considerable. In fact, he was a razor-thin giant. He was in sensible jeans and a white T-shirt that said "Carpe Mañana" across the front. I already liked him better than the big-breasted vestal virgin. "It's great to see you again," said Bill.

"Have we met?"

"No, no. At least you wouldn't remember me. It was at Palenque in February of '91. Merle's house? There was a little group of grad students down from Oklahoma?"

"Oh, yes," said Jan. "I do remember now."

"And your wife had us out to the house for lunch?"

"Yes, of course."

"How is she, by the way? If you don't mind my asking?" Bill's dark eyes touched on me for half a second, but not in any kind of judgment. More curiosity, I thought, than anything else.

Jan got quiet. I could tell he hated this question. "She's doing as well as can be expected," he said finally.

Bill stood there respectfully for a moment with his big bony hands hanging down at his sides, and then, when the right amount of time had passed, he said, "You know, she pointed out some stuff to me about the wing-shell death variant and the T585 death glyph—that business about them being semantically equivalent?—that wound up in my master's thesis. She was great."

"She is," said Jan.

Another short pause. Then Bill said, "Excuse me, I'm Bill," and stuck out his hand to me.

Jan started a bit at this sudden reminder of my existence. "My colleague, Eva Kovic. She's a photographer and artist."

"Albuquerque, right?"

"Pardon me?" I said.

"You studied with Garza."

"No, somebody else. Not me."

"Then you were working at Dumbarton Oaks for a while?"

"Not your girl there either. Sorry."

He was stumped. He stared at me, his black brows knitting in innocent bafflement. Nobody, I realized, truly existed for Bill until he'd successfully placed them somewhere in the Mayanist world. He made one last stab at it. "Maybe vase rollouts? With Carlson?"

I shook my head and folded my arms unhelpfully across my chest. I figured it was up to Jan to explain why he was hauling around an untutored bimbo like me.

"Ms. Kovic," said my trusty partner, "is a woman of many talents. She has been invaluable to me in the past few months."

"*Really*," said Bill. He looked me over, impressed. I could see his mind going a thousand miles an hour. Apparently, there was a secret passageway he'd never heard about in grad school that got you right to the treasure trove without having to do a master's thesis. And I, who was working hand in glove with the illustrious Dr. Bource, had found it, while he, poor Bill, was sitting behind the library desk at Na Bolom waiting for his archeological ship to come in.

"We are going to do some photography," said Jan, "if that is all right. In the Chilam Balam from San Miguel Mitontic."

"*Really*," Bill said again. "No kidding. You know what Reindorp said about it, of course."

"Of course."

"Well. Interesting." Bill was nodding his wiry head, thinking all sorts of things at top speed, and then he came to himself and said, "Listen, let me get it for you. We keep it in Special Collections, but I'm thinking that the art studio would be a good area for Ms. Kovic here to work in." He gave me a respectful look.

I said, "Call me Eva."

In time, the three of us were assembled in what was clearly an artist's work space, a room adjacent to the museum that had canvases stacked against the walls and Japanese-style paintings hung everywhere. We stood around a broad worktable on which lay a small, heavy-looking book covered in cracked leather. Instead of the usual binding, tightly wrapped cords held the two covers together. Bill opened it. "If it's genuine," he said, "which of course most experts don't think it is, then they would have used deerskin like this because that's what they always used. But inside, if you notice, there's handmade paper instead of the traditional bark of the Postclassic codices. The paper's been dated to the middle 1500s and is consistent with what the Spaniards would have brought with them. The question, of course, is how a chilan, a jaguar priest, would have gotten his hands on Spanish paper, which had to have been incredibly expensive."

"The intrepid Bishop de las Casas?"

Bishop de las Casas. Defender of the Indians. Stefan had talked about this guy in one of his letters. I was momentarily oriented to the conversation.

"Well, that's one theory, obviously," said Bill. "He didn't actually wind up in Chiapas until he was sixty, in 1544. But the date for the book would match up with his time here. And after his long battle in Spain to convince the king to outlaw slavery and the encomienda system in the New World, he wasn't about to let anyone dictate his relationship with the Indians. He spent a lot of time out among them, and he had friends. I wouldn't put it past him to have encouraged the writing of some kind of Chilam Balam, and even to have supplied the paper."

Jan was studying the first page. "These are Castilian characters, all right."

"The problem is where somebody from Mitontic would have learned to write the hieroglyphs in Spanish characters. There are no records of missionaries in that town, at least not during that period."

"From everything I've heard about de las Casas, if he wanted it done, he would have gotten it done."

Bill nodded. "True. But there's also the problem with the indigenous language. Tzeltal versus Yucatec. All the other Chilam Balams are from the Yucatán, so they've been able to correlate them, even when a lot is jumbled. There's nothing to hook this one to."

"And the consensus is?"

"It's a fake. It's too neatly done. The dealer who offered it to Trudi wanted a ton of money. When she wouldn't bite, he vanished for about twenty years. When the book turned up again, without him, it had somehow gotten into the hands of a collector in the States who died and left it to Na Bolom. So the trail is a little fuzzy, if you see what I mean."

"I do."

None of this made much sense to me, but I wasn't going to let old Bill catch on to that. So I nodded when Jan nodded, hmm'd every so often, and once even gave my chin a scholarly-looking massage. It was clear the poor guy would have given his eyeteeth to stick around and see what we were up to, but he was too polite to hang around without being asked. Eventually, he sloped off down the hallway to man his desk, and we were left on our own.

"Well," said Jan, picking up the book. "This is something. I have heard about it for years, but I have never actually seen it before. And nobody has bothered to do a translation yet, since the jury is still out."

"You mean into English?"

"Just into contemporary Spanish."

I checked down the hall to see if Bill was out of earshot. "What's Chilam Balam mean?"

Jan looked at me, musing, and then seemed to make up his mind about something. "Sit down," he said, closing the door. I sat and he pulled up a chair across from me. Evening was on its way. The room was small, with two of those great old windows shedding a jungly light on us and the deerskin-covered book in the middle of the table. I suddenly realized I was starving, that we hadn't eaten since before dawn. Both of us had forgotten all about food.

"The Chilam Balam books were written by Maya priests during the Colonial period to preserve the old prophecies and religion. This was after so many of the old codices, the original Maya library written in hieroglyphs, had been burned by the Spanish. The Chilam Balams were done much further north, in various towns of the Yucatán. All of them have confusing sections. People were working from memory, and Christianity had already had a big impact. But they represent the best information we have on what was left of the culture after the early years of the Conquest."

My brain, already worn out by Stefan's theologizing, was working overtime trying to keep up with all of this, but when he paused, I gave him a calm nod as though I understood what he was talking about.

"This one, however, came from a Tzotzil village in the Chiapas highlands. Very unusual. And also interesting, because the Maya culture hung on much longer in this area. The source, if this were real or even a good fake, would be much purer, in other words. It could tell us a lot."

Us. I wondered if he were about to take his wife's advice and finally fill me in on the project. He reached for the book and opened it with reverent hands. "I wish I was better at archaic Spanish," he said. "I wish Anne were here. She could do this in 50 percent of the time it is going to take me." He glanced up at me. "She was amazing that way. Like fire, when she was on to something. I was always the slow one."

"Bill doesn't seem to think so."

He gave me a half smile. "Bill. It is driving him crazy why a dirt archeologist like me would be studying a Chilam Balam book, especially one everyone believes is a fake."

"Or hiring some know-nothing instead of him."

A bird outside the window suddenly went crazy, like they do in the jungle at sunset. Surely they would be setting the table by now. I thought I could smell onions.

"Not a know-nothing for long," he said. "But not tonight. I want to spend time with this book after dinner, and then I am going to fill you in. That is, if you care to know."

Did I care? I sat there fiddling with the end of my braid. Up until today, I'd been plenty curious. But now all I could think of was Stefan. Here I was, in San Cristóbal de las Casas at last, only blocks from his church and itching to get over there to talk to Fr. Martin and Jorge. Maybe I could get there tonight, while Jan was busy with his book.

Something must have shown on my face. I could tell by looking at his. "It is all right," he said, closing the book. "You have heard enough out of me lately."

"Jan," I said. "You've got it wrong. I do want to know why I've been crawling through passageways for the last month, shooting k'in signs in strange places. But I've got something I have to find out here in San Cristóbal as soon as possible. Tonight, really."

"Tonight?"

I nodded.

He looked concerned, and I saw him remembering what I'd let slip in Flores the night of our disastrous dinner. "Do you need any help?"

I shook my head. "Not yet. Maybe later, though."

Somewhere, a little bell tinkled. Dinner, thank heavens. We stood up at the same time. "You let me know," he said, "if you need someone along. Or anything else."

"I will." Help was available, no questions asked. One herd animal watching the other's back. I liked that. It was something new in my life, having a reliable person around. Jan had been Mr. Reliable since I met him. The question was why he couldn't come through for his sick wife that way. Could you still be Mr. Reliable if you flaked out on something like that?

These questions afflicted my already aching brain. Which, I observed, had been stretched and strained more in one month than in my entire life. Before, there had been no limits: adventure, travel, new experiences, no matter how grisly at times. All I needed was what I already had in abundance: muscle and guts. But Stefan's disappearance had brought me up short, like someone pulling hard on reins I didn't even know I had. Then Team Bource had tied the reins to a big post, and I couldn't budge no matter how much I yanked my head around or wanted to be running again. I was stuck having to look at things from one spot, which was completely different than glancing around as you're flying past. As Anne had pointed out just that morning. By the time we got to the dining room door, my brow was furrowed with all this thinking.

Inside was a huge table that looked like it could seat forty, though fewer than half the seats were filled. Jan made a sound in his throat, which he probably thought I didn't hear, and then he touched my elbow with a couple of fingers, very lightly, and said, "Onward and upward."

It didn't take long to see why his hesitation. Dinner was a replay of the girl at the front desk and fawning Bill, times sixteen. Not all of them were grad students: a middle-aged German couple sat watchfully together at the end of the table, and a spiffy woman with a New York accent, obviously a tourist, sat to my right. I was so busy wolfing down the food, which was in the high-class vegetarian category but definitely tasty stuff, that I didn't bother keeping up with the conversation until it had focused itself entirely on my boss. Bill was leading the pack, with solid backup from a very pretty person named Muriel or Margarita, who wore fatherly-looking horn-rimmed glasses over her big black eyes.

When I stopped chewing and swallowing long enough to listen, Muriel/Margarita was saying, "You were at El Mirador in the late seventies, weren't you? Working in the El Tigre complex?"

Jan nodded and patted his mouth with his napkin. Most of the food was still on his plate, though he had to be as hungry as me. "The early eighties, for about six months."

"And before that you were at the North Acropolis?"

I was figuring she meant the North Acropolis at Tikal, where we'd made our crawl from hell.

"Yes," he said.

"You've been at Cerros too?"

"Again, very briefly. Most of my work during that time was at Tikal."

Margarita/Muriel took a fairly manly gulp of her red wine and pushed her glasses back in place. "But you've had a chance to compare Structure 5C-2nd with 5D-Sub.1-1st and Structure 34, right?"

I decided that if Muriel/Margarita were an IRS agent, I would not want to be audited by her. Jan, however, did not seem particularly put out, as though this were how archeologists carried on conversations. "You mean, I've had a chance to look at all three of the major lowland Preclassic sculptured pyramids."

"Yes." I've never heard such an eager yes, not even on dates in high school.

"I have."

Bill, who was leaning so far forward in his chair that he'd managed to get puttanesca sauce on his shirt, could not restrain himself any longer. "And what do you think, Dr. Bource? Do you accept Freidel's hypothesis? That the big polychrome masks on the pyramids coincide with an explosive development of ceremonialism in the lowlands? That this was an indigenous development and not some disguised import from the highlands?" The tourists had gone dead silent, trying, no doubt, to remember important tidbits for when they showed their slides.

"Oh, I think that's pretty clear."

"And that the symbolism was in service of consolidating the power of the elite?" This, I could tell, was a bigger question, and it was coming from none other than Ms. Vee, receptionist extraordinaire. The entire pack of grad students were now in various strained poses, awaiting the answer from on high. I could see them all rushing to the airport right after dinner to get to their departments before the news leaked out.

"Is that still an issue?" asked Jan. "I'm surprised."

"Not specifically," said Bill. "I think she's talking about the threshold effect."

"Ah."

"Structural impasse, collapse, transformation," said Margarita/Muriel. "The dialectical approach to the relationship between culture and society."

"I see." Jan reached out for a slice of truly fine homemade oatmeal bread and buttered it calmly.

"Well?" said Ms. Vee. "We'd really like to know what you think, Dr. Bource. It does explain this kind of disjunctive episode, this business of sculptured pyramids springing up all at the same time. And there are so many evolutionary implications."

"There are indeed," said Jan. "And it is clear you have all been studying very hard."

They looked around demurely at each other.

"But you are talking to an old-time dirt archeologist here. Not a theorist. Or not much of one, anyway."

A frustrated silence fell over the table. It was clear they thought he was holding out on them, especially tall Bill, who had personally handed over the Chilam Balam of San Miguel Mitontic to him. As Jan had said himself, what would a dirt archeologist be messing around with a Chilam Balam for, if he weren't on to something?

"Listen," said Jan, laying his unfinished piece of bread and crumpled napkin on his plate. "Thank you for the great dinner. Or thank the cooks, anyway. But I have some work to do before bedtime."

The New York woman leaned past me. "I've heard of you," she said to him, "though I can't remember where. But I read a lot. This is very exciting for me to be part of this." She raised her wine glass to him. Her fingernails were long and painted a deep burgundy. I could smell perfume above the onions.

I peered at him out of the corner of my eye. He looked hunted.

"Jan," I said, "if I'm going to run out to"—I raised my eyebrow significantly—"for you tonight, I'd better get a move on."

"Ah, yes, of course," he said. "Certainly." He looked around the table. "I do not suppose any of you are going out on the town tonight?"

"Where?" said Bill eagerly. "Do you need a lift somewhere? Directions?"

"Not for me," he said. "Ms. Kovic, here, could use a ride to the Barrio de Guadalupe, if someone is heading that way."

This brought me up short. I hadn't told him where I was going. Clearly, no matter how focused he might be on the whole Chilam Balam thing, Jan had one eye on me. He'd remembered my mentioning Iglesia de Guadalupe. I wondered what he thought I was up to. But I couldn't worry about that. It was too important that I get over there tonight.

Bill gave me a narrow look, calculating, no doubt, how much information he might be able to squeeze out of me during a fifteen-minute ride. I dropped my eyes modestly to my plate. "Britt," he said to Ms. Vee, "could I steal your wheels? I need to go see Tomás anyway. I'll fill it up."

Britt shrugged rather ungraciously. It was clear I did not inspire her the way Jan did. "Go ahead. I'm not going anywhere."

"Thank you," said Jan. "We appreciate this, believe me."

"Meet you in ten minutes?" Bill said, looking at me.

"Sure. No problem. I'll just grab a couple of things in my room."

Jan and I rose at the same time, nodding to everyone and making our escape. "That is the sort of occasion that makes me feel a hundred years old," he murmured as soon as we were out of earshot.

"Well, I won't fight you on that."

"It is why I never could stomach teaching. All those bright minds, and it feels like you are never teaching them what they really need to know."

"They're bright, all right. You can say that again."

He gave me a look over his shoulder. "No brighter than you are."

I made a noise. "Come on."

"I am serious. You pick up things faster than most of the graduate students I have ever worked with."

"Get out of here, Jan."

"No. It is true. The only difference between them and you is that they think they know more than they do, and you think you know less."

I snorted. "In a million years," I said, "I could never cut real grad school."

"You have an MFA, if I remember correctly?"

"That doesn't count. That was art and photography with some art history tossed in here and there. Nothing about disjunctive events or threshold effects that I can remember. But maybe I missed it somehow."

We stopped in front of my door. "Look," said Jan. "Whatever you are up to tonight, be careful, all right?"

"I'll be fine."

"Oh, I know you will. You are like a cat that way. But take care of yourself anyway."

"I will. Have fun with your Chilam Balam."

He gave me a small salute and went on, already, I could tell, absorbed in his thoughts. Partway to his door, however, he turned back and gave me an abstracted look, like when you are checking to see if your car is in the same place you parked it, or if your child is slumbering away in his crib, where he is supposed to be. I gave him a little wave and went into my room, thinking an unwelcome thought: maybe I was to Jan as he was to me. In some weird way, he was counting on me. This notion carried with it far too much responsibility, but when I tried to ignore it, I felt the pull of the end of a tether.

No one's ever counted on me in their life, I thought. But now someone was. Which meant I had to be different than I'd always been. I reached into the neck of my T-shirt and pulled out the water lily. A funny little silver pad and stem, with a single flower coming out of it, glimmering in the lamplight.

Chapter Fourteen

Old Bill, once out of the aura of Jan, was a more relaxed guy. He tried a couple of probes on me and got nowhere, a result he seemed to have resigned himself to ahead of time, so instead he talked about Illinois, where he'd grown up, and the Field Museum, where he'd first gotten inspired to be an archeologist when he was just eight. This was actually somewhat touching, and I tried hard to listen, but my mind was blazing now that I was finally headed to Stefan's church. Not wanting to get entangled in an actual conversation, I did not mention my own Chicago roots.

Who would I ask to see? Fr. Martin? Jorge? Who would give me the most information? My hunch was that Jorge was my man. From all accounts, Fr. Martin, the traumatized Salvadoran, would be leery of stirring any political pots. Even if he knew something, he might try to put me off. Stefan liked and trusted Jorge, that was clear from the letters. I would look for Jorge first.

Bill was now going on about his junior year in college and the first time he clapped eyes on a major Mayanist, Michael Coe, and how he had been inspired then and there to specialize in lowland Classic Maya culture, but the question was, in what capacity? His words ran into my questions: But what if Jorge isn't there? Do I try to get to Fr. Martin? Or do I just wait?

No. Now that I was finally here in San Cristóbal, I couldn't wait any longer. If Fr. Martin was the only guy around, I'd have to take a chance on him.

We went around a corner—a bit fast, because apparently Bill had reached a particularly exciting moment in the "making of an archeologist" saga—and Britt's tires squealed. I hung on to the door handle, trying to figure out, in spite of the darkness, what the neighborhood looked like. Not poor, but not wealthy either. Sort of like the old Croatian neighborhood around St. Silvan's. The kind of place where working families lived.

"It's up that hill," said Bill, right in the middle of a sentence. "You want the church, right?" From the car, I could see what he meant—the graceful old church at the top of a long, steep flight of stairs, the church described by Stefan in his first letter. I swallowed hard.

"Well," I said, and stopped. Stefan had said he lived in a house below the church, but how was I supposed to know which one? "I'm actually looking for one of the priests. Any idea where the rectory would be?"

Bill cast me a fascinated look. "One of the priests?"

Not about to reveal any more than that, I nodded.

But this was one resourceful man. When Bill realized I had no idea where I was going, he pulled over to the curb, opened the door, unfolded his long self, and jogged a half block to where I could see him having an animated conversation with two women and a little boy out for a stroll. He was back in a flash, and soon we were parked in front of a modest, traditional-looking house. I stared at it for a moment waiting for a wave of nausea to pass. Bill was being respectfully quiet, though I could feel him vibrating with curiosity beside me.

"So how long are you going to be?" he finally asked.

"I have no idea," I said. "I'm not sure the guy I need to talk to will be there."

"*Really.*"

"But if he's not, I guess I could go on up to the church?"

We both looked up the hill at the formidable flight of stairs. He squinted at his watch. "It's not that late. They usually don't lock up churches till later. People coming in and lighting candles and that sort of thing."

"Well, okay," I said. "How long are you going to be?"

"I'm just having a couple of cervezas with a friend. He lives a couple of miles from here. So what—an hour and a half?"

"Sure," I said. "That sounds fine." And then, finally, I opened the door and got out.

As he drove off, I could hear the muffler rattling. Britt needed a tune-up.

From the front, the house looked deserted, though I could see a light burning in one of the back bedrooms. I knocked, though I was not yet sure what I would do if Fr. Martin answered instead of Jorge. How would I introduce myself, for example? As Stefan's sister, or simply a close friend? I could say I was an American reporter on assignment, though that would probably make everything even more difficult. Would there be any advantage in trying to hide my identity?

Before I could decide, the door swung open. It was Jorge. It had to be. It was a young man, anyway, who looked like he was in his early twenties, the right age, and more than that, like the cheerful, honest sort that Stefan had described. He was only a couple of inches taller than me, but with a stocky, powerful body in civilian clothes: black shoes, gray pants, white shirt. Around his neck hung a hefty silver cross on a leather thong. His hair was so black it looked wet. He was carrying a book and a pair of gold-rimmed glasses. "Hola," I said, making an instantaneous decision. "Me llamo Eva. Soy la hermana de Stefan."

He stared for a moment, then broke into a delighted smile. "Stefan," he said. "You are his sister?"

"Sí."

He pulled the door all the way open. "Come into our little house," he said in English.

I went inside. The living room was tiny, smaller than the one in the yellow stucco house in Palenque. The walls were lined with mahogany shelves filled with books, and a hefty crucifix hung on one wall. The floor, bare wood, had a woven rug in the middle of it.

"You have come from the States?" he asked. He was watching every movement of my eyes, everything I was looking at, but it was not a suspicious kind of watching. He seemed thrilled to have me there.

"Yes."

"You have heard from him?"

Now it was my turn to stare. "Well, no. Of course not. That's why I'm here."

"So you have received no message?" He still had his dark eyes fixed on my face, as though encouraging me to remember something I must have forgotten.

"Should I have?"

"He has not arrived at your home? You have not seen him?"

"Jorge," I said. "You are Jorge, aren't you?"

He nodded.

"Tell me what you are talking about. Why do you think I would have seen my brother?"

The expectant look was fading from his face. He ran a hand through his impressive hair and then stuck his reading glasses on top of his head. "I hoped, that is all. I hoped you saw him."

I looked down the hallway at the light shining from the open bedroom door. "Is Fr. Martin here?" I said.

"No, he is visiting a sick man tonight," said Jorge. "He is administering the sacraments of healing."

"Good," I said, "because it's you I want to talk to, and I only have a short time."

"Yes," he said. "Please, sit down." He was urging me with his hands. I sat down on an old sofa with cracked leather, directly under the big crucifix. Jorge sat across from me in a wooden chair. Somewhere, a clock was ticking in a loud, old-fashioned way. I had not pictured it like this, not the room but the way it was going. I don't know what I'd pictured, but not this. If anything, Jorge seemed more at sea about Stefan than I was. We studied each other across the bright rug. The little room was lit by a single lamp, closer to him than to me, and the light flashed on his hair. He looked Indian, but broader and more powerful than most of the indios I had seen in Chiapas, as though he boxed or lifted weights. I had been prepared to trust him. Now I didn't know.

However, the minutes were ticking by. "Jorge," I said as gently as I could, "what do you know about my brother?"

His hands were on his knees. He leaned toward me, and I could see the muscles working in his neck. Also, that he was suffering some serious anguish, whether about Stefan or about something else, I couldn't tell. I decided to help him out.

"I know that my brother visited a guerrilla training camp in the jungle at least once, maybe more than once. The EZLN, am I right? With Mat." I stopped to see how he would respond. His eyes widened, but he gave me a reluctant nod.

"And that he has not been heard from since early September, nearly four months by now."

Another, more hesitant nod.

"But the Church will not even admit he is missing. Why?"

He looked away, then back. It was the transparent guilty look of an honest man who is trying to hide something but is not good at it. He seemed, in fact, resigned to my finding him out.

"Jorge," I said, "how do you think my parents feel?" This was stretching it. Bruno and Hana didn't have a clue about any of this, and as far as I was concerned, they weren't going to. But I couldn't let up the pressure at this point.

He gave in without a fight. "Excuse me," he said, rising. "I will get it for you." He went down the hallway and into one of the dark bedrooms. I heard him rustling around, then he came back down the hall with a piece of paper in his hand, which he dutifully handed over. It took only a moment to recognize Stefan's handwriting. A letter addressed to Jonah, dated October 26, nearly seven weeks after what we thought was the last time he wrote.

> Dear Jonah,
> Mat has been given an assignment, he and some others. If he carries it out, he is doomed. I mean spiritually. He will not be able to resist the chance to avenge his father's murder. I only know this because he slipped back into town long enough to tell me. Not in confession—he's through, he says,

with confession—but out of some impulse I doubt he under-stands himself to share with me what he's up to. I think I see what I need to do here. I can't say what will happen next. If it's not good, I leave the legendary Bruno and Hana and my beautiful sister in your hands. You have been the brother I never had. Thank you for that.

Stefan

"Who found this?" My voice was angry, even a little crazed.

"Fr. Martin and me. We thought there might be a letter, so we looked for it. We looked in his desk drawer and it was there, at the back."

"Why didn't you let someone know? Why didn't you send it on to Jonah?"

"Because it had been hidden, as though he had decided not to send it."

"Why wouldn't he have sent a letter he'd already written?"

"This is the mystery, don't you see? The letter was written, then hidden away, as if he did not mean to send it. So how could we send it? This, at least, was Fr. Martin's reasoning."

Fr. Martin, I thought with profound disgust. Yet another Catholic coward. "But it says very clearly that he was going away voluntarily."

"Excuse me," said Jorge, who was beginning to look very agitated. "Fr. Martin's reasoning was that if he really meant to go away, he would have sent it. Since he did not send it, therefore he decided not to go away."

This was getting surreal. "But he *did* go away."

"He disappeared, yes, but whether or not he went to be with Mat, we do not know."

I was finally seeing what he was getting at. I'd been too upset before. "You mean that something else happened, something he didn't plan."

He nodded miserably. "This is what I think."

"You mean he was kidnapped? But in that case, the Church should be raising an enormous stink, shouldn't they?"

"If this letter did not exist, they would."

"What are you talking about?"

"This letter implies he is going after Mat. Too many people already know that Mat is with the guerrilleros and that Stefan went to the camp in the jungle more than once. He is a priest. Both the Church and the guerrilleros insist that there is no connection between them. A very delicate situation, as you can see."

"But if he has been taken, say, by the Guardia Blanca, wouldn't it be far better to publicize this? At least he'd have a chance, then."

Jorge was shaking his black head stubbornly. "No. If the press becomes involved, they will waste no time uncovering his visits to the Zapatista camps. Not only would he then be in far graver danger, but others would too, especially those priests who have been working with the indios."

We both fell silent. I was thinking hard but kept running into blank walls. I could not believe I'd made it all the way to San Cristóbal, all the way to Stefan's church, and I was still on square one. "Jorge," I said at last, "let's give this your best shot. Say he wasn't kidnapped. In that case, why do you think he would write this letter if he did not plan to send it?"

He gave a gusty sigh, whether of pain or relief at finally being pinned down, I could not tell. Then he said, "I did not think of this until now, but if he left on his own, I believe he wrote it and hid it away for you. In case he never came back and you came looking for him."

Suddenly, the ring of truth. Stefan would have known I'd eventually come looking for him. That I wouldn't let the official silence stop me. That I would figure out a way to find him while circumventing the authorities he could not afford to put on red alert.

"Jorge," I said, straightening up on the sofa. "Here's what we're going to do. You are going to find me someone who can guide me to the camp."

"To the guerrillero camp?" He looked shocked. "You cannot go there. Nobody can go there without permission."

"But you know where it is."

He shook his head. "I do not."

"You do."

"No," he said. "If I did, I would join them, so I refuse to go. Your brother is different than I am. He is not indio, he has not grown up in this place. He does not know the rage that can build up. We have talked about it. We agreed that it is better this way. If you cannot control the rage. If you are trying to be a priest someday."

I gave a long quivering sigh. I could not remember feeling so frustrated. "Jorge," I said, striving to sound rational and patient. "Can you find me a guide? I will pay him anything."

"It is not a problem of money."

"Then what is it a problem of?"

He looked a bit embarrassed, then girded himself and said it. "You are a gringa. Nobody is going to trust you. Why should they trust you? You could be a norteamericano reporter, hoping for a big story. You could have interests in Chiapas."

"What if I were an ethnographer?"

"A what?"

"An anthropologist? Just out there to study the Lacandones?"

He actually smiled for a moment. "Those poor Lacandones," he said. "They have been studied so often that they are more famous than movie stars."

"Would it work?"

"Perhaps long enough to get you a guide to the forest. Not to take you to the camp."

"Will you help me find somebody?"

I could see him hesitating.

"Jorge, if I don't go looking for him, who will? You've already said you can't. Stefan wouldn't want you to."

"I will try to find someone for you. There is a doctor who sometimes goes there to treat the Lacandones. Perhaps . . . "

"How soon?"

"It may take several days."

"All right. I am staying at Na Bolom. You know how to reach me."

He pulled a small appointment book from his pocket. "Next Monday is the third," he said. "I will call you there on Monday, no matter if I can find a guide or not."

It was longer than I wanted to wait, but there wasn't any choice. "All right. You call me there. And Jorge."

"Yes?"

"Will you show me my brother's room before I go?"

Suddenly he looked very sad. "Of course," he said. "This way."

We went down the hall together to a small room at the back. When we got to the door, Jorge opened it to let me through, and then, good soul that he was, backed away so that I could be alone in Stefan's space. Since I had not anticipated what it would do to me, walking through that door, I was glad for the privacy. For all of a sudden I was swept back years, to the day my exiled brother returned to the house by St. Silvan's to pick up his meager belongings. The day I realized my brat was leaving me behind.

It took me a second to put myself in order. Then, as systematically as possible, I searched the little room, looking for any clues. I already knew that given who Jorge was, neither he nor the shell-shocked Fr. Martin had gone beyond looking in the desk drawer and discovering the letter. If Stefan really thought I'd come looking for him, then there had to be something else.

There was. I found it exactly where I'd found it the first time, well over two decades ago: the scuffed wooden box, pushed against the back wall under the bed. But this time there was a key in the lock. I dragged it out, then sank down on the edge of the narrow bed. For a long moment, I held it in both hands, a bit shaky. Because whatever was going on with Mat, I was beginning to see, was more symptom than cause. Mat was just the occasion. Whatever was in this box was the real reason for Stefan's disappearance.

Bill picked me up when he said he would. I was still shivering when he pulled up, though not from the cold, and I didn't feel like talking.

Bill, after several interested glances at the box in my lap, did not let my silence stop him from chattering away, but I was too engrossed to hear a thing he said.

After a few minutes of this, I saw what had to happen. I absolutely could not allow myself to dwell on what I'd found in Stefan's room. Instead, hard as it would be, I had to put it out of my mind completely and concentrate on the practicalities of how I was going to find my brother. Before I left, Jorge had told me we were about the same distance from the Lacandon jungle as we were from Palenque. Of course, the difference was that the road to Palenque was paved. Jorge said that there were small roads to the highland villages, but most of them trailed off into dirt tracks eventually or stopped abruptly at impassable mountains, and you had to get through the mountains to get to the jungle. Or you could catch the Carretera Ocosingo back to the unpaved frontier road along the Usumacinta, the one we'd taken from Corozal to Palenque—not a terrible road, but ten hours at least, and then you'd still have to make your way into the jungle, only this time from the east. You could also go down to Comitán and take the southern frontier road along the Huehuetenango border, but that, again, only took you to the very edge of the forest, which was vast.

The fact was, without a guide, there wasn't much chance of me getting anywhere.

Back at Na Bolom, I thanked Bill for his help and went through the courtyard and the back park to my room. I could see the light under Jan's door, and was momentarily overwhelmed by the urge to knock. All it would take was one look at that rumpled hair, that bemused face, and I would shove my way inside, run for a far corner, and assume the fetal position and shake for a while. And then, when I was calm again, show him the box and the letter inside and ask him what a person did with something like this. How they lived with it.

But I left him alone. I unlocked my own room and went inside and settled in a chair by the window. Pretty soon I felt hot—I'd been alternating between freezing and boiling for the past hour—and I opened the pane a crack to let in the chill, damp air. It had the same fertile, mulchy smell to it that the jungle had, though this was not the jungle, and the jungle wasn't fertile anyway, but thin and fragile and subject to instant destruction if you stripped away its green cover.

Finally, at 2:00 a.m., I crawled into bed where I proceeded not to sleep. At 7:00, Jan rapped on my door.

We spent the next several days in the art studio, photographing pages from the Chilam Balam of Mitontic. Between persistent insomnia and trying to come up with a plan, my mind was not on my work. Some kinds of photography lend themselves to routine, which means you can go along on autopilot. But not this kind. This was studio work, the kind you do for museums. I'd done some of it before, but it was slow, meticulous going. I had to keep pulling my attention back to the job.

Jan made an attempt to draw me into conversation that first day, asking me if my visit to the church of Guadalupe had been a fruitful one, but I skated away from the subject so quickly, he got the message. And besides, he was just as absorbed in his own project as I was in my plans for finding Stefan. I could tell by the big razor scrapes on his left cheek, evidence that you can't think hard and shave at the same time.

Every so often I checked a page for the k'in sign as we worked, but that didn't seem to be what he was after. Rather, he wanted me to photograph the whole book, page by page. We didn't talk much, just directional kinds of things, and the hours went by each day while I photographed, in minute detail, a supposed hoax.

By the afternoon of the fourth day, we were both dead tired, and I told him we should stop before I made a mistake. "Right," he said. "You take a break and then put on a skirt or something. I owe you a decent dinner with no young archeologists to dominate the conversation."

I wasn't going to argue. "What time?"

"Six?"

"I'll be ready."

We went to a place called El Fogón de Jovel, which couldn't compete with Na Bolom in terms of atmosphere, but at least gave you the feeling of privacy if you didn't count the tourists who occupied the courtyard tables. The linen was spotless, the outdoor heaters warm, and the waiters, though not Indian, wore glamorous versions of the native traje. "Fantasy land," said Jan, "but I will not have to answer any questions about the threshold effect, at least."

"It's fine." It was fine. I've never liked tourist places either, but a night away from Bill and Margarita, whose name I had finally gotten straight, was worth it. Sitting across the table from Jan, capless and actually wearing a sports coat, was almost like a date, especially when the marimba band fired up. I tried to remember the last real date I'd been on, but couldn't, not since the prom in high school. The guys I usually hung around with were either living in tents or drinking as much as they could get their hands on. Peter, of course, had been into the finer pleasures of life, but no matter how many high-end restaurants he dragged me to, I never felt as though the important thing at those places was my company. Peter was after experiences; it didn't matter who was with him. The same principle held true in bed.

There was a third shaving scrape on Jan's cheek tonight, fresher than the first two. "Wine?" he said, looking up from the menu. He must have sat on his glasses. One lens was riding lower than the other.

"Sure," I said, making a silent vow not to drink too much. I could not afford to relax and lose control of my mouth.

"They've got some decent Oaxacan dishes here if you want to try one."

"Great. You pick."

He went back to studying the menu as though it were the Chilam Balam.

I thought again about how everything had suddenly changed for me. One day I was trekking around Africa with the boys, and the next I was in search of a brother. What if he'd never disappeared? What if I'd met Jan and his family someplace else under different circumstances, before I'd seen how fast you can get the piers knocked out from under you? I would have breezed right past them, probably, on the way to my next adventure.

I was staring at Jan the whole time I was cogitating, and when he looked up from the menu, he must have been startled by whatever was on my face. "Eva," he said, "are you all right? Do you feel okay?"

"Fine. Hungry. Tired. Not enough sleep."

"You are troubled by something?"

"I have a lot to think about. And I'm not that good at thinking."

He narrowed his blue eyes at me. "Not about . . . all that, I hope." He made a little sweeping motion with one hand. "What we talked about the other day." He seemed uncomfortable.

"Your family? No. This was something else. But I'm fine."

One brow rose briefly behind the cockeyed lens, but he was too polite to push it.

"Order," I said, "and then tell me what we've been up to all these weeks."

Later, after the pollo ticuleño and tamales made with hoja santa and unsolicited serenading by a strolling guitarist, he made his first stab at it. "But first, do you mind the pipe?" he said, fishing it out of his sports coat.

"Have I ever?"

He stuck it between his teeth, lit the bowl with a match, gave a couple of experimental puffs, and settled back for a good long draw. "Oh, that is good," he said, closing his eyes. "Very good."

It was hard not to smile, but I didn't. This was not a man of pleasure sitting across from me, not some hedonist like Peter. All Jan did was work. So I guess he deserved a good pipe now and then without someone grinning in his face about it. He puffed for a few minutes in peace, while I gazed across the courtyard at the dance troupe that was threatening to assemble, and then he said, "All right, that is enough of that," and came back to reality, though he hung on to the pipe.

"Just a word of warning," I said, nodding at the dancers.

"They could not be any louder than the marimbas. Look," he said, leaning forward, "it is not that I do not want to tell you. The question is where to start."

"Because I have no background."

"That, and not knowing what the controversies are. This is why I have been so anxious about your not letting on to anybody."

"We're talking about your profound trust in me."

He gave his faint smile. "Sometimes I can be very flattering."

I shrugged. "Most people wouldn't lay a nickel on my trustworthiness. You've gone a lot further than that."

The dancing began, swirls of magenta and hot pink. Some of the tourists were taking flash photos.

"Well, then," said Jan. "The k'in sign. What can I say about the k'in sign? Let me see . . ."

He was starting to hem and haw. I decided to help him. "You noticed the k'in sign in odd places by itself. You started wondering if it was being used in some kind of special way."

"That is true. How . . .?"

"You decided it must be a code sign. But people only use codes when they're involved in something that will get them into trouble. So you had to figure out what that might be."

He'd gone from looking impressed to looking stern. "Did Rikki tell you all this?"

I shook my head. "Obviously, it had to be something that might bring down the wrath of the powers-that-were. Like the king and all his henchmen or the gods themselves. In other words, some kind of competing movement, maybe political, maybe religious. Something with enough revolutionary punch to topple the system if they didn't squash it fast." I smiled. "How am I doing?"

"Very well. Though I would like to know where you got all this if it was not from Anne or Rikki."

"From life," I said. "Don't you know what kinds of places I've been hanging out in for the past ten years? There's always a dictator, always a rebel movement, almost always some kind of competing ideology that has to be stamped out. Why not the Mayas?"

"Well, yes," he said somewhat ruefully. "Is it really that obvious?"

"You mean do I think Bill and the rest of them will figure it out?

No. They're too busy reading and gabbing about the latest. But here's a question for you. Why have you been so concerned about anyone finding out about this project? Why didn't you hire one of those bright grad students right at the beginning?"

He put his pipe to his mouth. Blue smoke went in a lazy shape over his head. "When I decided I had stumbled on some kind of political rebellion or dissenting religious group, as you say, I could see all kinds of worms coming out of the can if I opened it in public. It is not the thing to come up with a new theory about the collapse of the lowland empires, which has been done to death already. Sometimes in scatter-brained, romantic ways, thanks to the nineteenth-century archeologists who dominated the discipline for so long. People in the field today pride themselves on their scientific techniques. No more big theories, just a lot of fine-grained chipping away. And I am not just talking about archeology. It is the way that linguists and ethnographers work too."

"Not grad students, apparently."

He took another puff. "They will learn. People who try to shift the reigning paradigm often pay dearly. For example, when Tatiana Proskouriakoff first proposed that the dates on the stelae were connected with real historical events instead of prophecies, as everyone believed up until then, she was dismissed until they saw she was right. And then, of course, there was Knorosov, who figured out a major key to glyph translation back in the 1950s but was ignored by a leading Mayanist and his supporters for years, mostly because Knorosov was a Soviet."

"And so?"

"I do not have the linguistic training to be doing something like this. I am an amateur in this area. Anne was not, but she has not been in the field for a while and people know she is no longer active."

"But she thinks you're on the right track?"

"She is getting it all secondhand, of course, but in its broadest outlines, yes."

"Broadest outlines?"

"She cannot agree or disagree with the specifics. There is not enough evidence for anyone to do that yet. But she has always said it was worth pursuing."

I paused, meaning it to sound pregnant, then said, "Well, wouldn't she?"

There was a long silence.

"No matter what she really believed?" I added helpfully.

He'd gotten his brooding look back.

"Just a thought," I said, "but what else is she going to say under the circumstances? That what you're doing isn't important enough for you to stay away from home?"

"I see your point."

"It would look pretty self-serving, wouldn't it?"

"Eva," he said, "I do see your point."

"Well, all right." And for a moment I felt a little surge of anger on behalf of Anne.

"You, on the other hand, have nothing to win or lose, do you?" He had me in his blue gaze. There was a touch of anger coming from his side of the table, too.

"That's probably true."

Just then, we were engulfed in dancers, a spinning pink mass of them. Some of the tourists were stamping their feet. Our table was suddenly the center of attention.

"Time to get out of here," he said.

On this, we were agreed.

Chapter Fifteen

Away from the courtyard heaters, it was a bit cooler, even nippy. But at this hour, the other restaurants in the area were probably in the same fiesta mood as El Fogón.

"No quiet little cantinas around?" I said.

"None that I know of."

The jeep was sitting half a block away, we could see it, but by mutual silent agreement, we headed down the street in the opposite direction, in hopes that a cantina might magically appear. In a few minutes, I was hugging my arms to my chest.

"Take my jacket," he said, pulling it off.

I objected, but it was already over my shoulders, heavy and warm. Now he was the one shivering.

A church bulked up on the right, dark and imposing, but I could see light under the door. "They keep these open late. Or at least that's what Bill told me," I said. "People come in to pray and do candles."

The big wooden doors were locked, but the smaller doors cut into them were not, so we slipped inside. The place was empty and full of shadows, but there were rows of flickering tapers in statue alcoves on either side that cast some light. We edged into one of the back pews and sat for a while in silence. You could taste the incense and the church dust hanging in the air. I'd spent a lot of time inside St. Silvan's as a kid—which, like this place, had a massive crucifix and mournful dark paintings of the Virgin and the wizened Child—but never alone and at night. I wondered what Jan thought of it.

He seemed to be okay. Or at least he was looking around calmly as though he'd just broken into a new burial chamber and was taking account of what was there. Maybe because of all the candles, it was warmer here inside the church. He'd stopped shivering, at least.

"Sooner or later we'll either be locked out or someone will come a'praying," I said, "but this is fine for now."

"Look at that crucifix."

I'm used to crucifixes, but this one was indeed impressive. Larger than life, with painted blood streaming brightly from the forehead and the other usual places, it hung over the altar in splendid agony. I thought about Stefan's French guy and what he'd said about all that. That it was meant to be a protest against the status quo, sort of like performance art, only bloodier and deadlier, so that people finally wised up about sacrifice in general. I'd never thought of that before. I supposed most people hadn't. I wondered if the French guy would get burned at the stake for saying it.

"I do not know why they do that," said Jan.

"You mean the whole body on the cross bit?"

"I mean using it as their major focal point. Something like that"— he nodded at it—"lends a certain tone to the proceedings."

"I guess," I said a bit grumpily. Under normal circumstances I would have been mocking away, playing off Jan's distaste, but at the moment this felt disloyal to Stefan.

Suddenly I could see him getting it. "You are Catholic," he said apologetically.

"Born and bred."

"Sorry."

"No need. Haven't been to church in years," I lied.

"But I know Catholics," he said, "and they tend to get very touchy about outside criticism."

"Not this one."

"It is not that I mind it. The crucifix, I mean."

"I wouldn't care a bit if you did."

"I just have not seen one quite like it before."

"Jan," I said, "will you just drop it please? And here." I pulled his jacket off my shoulders, the warm weight sliding down my arms, and suddenly I felt cold again. We fell back into silence and I remembered we'd been on the verge of a tiff back at the restaurant. What had it been? Anne, of course. Bringing up Anne was like prodding him with a hot fork.

"Well," he said finally, awkwardly, "maybe we should continue this conversation about our past month's adventures later."

"Why? We're here, aren't we? We've got time. Shoot."

He sat studying the crucifix. I couldn't tell whether he was just thinking or on some kind of escape route. If so, it was pretty clear whose fault it was.

"Jan," I said, "sorry. The whole Catholic thing doesn't bring out the best in me, especially right now." He went on looking at the cross. "Someday I'll tell you all about it," I added. Was that enough? Should there be more? I wasn't good at apologies—not enough experience. It was hard to judge, but something still seemed to be missing. Then it came swimming up at me: the tone of my voice. There was nothing inviting about it, nothing that would inspire someone to relax and open up, especially about an enormous secret he'd been harboring for years. Actually, my voice was missing that quality entirely. If anything, it communicated to people that they should have never been born.

I tried again. "Jan, I know at times I can come off as somewhat coldhearted." This wasn't the exact truth. The "at times" was clearly hedging. "No," I corrected myself, "I mean that I *am* coldhearted. One guy told me years ago that you could chill a six-pack if you put it next to my heart." He had turned from the crucifix to look at me. "Yes," I nodded at him. "I thought he was the biggest jerk who ever lived. But he was right. I don't know why I'm like this, but it's been going on for a long time. Maybe it was my parents' marriage. That's what the shrinks always tell you, anyway."

"You are not *that* bad," said Jan.

"Thanks."

We looked at each other in the almost-dark. The candles flickered like the ghosts of the dead. One of the doors creaked open. A family came in, a mother and her two children, both boys, and dipped their fingers in the water and crossed themselves, then went up the center aisle past us and knelt on the steps in front of the altar. One of the boys prayed with his mother, while the other, too young, craned his neck to look around at us. We didn't talk while they were praying, but sat and watched them. They prayed for eight or nine minutes, and I thought they would light a candle—they always light candles—but they didn't. When she was done praying, she stood up and then genuflected in front of the altar, pushing down the small boy so he genuflected too. Then she turned and took both the boys' hands in hers and came down the aisle again. I watched them all sign themselves a second time as they went out.

"That is something," Jan said when they had gone.

"Do you mean people who really believe?"

"Yes."

I thought about this for a minute. Though it was just as hard for me to imagine such a thing as it was for Jan, I could not discount the fact of Stefan. "Well, I think some can. But most can't, not really."

"Anne would disagree with you."

This intrigued me. I had thought the subject of Anne's faith was off limits. "What does she say?" I asked him.

He told me she believed it was all there in front of us, open to everybody, and it was only a matter of learning how to see it, which sounded exactly like what she'd told me about Quaker meditation, not to mention a recap of Stefan's looniest letter. Jan told me that she believed we're born with the capacity to recognize some mysterious reality that's there, but that life hurts us and makes us wary, and eventually we screen ourselves off from things to the point where we lose the vision entirely. Again, echoes of my brother. Between the two of them, Anne and Stefan, it all sounded pretty spectacular, this mystical reality they were so sure of.

But my inward response to Jan's recital was the same as it always was: how does that vision remotely help? Because between the two of them, one had managed to contract a degenerative neurological disease that would lead to an early and horrible death, and the other a form of advanced idiocy that would almost certainly get him shot, if he were not already moldering in a shallow jungle grave. I shuddered.

"I will admit this," said Jan. "In some ways, I envy her for that. For seeing what she sees."

"Okay," I said. "I'll admit it too, much good it's going to do us."

For a moment, we sat in glum silence. Then I said, "So tell me what you've been working on for so long."

He looked down at his hands. They were big hands for a man his size, the hands of a dirt archeologist. The light from the candles went over him. "All right," he said. "Do you remember that very first temple at Tikal? The one near Mundo Perdido?"

I said, "The one with the open pit in front of the bench? And the really faint k'in sign on the wall?"

"That is the one. I happened to be heading a team that was opening that temple. Anne and I were working with the Corpus of Maya Hiero-glyphic Inscriptions study. The idea was to photograph and draw every extant piece of Maya epigraphy in its own setting before it was further corroded by pollution or completely defaced by robbers. We knew that many important inscriptions had been lost already. The nineteenth-century explorers Stephens and Catherwood had done a good job of recording everything they could get to, but by the time the study was launched in the late 1960s, much of what those two found had already been carted away to museums or had vanished. We thought it might be worthwhile to see what was inside that little Preclassic temple."

"So what did you find?"

"A kind of burial, but not of a king."

I turned so that I could rest one elbow on the back of the pew and my chin in my hand. "What do you mean?"

"It was the site of a ritual sealing. A temple whose power had to be contained and sealed off forever. It appears that the transition between Preclassic and Classic society was fairly abrupt and dramatic. Almost overnight they went from a modest agricultural civilization with a fairly simple religious and political system to what you saw in the central plaza at Tikal. All this was supposedly set off by the perceived need for kings. The minute true kings came into being, they did what all the medieval European heads of state did—they invented rule by divine right. Only in their case, they took it a step further and became semi-divine themselves."

"So why did they seal off this temple? Rikki told me something about it, but not a lot."

"It was part of the transition. The new structure of society required bigger, more impressive temples. More often than not, they simply built over the top of the old ones. You saw that in the North Acropolis at Tikal. The inner structure, the one with the masks, was covered over by a later, much larger Classic pyramid. But all the temples, even the older ones, were portals to the spiritual world. So they could not just cover them over. They had to seal them ritually so they would not be sitting there as uncontrolled passageways between the Underworld, the world of death, and this one."

The dark church we were sitting in, with its flickering candles and bloody crucifix, could, if you looked at it a certain way, be one of those very portals. "So how did they seal them?"

"They went through a ceremony of 'killing' certain items, like incense pots. They purposely defaced inscriptions. They built fires and burned everything to purify the place. It was like holding a funeral for the temple. Then they very carefully jammed the passageways with rubble and closed them off forever. Or at least until robbers found them."

"Then that wasn't a real grave in there?"

"Unfortunately, yes, but not of a king. It was two children, sacrificed to propitiate whatever spiritual beings may have been upset at the sealing of the temple."

More points for the French dude.

"Besides the bones of the two children," Jan was saying, "we found plenty of evidence that this temple had been ritually sealed, and it did not look like a soul had been inside for eighteen hundred years. Except for the fact that the passageway had been cleared of most of the rubble, which we assumed meant robbers had beaten us there. But nothing else had been touched. It was all still intact: graves, ritual paraphernalia, smashed pots. And then I noticed that k'in sign on the wall. Nobody else seemed to see it, and at first it did not really register as significant. But then, four years later in Yaxchilan, I stumbled across an almost identical situation, a small, Preclassic tomb that had been ritually sealed and then reopened without being robbed. And there was another faint k'in sign on the wall. The coincidence was too bizarre. Especially since the sealed temple was off on its own, like the one near Mundo Perdido. Far from the big ceremonial center. It was then that I started to look for k'in signs in unusual places. And I started finding them."

"Like in that strange tomb with the teddy bears on the wall?"

He nodded. "After a while, I found the first carved example, and that really got my attention. The painted or drawn signs could have been done by anybody. It would not have been a difficult sign to copy, even if you were illiterate, which most Mayas were. But actual carvings had to be done by a scribe, an expert. In fact, it is now believed that the scribes themselves were ahauob, members of the aristocracy. So I knew that the carved versions of this code symbol had to have been done by people with some real political power. This threw a new light on the problem."

I studied his face, how animated it had become, the most I'd ever seen it. "And you started to think you'd uncovered an underground movement of some kind?"

He nodded. "At first, I thought it was a dissenting religion. Maybe it began as a rebellion against a particular ruler, one who was perceived as grabbing illegitimate power. We have evidence that Pacal in Palenque and Shield Jaguar and Bird Jaguar in Yaxchilan all manipulated the cosmology and mythology to validate their right to rule. This idea of a religious rebellion was interesting, but if that had been the case, the code signs would probably have been nothing more than evidence of a puritan impulse that was quickly wiped out by those in power."

I've never been much of a student, but listening to Jan go on this way, I thought maybe I'd be able to stand a class if he were teaching it.

"The more risky thesis, of course, was that I had stumbled across evidence of a monotheistic movement, the belief in a single god. The k'in symbol was incredibly rich. It stood for the sun god, for days, for time, and it was probably one of the more ancient glyphs, even then. For them to adopt it seemed significant. They did not have to use an old symbol, after all. They could have invented a new one. But to choose one that encompasses as much as k'in does seemed to me like another piece of important evidence. They were looking for a symbol that would stand for everything."

I was getting more and more interested.

"There is evidence of other ancient cultures, Egypt for one, having tried out monotheism," he said. "The pharaoh Akhenaton made the worship of a single god, Aton, the official state religion in the four-teenth-century B.C. But it is a hard belief system to get off the ground when the tradition has always been polytheistic. Look at the Hebrews. Every time their leaders turned around, someone in the tribe was build-ing a golden calf or putting up an Asherah pole."

"A what?"

He made a dismissive gesture. "The point is, for me to come for-ward and suggest that there was a dissenting monotheistic religion in Classic Maya times, maybe even one that contributed to the collapse of the civilization, would have been stupidly bold. Not that it had not been thought of before. Even Sir Eric Thompson gave hints that he was pondering the possibility. If I had come up with this idea while he was still the reigning power in the Mayanist world, I might have gotten further with it. But after his death, many of his theories were entirely discredited, so the last thing anyone wants to be proposing in this day and age is a hypothesis that sounds like Thompson."

This explained Jan's exaggerated reticence. At least, beyond his natural Dutchness.

"Besides, something was still bothering me," he went on. "I had seen the k'in sign in a number of locations by then, but the two I kept thinking about were the ones in the ritually sealed temples. Why would somebody go to all the trouble to clear those passageways and then not steal anything? Clearing passageways is grueling work. In ancient times, if you were caught, you might be killed for it. You would really have to want something inside to take such a risk. I could not figure out what that might be."

Jan's voice had a little throb to it. I had never seen him so lively. He looked like a coach with an unpromising team that was actually winning.

"What was it?"

"I decided it was the place itself. The room. Nobody in his right mind would go near a ritually sealed temple, so if you could get your hands on one, you would have a secret meeting place. A place to gather in the night. Anybody who gave his allegiance to a single god would automatically be guilty of insurrection. So a safe meeting place would be essential. What I could not figure out, though, is how they would have dared to go inside a sealed temple."

"Because?"

"It would be like early Christians meeting secretly in former shrines to Moloch, the god who demanded child sacrifice. Even if they believed his power had been broken, the place would have been permanently contaminated for them. Or at least it seems so to me."

I nodded. That made sense.

"And then there was the fact that this sign more often than not appears in upper-class habitations. You remember the sleeping room in the North Acropolis at Tikal? With the teddy bears, as you call them, on the wall? Again, that pointed to an aristocratic graffiti art-ist, someone of the educated class, perhaps even close to or part of the royal family. This might have been a person privy to the secrets of Maya prophecy, astronomy, mathematics. Someone in the know, and perhaps someone not as awed by the dramatic rituals of the kings as the common folk would have been. It is one thing to be a member of the crowd, watching from the great plaza while a supernatural-looking being in a three-foot-high feather headdress emerges from the sacred portal, his white loincloth stained with blood. It is another to have that supernatural figure, under all his feathers, be your Uncle Hans."

"Uncle *Hans?*"

"You know what I mean."

"So what you're saying is that if this was a movement of some kind, it was an educated one, and one close to the top of the power structure."

He nodded. "Exactly. No one else would have had the leisure or the skills or the insider's knowledge to have figured out a system to oppose the reigning one. Revolutions from the other end, the great masses, are not quite so sophisticated and do not go on for so many years. They explode. And at the height of Classic Maya civilization, with its ritualized public torture and human sacrifice, I cannot imagine a group of commoners getting together with sticks to oppose the king."

The pew was getting hard, which once again reminded me of happy days at St. Silvan's. I drew one foot up under me. "So what did you decide?"

"It was not until I put my hand under the edge of the lid of Pacal's sarcophagus and found that perfectly carved k'in sign that it started falling into place. It was so clearly a deliberate act of extremely dangerous defiance by a high-ranking individual, and it took place in Palenque, which was an enormous distance from Tikal or even Yaxchilan back then. Whatever the movement was, it had spread even to the domain of the most powerful king who ever reigned in the lowlands: Pacal. And a great deal of that power had fallen into Pacal's hands because he had figured out how to manipulate religion to serve his own ends and the ends of his son, Chan Bahlum. The whole building project in Palenque was in service to affirming his divine right to rule."

He paused, running his hand over his hair, thinking hard. "Pacal's scheme must have been blatant to anybody who was in the know. And I think that person, or one of them, was willing to risk his life to call him a liar, right there in the magnificence of his final resting place. This person did not clear out any rubble to hold meetings in a ritually sealed temple. Instead, he carved the secret sign right under their noses, maybe on the day they put the rubble in, the day the funeral ceremonies ended. The day they stuck the knife into the chests of those five captives and threw them in a box outside the tomb. If anyone had seen him carving the sign, he would have been a dead man. Maybe he was, though I think that if they had caught him at it, they would have defaced the symbol itself."

"How did you find it?"

"I looked for it. I had already seen evidence that the movement was alive in Palenque. You remember some of the other sites you photographed during that week before Christmas. I figured that somebody might have tried to make a final statement on Pacal's sarcophagus. I did not have the skills to decipher the lid, and I did not try. But I ran my fingers all around the underside to see if I could feel anything. And there it was. The one you got on your back to see." He sighed and clasped his hands behind his neck, stretching his spine. "I have never tried to tell the whole story before."

"It's a great story. Don't stop now."

"Well, there is not much more. Just that I decided that it was not a religious movement at all. But at the same time, it could not be simply political. Not if it were that widespread. Overthrow of a particular king would be one thing, but this seemed to be a movement that was slowly seeping into the very top ranks of a number of different lowland kingdoms. It was something else entirely."

Now he was taking off his glasses and rubbing his eyes, evidence that he was as wiped out as I was and that we should probably stop and get some sleep if we were going to get any work done tomorrow. Yet I hated to halt the momentum.

"I had a hunch," he said, "but I did not know enough yet. I realized I had to find an ancient corollary, a culture that had enough parallels to the Mayas to be a good comparison. And the two ancient cultures we know a lot about, thanks to the written record, are the Greeks and the Hebrews. Hebrew history is fascinating because it shows us the rise of king culture, the same phenomenon that took place so rapidly during that juncture between Preclassic and Classic Maya times. In the Old Testament, it is the people themselves who demand a king. Their god Yahweh does not want them to do it. He tells them that having a king will lead them into temple building and warfare and trying to make a name for themselves, which is exactly what it does. But they want what everybody else has."

Jealousy leads to violence. The French guy was batting a thousand so far.

"It is also interesting that every time a dissident came along, a prophet who called the reigning political power into question, the people themselves killed him. Not the king, the people—and usually by stoning. They did not want to hear the system challenged. They needed it for their own sense of security. Just as they seemed to need the huge temple in Jerusalem, even though their god said he wanted nothing to do with it. A temple at which rivers of animal blood flowed on the great sacrificial days."

So what was Jan saying? The Mayas were a lost tribe of Israel? My mind, already pushed far beyond its normal capacity and also in a state of protracted shock—Stefan's box—not to mention impaired by insomnia, was threatening to shut down entirely. But in spite of how tired I was, all this was making some sense. People need strong rulers and major religious hoopla to feel safe. And they want somebody else to run the show, so they won't have to decide what to do on their own.

"In time, however, I set aside the Hebrews precisely because of their monotheism," Jan was saying. "The Mycenaean Greeks, Homer's Greeks, were another matter. Like the Mayas, they were highly aggressive warriors. They had a pantheon of gods to please, and at times their gods required human sacrifice. Read Patroklos's funeral scene in the *Iliad*, when his best friend Achilleus sacrifices twelve young Trojan men on the pyre. They also went through a cult of heroes phase when their great kings and warriors were semi-deified and blood sacrifices were made over their tombs to nourish them in the spirit world. Even more, the Greeks had a strong tradition of religious ecstasy, during which they would put themselves into trancelike states, usually with wine enhanced by other drugs, and go out of themselves to meet the divine. Some of these cults hung on for centuries, such as Dionysianism and Orphism. A Maya king in ecstasy might have jammed a stingray spine through his penis, but the Maenads, female Dionysian worshippers, are on record as having torn apart living human beings and eaten their flesh during the sparagmos."

"Jan," I said, holding up one hand. "Enough. I believe you. There are parallels. And so?"

"And so one of these Greeks discovered reason. The seedbed of speculative philosophy is Greece, right in the midst of all these wild goings-on. Maybe, I started to think, in response to them."

He paused. "I thought of Shield Jaguar of Ucanal, who was held captive by Smoking Squirrel of Naranjo, according to the stelae dates, for eighteen years. On big occasions, he was dragged out in public and tortured in front of the crowds. What would it have been like to be him? Even more importantly, what would it have been like to watch this going on? Year after year, knowing he was of noble birth, just like you, maybe, and how easily his fate could be yours. Because the whole purpose of war was to capture kings, or the highest noblemen you could. You even wore ropes wrapped around your arms to make it easier for them to capture you; it was considered a sign of courage. So there you are, the nephew of a major king, and you watch this other king being ritually degraded the whole time you are growing from a child to an adult. At some point, it seems to me, you might start wondering if there was another way to think about things."

"Are you saying that somebody suddenly decided to pass judgment?"

"Yes. It seems inevitable that someone would, out of all the kingdoms that flourished for those six hundred years. Somebody would have passed judgment. And if that person were gifted enough intellectually and educated enough and powerful enough, he may have set into motion a movement that could destroy the power of kings. He may have invented reason."

"Which was not a dissenting religion."

"No. In Greece, the first thing Socrates had to do was challenge the gods. He had to point out the immorality of celestial adultery and deceit and cruelty. And in the process, he shone a light right in the faces of the corrupt politicians of his day. That is why they killed him."

I remembered few facts from high school—Alexander and his eager hands had drawn most of my attention—but I did remember this one. "The hemlock scene."

"Yes. And Plato was there. He saw his mentor die for a principle, reasoned goodness. And he went on from there to lay the foundations of Western thought."

"So if some high-level, educated Maya had come to a similar conclusion, he might have gone the same route, teaching other people what he'd figured out. Only maybe in secret for a while."

"And it spread. Three kingdoms, at least."

"But Jan," I said. "How do you think it brought them down? Those Classic kingdoms?"

All of a sudden, he looked exhausted. "This is where I hit a wall. Beyond the stray k'in signs, there is no evidence that any of the major kings were actually overthrown. Or that this dissenting movement, if one existed, had any lasting effect on the system. Yet within a relatively short time, the entire culture fell apart. And we do not know why."

Okay. What would the French guy say here? Come on, Eva. Think.

"Jan," I said carefully, "what if all they did—the dissenters, I mean—was to call bullshit on the hoopla? To just cast doubt? Because if those kings in all their feathers with their bloody penises started looking like idiots instead of gods, then the magic fell apart, didn't it? And if people need magical kings and hoopla to feel safe and suddenly it doesn't seem to work anymore, then what do they do?"

He was staring at me with something close to amazement. "Tell me," he said.

"They turn on each other, that's what," I said. "There's nothing left to pull them together as a team. And it all crumbles in a heap, the whole production."

We sat there for a moment, somewhat astonished. I, because I couldn't believe I'd actually remembered enough of Stefan's incomprehensible letters to make a rational conjecture, and Jan because he'd probably concluded long ago I was an airhead.

"That is good," he said finally. "Very good. I will think about that.

Thank you."

"So what's next?" I said. "I mean for your project? What are you going to do with all the drawings and photos and everything?"

"I am still not sure. I decided that if I was going to record the sign in its various settings, then I would do it correctly so that if I do decide to publish my findings at some point, I will have good camera-ready material available. But I am still a very long way from that at this point, though the Chilam Balam may help. Meanwhile, I wonder if all this is worth anything at all, even if I am right."

"Especially if the price of it is Anne sitting there alone in her wheelchair in Palenque while you're out hunting down k'in signs?"

Normally this would have made him angry. But he just gave me a sad glance. "My project is not the real cause of that," he said, "but it is a part of it. It is the excuse, but not the real reason. It gives both of us an explanation for Rikki that leaves us with our dignity."

"You mean you'd give it up."

"If I thought I could stand being at home right now, I would give it up in a minute."

"That doesn't make a lot of sense, Jan," I said. "Sorry, but it sounds weird to me. I thought it was mostly work that kept you away. That's what Rikki thinks. And then you got used to being gone, is what he says."

He pushed his hand through his hair again. "That is because he has heard it since he was a little boy. His father's work being so damned important. She has been covering for me for years that way."

I stared at him perplexedly. I wasn't much good at this, but even I could see that there was something here he hated himself for. I could ask or not ask what it was. If I didn't, though, who else would? Anne? Rikki?

"Jan," I said, "what's holding you back? Especially now, when she's really starting to lose it?" I thought of her crying in the bedroom, shamed.

"I told you. I am a bloody coward."

"Fine," I said. "Why don't you get over it?"

My voice, which had softened up, was back to its usual self. This might be it, I thought. The end of the conversation. The friendship.

But he said, low, "This is not an excuse, just an explanation. My mother died of cancer when I was eleven. It took her two years. Breast cancer. It went from her lungs to her liver to her brain. They did everything they could do back then, which was quite brutal. She had a radical double mastectomy and lost most of the muscles in her chest and shoulders. She had radiation burns all over her torso. My father was like Rikki must think I am now. He could not watch her suffer, so he hired a part-time nurse and kept clear. Business trips, he called them. She was my job. Every day before school and afterward, I sat with her. Did my homework on the floor beside her bed. Talked to her. Held her hands when she cried." He gave me an intense look. "I was glad when she died. Happy. I could play outside with my friends again. The ones I still had. And I was glad to have my dad back, too. It took a few more years to figure out I could not stand him."

My foot had gone asleep. I carefully pulled it out from under me. "Anne knows all this?"

"Of course she knows."

"You told her after she got sick?"

"My father told her sometime shortly after we got married. By way of explanation. She could never figure out why I did not want to see him."

"So when she found out what she had and what it was going to be like, she made you promise not to give up your work."

"She was not going to let me be a martyr. She said it would do bad things to me to have to pretend that way."

"Rikki told me some of this."

"We informed him of the plan together. After I so reluctantly agreed."

I studied him. "You put up a fake fight about it, didn't you?"

"I did."

"It's what I probably would have done. To keep from feeling like a bitch."

He shrugged.

"But now it's different," I said. "Now she's going downhill fast."

He nodded. "And now there is no excuse anymore. But I still do not think I can do it. Nurse her through her last years."

It was flat, the way he said it. No drama. I believed him. I didn't know if I could have done it myself, much as I thought of Anne. She was going to get crazy, maybe, before the end. Rikki told me she might lose her ability to speak. She'd have to write things down with those shaky hands of hers. Unless, of course, she went blind, which some of them did. Her body would start to shrink down into itself, a bundle of wasted fibers. There would be rubber sheets and needles and force-feeding.

"It is easier just to stop loving her," he said simply. "Before Christmas, I thought I had. Just to have no feelings at all anymore."

"And now?"

He didn't say anything for a few moments. "Now, I do not know. Except that I know it is not right, willing your heart to go dead like that just to spare yourself pain."

A year ago I might have objected to his use of the word "right." Who's to say who's right? You never knew what you would do in someone else's shoes, so how could you judge them? I was breezy about it—you go your way, I'll go mine. No sense getting too stirred up. But that was before I met her. Before I watched her struggle to get the orange juice out of the refrigerator and never whine about how hard it was. Before I met her kid.

"What are you going to do?" I asked him.

"I do not know," he said. "Right at this moment, I honestly do not know."

A door opened back behind the altar. A man came out and looked at us. Then he rattled some keys in his pocket and looked at his watch and looked at us again. We got up and went sideways out of the pew, and I gave the man with the keys a little half wave so he'd know we didn't mind. He was standing right underneath the big crucifix, and it looked, in the yellow light from all the candles, like Jesus was looking down on him with a face full of pity. It was the same look Anne had given me once or twice, as though there were something about me that broke her heart. As though I could possibly be worse off than she was in her wheelchair.

Outside, it was really cold.

Jan made me put his jacket on again, and we hurried up the street to the jeep. Even though we were parked close to the central zócalo, the city seemed deserted, and the jeep looked lonely sitting there. We got in and I tried to make him take his jacket back, but he ignored me, turning on the engine and letting it idle for a few minutes to get the heat going. While we were sitting there, looking out through the windshield without speaking, tired of so much talk, an army truck came around the corner, going very slowly and without its lights.

"What's he doing?" I said.

Jan was watching out the window. "I do not have any idea. But I am going to just stay put here so he can see who we are and what we are doing."

He sounded calm, and that was good, but already I was running down the list of what I was carrying on my person: lip gloss, room key, pesos, passport. The two fakes, Stefan's and mine, were hidden in my room at Na Bolom, thank God. So were his letters. Hopefully, none of these goons—because army trucks cruising downtown without any running lights were always driven by goons—would recognize my last name. If one of them did, then Jan was going to be my one and only ticket out of this. My fake boss and my fake job would finally have to come through for me.

I couldn't have been more thankful that Jan didn't know a thing. Lying was clearly not his forte.

Chapter Sixteen

The truck rolled slowly to a stop beside Jan's window, blocking the street. Before I could get a good look at who was in the front seat, the guy riding shotgun turned a big flashlight on our faces and asked in Spanish who we were and what we were doing. Jan explained that he was working at Na Bolom and I was his assistant.

The guy did not seem impressed. "Sus papeles?"

"Momentito."

They still had the light right in our eyes. It looked to me like there were four of them. Jan reached back to get his wallet.

"Señor. Alto."

Jan halted.

The boss man told us to get out of the jeep.

"Slowly," said Jan, muttering. "Let them see everything you are doing."

"Señor, cállate."

We got out. It was cold, but at least the light wasn't right in our eyes. I was still wearing Jan's coat. I could hear a truck door opening on the driver's side and somebody's feet hitting the street. Two soldiers, both carrying rifles, came around the front of the truck and stopped beside Jan. A third guy, presumably the one in charge, followed them. The driver stayed behind the wheel. I was standing on the sidewalk. One of the soldiers motioned me over with his rifle, so I went around the jeep and stood in the street along with the others.

"Los papeles," said el jefe. He directed the light on Jan's hands. Jan reached back and pulled the wallet from his pants and then held it open so that the soldier closest to him could see his driver's license. The guy squinted down at it, leaning forward and letting the rifle relax down against his leg. The other guy, however, was still in full alert position.

"Y la señora."

So now I'd find out whether the family name was floating around out there on somebody's bad list. I took a breath, realizing I was going to have to lift my skirt in order to get at the money belt and not relishing being on display in the blinding light.

"Eva," Jan said quietly. "Your passport. Do you have it?"

"It's there." I pointed to the bulge at my waistline where the belt was strapped.

He saw the difficulty. "La luz," he said. "Es necesario que la señora levanta su falda."

This took some thinking on el jefe's part. If he lowered the light, I might turn into a revolutionary with a gun and blow off his head. If he didn't, and I proved to be a genuine American citizen with a genuine set of papers, then I might go complaining to the embassy about my indelicate treatment at the hands of the military. But all political considerations aside, turning off the light also meant that everybody missed the show.

I waited until he made up his mind. It wasn't like I'd never had a gun trained on me before. Your best approach in these situations was to imagine yourself an ox, patient and dumb and immovable. Eventually, somebody gave you an order you couldn't resist, and then you did it, but there was no use getting wound up until that happened.

The light went off. The soldier beside me flicked me on the shoulder with the top of his rifle, a gentle reminder not to play any games. I pulled up my skirt, unzipped the bag, which was resting cozily against my bare abdomen, and pulled out everything, including the pesos, which might come in handy. "Okay," I said. The light glared on again, and I held my passport open on the hood of the jeep with the edges of the pesos showing underneath so the soldier could look everything over, hoping that el jefe would not ask to see any of it.

My soldier bent over the hood, scrutinizing. The pesos, as far as I could tell, didn't impress him in the least. He could read, but it was slow going. Good, I thought, but not too slow. Not slow enough that our friend over there gets impatient.

Finally, the soldier straightened up and gave a snapping nod at the boss man. El jefe didn't say anything, but the light started moving, first into the windows of the jeep, then over Jan, and then, very slowly, over me. My skirt was thin enough that he probably saw everything he'd missed during the money bag routine. A whole minute crawled by without anybody speaking. This was the worst stage—when they'd decided there was nothing going on but were reluctant to let you go back to your life in a state of false relief. This guy wanted us to know that something was up in San Cristóbal and that there were people in charge, including him, who shouldn't be taken lightly.

The light went off. "Bueno," el jefe said abruptly. The two soldiers stuck their rifles under their arms and went off around the back of the truck. The boss followed them. I heard them all climb in, and then the doors slamming. The engine turned over, a low rumble, and the truck went crawling off, still without its headlights on. Nobody in the cab gave us a backward look as we stood there shivering, still stunned, in the street.

"That was strange," said Jan, when they'd gone around the corner at the end of the block. "I have been coming here for a long time, and that was an unusual event." He reached over and took me by the upper arm and held it lightly for a moment. "Are you all right?"

"Fine."

We got back in the jeep, and this time he started it up and pulled out into the street. Before we got to Na Bolom, he turned and said, "This may not be the time to be in San Cristóbal. I am considering calling Anne tomorrow and telling her to keep Rikki home."

I hadn't thought of this, the fact that he might want to bail out of the project for a while. But I couldn't leave, not now. Especially now. If something was going to happen and Stefan was with the Zapatistas, this is where I had to be. Waiting for Jorge's guide.

"What about us?" I said. "You mean we'd go back to Palenque?"

He pondered this. "I think we will be okay," he said, "but I want to be ready to leave if we need to."

We walked through the front courtyard, and even though it was almost 10:00, people were still talking in the dining room. I wondered if they had any idea that something was about to break in San Cristóbal. We stopped together in front of my door. Suddenly, I felt completely beat. No sleep all week, the big heart-to-heart in the church, the surge of adrenaline wondering whether the goons would recognize Stefan's last name on my passport. My key wobbled in the lock, and I had to try it again.

"You are sure you are okay?" said Jan.

I gave him a weary nod.

"Well, good night then."

This is where he should have left me and continued on to his own room. Instead, he lingered as if there were something more to say, and we looked each other full in the eyes. The moment stretched out, first into awkwardness and then past it, into a strange nakedness between us. I had no idea what he was thinking, though I could imagine certain things. And then he was gone.

It turned out to be yet another night when tiredness had progressed too far for sleep. The minute my head hit the pillow, I was jerked out of my semi-coma by some generator pumping the jitters through my nervous system. Which got me to thinking that Jan might have been useful after all to help work out some of that energy, if that were actually the signal I'd read at the door. I never take sleeping pills, and there aren't too many other natural options available. I didn't have anything to do but fantasize as the night went crawling by, and pretty soon I found myself imagining he was in bed with me. What would it be like? Well, there would be no red cap, of course—such a shift in routine that both of us might become irreparably flustered. And considering the change of venue—neither jeep, nor church, nor tomb—conversation would be stilted, but we could get past that.

The real difficulty of imagining the two of us together was something else. It had to do with that moment on our first day in San Cristóbal when we became a two-animal herd, committing ourselves to mutual aid and protection. Whatever this was—friendship, I thought, though it was hard for me to judge—it had brought new barriers with it. Theoretically, you could trust each other in a more essential way than you'd ever trusted anybody before. But that came at a price. You couldn't just run on instinct anymore. You had to think things through.

I turned over and ran into the spare pillow, which I stuffed between my thighs like it was somebody's leg, somebody sleeping on his stomach right next to me.

It was not that I had forgotten Anne. She was right there in the middle of it, more present to both of us, maybe, than we were to each other. Our better half, so to speak. But I suspected that Anne would understand. It would cut her heart out—how could it not?—but she would understand, because how many years had it been for them by now? I knew her. And she'd manfully set it aside, the hurt she was feeling, if it meant that her spouse, so clearly dying of loneliness, could find a little comfort with a friend. She would not condemn us, I was sure of it, and I didn't think she'd stop liking me either. That was Anne.

Which meant the ball was fully in my court.

What would Stefan say? What would he even know about sex? I turned over again, dragging the pillow with me. Then again, maybe he knew quite a bit about it. When you'd made a vow never to do it your entire life, then it was bound to be a fairly serious business for you. You'd think it over. Maybe on sleepless nights. Maybe just wondering about it. Jonah and I had had a little talk about that once. He was curious, and in his Jonah way, didn't try to hide it. But not curious in a perverted way, like a guy drooling against the window pane with his fingers spread out on either side of his face. He said, Is it all it's made out to be? I told him the truth: No. People tended to mislead you on that. But it was plenty good all right.

Or maybe when you'd made a lifetime vow like Jonah and Stefan, it was actually easier. Like becoming a full-time vegetarian. You didn't have to go through the little should-I-or-shouldn't-I shuffle every time somebody offered you a bite of turkey or steak. You already knew you wouldn't. It was out of your mind, no longer a question you had to keep answering.

Maybe I had a fever. I sat up in bed with the sheets wound all around me and the pillow still jammed between my legs and put my hand on my forehead. There was sweat there, but that wasn't definitive. I untangled myself and went over to the window and opened the shutters. Na Bolom was buried in its own private little jungle, but it was a cold, clear night, and you could see the light of the moon falling through the trees and making pale silver patches on the grass. A nice place to frolic, the gardens of Na Bolom in the moonlight. Though old Bill would probably be peering through his spyglass at the whole event.

This was awful. I closed the shutters and went to the bathroom, trying not to look at the clock but seeing out of the corner of my eye that it was 3:30 already. Maybe another shower. I could get rid of the sweat. But then I'd wake up the entire place, including the guy I didn't want to sleep with.

I peed and went back to bed. Sometime near dawn, I fell asleep.

You would think I'd have been a wreck the next day. No sleep again, and the sheets were a sweaty mess. But I was actually in pretty good shape. Alert. Cheerful, even. I couldn't figure it out. Then another habit of the monks crossed my mind—fasting, which I couldn't imagine doing through even one meal. Stefan was big on it. Once a week while he was still at the Hermitage, he had eaten nothing but bread and water. I asked him once, wasn't it sheer hell? And he had said no, it was actually a relief when his fast day came. It simplified things so much. You didn't have to decide between oatmeal or granola, you didn't have to waste an hour eating dinner, you just went through your day on your chunk of bread and whatever you had stored up in your fat cells. I asked him if it made him weak, and he said, actually, it made everything come into focus.

Maybe that's what had happened to me. Maybe I'd pulled off an unintentional fast. In any event, I felt like I had X-ray vision this morning.

Jan was where I figured he'd be. I checked him over for signs of nighttime restlessness, but he looked fine. He was already, in fact, deep into the Chilam Balam. "Oh, hello," he said, turning his head, but his eyes barely touched on me because he was so far into what he was doing right then. It's a good thing, I thought, that we hadn't wound up in bed last night, because after that, even if you don't mean to, you start getting touchy about certain things. Such as not being looked at when you're being talked to. Small stuff, but postcoitally significant.

He turned the brittle pages of the book carefully, and then even more carefully, held the book open so I could see. "Here," he said. "Take a look." There was a chair beside him and I sat down in it. The handwriting was beautiful, if smudged, but of course I couldn't understand a word. He read a bit of it out loud to me, translating as he went. "This part here about the 'contrary priest' and the 'ancient priest'—I've seen the phrase before, in another Chilam Balam."

"What does it mean?"

"Well, the Chilam Balam books were written well after the Conquest, and the Church had been busy among the Maya for a long time by then. So the obvious reading is that the contrary priest is a Catholic one, trying to convince a Maya Jaguar priest to change his ways. Except that the section it's from is a very confused one, which some scholars believe could be bits and pieces of much more ancient material. If so, the contrary priest might not be a Catholic priest at all. The significant thing is that the wording in each of the two books, this one and the Chilam Balam I remember, is almost identical."

"Read me the one from ours."

He took his glasses off and rubbed each lens with the tail of his shirt. I didn't often see him without them. He had a raccoon-style white tan line around his eyes from the frame. He put them on again, then continued to read to me slowly: "'The contrary priest comes before him. His arms are bound and he wears no ornaments. The great priests lead him to the altar. Show us, they say, or become a rock which we will crack. The contrary priest says to them, Justice exists. O fools and children, why are you blind?'" He looked up at me. "Do you know what that means about cracking the rock?"

I nodded. Rikki had filled me in on that one. It meant they were about to carve open your chest with an obsidian knife and remove your beating heart. "So this is one of your guys? One of your dissenters?"

"Maybe so. If this Chilam Balam book is not a fraud, like most people believe it is. If the reference to the contrary priest in the other Chilam Balam is indeed part of a much more ancient record. If, if, if."

"But you think it is."

He sighed. "I can feel it all the way to the bottom of my stomach. It is that word justice, probably. Have you ever read Plato's *Republic*?"

I scanned the part of my memory bank where great philosophical works might be stored. The search did not take long. "No," I said somewhat defiantly.

"Well, in the first part, Socrates is talking to a man who insists that the meaning of life is to be found in satisfying our own desires—you know, for food or fame or sex, that kind of thing."

That kind of thing.

"And Socrates keeps pushing him to justify this position, which of course he cannot. So then Socrates gets people to start thinking about the concept of justice and what it really means. Justice, Eva."

"Just like your contrary priest."

"Not 'just like,' but it certainly got my attention the first time I spotted it."

"Anything else you found in there?"

"Yes." He turned back to the section I'd photographed the day before. "Listen to this: 'Then the clouds in the sky were divided, as if by a powerful key, making way for the light of the sun.'"

"K'in," I inserted.

"K'in." He nodded. "Our quarry. But there is more: 'And the contrary priest said to them, Look to the shadows lest your eyes fail you. As k'in moves his face across the land, so does true knowledge cast its burning light.'" He glanced up at me. "I don't suppose you've read the

Allegory of the Cave? It's in *The Republic*."

"As I matter of fact, I have," I said, trying not to sound smug. "At St. Silvan's. You could not be a legitimate eighth-grade Catholic kid without getting that one under your belt. The cave, the shadows, the sun."

"Exactly," he said. "The sun, the great metaphor for enlightenment. For truth. For the Good. But it is so bright that it will blind you unless you are prepared to see. First you have to wean yourself from all sorts of illusions—for example, that you owe it to yourself to satisfy every sexual urge, or that your belly should rule over your mind—or you are not even capable of realizing that there is something better than the half light of the cave. And then you still have a long way to go before you are able to look toward the light without harming yourself. At least this was Plato's view. But if this is indeed a reference to a Maya dissenter movement, perhaps they had a similar insight."

I caught the reference to the illusory mystique of sex—got it, Jan!— but what I was really gnawing on was the connection to Stefan's ecstasy letter, the one that made the quickest of references to our man Plato. Also the connection to Anne and her Quakers. Everyone talking about seeing versus being blind. And here it was again, maybe, popping up in the middle of the Central American jungle. Who would have thought? I could feel myself teetering on the edge of my very first, invented-by-me-myself-and-I theory. What if the world were divided into two kinds of people? Group A being the ones like me—let's face it, most sane human beings—who put their faith in what they can actually see, hear, taste, touch, and smell, and Group B being like Anne and Stefan and possibly a small number of ill-fated Maya dissenters, plus Plato and company, who look upon the world as one giant finger pointing toward the beyond. Toward what the rest of us can't even begin to envision. Holy fools, one and all, but still. For a moment, I was swishing around in the sadness tank.

And then I looked down at the Chilam Balam, open on the table before me, and my cameras on their little stands, and my various lenses in their bags, all my beloved and damned costly photography equipment, and I thought about the best photos I've ever taken. My one and only prizewinner, the Afghan child in front of the burning house. Those stick kids in the Darfur refugee camp. That Kurdish girl, maybe fourteen, holding a white baby goat. The abandoned hut in Burundi, after a machete-wielding mob of neighbors swept through. By now, I'd taken thousands, and some of them were pretty good. But there were a few that were more than good. I'd known it before I even put my finger on the shutter button, when they were still in my viewfinder, still a gleam, as they say, in the photographer's eye.

I glanced up at Jan, who had noticed my extended mulling and was looking quizzically at me. "Just a minute," I said, holding up my hand. "Something's beaming through here."

Why were they so good? How could I tell? Because it wasn't just beauty, though all of the really good ones were beautiful. The color, the light, the composition—everything was there, even when they were incredibly sad, like the one with the Afghan kid. It was something more.

"Jan," I said, repositioning one of the cameras over the open Chilam Balam. "Take a look through this viewfinder and tell me what you see."

He looked surprised, but bent over obediently, squinting, and I could tell he was a man not used to taking photos. "Well?" I prodded him.

"I am not sure what you are asking," he said. "I see the page. I see the Cholan that has been written down in Colonial Spanish characters. I see . . ."

"What I mean is, what is in the picture that you *can't* see? For example, what about the Jaguar priest who wrote those letters in the book? And the dissenting priest who might have gotten his heart removed shortly after he pronounced those words hundreds of years before anybody wrote them down? And the Spanish peasant who made that paper before it was loaded on a boat to the New World? And the sailors on the boat, and how thirsty they were when they got becalmed for three weeks?"

He sat up. "Okay," he said. "I am listening."

"A photograph is never just a photograph, that's what I'm trying to say. It's a window onto something else, another reality. A completely invisible one, but always there. And what makes a really great picture is how much of that comes through, even though you can't see it with the naked eye. And the part you *can* see doesn't just *suggest* the part you can't see—it *is* that part you can't see. Or at least it's a piece of what it's rooted in. Does that make sense?"

He looked a tad bewildered. I could understand that.

"I'm trying to get a lock on this vision thing, Jan. Plato talks about it in the Allegory, the nuns talked about it at St. Silvan's, Anne talks about it when she talks about the Quakers, my brother . . . well, anyway, and now you've got some Maya priest alluding to it, or possibly, and what I'm thinking is that this intuition, if you want to call it that, is some kind of universal human trait, or maybe not universal but widespread among certain kinds of people, that's going to pop up in strange ways no matter where or when you go looking for it." Group B people.

"Your brother?"

"He died," I said quickly, and flapped my hand at him when he started to offer his condolences. "Jan, listen up here. This is important. I've never had a clue what these people are talking about before. And now I'm getting a hint. What did you say about that guy in *The Republic*? The one who had all his bets on food and sex?"

"Thrasymachus? Only that he believed the meaning of life is to be found in satisfying our desires."

I thought about this one for a minute. We were talking about urgent Alexander here, and Peter and the USIA man and Robert and the Italian on the trail at Tikal. And moi. Last night being the first time in my entire life I had denied myself the solace of sex for the sake of something that seemed to trump it—friendship. "Jan," I said, giving him a sadder but wiser smile than I'd ever smiled before, "there may be hope for me yet." And before he could respond, I added, "Now tell me why this project is so important to you. Because I don't believe it's just an excuse not to go home and be with Anne. There's something here that's really got you fired up. What is it?"

This silenced him. After a time, when he couldn't seem to think of anything to say, he got up and went to the window while I patiently waited for him to justify the past twenty years of his life. Finally he came and sat down in a chair next to me. "Okay," he said. "I have been fascinated by the Classic Mayas since I was a young man. I have spent my best years digging up bits and pieces of their history. And the more I—we—learned about them, the more I admired them and appreciated their love for beauty and their accomplishments in math and astronomy and architecture, and the more I wanted them to be better."

"Better?"

"I wanted them to at some point stop the ritual bloodletting. I wanted them to stop torturing and sacrificing those war captives. They were an amazing culture—look what they built in such a short time—and I wanted them to measure up to their own accomplishments. And so maybe I set out looking for evidence that they had."

"I can get that. They're practically your family members by now, right? And you want . . . you *need* your family to be decent human beings."

"This is true," he said simply. "I wanted them to be good."

All at once, I was completely worn out. Multiple nights without sleep, a brief run of X-ray vision, and then total mental shutdown. I was about to suggest a break when someone said, "Dr. Bource?"

We both turned. I'd forgotten to close the door, and in the doorway stood Margarita. Who knew how long she'd been standing there or what she'd heard. I could see the same thought running through Jan's mind, but he sounded calm as he said, "Is there something wrong?"

"A phone call for you," she said. "Your wife. You can get it in the office if you want."

"Thank you." He turned to me. "I put in a call this morning, but nobody answered. Rikki must have been out and Anne sleeping. I will be right back."

He went, and after a long, speculative pause, so did Margarita. I spent the time till he got back trying to read the page he'd been translating for me, just to see whether, by osmosis, I'd picked up a bit of ancient Cholan. I hadn't. He wasn't gone long, not as long as you'd think a man who hadn't talked to his wife in five days would be. I couldn't tell by his face what he was thinking. He said, "I just missed Rikki. He was offered a ride down here this morning with one of the American Friends from Mexico City, and since Felice is due back later today, Anne convinced him not to pass it up. The bus ride can be very slow."

"But who's taking care of her right now?" The thought of her being all by herself made me feel indignantly maternal.

"One of the women from her class offered to stay with her till Felice comes. I told her about last night with the soldiers, but she had not heard anything on the news."

"Are you wishing Rikki weren't heading this way?"

He sat down beside me. "Frankly, yes, though it is too late now. But I would actually prefer he were riding in a second-class bus than a private vehicle, if you want to know the truth."

"Because?"

He flicked his eyes at me. "They have to pass through the mountains. If they get stopped, there will not be any witnesses."

Maybe I should have said something reassuring, but it would have been a lie, and I'd already used up my quota with the one about Stefan. As if we have a quota. I paused for a moment, giving myself a hard appraisal. What was wrong with me? I'd never used to think twice about lying if it gave me the edge. I looked over at Jan. Maybe it was one more of those boundaries that fell into place when you got yourself a friend. Would I want him lying to me? No way. So what point was there in lying to him about his son, telling him there was nothing to worry about?

It would have been simpler if I believed, like Anne and my brother, in the power of prayer. As it was, all I could do was cross my fingers and hope the kid showed up.

At 2:30, Rikki and a woman about Anne's age pulled up at Na Bolom. I spotted them through the studio window as they came through the entryway into the courtyard, Rikki's long legs and bright head, and I was shocked at how happy the sight made me. Like someone had just handed me five hundred million pesos, like it was Stefan on that path. "They're here," I sang out to Jan, and whizzed out the door and stood there bouncing like a fool on the veranda till Rikki spotted me.

"Eva," he said, striding over. "Hey." He bent down and gave me a teenaged-boy hug, nothing touching, and I gave him a smack on the shoulder, and I don't think I'd remember that poor Quaker woman even if she turned out to be a long-lost relative of mine. I was too busy being grateful that they'd made it through without mishap. That nobody had disappeared.

Chapter Seventeen

We caught up with each other that evening over dinner, this time at a place called the Unicornio, which specialized in the kind of burgers and fries I hadn't had for a long, long time. Rikki sat beside me in the little booth with Jan across from us, and I could tell by the way that he wolfed down his burger that Rikki had shaken off some of the worry he'd been carrying around in Palenque. Some kinds of worry don't change no matter where you are—worries about money, how old you are getting, if you are doing the right thing with your life—and other worries are dramatically increased or decreased by a change in scenery. Anne was the second kind of worry; you never forgot about her, but the situation was easier to bear at a distance, which went some way toward explaining Jan's less than exemplary behavior, I suppose.

Rikki probably loved her more than anybody else did, but he was ready for a break. And he was glad to be back with his father and out of the tension that flared when the three of them were together in the little yellow house. So I kidded with him, and he with me, and Jan sat across from us with that faint smile of his, and it was almost like the good old days in Tikal—just the three of us, and Rikki and I spending whole days together in the ruins like a couple of siblings on vacation from their parents.

"Tonight," he told me, "it's going to be wild around here. New Year's Eve—crazy, right, Dad?"

Jan rolled his eyes.

"Firecrackers," Rikki went on. "Whole strings of them. The kind you can't get in the States. And everybody drinking."

"Except you," said Jan.

Rikki said, "I miss Trudi."

"Well, of course," said his father.

"It's like coming home to Grandma's and she's not there anymore. I keep thinking about being a little kid here, and Mom . . . anyway," he finished lamely. "It's not the same now. Especially with all the tourists."

"Nasty creatures," I said. "Dangerous fingernails."

It turned out Rikki was right. Sedate San Cristóbal went a bit berserk on New Year's Eve. Considering the scare we'd had the night before with the soldiers, I was surprised at all the festivities, but though we walked for blocks through the city, we did not see any military vehicles. Instead, there were crowds in the streets that were usually empty before eight, and people, both tourists and locals, looked happy and already a bit smashed though it was early. Firecrackers were going off here and there, and I was glad we were not staying in one of the downtown hotels. It looked like it would be a noisy, long night.

Our walk took us in the direction of Iglesia de Guadalupe, and I thought about going all the way to the church and checking in with Jorge to see if he had found me a guide yet, but this was impossible with Jan and Rikki on either side of me. People kept passing us, some of them singing, and even though it was a long time until midnight, the feeling of the new year was all around us. We stayed out till 10:00, and then, by mutual, sleepy agreement, made our way back to the jeep and drove to Na Bolom. We were greeted by a group with some big bottles of wine who had gathered in the dining room and wanted us to celebrate with them, but we waved them off and went to bed.

In spite of the noise, I finally got a good night's sleep, only waking when a strand of firecrackers went off close by, and then to the baying of what sounded like all the dogs in the city. At 6:30 I opened my eyes to the morning light with the thought of Stefan weighing down on me. The waiting was becoming unbearable. It was only Saturday, and Jorge had told me to give him till Monday, but suddenly I wanted to go check. Maybe he'd been lucky. Maybe he'd tried to call me but I'd been out.

I got up, dressed, and jotted a little note for Jan, which I slipped under his door. It was probably too far to walk all the way to the rectory, but I could get a taxi if I needed one. I peeked in the dining room on my way out; nobody awake yet—too much celebrating—but the coffee was on, so I had a cup for the road and then went out to face the chill morning air.

From the oldest parts of San Cristóbal came the deep booming of bells, ringing in the half hour and announcing the 7:00 a.m. Mass. As in every old city, all the bells were on a slightly different schedule, and so what could have been beautiful was clamorous. Twenty minutes into the walk, I heard more firecrackers. They were still celebrating in the villages, maybe. Five minutes later there were more, but individual ones this time, not like the crackling strings of them we'd heard all night. Then something really big went off in the mountains. The sound echoed, deep and rumbling, and suddenly I was back in El Salvador, and I knew what I was hearing. Rockets.

I stopped with my hands in my pockets and looked all around me. It was almost 7:30 by now, and the town was starting to wake up after its long New Year's Eve celebration, but nobody was on the streets but me. Maybe they couldn't hear what was happening from inside their houses. I knew they might not be able to hear it through the thick walls of Na Bolom. I was twenty minutes from Stefan's church. I was twenty or so minutes from Jan and Rikki. Which way to go? I strained my ears, but could not tell for sure what was happening. But I knew the revolutionaries would almost certainly strike at San Cristóbal first.

I threw a last, longing look in the direction of Guadalupe, and then turned and jogged in my sandals back to Na Bolom. Those two could still get out, maybe, before all the roads were blocked, either by guerrilleros or the army. They could get back to Anne, who would be going nuts with worry the minute she heard. Once they were on their way, I'd find Jorge and figure out what to do next.

I ran, huffing a little, my camp body ruined by last night's burger and fries, until Na Bolom came into view. Then I slowed. How would I handle Jan, who would not even consider leaving me behind? Would it be better to pull Rikki aside and tell him what was going on, and then disappear before they could stop me? I was still thinking about what to do when I burst through into the courtyard and saw a cluster of people milling around on the veranda outside the office: Jan, Bill, Margarita, Britt, several of the other earnest grad students, the woman from New York. Somebody besides me had heard the rockets.

"Eva!" called Jan when he spotted me. "Where have you been?"

Everybody on the veranda turned toward Jan, then toward me, waiting expectantly for my answer.

"I left you a note," I called back as quietly as I could. "Didn't you see it?"

"You call that a note? 'Gone out'? Do you know what is happening here?"

This was embarrassing, being dressed down in public this way. "Jan," I said, "just hang on a minute, okay? I came back because I wasn't sure you people heard anything from the inside."

"Oh, we heard it all right," said Bill. He seemed particularly wound up. "They attacked a half hour after midnight, and they've been swarming around the zócalo ever since. The municipal palace and police station and even the public justice ministry headquarters down at María Auxiliadora are all torn up. The road to Tuxtla is blocked with trees they've cut down."

"They're fighting in Ocosingo, too," said one of the grad students. "We heard it from somebody who's been working at Toniná."

"They shot three policemen in Las Margaritas."

I said, "Is anybody trying to get out?"

"Not yet," said Jan. "We do not know yet what else might be going on."

"But wouldn't this be a good time to go? Before all the roads get blocked?"

"I agree with that," the New York woman with the fingernails spoke up. "I'm for packing up and getting out of here as soon as possible. All we need is to be cut off, and then God knows what will happen next." She seemed extremely tense compared to only a few nights ago, sitting across from Jan and toying significantly with the stem of her wine glass.

Bill said, "Well, that's certainly a valid perspective for some of you."

"Some of us?" said the woman.

"Those of you who aren't responsible for this place. You know." He didn't say the word "tourists" but he might as well have—it was ringing in the air all around us.

Just then another big one went off, a deep, distant thud. The woman from New York said, "Look, I want somebody to take responsibility here. I'm going to pack and when I get back, I want you to have figured out how we're getting out of here, do you understand?" She jabbed a fingernail at Bill. "I mean it," she said. "You figure it out. That's your job." She turned and hurried off down the veranda, and we could hear the sharp click-click of her heels on the tile floor.

Bill looked around at the rest of us. His black hair looked wilder than ever this morning. "Damn," he said. "Damn. Why did everyone have to be gone right now? I'm supposed to be in charge of the library, not the whole damn place."

Margarita said softly, but still loud enough for us all to hear, "What a bitch. Let her hire a helicopter if she wants."

"Where's Rikki?" I said to Jan.

"Still sleeping. Though you would think he would be awake by now."

"He's sixteen," I said. "He could sleep through a bomb."

One of the female grad students blanched.

"Jan," I said. "Seriously. You guys need to pack up and get out of here. Anne will be worried sick."

He stared hard at me. "What is this 'you guys'? What about you? Do you think I am just going to leave you here?"

Everybody was once again shamelessly listening in.

"Jan," I said, "come on inside a minute, okay? Excuse us," I said to the rest of them. I took his arm, which I'd never done before, and marched him into the currently unmanned office. "Look," I said when we were out of earshot, "this isn't going to make any sense to you, but you're just going to have to trust me. I can't leave. Especially now, I can't. The whole reason I'm here in Central America is happening right now. If I left, I could never live with myself."

We were leaning our hips on the edge of the desk. He was giving me his blue stare. "Jan," I said, "this is the bottom line. I'm staying. In fact, I quit. I'm no longer your employee, okay? You need to get your kid out of here and get back to your wife. Who knows where this thing might spread? What if she's all by herself in Palenque and they bring the revolution there?"

"No," he said.

"No?"

"No. I will not drive out of here without you with us. You are crazy if you think I am going to leave a woman here by herself under these circumstances. And do not talk about Anne. She would not do it either." His mouth was clamped down in a way I recognized. I didn't like that look. It was inflexible, and from my angle, highly irritating. But I could see I wasn't going to get around it, at least not by direct confrontation.

"Fine," I said, shrugging.

"What does 'fine' mean?"

"Fine. You call the shots, boss."

The blue stare got narrower. "I mean it, Eva."

"What do you think I'm going to do? Run off?"

He reached out like he was going to take hold of my shoulder, then dropped his arm. "I hope," he said, "that you respect me enough not to lie to me."

That got me. I swallowed, but surreptitiously, and shook my head. "Look," I said, "the most important thing right now is to get Rikki out of bed, and for us to get packed and be ready to go, don't you think?"

"We will get ready," he said, "but we are not making any moves until we get more information about the roads. The safest place might be right here at Na Bolom. It has a good reputation among the Mayas, anyway. And the rumor is that the Zapatistas are heavily Maya, if that can be believed."

"Have you ever been in a revolution before?"

He smoothed his hair with the flat palm of one hand, and for the first time I could see how rattled he was. It made sense he would be—a sick wife by herself three and a half hours away, a sixteen-year-old kid to think of, and unpredictable me. "I was in Central America during the Soccer War in 1969," he said. "We were working at an Olmec site in El Salvador when it decided to attack Honduras. And of course we were at Tikal during the Guatemalan Civil War of the eighties. But if you mean have I ever been right in the middle of an attack, no."

Another big one went off. I could hear, far off, the whack-whack-whack of a helicopter, maybe coming from the army base. "Well, I have," I said, "and we need to come up with a plan. Because there's no way the army's not going to show up soon."

"I know. And phone lines will be down if they are not down already. You get Rikki up, will you? I am going to try to get through to Anne. We will see what it looks like up there before we make any decisions."

He hurried off and I went to their room where, amazingly enough, Rikki was still sleeping peacefully, one big hand curled into a fist and resting beside his blond head. He was so tall that both of his feet hung over the end of the bed; I could see them through the sheet. I stood looking at him for a moment, the half-open mouth, the long eyelashes quivering with each breath. Such a beautiful man-child. The same age as Stefan when Bruno threw him out on the street. "Hey, Rikki," I said, and put one hand on his bare shoulder. His skin was as smooth as Anne's cheek. "Hey, guy, wake up." I shook him gently, and he moaned and raised his head, still asleep, and then let his face fall back into the pillow. His feet made little rubbing motions against each other under the sheet. The room smelled faintly of sweat.

Then came more gunfire, sharp and hard and fast, and much closer. I pushed him with both hands, and this time when he raised his head, he opened his eyes and looked at me without quite knowing who I was. My throat began aching at that unfocused look, and energy rushed through me, a weird, fierce desire to take the bullets for him, if that's what it came down to. "Get up," I said sharply. "Get dressed. We've got to pack."

"What's going on?" His hair was smashed flat on one side and stuck up on the other. He raised up on his elbows, and the sheet slid down to his waist.

"The EZLN moved in last night. They're fighting," I said. "It's the revolution." That sounded more dramatic than I meant it to. "Get dressed." I turned and went out to find Jan, who was standing beside the front desk phone, head bowed, with the receiver at his ear. One hand was hooked on the back of his neck, as though it were stiff. As I came toward him, he glanced up, one of those intense distant looks that didn't have me in it but something else he was thinking hard about. "Here," he said, and thrust the receiver at me. "She wants to talk with you." Then he walked off, his heels going hard into the floor.

I put the receiver to my ear. There was a lot of static on the line. "Hello, Anne," I said. "It's Eva."

"Hello," she called to me from three and a half hours and a revolution away. I could hardly hear her, but it was definitely her voice, thin and strong, with that curious sweetness to it that was never faked but the most real thing I'd ever heard. I hadn't realized how much I missed her.

"Are you all right?" I said loudly. "Has it come to Palenque?"

"I'm fine," she called back. "But I can't get that through Jan's head."

"Is Felice there?"

More static. I couldn't hear anything.

"Anne? Is Felice with you?"

"She called me earlier," she said. "There's apparently a lot of fighting in Ocosingo, but she's all right."

"Then who's with you, Anne? Is the lady from your class still there?"

Silence.

"Anne?"

"When we heard the news this morning, I told her to go. Her mother is eighty-five and lives in Ocosingo too."

"Oh God, Anne."

"I'm fine, Eva. Really. And there's no indication Palenque's in danger."

"But who's helping you up? Who's feeding you?"

"I have to go slowly, but I can do it."

"What about Fr. Miguel? Could he send somebody?"

"If I need someone, I'll call him. And Felice will be back as soon as she can."

"But Anne, what if you . . . ?" I stopped. I could see her lying in her bed with the phone in one thin hand and the open window and a little breeze stirring her brown hair. I could see the blue veins on her eyelids. "What if you have one of those spells?" I asked her.

She was quiet for a moment, and I thought I'd lost her. Then she said, "It won't be the end of the world, Eva. One way or the other. I'm not afraid, anyway. I was for a while, but I'm all right now."

I started to speak, but she broke in. "Listen, Eva," she said, and I could tell she was getting tired. "Jan told me he was coming. Please talk him out of it, would you? I can't get him to listen. It's probably safer for you all to stay at Na Bolom, or to get out to the west, to Tuxtla, maybe. But don't try to come here. You'd have to go through Ocosingo—it's much too dangerous. Just take care of Rikki, will you?"

I didn't know what to say to her. She was right, but it didn't seem right. She should have never let Felice go off for Christmas, or Rikki leave with the Quaker woman. She could die by herself in that yellow house, and not from any revolution.

"Eva?"

"All right," I said. "I'm going to do my best, but you know Jan."

She laughed. "I don't envy you."

"We almost had a fight already this morning."

She laughed again.

"You take care of yourself, Anne, okay?"

"I will."

I could see Rikki coming down the hall. "Do you want to talk to that son of yours?"

"Put him on," she said.

I handed the phone to Rikki, who had wet down his hair and was looking both wound up and sober at the same time. "Mom?" he said.

I went off in search of Jan. Inside my head was her voice, and the words "I love you," though I couldn't have told you who they meant. I could see why soldiers with families have such a hard time. It screwed you up, caring too much about the people at home.

I found Jan on the veranda where he had clearly been elected, however unwillingly, leader of the group. He turned when I came out. Guns cracked close by. "That sounds like the southeast side of town," he said.

The woman from New York was back, fully packed, and taking short hard breaths whenever the guns went off. If she kept that up, she would pass out. "Isn't somebody going to do something?" she said, panting a little. "This is utterly ridiculous, that nobody's doing anything."

"What do you want us to do?" snapped Margarita. I noticed she'd lost the glasses somewhere and was all business this morning. Britt was standing right behind her, looking equally fierce. I wouldn't have wanted to be from New York right then. "You have a brilliant idea on that?"

"I demand to be taken out of here. I refuse to stay."

"Go," said Margarita. "Scram. No loss to us."

"Margarita," said Bill. Britt looked like she was about to high-five someone.

Jan said, "My guess is that the downtown hotels are all facing the same situation. People who need to be moved to someplace safe."

"You mean tourists," Britt spat out.

Jan said, "I am pretty sure that the rebels will not be interested in civilians. In fact, it would be easier for them if civilians cleared out. So I think if we get the people who would like to leave down to one of the big hotels, they will be taken care of."

"Fine," snapped the lady from New York. "I'm packed. Let's go."

"*Brother*," Margarita muttered to Britt.

The woman whirled on the two of them. "You should be fired," she said, panting. "Both of you, and him too." She pointed at tall Bill.

Margarita put her fists on her hips. "We're volunteers. Too bad, isn't it?"

Bill said to Jan, "I'm staying. Margarita, Britt, will you stay too?"

"Of course," Margarita said, tossing her hair like a spring filly. I was beginning to like that woman better.

Britt said, "Do you need to ask?"

"The rest of you," said Bill, trying to sound authoritative, "better go soon. Take the cars. Leave one for us. Dr. Bource, would you be in charge of this part?"

Jan looked at the woman from New York, who was sitting by herself, stewing, on top of her luggage. He sighed. "Yes. We will leave as soon as everybody can get ready."

The other grad students scuttled off to get their backpacks, and I cut through the park in back to get mine. Rikki was just coming out of their room with both packs and his hiking boots on. "Meet out by the cars," I said to him on my way past.

In my room, I stuffed everything including the camera equipment into my pack, except the envelope with Stefan's letters inside. I wasn't sure what to do with them, whether to carry them with me or hide them somewhere. If we were stopped by the rebels or more military, I wouldn't want to be carrying anything with Stefan's name on them. On the other hand, if I got myself into the Lacandon jungle where I thought he was, I might need them the way you need letters of introduction. Finally, I decided to save one, the last one he'd sent Jonah, since it was short and mentioned Mat. Then I reached under the bed and pulled out the box and stared at it with a cold and practical eye. The thing inside might actually come in handy. The leather half glove would no doubt be too large for my palm, it was designed for Djed's after all, but the curved blade, as old as it was by now, still looked very businesslike. Should I take it with me?

I decided no. If I were caught and searched, it wouldn't look good to be so wickedly armed. And it was a very odd item that would automatically raise questions. If it were taken from me, which it surely would be, then I'd have lost it forever, and even though I could hardly stand the thought of it, much less its ugly presence, my brother had carted it around with him since he was fourteen. Besides, I had the boot knife. So I opened the lid, drew out the letter inside, which I'd only had the stomach to skim once, that night in Stefan's room at the rectory, and locked the box back up, keeping the key. I would shove the thing back under the bed where it belonged, and if neither Stefan nor I ever returned to get it, at least there was nothing inside that would link it to us. To our family.

Then I stuffed both letters, the two fake passports, and some pesos into my bra, incredibly uncomfortable but safer than any other place on my person, and my real passport and more pesos into the money belt around my waist. Even though I was still wearing my skirt, I pulled on my boots, like Rikki had. If nothing else, one of them would serve as a sheath for the knife.

Before I went back to join the others, I took one last look around and was glad, more glad than I could ever say, that I had not done anything in that room I would have been ashamed of if and when I ever saw Anne again. I was glad that I had not tried to capitalize on her husband's terrible loneliness, and that he could still look her in the eye if indeed he made it through to Palenque. Possibly for the first time in my life I was experiencing the rush of sheer gratitude and relief that follows not wrecking something good when you could have.

We went to the Santo Tomás Hotel because Bill knew the manager and told Jan to go there. The place was in a state of subdued chaos, a typical scene when wealthy Western tourists find themselves trapped behind the lines during armed insurrections in ex-European colonies. I had seen it all before: people with flushed, responsible-looking faces wandering around the lobby, asking questions that were impossible to answer, while others, pink with worry, tried to make calls on the now-dead phone. Our woman from New York fit right in and, somewhat paradoxically, seemed calmer now that she was with masses of semi-hysterical gringos. Under normal circumstances, I'd be standing somewhere off to the side with my camera equipment tucked safely between my feet, shooting the breeze with some fellow photojournalist while we professionals waited for the angst-ridden bourgeois to be cleared out so we could get to work. Thanks to my two compadres from Palenque, however, I couldn't seem to get the same distance on the scene this time around.

The gunfire appeared to be moving from one part of town to the other, though it was still several miles off. Nobody was leaving the hotel. Jan went off to talk to the manager, and I could see the two of them through an open door and hear Jan's voice going on and on in Spanish that was too soft for me to translate. The manager did not want the responsibility of our little group, that was clear. He had his hands full enough with the hundred or so folks who were jammed in the lobby, and here Jan had brought him fifteen more.

Pretty soon another man came bursting in through the main doors and strode down the hall to the same office, and Rikki, who was eavesdropping, told me he was the manager of the Posada Santa Clara, on the southwest corner of the square. More talk, with Jan gesticulating, which he never did. I could hear what we used to call backcountry radio crackling away somewhere. A woman who looked a bit like Felice, only older, was calmly measuring ground coffee into a big coffee maker in the lobby. She'd already put out Styrofoam cups.

"What did the manager say?" I asked Jan when he returned.

"He is going to try to get everyone to Tuxtla Gutiérrez as soon as he can. If they can get a military escort, they will move these folks out of here."

"Us too?"

"You too," said Jan.

"But not you?" said Rikki.

"I will stay until I know what is happening. Then I will leave for Palenque." He was looking at me as he said this, that hard stare of his.

"How are you getting through?" I asked. "All the roads north and east will be blockaded by now, I bet."

"I will take my chances," he said, "because I am not totally convinced that Palenque is going to remain untouched. Nobody knows how large the rebel army is or how far it might extend its operations. I am not too worried about the Zapatistas themselves—I cannot imagine them being interested in civilians—but if they take a town like

Palenque, the military will move in very quickly. I do not want Anne by herself in the middle of a firefight."

"Why can't we go with you?" said Rikki. "I'd rather go with you."

"You cannot. You are staying with Eva."

I didn't say anything. I could see what he was thinking and it made sense. If something happened to him, Rikki would at least be safe. Somebody would be left to deal with Anne. If we were all together and something happened, then she was completely on her own.

But the dilemma for me was clear. How was I going to slip away if I had Rikki to worry about?

"You should go now," I said to Jan, "if you are going. It's only going to get more crazy."

"No, I will wait," said Jan. "At least until I know what they are going to do."

So we waited in the hotel of the doubting saint. Off and on, you could hear the fighting, sometimes close and sometimes far off, with the occasional thudding explosions off in the mountains. Shortly before noon, several tourists came in, excited, and said they'd been in the plaza and seen the rebels for themselves, that the plaza was jammed with locals and tourists, and that the rebels were actually talking with people. Jan decided to go find out what he could. Rikki and I insisted we go with him.

Everywhere there were leaflets, either drifting along the cobblestone streets or crushed under boots or slapped up on walls. In the zócalo itself, morning bonfires fed by piles of furniture from the government palace still burned, and heaps of documents, dumped out onto the patios, ruffled fitfully. In the center of the plaza, high above the crowds, flew a stern black flag with a red star and the letters EZLN emblazoned across it. The doors of the palace had been hacked open with marros, the sledges, Rikki told me, of Indian street laborers. Everywhere we heard the din of speculation, the protests of affronted San Cristóbal natives who could not imagine such goings on in their spectacular city, the jeering of men sitting together on tops of kiosks, drinking out of flasks. In among the crowd were the Zapatistas.

I was startled when I first realized who they were, most of them so small I would not have noticed them except for their ominous black ski masks, pasamontañas, I was informed by Rikki. They also had (dead giveaway) bandoliers of bullets across their chests. Some of them wore red bandannas (paliacates) tied across their faces instead. Every one of them had rubber boots. I thought of them streaming into the city after midnight, those boots smacking against the cobblestones, while everybody else was sleeping off the New Year's drink-fest. If you were going to start a revolution, I thought, it was definitely perfect timing.

Just then one of them appeared at a balcony railing, high above us, and unfolded a document, which he began reading out loud. I could not follow him well, so Rikki leaned in close, translating. "It's a declaration of war," he said, his eyes wide. "They say they're from the Lacandon jungle, and they demand that Salinas resign the presidency." There was more about the exploitation of the indigenas and the five hundred years of oppression already suffered, and then the comandante shouted, "¡Ya basta!" and some of the crowd began to cheer, though the tourists merely grew increasingly baffled and anxious-looking. What would happen next?

One by one, women comandantas stepped forward at the balcony rail. Women, I thought. Wow. One of them began a chant: "Trabajo, tierra, techo, pan, salud, educación, democracia, libertad, paz, independencia, justicia." Over and over and over again: work, land, shelter, bread, health, education, democracy, liberty, peace, independence, justice. Perfectly reasonable things. Yet they were causing San Cristóbal's landed aristocracy, some of whom were now moving imperiously through the crowd, to quiver with indignation.

Then, as though the last slot had been saved for the best, a tall Zapatista dude wearing the same black pasamontaña stepped forward and addressed the crowd in Spanish. Instantly, my radar began transmitting. He might have been the Italian on the trail, the immigration officer in Corozal, a good-looking photojournalist just about anywhere. Masked though he was, something was happening, and not just to me. I could see other people in the crowd responding with equal fascination. I wondered, for a confused moment, if he might be the mysterious Mat himself, with Stefan close behind him. But no: Mat was Tzeltal and this man was obviously, by his fluent Spanish, ladino. He invited the crowd to ask questions, and then, when he could not hear well enough, came among the people.

I watched him from fifty feet away. These were the guerrilleros Stefan had visited in Las Cañadas, according to Fr. Miguel. This was the army of the jungle. But so far, they hardly seemed real, more like performance artists staging a fake revolution in order to raise money for any number of approved liberal causes. I kept expecting a movie director with a bullhorn to come barging through the plaza. And like an old coonhound scenting quarry, I found myself slipping a hand into the pack I refused to leave amid the jumble at the hotel and pulling out one of my Canons.

The dashing young Zapatista might have been running for political office. Gracious and self-contained, he actually seemed apologetic when tourists pressed close to him, begging for safe passage out of the city. I took pictures of him writing in a notebook and tearing off leaves, passing them out to people. "Salvoconductos," someone close to us said. "So you can get past the roadblocks." Jan pushed forward to see what he could do for our group from Na Bolom, but it was impossible to get closer.

Then, suddenly, it got real. In the western sky, four Pilatus fighters lined up, taking their look, letting themselves be seen, then made a whining circle back toward their base. "We are going," said Jan at my elbow, and without quibbling but still shooting photos as fast as I could, I forged along behind him to the Santo Tomás, Rikki trotting in my wake.

When we got back to the lobby, many of the hotel guests had gone off to their rooms, and the ones who did not have rooms were huddled on the floor, staking out places to sleep for when the time came, even though there were still hours to go. The woman from New York had not spoken to us or acknowledged us since we had arrived that morning, but now she came over and asked what was happening in the square.

She had heard the planes, she said, and wondered if we were going to be bombed. Her hair was all undone, her lipstick gone. She did not look angry now, only fragile and afraid. Jan was very kind to her and assured her that the rebels seemed like courteous folk, not berserker Vikings, and that the planes had only looked and turned around again.

Our own little group was on our minds, however, for the long hours that came next. Had we made a mistake by coming to the center of town? Would everyone have been safer at Na Bolom after all? Would the Mexican Air Force distinguish between guerrilleros in the plaza and tourists trying to stay out of the way? No other planes came, however, and as night fell the three of us, Jan and Rikki and I, found a spot in one corner and made pillows of our packs and pulled our jackets over us for blankets. Even though I didn't sleep much, it was a restful night, lying there between the two of them. Sad, too, because I knew what I was going to do next, and it meant that I might never see either of them again.

At 6:00, with the dim morning light filtering through the hotel windows, people began stirring around on the floor, moving their stiff limbs, and the hotel staff, who had to be the most loyal hotel staff in the world, brought out more coffee and platters of cut fruit and leftover chicken before anyone was really up. Rikki, of course, was completely unconscious, and Jan and I sat beside him on our packs, sipping coffee and thinking our own thoughts. Everything outside was very quiet.

After a while, a young man came in through the main doors and went back to talk with the manager, who had never left. Then the manager came down the hall and over to Jan and me. "The rebels have pulled out," he said in English. "They looted a government store and some pharmacies, but now they are gone. I do not think there were enough of them to hold a city this size."

"Do you think they will be back?"

He shrugged. "I do not think so. But this town is not a good place for tourists until we know more. We are too central here. They are all around us in the mountain villages. They have taken Ocosingo, Las Margaritas, and Altamirano, and now I hear they have Chanal. All the radio stations and roads are in their hands. We will have a hard time getting supplies now, even if the Zapatistas are not here. If the army will help, we will get these people out today."

"Good," said Jan. "How soon will you know?"

"Soon."

Two hours later the military showed up, a small convoy of trucks filled with soldiers who looked much like our rebels only better fed. Meanwhile, the hotel manager had gotten ahold of some combis, some of the guests had vehicles, and it was clear this exodus was going to take place. The army trucks waited outside the hotel with their engines rumbling while we all assembled around the different vans with our luggage. Jan waited until he was sure that we both had a place in one of them. Then came the goodbyes.

He stood facing us in his usual jeans and work shirt, the red ball cap pulled down low over his eyes. Rikki and I didn't have much to worry about—not with the military escort and the giant pack of gringos we were traveling with—but who knew what Jan might run into on his own? He didn't seem to be thinking about that, though, but about something else he wasn't having much luck saying. He hooked his thumbs in his back pockets, dropped his head, scratched back and forth on the street with one boot, then glanced up at us again. Behind him thronged a chaos of tourists, soldiers, and flapping pigeons, settling and rising and settling again on the roofline of the Santo Tomás. It was a beautiful bright morning, cool and clean, and for once the green mountains were free of clouds. Also gunfire. I wondered how long that would last.

"Son," he said finally, looking up from under the cap at Rikki. "You get in touch with your mother as soon as you get into Tuxtla. Let her know where you are and make sure she can reach you. Tell her I am on my way. You will be fine in Tuxtla, they will never attack there—it is too big. We will wait a bit until things calm down, make sure that Palenque is not on the list, and then we will probably send you two up north to Villahermosa and I will come and get you." He looked at me as he said this. I was supposed to nod, but I didn't. "Eva?" he said.

"Villahermosa sounds like a plan."

He turned back to Rikki. "You take care of yourself. No trying to be a hero. Just wait there until we are ready to make the next step." He put out his hand and Rikki shook it, and Jan held Rikki's hand in his for a little longer, then gave it a squeeze and dropped it and turned to me.

"Eva," he said. "I am grateful. I am glad you are with him. And I am sorry for all this. It was not in your job description."

I shook my head. Anything that came out of my mouth at this point would have been more dirty lies. And the only true things I might have said, I couldn't. Things like, "Don't die," or, "Don't hate me for breaking faith with you."

He stuck out his hand, just as he had done with Rikki. If I'd been a normal woman, I probably would have felt compelled to lunge into his arms for a sentimental hug. The handshake was fine, though, and much more true to our natures. And neither of us lingered over it, which was a relief because something painful was rising up in me that might have spilled over if we'd drawn it out for even two more seconds. Instead, Jan touched the edge of his ball cap and turned and walked away from us at a steady pace, not looking back, and got inside the old red jeep, fired it up, and drove away.

I looked up at Rikki, who appeared to be crushed around the edges. This was going to be even harder than I thought. He was a big kid, competent and responsible—he'd be fine on his own in Tuxtla—but still and all, he'd just watched his dad drive off into a war zone to go be with his mother who was dying. How was I going to turn my back on that one? But if I didn't, I might as well give up my search for my brother; in San Cristóbal, I was within a half day's travel to the jungle, but Tuxtla was in exactly the opposite direction. If I left now, I might never know what happened to Stefan, whether I could have helped him out, whether he was alive or dead. There was only one thing for me to do and I had to do it.

Then I thought about my photography equipment. Not just that, but all the canisters of film I had stored in the pack. K'in signs of all shapes and sizes from any number of different sites. Pages of the Chilam Balam of Mitontic. Jan's entire project, for which I'd been paid good campesino wages. Not to mention the whole series of photos I'd taken of Anne on Christmas, and the photos of all three of them in front of that pathetic little Christmas tree. I couldn't just leave without turning all that over. But if I didn't give him the cameras too, Rikki might figure out I was splitting.

People were starting to get into the vans, and he stood aside so I could crawl into ours ahead of him. This was it. I was still not sure how to break away without him following me, but as I scanned the crowd, I spotted the woman from New York trying to load all her luggage into another combi. I squeezed his arm and said, "Rikki, I'm going to ride with her. She's a mess; she needs somebody. You'll be fine with this group. I'll see you in Tuxtla, okay? And by the way," I said, dropping my pack to the ground and pulling out my camera gear and film. "You keep this for me, okay? She's got a cartload of stuff. We'll need the room in the other van."

"What?" he said, but before he could react, I stretched up as far as I could get, gave him a kiss on the chin, thrust my entire stash of beloved photography equipment plus canisters into his arms, scooped up my pack, and darted away. There was an army truck blocking the way, and when I got around it so I was hidden from him, I inched out just far enough to see what he was doing. Poor thing. He stood there completely lost for half a minute, looking for me in the crowd, then slowly picked up his pack and my gear and climbed into the van after the others. I was home free.

I waited behind the army truck just long enough to see his van grind its way into the convoy, and then I went back inside the empty Santo Tomás and talked them into letting me have a room for the night, even though I think they'd expected to close the place down.

Chapter Eighteen

Once I had a place to store my pack, I set off to find Jorge. The convoy was gone, but the streets were still full of people: the curious and the fearful, come out to see what the rebels had left behind. I cut through the plaza, where people had crowded inside the damaged government palace, craning to see what had been done, then back into the streets toward Guadalupe.

Two kids came out of a house, hand in hand, and stood staring at me. The little boy was not wearing any pants—his diaper had fallen off or never been put on—and his penis showed like a pink bud under the bottom edge of his shirt. He had one finger in his mouth and kept glancing at his sister to make sure everything was all right. I thought of Rikki in the combi headed for Tuxtla, not yet knowing he'd been abandoned.

Three blocks later I saw it, the big church rising up over the houses, the little rectory where Jorge and Fr. Martin lived. Where Stefan's bedroom sat empty. I stood looking up at the church for a few moments and then went on down the street to the rectory door and knocked.

Forty-five minutes later, Jorge and I had gotten nowhere. He had not yet been able to find me a guide and he absolutely refused to take me himself, not because he was worried about his own safety but because he was worried about mine. We sat in the living room eyeing each other with weary rage, this time him on the sofa and me on the chair, and it crossed my mind that if I weren't so angry, I'd probably feel sorry for him.

"You do not know what you are asking," he kept saying. "This is a tense time, very tense. Everything could break out again tomorrow, do you understand?"

"I understand."

"You cannot go into the forest right now. The gun battle yesterday was all in the forest. Here in San Cristóbal is the safest place to be."

"I'm not interested in safe. I need to find Stefan."

He flinched. "Do you know how the battle started? An army patrol ran into a minivan carrying some of the rebels. What if you were out there on the road?"

I'd noticed something. Every time I said Stefan's name, he reacted. I tried it again. "Jorge, just think if you were out there. If you were Stefan."

He was leaning forward with his elbows on his knees and his hands clasped together in front of him, but when I said my brother's name, he sat back up and looked away. The old clock ticked loudly. Above him was the crucifix. He couldn't lie under the crucifix.

"Jorge," I said, "what do you know?"

He still wouldn't look at me.

"Jorge?"

He sighed and got up and walked to the window. He peered out at the street for a moment, then turned back to look at me and leaned against the edge of the windowsill, crossing his arms. "All right," he said. "I got word this morning after Mass. Some friends of Mat's were here."

"And?"

"They said Mat's group is special. Like a special forces unit. Not stationed with the Zapatista army. They are separate. They have their own jobs.'

"Like?"

He sighed again. "Sabotage. Kidnapping. Yesterday night, they captured Donaldo Aguilar."

"The latifundista who killed Mat's father?"

"Yes."

"Oh my God."

He rubbed his eyes as though they hurt. "Yes," he said. "That is the correct person to call upon. God."

"Jorge. You think Stefan is with them?"

He raised his burly shoulders and let them drop. "God knows."

"Why would they kidnap Aguilar? I mean, what good is he to them?"

"Ransom. They will need important people to trade for captured rebels. They already have comrades in jail in Ocosingo and Tuxtla and maybe other places. And there will be more as this goes on."

"This is what Stefan meant in the letter, isn't it? About the assignment for Mat he was worried about? And he's been out there for two months, and he still couldn't stop it. So why should he stay any longer? They're going to do what they're going to do."

Jorge was watching me, a bit confused, maybe even a bit horrified. I didn't think like these people, these priests who love Jesus. I could see Mat pretty clearly, though, a normal young guy with normal amounts of justifiable fury who'd been saving it up for years. Now he had his prey in his hands. Donaldo Aguilar was not going up on the auction block. Donaldo Aguilar was going nowhere, except maybe to hell. And Stefan was a fool if he thought he could stop it.

"Look, Jorge," I said, "if you don't help me—if you don't get me someone who can lead me there—then I'm going out to the highway and sticking my thumb in the air until somebody, army or EZLN, I don't care, picks me up and dumps me in the jungle. You got that?"

"You are loco," he said.

"Fine. But that's what I'm going to do."

He slapped one of his palms down hard on the windowsill, harder, probably, than a would-be priest should slap something, and then pushed himself away from the window and up on his feet where he stood staring across the room at a place where two walls came together. He stared for a long time, maybe half a minute, and I thought he might be praying for advice, though he looked much too frustrated to be talking to God right then. If anything, he looked like he was thinking about punching one of his formidable fists through the wall he was glaring at. There was definitely something of a middleweight boxer in Jorge.

Finally, he turned away from the wall and back to me. He didn't look much happier, but it was clear he'd come to terms with the situation. "All right," he said. "There is somebody. Not one of Mat's friends," he added, a bit of mind reading on his part. "That would be better, but they would not do it. Too dangerous for Mat."

"Even if you told them that all I want is to see my brother?"

He shook his head. "They would not do it." Not for some gringa anyway, he was no doubt thinking but not saying.

"Then who?"

"A sick man. A bad man. A man I do not trust, though I have pity for him." He said this quietly, considering the long argument that had preceded it and the mood I'd put him in. He said it with no drama. Which, for some reason, affected me more than if there had been. That way, I could have discounted it. I felt the hair on the back of my arms rise a little.

"He lives here in San Cristóbal now, in one of the poor barrios," said Jorge. "But for many years before that, he lived in the jungle in his own hut. A white man trying to be Lacandon. They had mercy on him, a man without a family, a country, a religion. They thought he was a poor fool. He believed himself to be their brother. They gave him balché and tobacco and let him sit in on some of their rituals, the smaller ones. He fed on that for ten years, thinking he was Lacandon in spite of being white. If spite of being a drunk and covered with lice and half crazy. Then timber companies went after the trees in his part of the jungle. He tried to damage one of the bulldozers with his machete. They put him in jail in San Cristóbal. When he got out, he would not go back. So now he lives here, still a borracho, still convinced he is an Indian."

I stared at him, considering.

"This is your guide, if you want him. For money, he will do anything. Even take you into the war."

None of this sounded very good, but it would have to do. "What's this guy's name?"

"He calls himself Ah Pek, which is Lacandon for 'he of the lightning.' He does not seem to realize that this name is an offense to them. It is the same as one of their rain gods, Ah Peku, and they do not believe a man should be named for a god unless he is a chief. Surely not a white man. So they call him 'Jet.'"

"Jet?"

"Some of them are old enough to remember the first time they heard a jet airplane cross the sky over the forest. It was the beginning of the invasion of their home."

"So obviously they're not fond of him."

Jorge shrugged. "They have been very tolerant all these years."

"Take me to him, Jorge."

"You are sure?" He actually looked anguished.

"I'm sure."

Jet lived in a shanty in a neighborhood one step up from La Hormiga, the notorious slum on the edge of San Cristóbal. It was the kind of shanty where knocking on the door causes all the walls to shake, and it was in the kind of barrio where the kids never want to go indoors because their houses are falling apart. As we stood on the sagging boards of Jet's front porch, kids swarmed around us, buzzing like they'd found a brand-new toy in the dump.

By now, the afternoon was on the downslide, and even though the sky was still filled with light, it was coming at us over the tops of the trees from just above the mountains. Big cumulus clouds were piling up in the south, layer on layer, their edges etched in silver. The smoke from a hundred cooking fires rose up to them. I hadn't heard any guns for a while, just someone trying to play a wooden flute, and you'd almost think—with the gang of big-eyed kids huddled close, their fingers stuck in their smiles, and the far-off flute player, and the sun slanting down on us that way—that poverty made us all better people.

It was a nice thought, which Jet dispelled the minute he opened the door.

Lord, I thought to myself, and almost gave up the whole plan right then. He stood there barefoot in the slanting sunlight, scratching his balls through his ragged jeans and squinting out at us. His hair, which had probably once been blond, sprayed out of his head in two-foot-long matted dreadlocks. He was tall, over six feet, but his shirtless chest was caved in like a TB patient's. It would have been easier if he were old. What I was looking at was a burned-out Union Square ex-hippy who'd been on the streets for twenty years with maybe one bath the entire time. He smelled like rotting alfalfa. His eyes seemed incapable of focusing.

"Hola, Señor Jet," said Jorge politely, and stuck out his hand. Jet put out his scratching hand and shook Jorge's, while a battle, you could tell, raged within him as he tried to drag Jorge's face from the vandalized archives of his memory. "I visited you in jail," said Jorge, helping him out.

The word "jail" started one of Jet's legs bouncing. But apparently it was also the open sesame to the right file.

"*Hey*, man," he said. "How've you been?"

"Muy bien," said Jorge.

"Cool. Cool." He kept nodding as if he had a palsy, and I thought, This will never work. This guy couldn't find his way across the road, much less around the jungle. Meanwhile, the kids had crowded even closer, not afraid of our man Jet, and in fact seeming to expect that if they stood there long enough, there'd be something in it for them.

"Señor Jet," said Jorge, "this woman is called Eva. She is looking for somebody to hire." He looked down at the kids, who were all ears. "May we go inside?"

"Sure," said Jet, who had brightened even more at the word "hire." "Cool. Come in, man." He stepped back and swung the door wider, and Jorge waited for me to go in first. The air was filled with the essence of Jet, the same rotting alfalfa small, only stronger, and through the open kitchen door you could see a horrifying pile of scummy dishes stacked on the small counter and filling a bucket of dirty water.

"Sit down, man," he said to me, sweeping a hillock of old newspapers off the seat of a wooden chair.

"Thanks," I said, and sat. Beside me on the table were things I didn't want to look at, more foul plates and silverware, empty booze bottles, a Kerr jar half-filled with slimy water and charred-looking flowers that must have been there six months at least. Two feet away from me on the floor was a cage with some kind of odiferous, chipmunk-sized animal in it, sleek and beady-eyed and disgusted. It emerged from a pile of urine-soaked newspapers, presumably to get a better look at us, and after a few minutes of steady musing, went back to bed.

Jet noticed me noticing the cage. "That's Uo," he said. "She sleeps a lot." Then he grinned, displaying teeth that were decayed brown or disintegrated to stumps in what, by the squareness of the jaw and the curve of the lips, could have been a handsome mouth. This was someone with attractive parents, L.A. by way of Sweden. What a waste.

Jorge, who was standing off to the side with his arms folded, was clearly hoping Jet had given up all active employment. Or perhaps that the image of his nemesis, the bulldozer, hacked up but still running, and the memory of his jail cell were still present in his mind, and he'd refuse to go back to the jungle. I was almost hoping the same.

But Jet was obviously intrigued by our visit, and by me in particular. "So," he said, "what's this about a job?"

I held out for fifteen more seconds, locked in a silent but fierce debate with myself about whether or not to really go through with this. There didn't, however, seem to be any other way. "I need to get to the Lacandon jungle," I said. "I'm looking for someone there."

"Who?" Jet was staring at me, goggle-eyed.

I swallowed. Was I really going to hand the burden of my lost brother over to this loser? "It's a priest," I finally got out. "He's with the rebels."

"*No shit.*"

"No shit," I said.

"He's *with* them? As in the G.I. Joe routine?"

"Of course not," said Jorge, who had moved as close to the open window as possible. "Most armies have chaplains. Why not a rebel army?"

Jet laughed. "Come on, man. A chaplain? The Zapatistas?"

"Why not?" I said. "What do you know about the Zapatistas?"

"Well, they ain't Baptists, I know that much. They ain't carrying around the Bible. Mao's *Little Red Book*, maybe, but not the fuckin' Bible."

I looked at Jorge.

"That is not necessarily so," he said to both of us. "Think of the priests in Guatemala and El Salvador who supported the rebels' cause without picking up a gun."

"G.I. Joe priests," said Jet. He seemed pleased with himself, as though he'd scored big on some TV game show. "Priest-os desperados," he added, trying out the sound of it. "So where is this dude?"

"With a special forces unit."

"Special forces. Whoa."

"My guess," said Jorge, "is that this particular group is in the Laguna El Suspiro area."

"El Suspiro," said Jet with sudden seriousness. "That's two mountain ranges away."

"But there are roads?"

"Dirt tracks up to the edge of the jungle. And the rebels will have every damn one."

"What about the other way?"

"What other way?"

"So how do we get through?" I asked him.

"We?"

"If I hire you?"

Jet suddenly got a crafty look on his face. Now we were talking turkey, or as Rikki would say, kutz. This was where the money came in. "Hire me to do what?" he said casually as though it didn't matter a whit to him one way or the other.

"To be my guide. To get me to"—I looked at Jorge—"Laguna El

Suspiro. To hook me up with the group."

He put on a somber expression. "You're talking major danger, man."

"How so?"

"A special forces unit? They'll blow us up before we put one foot near that lake."

"I don't think so."

He shrugged. "I ain't interested in dying."

"Then don't die." I gave him my most aggressive glare.

"*Whoa*," he said, and glanced over at Jorge, a man-to-man, bitch-on-the-rampage kind of glance. Jorge, knowing which side his bread was buttered on, didn't bite.

"So do you want the job or not?" I said.

Jet went into deep thought and I could see, like numbers on the cash register of his face, the various pay scales he was proposing and rejecting. Beside me, Uo woke up and scratched violently at the soggy mess of newspaper, re-forming her nest. "How many days?" he said at last.

"I have no idea. I don't know how long it takes to get there."

"No, I mean how long are you going to want to stay, once you get there?"

I lifted my shoulders. Who knew? If Stefan was there, I wasn't leaving without him, that's all I could say for sure. "You just lead me there," I said, "then you can go. I'll get back on my own."

"No way."

"I'm not worried."

"You should be. You can get lost in two seconds out there. If a snake doesn't get you, a jaguar will." He looked at Jorge and laughed.

"I've been in the jungle."

"You haven't been in this one."

"Look," I said, "don't worry about impressing me, okay? Just answer the question. Do you want the job or not?"

He fell silent for another moment. "How much?"

"You tell me."

"So, okay." He proposed an amount far smaller than I'd expected, which let me know he hadn't had a job in some time.

"Fine," I said quickly. "No problem." I put out my hand to seal the bargain. We shook. His palm was dry and calloused, like a farmer's, and he looked quite pleased with himself at the tough negotiation he had just pulled off.

"So when?" he said.

"Right away."

He took a step back and almost tripped over a chair. "Whoa," he said, putting up both hands. "I got to make some plans."

"Such as?"

He pointed at the cage. "Someone's got to feed her. I have to get some food together. And there's the caballo problem."

"Caballos?"

He gave an exaggerated sigh. "How the hell do you think we're getting to El Suspiro? We ain't driving no red Porsche, man, I can tell you that much."

"Horses? You are going to ride horses all the way from San Cristóbal to the jungle?" Jorge looked incredulous.

"Why not? We can get around the blockades that way, and from the air, we'll look like a couple of peasants."

"Not with *that* hair," I said.

"I got a hat."

"How long will it take?"

"A few days, probably. We have to cross the mountains."

Jorge started to object, but I cut him off. "Can you get them?"

"I know a guy on the edge of town."

"Well, get them, then. Tomorrow, if you can. And don't forget, we made a deal. I'm counting on you to be my guide." I'd come prepared; I pulled the roll of pesos from a pocket in my skirt and handed it over. For a moment, I thought he was going to faint from sheer astonishment at this unexpected good fortune. "Down payment," I said sternly. "Find me those horses."

"I'm the guide," said Jet happily. "Holy shit, I'm the guide."

On the way back to the hotel, I thought again about what I was getting myself into. Three days with Jet might be tougher than stumbling upon the whole Zapatista army. But there was Stefan. And now that Jan and Rikki were gone, Stefan was all that mattered.

Just as he promised, Jet had the horses by nine the next morning. Jorge drove me to the edge of town where there were small truck garden farms and cattle grazing along the edge of the pine and cypress forest. Everything looked peaceful, though I had learned last night at the hotel that a gun battle that killed a cop and thirteen others had taken place right in those trees a couple of days before. Jorge told me that a half mile further down the highway was a military blockade. He said he hoped Jet knew what he was doing. I said I hoped so too. He said we had at least seventy-five miles to cover, much of it steep terrain, and that the caballos would be skinny worthless creatures without any wind—I hoped they weren't, but understood that he was probably right. He said we would have to avoid Chanal and El Niz and especially Altamirano, which would be highly suspicious areas to the military, and that we'd have to go overland to do this, without any roads to follow. I told him I had a compass. He wished I would rethink all of this. I said that I couldn't.

The farmer we were getting the horses from was named Manuel, and he had many children, all very young, a young pregnant wife, and an assortment of barnyard animals who were quite comfortable in a domestic setting, particularly in the kitchen area of the hut. He was not there when we arrived, and neither was Jet. We sat inside on a wooden bench Manuel had built, sipping the black, boiling-hot coffee made by his wife and waiting for the two men. A big sow twitched in her sleep on the earthen floor beside us while flies buzzed around and red chickens wandered in and out of the open door, which was actually a pulled-back blanket. Manuel's wife was behind on her morning task of frying tortillas for the day, so after she greeted us and served us coffee and explained that they were out catching the horses, she went back to her slapping and sizzling.

Little kids watched us from all over the room, some of them on one leg, like storks, and some of them hanging on their mother's skirt. Surely these could not all be Manuel's children, I thought. It turned out they were not; his brother had been killed a month ago in a truck accident on the main highway, and his widowed sister-in-law had moved in, along with her kids. In this room, I calculated, must live three adults and at least eight children, soon to be nine. I wanted to ask where they had all gone during the gun battle, but that seemed rude.

After a while, Jet and Manuel came back, each of them hauling a horse no better than the ones Jorge had described. The men were sweating—they must have had to chase the animals—and the horses looked distinctly reluctant, barely managing to clear the ground with their clumsy, untrimmed hooves. In their winter coats they were as shaggy as dogs, which at least disguised their jutting ribs. Jorge turned to me and said in that anguished voice of his, "Do not do this."

"I have to."

We got up from the bench and went out to greet them, the kids flowing around us like a river. Jet was clearly relieved to see me, as though a paying job might have turned out to be a pipe dream after all, and gave me a grin that showed all his bad teeth. "Look, man," he said, and pointed skyward. "Just like I told you." Sure enough, he'd stuffed his filthy lion's mane inside a straw cowboy hat, the same kind Manuel was wearing, the kind you saw on campesinos all over Mexico. He was also wearing the white pants and white shirt of a working man, though the pants came halfway up his calves. I didn't think he'd fool anybody—he was much too tall and skinny—but I didn't exactly look like a farmer's wife either, in spite of my sandals and skirt. We'd just have to take our chances.

"Very snappy," I said.

Manuel, who must have spoken a little English, smiled under his own hat brim. I wondered if he'd ever see his horses again.

It took an hour and a half to get loaded up, mainly because of all the kids in the way, but by 10:30 we were swaying along a small track in the forest with me turning and waving back at the disconsolate Jorge and the receding hut with Manuel's entire double family standing in front of it. Jet was ahead, which was fine. I'd rather be watching him than have him watching me. I hadn't been on a horse in a long time, but it doesn't take much to get used to them again, except you know you're going to have trouble walking after the first day, and that it will be worse on the second, and even worse on the third, until it can't get any worse and starts getting better. The saddle, an old-fashioned, high-pommelled affair, didn't help in that regard, but at least it had a horn and some strings to hang bags from. Which is what we were carrying now, part of the peasant outfit. All my earthly goods, not much without the camera equipment, had been transferred out of the gringo pack and into woven pouches for the journey.

The forest path was soft with crushed pine needles, and the horses soon found their rhythm and settled in for the long ride. The sun came down through the big trees in long beams of yellow light, and you could hear the wind, though it wasn't much yet, moving through the boughs. From our right came the sound of a stream running over rocks.

In fact, we were moving parallel with the stream, the track following its curves. Jet's lanky body, obviously unused to horseback riding, jackknifed with every step. Today he seemed disinclined to talk, which was fine with me. We had a long way to go. But I knew this was the easy part. We were in the mountains, out of the way of the fighting, though maybe not so safe if fighter planes came over the ridge.

The saddle complained, and my horse, a mournful roan with a patchy coat and a roached mane, rolled the bit around in his mouth and flicked his tail at the flies, sometimes snapping me in the back of the ankle. On we went, climbing steadily, while the sun got higher and hotter and the horses began to sweat under their burdens. I had my skirt twisted around my legs, as close to pants as I could make it, but still I could feel the salt from my own sweat starting to make red, hot places on the inside of my thighs.

I was thinking about Jan, whether he'd made it through or not, whether he was there with Anne by now, and what was happening in Palenque. I was thinking about Rikki, what he must have thought when the gringo convoy arrived in Tuxtla without me, and him with all my equipment. I was thinking about what would happen if I found Stefan and made it back, if I showed up at the yellow stucco house one day to reclaim the tools of my trade and see how everyone was doing—what they would say to me. If I'd still have some kind of place in their lives. I would in Anne's, I knew that, even though I'd left her only son on his own in the middle of a revolution. She, at least, would listen and try to understand. Rikki too, probably, though I was sure he was plenty worried about me at the moment. As for Jan, I couldn't say. He'd told me that he hoped I had enough respect for him not to lie to his face. Well, I *had* lied to his face. Which might mean no more friend.

I was surprised at how sad that made me. How purely sad, as in the grief when someone you love and count on dies and you are left, once more, on your own. I hadn't had that experience of pure sorrow at the end of a relationship before. I'd been hurt, true, when Robert called it quits. My biggest investment of the heart up till then. And I had been angry, or conversely, relieved, when the rest of that motley crew—Alexander, Peter, the USIA man, those strangers in between—moved on, as I always knew they would. That was how the game was played, and everybody knew the rules.

But a friend was a different thing. Someone who helped you see who you are without having to slam the door behind him, who could point out those gaps inside of you, the rotted planks you're in danger of falling through into the black hole at the center of yourself if you don't look around. Maybe I needed, more than most, someone who could do that for me. Because look at the family I came from.

Jet and I rode along through the pines, and the scent of them was sharp and resinous in my nose. I thought about my pregnant grandmother on a sunny morning in Croatia, taking a day off from her eight-year-old son in order to visit her friend. She must have loved that friend a lot to make that lonely walk, knowing, as she probably did, that it was dangerous. By the end of the day she was dead. When they shot her at the edge of that ravine, they no doubt thought that she was just another peasant, nobody who mattered much. But look what that murder set in motion.

Tonight, I determined, I would finally reread the letter from the box. The story Stefan had been carrying around by himself all these years.

By 5:00 we were in the mountains with a cold wind blowing. Somewhere in the valley to the south of us had to be El Niz, and though I could see that the brilliant green valley floor was a patchwork of small cornfields and banana trees, the village itself was invisible. Whatever thatched farmer's huts were scattered among the corn below blended into the landscape as well. We'd been on the trail for almost seven hours, and the horses had not only cooled down, they were shivering from sweat and fatigue. Jet said we should stop before it got too dark to make camp, so when we came upon a sheltered spot among the rocks, we climbed off the animals with great difficulty, got them unpacked, and waddled to the nearest tree to tie them up before they could lumber, saddleless, back down the mountains to Manuel. Then we sank down on separate rocks, both beat, and tried to work up the energy to get organized.

In spite of the sharp wind, it was a beautiful evening. The sun, mango orange, was setting over where I knew San Cristóbal must be, firing the thunderheads to the north with coral and flamingo pink. Below them lay the dark, folded mountains, covered in pines. Hours before, we'd heard distant gunfire, again from the north near Ocosingo, but now, except for the soughing of the wind, everything was quiet. A hawk turned above us in the pink sky.

I had my single-man pop-up tent along and thought about setting it up just to have a way to zip Jet out if I needed to. But even though we were in the rocks, we would be visible to any nosy Huey helicopter that took the hawk's vantage point. Better not to risk it.

Jet roused himself and went off to find an armful of wood for a cook fire. I was of two minds about that—the smoke could give us away—but we needed a real meal. I looked around for a way to make myself useful. Luckily, we didn't have to worry about the horses; even though the vegetation was getting sparse, we were still below the tree line, and there was plenty for them to eat. They strained at their lead ropes to get at the thickest clumps of grass.

I got off my rock and starting unpacking the bags we'd hung from the saddles: food, the cook set, utensils, matches. If Jorge were right, I might be within two days of seeing my brother. After the ground we'd covered during the day—probably twenty-five miles or so—we were fewer than fifty miles from Laguna El Suspiro. Jorge had heard from his sources at the parish that the main body of the Zapatista army was nested further south, in and around the jungle village of La Realidad. Mat's special forces unit was purposely keeping its distance in order to be able to operate independently. If Jorge's sources were accurate, and if Stefan were still alive, then El Suspiro was where I would find him.

How would he react when he saw me? I hadn't let myself think about that before. Would he be angry?

I didn't think so. But I knew he'd be upset. I was putting Mat and the rest of the unit at enormous risk, not to mention myself. Somebody could be following me. I could be picked up by the military at any point. The guys in the jungle were holding an important hostage, and I could be leading the army right to them. Stefan, being Stefan, would be thinking of that first. And then would come the arguing, me telling him that he had to come back with me, him telling me he was staying. If he were alive, why hadn't he already walked out on his own if he wanted to leave? I didn't have a clue how I would pull it off.

Suddenly, the horses' heads went up, their ears flicked forward, and then I heard somebody coming through the rocks. Jet, I hoped, but maybe not. I drew back into a crack in the granite, pulled out my boot knife, and waited. The horses lifted their heads higher, drinking in the wind, and then, after a few minutes, went back to cropping grass. I strained to hear the sound of footsteps over the rhythmic grinding of their teeth, but whoever it was seemed to have stopped. Whoever was there was standing on the other side of the boulder I had tucked myself into, out of my sight.

I am at my best under threat. Everything slows down and becomes intensely clear. My breathing gets light and efficient. I am stronger and filled with infinite patience. If need be, I can wait forever.

This time, though, waiting would have been silly. If someone were stalking us, I didn't want him to linger until dark to make his appearance. If Jet had gone completely feral on me and was lurking behind the rock to hammer me on the head, then that would be good to know as soon as possible. Given either scenario, cowering indefinitely in a cold crack of granite was not going to do me much good. I fingered the knife blade to remind myself how to thrust, then launched myself from my hiding place in a direct line for the horses, who plunged sideways, snorting and wild-eyed, as they saw me coming.

"Whoa," said Jet, stepping out into the open. "It's just me. What the hell are you doing?" I caught the tail end of his left hand tossing something behind him.

I stood behind one of the horses, watching him, deliberately holding the knife where he could see it. I didn't say a word.

"What are you doing?" he repeated plaintively. "What are you packing that thing for?"

I shook my head at him and bounced the knife a little, letting him think about things. He stood staring at me from fifteen feet away, and I studied his expression, trying to decipher what he was up to, but all I could pick up was hurt bafflement.

"You are one weird chick, you know it?" he said, and the hurt was not only on his face but in his voice as well. "What did I ever do to you?"

"What'd you throw away, then?" I said in a hard voice. "Show it to me."

He made a disgusted, oh-so-that's-it gesture with one hand and heaved a dramatic sigh. The last of the sinking sun turned his dreadlocks to gold, though the sudden flare of beauty didn't impress me one bit. "A fuckin' joint," he said. "That's all. A little mota for the road."

"Show me."

"Shit," he said. Then he turned, lanky and irritable, and went back around the rocks and picked up something, holding it up and pointing at it with his other hand as if I were too stupid to see for myself. It was a joint. No doubt about it. A sloppy-looking joint. I'd interrupted a man about to have his evening toke.

"Sorry," I said, and let my knife-holding hand drop down to my side.

"You're crazy," he said. "Shit."

I shrugged. "I've been in some tight places, is all."

"If that priest is anything like you . . ."

"What?"

"He's probably a fuckin' rebel general by now."

One of the horses, not the roan but the shabby bay that Jet rode, butted me in the thigh, and I smacked her hard on the nose, which got the other one all stirred up. They both backed off with their eyes rolling and their heads going up and down like pumps, whuffling things at one another through their nostrils, and you'd think, to look at them, I'd just administered twenty lashes. "You're not very good with animals either," Jet said accusingly.

"Anything else?"

We glared at each other in the dropping twilight. He gave first, which was usually how it went. But for once, this little victory didn't do much for me, only made me feel smaller and colder and meaner than usual. So I wasn't even good with animals, was I? I guess because I didn't keep some stinking rodent in a cage like he did. Well, the hell with him.

That night we slept as far apart as possible, me on one side of the rocks, him on the other. Our little set-to had spooked me enough that in spite of Jet's cranky objections, I nixed the cook fire after all. The last thing we needed was some stray asshole in a helicopter deciding to make a target of us. I thought briefly of the letter before I rolled over and went to sleep. Not tonight, not in this mood.

By midmorning of the third day we were two miles from the village of Las Tacitas, which meant we were getting close to the edge of the Lacandon forest. The horses were worn out from the long climb and descent, and it was much hotter at this elevation than it had been in either San Cristóbal or the mountains. We were also getting low on food. Jet thought we should go into the village, where he claimed to know people, and get ourselves some lunch and some information. I wasn't sure. All morning we'd heard bombing, some of it close by, but most of it in the general direction of San Cristóbal, and the rat-tat-tat that could only mean strafing from the air.

Toward noon, a Bell 212 helicopter came whacking across the sky, and even though it was not close enough for us to be visible from our hiding place in the trees, my guess was that the villages near the edges of the jungle were under watch. From here on in we would have to be very careful. Finally we decided that I would stay put, and Jet would go into Las Tacitas on his own to see what was happening. If he didn't return in two hours, I was soloing the rest of the way.

I didn't much like the idea of splitting up, but I had a bad feeling about Las Tacitas for some reason. Not so much for Jet's sake but my own. And I'd learned to trust that kind of hunch over the years. "You go," I said. "I've got some knitting to catch up on."

After three days on the trail together, you'd think he would have developed a sense of humor about how badly we got along, but he still hadn't forgiven me for the "Rambo attack," as he called it. Apparently, because of his years among the Lacandones, he was used to being treated with a great deal of patience, a virtue I did not possess. Looking at him, his horrifying hair, his conviction that somehow he'd been set apart from the rest of the world, made me depressed. With a bath, two hours at the barber's, a new set of teeth, and some safari clothes, he could pass for one of the guys I'd shared tents with over the years. Born to be wild. But I couldn't afford to cut loose from him until we found the rebel camp. And I was counting on the fact that since I wasn't paying him the balance of his fee until then, he couldn't afford to cut loose from me either.

We'd been following yet another stream, so after Jet headed off for Las Tacitas, I tied up the roan and went down to the bank to watch the water flowing by. This was not a fast, bright stream like the one high up in the mountains, but a slow, shallow watercourse, green with algae speckled gold by the sunlight through the trees. In the shade it wasn't as hot. I sat for a while with my back against a rough tree, watching the water and listening to the horse ripping grass from the ground. It was the first time I'd been alone since the morning of the attack—actually, the first time in almost six weeks for any length of time. Alone was my natural state, or had been for years, even when I was with somebody. But that had all changed with Team Bource.

The bark was scratching my back, waking me up to the fact that if I were going to reread that letter, now was the time. I needed to get as clear as I could about what was driving Stefan so that when I finally caught up with him, I'd have half a chance of swaying him. He had to know that I wasn't simply there in my old role as his bossy little sister—that I was a person who thought about things too. Otherwise, we'd just revert to our old roles and I'd get nowhere with him. I rooted around inside my bra until I'd found the letter, damp with sweat, then pulled it out and spread it open in my lap. It was, hands down, the worst news I'd ever gotten, and I wasn't keen to read the whole thing again, but if I were really as close to Stefan as I thought, and if he were really alive, which was in no way guaranteed, then I needed to get my mind wrapped around it, no matter how horrible it made me feel.

Significantly, it bore the same date as the unsent letter to Jonah, the day, I conjectured, when Stefan realized he was really going to head for the jungle and not come back unless Mat was with him. Or unless something happened to detain him.

I'd gotten a lot of letters from Stefan over the years, and he'd always tried to keep them breezy and light, in deference, no doubt, to my superficial nature. What was the point of laying his convoluted theological theories on the likes of me?

But this one was different. The tone was different. He didn't want to write me this letter, maybe even more than I didn't want to read it. In a sense, it constituted his last will and testament to me, if that's what it came to. This was something he thought I needed to know, no matter how unsettling or devastating.

Dear Eva,

If you are reading this letter, then you have done what only you would do: come down to Chiapas to find me. Which means I've been gone a while, long enough for people to become alarmed. Which is probably not good. And which is why I feel obligated to leave you the box and this letter. Maybe I should have told you all this years ago, but I couldn't see why. I've found a way to live with it. Not just live with it, but in a strange way, make it the central reality of my life. A touchstone that helps me stay connected with what is. I don't know how you'll handle it, but I've decided I don't have the right to bury this story with me, if that's how it all works out. He was your grandfather too.

The thing in the box is called a srbosjek, or "Serb cutter." As you can plainly see, it's a curved blade strapped to the hand with a leather half glove, designed to make killing speedier. This one belonged to our djed, who spent World War II working at one of the divisions in the Ustaše-run Jasenovac concentration camp in Croatia—one of the only known death camps outside of Nazi Germany—called Stara Gradiška. The inmates were mostly women and children: Serbians, Jews, gypsies. Hence the euphemistic family tale about Milo working in a kid's camp during the war.

They don't know how many people died there. They've confirmed nearly 13,000 but there may have been a lot more. Something that distinguished this camp from the others in the same system was its cruelty. They specialized in starving victims to death, or starving them, torturing them, and then strangling them with piano wire. They also did medical experiments on children to see which kind of gas was the most effective. One of these "experiments" wiped out 2,000 kids in a few hours.

In late August of 1942, some of the guards made a bet: who could kill the most people with his bare hands in a timed event? The guy who won, using a simple butcher knife to cut the throats of some 1,300 prisoners, was awarded a gold watch, among other crass and inconsequential things. The most notorious of them all, however, was the camp commandant, a defrocked Franciscan friar called Miroslav Filipović-Majstorović, aka Father Satan, who specialized in the use of the Serb cutter. Our dad, fifteen when Djed was assigned the job at the camp, no doubt met him. Because I'm pretty sure Bruno's first job was not a paper route.

How did the two of them, Bruno and Milo, make it to America after the war? A Franciscan seminary in Rome became a conduit for Croation émigrés, never mind whether they happened to be war criminals. The choice must have seemed simple: Croatia under the Ustaše was a staunchly Catholic country, and Tito's Communist Partisans were atheists. And so our grandfather and his traumatized son arrived in Chicago, thanks to the generosity of St. Silvan's, and took up their new life.

Did you ever wonder why Bruno was so anti-religion, given what the Church had done for him? Father Satan may have had something to do with that. Did you ever wonder why he got so agitated when Djed began pouring out his heart to me? He was totally paranoid about his tata being arrested, however many years later, as a war criminal.

I don't know how we survived it, Eva, but we did. When Djed began to confess all this, I thought I couldn't stand it, and that's when I went off the rails. I wanted to die. Thank God for Fr. Anthony, who'd been an Ustaše captain during the war before he repudiated the fascist insanity. He's the one who kept me going. I hope you will go see him when you leave Chiapas.

So why did I hang on to the srbosjek? Believe me, I thought more than once about throwing it into Lake Michigan. But then it came to me that there was something sacred about it. Something holy. In some way, impossible to explain in this letter, it has become a holy artifact for me. When I take it from the box, which I do every year on the day Djed killed himself, the blood of every person who died under that knife cries out to me. Not for revenge. Not even for justice. Instead, to be made meaningful, to become a sign of the love of God, even in the middle of hell.

I want you to know that for many years now, almost every decision I've made, including the one that brought you here looking for me, has come out of my prayers for Djed and his victims. This srbosjek has become the crucifix for me. I'm sorry, however, that this is the only legacy I have to pass on to you.

Be well. I love you, Sister.

Your Brat

Once again, my blood was running icy-cold, fiery-hot. And my stomach was in major rebellion. Thank God Jet rode up right then, fast, with his cowboy hat in one hand and his dreadlocks flying free. He looked like somebody in a movie, and he was pretty caught up in the scene he was shooting, too caught up to notice the expression on my face. I jumped up and waved, then made a half turn away from him, ran a palm over both cheeks, just checking, and took a couple of wobbly breaths. The letter was already back under my shirt. Yank yourself together, I told myself. I could not afford to be weak and sick around the likes of Jet.

He reined up in a cloud of dust, the bay looking bewildered at all the sudden action. "Eva," he said breathlessly, still on the horse. "I almost got snuffed. You're lucky I'm still here."

"What happened?"

"The Indians. They had guards posted outside the village. Look at this! They took a swipe at me with a machete." He held out one skinny arm and let go of the reins long enough to pull up the sleeve of his white shirt, which I could now see was stained with blood. "Damn," he said, fascinated. "Would you look at that?"

I stepped closer to the horse and peered up at his arm. It was a mess, but that could have been because of the dirt mixed in. And sometimes the most superficial flesh wounds can look the worst, especially if there's much blood. "Hurt?" I asked

"Shit." The word was emphatic, but still full of fascination. I couldn't tell if he was in pain or simply caught up in the drama of it all.

"Maybe you should wash it," I said, gesturing toward the algae-infested stream. "Then we could tell better."

He glanced at the water, then back at his arm. "I don't think so," he said. "You want me to get gangrene or something?"

I shrugged. If he wanted to ride the rest of the day with an arm that was starting to smell like a butcher shop, that was his business. But I didn't want to run into whoever had done this to him. "What happened?" I said. "What ticked them off?"

He looked amazed then, as though it had only just occurred to him that nothing had gone as planned. "I know people in that town," he said, shaking his head. The bay took a step backward and he reined her in. "I figured it was fine."

"Did you know the guy who cut you?"

He shook his head. "Never saw him before. But it was a kid, so what the hell. Maybe he was too young last time I came through these parts."

"Did anyone else see you?"

"Hell, yes. People came running out from everywhere when I yelled. All of them swinging machetes. I kept yelling out 'Ah Pek,' and finally somebody woke up and figured out who I was. They wanted to take me into the village and clean me up, but I was afraid someone might come out here and find you. So I said no, I was just looking for information about where the army was."

"And?"

"They told me about Ocosingo." He said this calmly, not panting anymore, and using his bad arm to settle his hat back over his dread-locks. Good, I thought. The arm can't be that serious, then. "Could you hold her a minute?" he asked me.

"Sure." I stepped forward and took the bay's bridle in my hand, low down by the bit. She didn't like it—she wasn't a mannerly horse, I'd noticed—but she put up with it long enough for him to climb down off of her.

"Whew," he said. He was holding his arm as though it were in a sling, crooked and tender. I saw him glance at the green water again. It would be cooling at least.

"What about Ocosingo?"

He turned back to me. "Twenty-five people, plus a baby, lying in the street. Five with their goddamn hands tied behind their backs. Gunshots in the back of their heads."

"Executed."

"You got that right."

"What about the baby?"

"They don't know."

I thought about this. On-the-spot executions by the military. No wonder Las Tacitas had attacked Jet. They had to be terrified. It was like kerosene running in the streets, ready to ignite.

"What did you tell them you were doing here?"

"Well, shit, what do you think the San Cristóbal cops did, first thing, after the rebels pulled out? Went house to house, that's what, rounding up anyone with any kind of Lacandon jungle connections. That's why I had to split."

"And they bought it?"

"Well, it's true," he said defensively, squinting at me from under his brim. "They sure as hell did."

"Okay. Where did you tell them you were headed?"

He pulled the bay's reins over her head and walked her over to where the roan was obliviously chomping grass. "There," he told her. "Stay put." Her head went down so fast I could hear the bit jangle. Jet came back to where I stood, giving the stream a look of horrified longing. I knew it was only a matter of minutes before he'd have that arm plunged in up to the shoulder, the algae cooling him off like a nurse's sponge. "I told them," he said, "that I was heading back to my place in the jungle. My own little hut. They'd heard of me, and it made sense to them. It's what they would do if they could. Not sit out here waiting for the helicopters or Humvees to show up. So they let me go."

I knew it was probably a hopeless question, but I asked it anyway. "Did you get any food?"

"Bananas. And some aguacates, believe it or not. Some pan dulce and a stack of tortillas."

"Good job."

"Well, look what they did to me."

The funny part was, Jet was so indignant that I knew he wasn't after sympathy. He simply wanted acknowledgment. Look at my fuckin' arm. So I nodded solemnly. It didn't cost me anything. And suddenly we were on better terms than we'd been the entire trip.

"You think you can ride with that?" I asked him, knowing he could, he was probably fine even if he didn't realize it, but also knowing it was going to be up to him.

"Sure I can." He glanced for a third time at the sluggish water. "I'll just give it a little wash up before we get moving."

So I stood by, watching as he took off his bloody shirt, pulling the one sleeve gingerly over the knife wound and then cradling his arm over to the water's edge where he stood for a minute, still grossed out by the green slime. Then, with a grimace, he got down on his knees and laid the arm horizontally in the water, all the way up to the armpit. I don't think I could have done it, not in that much algae, and Jet's stock climbed a little higher because he had.

He swished it around for a bit, gritting his teeth, then asked me for the bloodstained shirt, which he balled up and dunked down in the water, then used to slop away at the wound, clearing it of blood. I leaned in close, smelling him above the sluggish stream, and took a look. Like I thought, it wasn't as bad as it had appeared with all the war paint on it. Long, but shallow. Whoever hit him with the machete was trying to scare him, not cut off his arm. I said, "You'll live."

"I know I'll fuckin' live," he snapped irritably. I don't think he liked me standing over him that way, looking healthy when he was feeling so woozy right then. "Hey," I said. "I'm sorry I let you go off alone that way. Maybe they wouldn't have gone for you so fast if you'd had a woman along."

"Don't count on it.

"Well, anyway." I flipped the braid back over my shoulder and looked around for the food, which was still tied up in a net bag hanging from the saddle of the bay. I was starving. "I'll rustle up some lunch," I said. "And then, if we're going to go, we'd better get moving."

"No problema," he said, still irritated with me. One thing about Jet, though: his brain was a bit of a sieve. Besides the grudge for my Rambo attack, nothing lasted long in there. Two hours from now, he'd have forgotten this entire conversation. Two hours from now, I'd probably be leading his horse while he slept. Two hours from now, we'd be very close to El Suspiro. The thought was starting to send jolts through me.

Chapter Nineteen

It took us longer than two hours to reach the lake. In fact, once we hit the jungle, we found ourselves lost for the first time in three days. I knew by my compass that the lake had to be nearby, but the sheer wall of green was disorienting. It became clear that we could no longer afford to stay off the tracks; there was no way to penetrate the dense foliage short of clearing our own trails with machetes we didn't have. Suddenly, everything got tense. We knew that whatever footpath we took could lead us straight into an ambush, questions asked later.

If we could even find a footpath. I hadn't been in heavy jungle since Tikal, and I found myself wishing my companion were Jan or Rikki instead of the melodramatic Jet. It didn't help that Jet himself seemed somewhat overwhelmed. "You've been in this neck of the woods before, right?" I asked him.

"Kind of," he said. "My hut is a ways from here, over by Lacanjá. I used to go more southeast from Las Tacitas to get there." He bent over his little map, a scene he'd been replaying for the last hour or so. His map did not look very official; from two horse-lengths away, it appeared to be nothing more than a hasty pencil drawing on a piece of yellow legal paper. "There's supposed to be a chicle route right around here, like a footpath. But who knows if it's still here."

"What do you mean, 'who knows'? Don't you know? Isn't that why I hired you?"

"Look, man, a track like that can grow over in two weeks if no one's using it. It used to be here, is all I can say."

"Isn't it marked?"

He turned to give me a look, his saddle squeaking. The bay swiveled her ears to keep track of the conversation. "With what? A traffic light?"

How could I have ever worried about zipping Jet out of my tent? Less chemistry between two people there had never been. "Look, Jet," I said. "It's obvious we're lost. We can't afford to be lost. We can't be wandering around in here when it gets dark, for one thing."

"You're telling *me*?"

"So how do we find this path?"

I'd never met anyone before who so literally put on his thinking cap when you asked him a tough question. Jet pondered with his eyes closed for half a minute, and I feared he might have dropped off. Then the lights went on and he gave me a big, tobacco-colored grin. "No problema," he said. "We let the horses find it. Horses always pick the easiest route."

Not having any better ideas, I shrugged and clicked to my roan, who stepped disdainfully around for a few minutes, sniffing the air, and then flicked his ears forward and lumbered, according to my compass, south. "Should I pull him up?" I called to Jet over my shoulder. "Aren't we going the wrong way?"

"Let him go," he called back. "I'm behind you, man."

Green fronds laced with water lashed against me, and I ducked down and held one arm over my face while the horses plunged ahead. I could hear things racing away from us through the trees, flapping and scuttling, and the distraught cries of birds. We'd stirred the whole pot, and if anyone was sitting there, waiting to pick off trespassers, we were dead. Or if a víbora got upset. There were also poison frogs, spiders so big they wore spelunking lamps on their foreheads, worms that burrowed under your skin and made giant boils . . .

Suddenly, we were gallumping along a thread-like trail, my roan so excited to be out of the undergrowth that he couldn't control his exuberance. I reined him in, and Jet almost ran over me. We were both panting, as happy as our horses to be out of that nightmare of green, and it took a minute for everyone to calm down. The horses stamped and jingled and shook their ears, their skinny ribs heaving, while a toucan, looking like a Frenchman with a big green nose and a yellow bib, sat staring at us from an overhanging branch. It didn't take long for us to sober up, though. Now that we were on a footpath near Laguna El Suspiro, we were moving targets and we both knew it.

"You got any plans about this?" I asked Jet.

He shook his head.

"You speak any of the Maya dialects?"

"Lacandon. A little Tzeltal. That's it."

"What if they're something else?"

"Well, hey, we don't look much like the ejército, you know. They've got to know we're not military."

Occasionally Jet said something wise. We would surely be surrounded by masked men with rifles very soon, but unless somebody shot without taking a good look at us, we would probably be okay. At least until they got us to their camp.

"I think we should keep talking," I said. "Like you do with grizzlies, to let them know you're coming."

"*You* talk," he said. "Talk like a gringa."

So as we rode along, not fast, not slow, I quoted the lyrics from "Soul Kitchen" and "Crystal Ship," and by the time I got to "Twentieth Century Fox," they were on us, just two of them, but that was plenty. One stepped out of the green wall ahead of us, his ancient .22 up and ready, and the other, cradling a shotgun, materialized behind us on the trail. Clearly Maya, their dark eyes were fierce above the red paliacates that covered their faces. They didn't say a thing. They didn't have to. We reined up and each put a hand in the air, waiting. They studied us for a long time while our horses circled restlessly, and every time I found my back was exposed, I closed my eyes so I wouldn't be surprised by the darkness if a shot went off and buried itself into my spinal column or the back of my neck. It was eerie, and went on and on. All we could do was circle like fools until they'd made up their minds.

Finally, one of them came forward while the other one covered him. He stopped about five feet away and snapped out some words I didn't understand, words with clicking "k's" and "t's" in them. Mayan of some kind. Everything Rikki taught me had departed.

"He says to get off the horses," Jet muttered, "so get off."

I dismounted and stood beside my roan, holding his bridle. My hand against his cheek calmed him down, and he stood docilely by my side while the guy who had spoken came up and thrust his hand into the various bags I'd tied to the big saddle. He must have been looking for weapons, because nothing he found seemed to interest him. Then he was standing in front of me, snapping out more click words.

"Hands in the air," said Jet sharply.

I moved my fingers from the bridle to the reins and raised both hands above my head. The roan tossed his head and tried to step away from the man when he came forward to pat my sides. I closed my eyes for this, but in this too he was extremely professional, only interested, apparently, in whatever guns I might be hiding. I wondered whether he'd think to check my boot and whether I should just give up the knife voluntarily before he came across it and got upset. "Jet," I started to say, "tell him . . ." But he'd already reached for my calf, which I lifted obligingly while he worked off the boot and drew out the knife. He never even looked up at me, but hefted it in his hand as though determining its value before sticking it through his belt. Then he scooped up my muddy boot, examined it carefully, and tied it to his belt beside my former weapon, where it swung like some war trophy. I stood there unshod, hanging on to the reins with my hands still high, while he searched Jet.

Once they'd disarmed us—Jet had to turn over his Swiss Army knife—they let us assume an at-ease position, which was a relief because my arms had started to ache. Then they put the two of us, on foot plus horses, single file between them on the trail, the one in the back prodding my shoulder with his rifle until I got the idea that we were to begin marching. I just hoped that we had run into the special forces group and not some splinter of the main rebel army, because it was a long, long journey to the Zapatistas in La Realidad. We went on this way for twenty minutes or so, me limping along on my bootless foot, the monkeys following us through the trees. A wakeful kinkajou skittered across the trail.

Then the guy behind us barked out something, and Jet told me to stop. This time both of them closed in, the one keeping his rifle on us while the other took off their red bandanas and tied them over our eyes. It was strange to be blind in the jungle. I felt suddenly helpless and didn't want to give in to the feeling. Then I felt the tip of the gun again, this time in my lower back, and I went back to marching, still hanging on to the roan's reins, but stumbling along now because I couldn't see. I hoped the horse would not step on my bootless foot and break it.

Without my eyes, the jungle came alive with sound: the dense rustle of leaves, the raucous chittering of birds and the whine of the insects. It was oppressively hot, hotter than Tikal had been, and it seemed wetter here, more like Thailand. I stumbled along, thinking that it would be fitting if I did die in a jungle, considering how much of my life had been spent in them up to this point. The horses blew through their noses, and the roan switched me with his tail. I thought that I would hate to die before I saw Stefan, that it would be a terrible shame, though not really for anyone but him and me.

We walked for a long time, far too long, making exaggerated turns on the way, likely made to confuse us, and then one of our guards called out something in their language, and another man called back. At almost the same moment I smelled the marshy stink of lake water, I felt the blindfold being pulled from my face.

The rebel outpost looked more like a hunting camp than a military establishment. It was so small that it could not possibly have supported more than seven or eight people. As we were led into the tiny clearing, I squinted into the surrounding trees to see if I could spot Stefan, though I was sure it would not be as easy as that. Aside from a young woman in blue sweatpants and a green military cap who was squatting by a fire over a lump of tortilla dough, there was no sign of anyone, not even the man who'd shouted back to our guards. In the clearing were two makeshift fires with pots hanging over them, a couple of camouflaged twenty-gallon water containers, and three hammocks slung from the trees.

Our guards directed us to sit by one of the fires. The woman gave us a searching, fearless look and went back to her work. Neither of our two captors, who were younger than I'd guessed, had bothered to put his bandana mask back on. I wondered whether this was a good sign or bad. I also wondered where everyone else was. The stillness after all this buildup was unnerving. My bootless foot was aching. I wondered how Jet's arm was doing.

One of the rebels, the one who had patted me down, took the horses and went somewhere with them. We could hear their obedient hooves moving away across the underbrush and through the trees, and all of a sudden I got sad for them, which was silly. They weren't bright animals; they'd never notice the change in ownership. But still. Maybe they'd spent their entire lives in Manuel's field on the outskirts of San Cristóbal. Maybe they were used to everything the way it had been.

The woman got up without looking at us, went over to the other fire, and with her bare hand, grasped the handle of a big metal coffeepot that looked like it could blister your skin. She carried it over to another flat stone and set it down, then reached behind the stone and drew out three metal cups, army issue, and poured out the steaming brew. The smell of it struck me hard and I realized I'd pay about a million pesos for a cup of that. I didn't have to, though, for she brought them over to us, handing one to each of us including our guard, nodding when I said "gracias," but not saying anything herself. Then she went back to her tortillas.

I took a couple of burning sips, closing my eyes against the hot, delicious pain, then sneaked a look at Jet. He seemed pretty relaxed, all things considered, and his arm, which had leaked more blood on the long hike, didn't seem to be bothering him much. In fact, he actually looked happy, as though the Lacandon jungle was where he belonged after all, and it had taken this trip for him to finally put his enemy, the bulldozer, behind him. We drank our coffee, taking our time, and it was good to sit there on the jungle floor, insects and all, in the weak, shadowy, underwater green of the jungle light, watching the woman work and smelling the tortillas. An interlude. After three days in a saddle with no shower and not a lot of sleep, it was good to just sit, though I didn't know what would happen next or what awful thing I might find out now that I was here.

At last, the first guy came back and held up my boot by its laces, swinging it in the green light, and made a gesture for me to get up and follow him, as though I were one of the horses he was going to lead off and hide. I stared up at him for a moment, putting on a stupid face to give me time to think. Why were they separating us? If I were them, is this what I would do? I glanced at Jet again, who wore the same stupid expression on his face that I did, though possibly in earnest. No help from that quarter. I decided that if I were running a rebel camp, I'd probably want to question anybody who happened to show up unannounced at the front gate one at a time. They were just being logical. I got up onto my sore foot and followed the guy without a backward look at Jet, and without, I noted, any cry of protest from his side of the fire.

The footpath was so tiny I never would have noticed it. It snaked through the forest, a little rivulet of bare, soft earth with a mind of its own, and I thought it was probably an animal trail that they were borrowing. Every so often there would be a flash of blue off to the right—Laguna El Suspiro through the trees—but we didn't seem to be headed there. If I had to guess, I'd have said we were going north.

My guard, still luring me on with the swinging boot, never looked back, as though he knew I was not going anywhere. I kept my eyes fixed on his sweat-stained back and his thick black hair that needed washing. I could see the swollen insect bites on his neck. The edge of one of his ears was ragged, as though something had caught it in its teeth. He smelled like Jet. Well, camping in the jungle was not easy. I'd done it myself, but the accommodations had always been somewhat more high class. This fellow could have been out here for months—years, maybe. I wondered what he and the rest of them did for food, besides tortillas.

Whether the Lacandones, Trudi's long-haired pals in the white shifts, helped them out at all.

Some place beyond the steady ache in my bootless foot was the image of my brother's face with his deep-set brown eyes and thick, no doubt filthy hair, the same shade as mine. Was I minutes away from seeing him or was he dead after all? Had I come here only to die myself? Would it be such a huge loss if I did? Anne would be sad. Rikki would mourn me. Jan . . . who knew? It might be a relief to have me off his chore list. I hoped not, though. If I died.

These disconsolate thoughts kept me occupied for some time, and when I looked up, I realized my guard was watching me over his shoulder. His helpless, shoeless captive. Suddenly, he seemed to make a decision, walking back to where I'd stopped and thrusting my boot at me, as though to say that my punishment for carrying the knife in it was now over. I cleaned off my foot as best I could and slipped it back inside the boot. Then I stood up, testing a little. It was sore and tight, but better than it had been. We began to walk again.

After a while, we came to another miniature clearing. My guard made a "stay" gesture and left me, vanishing into the trees. When he came back, he had someone with him, a man in a black ski mask like the ones worn by the Zapatistas in the plaza in San Cristóbal, with horn-rims like Margarita's over his watchful indio eyes. This was all I could see of his face. He stood studying me for a moment, then looked at the other guy. Everything got very quiet. Even the jungle seemed to hush. Something important was being communicated in that look between the two of them that I couldn't interpret. It could have been benign or it could have been the precursor to a death sentence. I couldn't tell. All at once it felt like the moment back at the pass when I didn't know who was hiding behind the rock or what he wanted, and I had to decide: wait him out or take action. I decided I couldn't wait. "Mat?" I said.

For a second—less—he froze. His eyes behind the thick lenses locked onto mine. His breathing caught for a second. Someone else might have missed it, it was so brief, but it was the reaction I'd been hoping for. "I'm Eva Kovic," I said quickly. "Soy Eva Kovic. Do you understand me?" He narrowed his eyes but didn't say a word. Cautious. What you'd expect if this really was Mat, a young man who'd captured his father's killer, a young man leading a special forces unit. I didn't know if he'd recognize Stefan's last name. "Do you know where my brother is?" I asked as humbly as I could. "Padre Stefan? Mi hermano?" Again, he narrowed his eyes, no doubt trying to figure out how I'd found them, where the leak had been. I hoped Jorge would not pay a price for this, but Jorge knew the score. He wouldn't have helped me if he thought it would bring the wrath of the Zapatistas down on Iglesia de Guadalupe.

The silence went on for a long time as Comandante Mat thought things through. At last he gave the other man another of those eloquent looks, and my guard turned and disappeared into the trees.

The two of us stood there in the little clearing, watching each other. Apparently, he was not going to speak until something else happened, and I didn't have a clue what that was. But I knew I'd flushed them out. I'd found my brother's keepers. Whether or not they'd kept him well, I couldn't say yet. But if I'd gotten my boot back, maybe I could get Stefan back too.

Footsteps were coming. Mat did not freeze this time, but I knew he could hear them too, people moving through the forest. The foliage was so thick behind him, I couldn't see a thing. Some insect was biting my arm. The sweat was running down the back of my neck and trickling between my breasts. I felt both soggy and dizzy, like you do with malaria. The light kept moving with the shifting of the leaves. And then there he was, coming out of the jungle behind the guard, head down so that I couldn't see his face, but no matter. I would have recognized those runner's legs, that uniquely Kovic head of hair, anywhere.

My brat.

He held me in his arms for a long time, his chin resting on my head. I could feel his ribs against me and the unnatural sharpness of his chin against my scalp; as in Nepal, he'd grown very thin. Then he stood me away from him to take a look, holding on to my braid with one hand as if to keep me there in front of him. He was wearing a coffee-colored shirt and dark pants, like the other Zapatistas, and the red paliacate loose around his throat. His hair was too long and had some early gray in it. The biggest change, however, showed up in his eyes: they seemed doleful and heavy lidded, as though he never got enough sleep. "You look older," I said. "Eons, in fact."

"Thanks much." He flipped my braid up and down, then let it fall.

Mat was still keeping his silent vigil without a flicker of expression in his black eyes, but something about the tense way he stood there made me think he loved my brother like you love a father whom you respect but disagree with. Frustrated love. And that if my brother had known sadness, it didn't touch what was going on in the young comandante.

"How did you get here?" Stefan asked me. "Aren't the roads all blocked?"

"Caballos," I said smugly. "Three days over the mountains."

"By yourself?"

I told him about Jet.

He shook his head. "Poor old jailhouse Jet. I'm beginning to see how all this went. Did you leave Jorge any sense of self-respect whatsoever?"

"I did what I had to do."

"Congratulations on arriving alive, Sister." He wasn't smiling when he said this, and I could see that it was just hitting him, my showing up so suddenly in the middle of his jungle hideaway. "Does anyone besides Jorge know you're here?" he asked.

I shook my head.

"Jonah?"

"He knows I'm in Chiapas, but that's all. I called him from Palenque."

"*Did* you."

"I wanted to find out if he'd heard anything from you."

Stefan touched his forehead, grimacing. "Nobody's heard anything from me. That's the deal, right, Mat?"

"Si." The voice beneath the ski mask was as grim as the eyes, and also somewhat hoarse. I couldn't tell which of them was more tired. One thing I'd figured out, though: Mat understood quite a bit of English.

I dropped my voice. "What are you doing here?" I asked my brother.

"I'm here as a priest," he said in his normal tone. "No mystery."

"But in a special forces Zapatista camp? The Church probably thinks you've gone guerrillero on them." I was practically whispering.

"Eva, there's no need to keep your voice down. Everyone in this place knows why I'm here."

"Are you one of those liberation theologians now? Is that it?"

"You've been reading!"

"I'm serious, Stefan. I don't understand this at all. How can you just disappear like this and leave everybody behind?" What I meant was, how can you just disappear and leave *me* behind.

Stefan stuck his fingers into his hair and stared down at the ground for a few moments, then raised his head and looked me in the eyes. "Listen," he said, "I'm going to tell you, I owe you that, but I need to clear it with Mat first. I need to get it straight with him why you're here."

I thought to myself that if I were Mat, I'd be thrilled out of my gourd that Stefan's little sister had just shown up, determined to cart his persistent priestly presence out of there, but I kept my mouth shut. Better to let my stubborn brother figure it out on his own.

Two hours later, the initial joyous reunion long over, we were already at total loggerheads. I wanted Stefan to leave with me ASAP, as in the very next morning. And though Mat hadn't said it out loud, I'd been right about him. Mat and I were on exactly the same page. I knew this by the way he'd so quickly agreed to this uninterrupted sibling gabfest. Clearly, he'd figured out I was his best shot at getting rid of Stefan.

Of course Stefan himself was having none of it. And we'd been going round and round for long enough that I was beginning to suspect it wasn't going to happen. We were too much alike in our stubbornness, and from his perspective, his stake in all this was even higher than mine. No way, I told him. How could his concern for a friend trump mine for a brother? But mine, it appeared, was a lesser thing, fueled mostly by personal need (he implied though did not say), while his involved the spiritual life or death of a fellow human being. Could I possibly understand that?

I could not. Or to be more accurate, I would not. I simply didn't buy it, this life or death gloss on what looked to me like an open-and-shut case of perfectly justifiable revenge. For somewhere nearby, bound and gagged and no doubt quaking in his $500 snakeskin boots, was concealed the notorious Donaldo Aguilar, beheader of Mat's father— or at least the instigator and financier of that beheading—no doubt one of the cruelest bastards to ever walk the earth. And Stefan was there to keep Mat from wreaking bloody vengeance.

"So what if he does?" I asked wearily and for the hundredth time. "Good riddance to bad rubbish. The universe would be a better place."

Stefan went straight back to his patient explaining, recast this time in even simpler terms for someone who lacked the ability to recognize a spiritually momentous situation when it was staring her in the face. The gist was that Mat had every right to seek justice for the murder of his father, was in fact morally required to do so, but that the moment he went after Aguilar for the satisfaction of hearing him scream, he'd lose his soul.

"He'll become what he most despises," said Stefan. "The image of the man he hates."

"So what's a guy supposed to do?" I asked, trying my best to keep the sarcasm out of my voice.

More patient explanations. It seems that when you are one of the Mats of the world, i.e., someone with neither political power nor the money to hire it, and you run afoul of the powers that be, you have three choices: you can comply out of fear and wind up so degraded you lose your personhood, you can strap on the weapons and become equally degraded, or you can speak the truth and take the consequences. In other words, become a martyr. The bottom line was that all three involve death, literal or figurative.

"But the most dangerous option is to pick up the gun," Stefan said. "Not only do you wreak havoc on others but you become the very evil you are fighting."

"So—what? Just let them kick you around? Watch them slaughter babies? Aren't you being incredibly idealistic, Stefan? Given who we come from?"

This was the first time I'd mentioned his revelation about Djed. We both fell into a brief, stunned silence. At least it was finally out on the table. Not that it would change anything.

"Of course not," he said at last, his voice low. "You never watch them slaughter babies, Eva. But this is different. We're talking about vengeance here. And what I'm saying is that taking vengeance only leads to hell."

I gave a disgusted, I-give-up-on-you shrug.

He sighed in return. Just as with Padre Miguel in Palenque, I was testing his Christian endurance. But being Stefan, he simply took another tack, urging me to think through all the best war photos I'd ever seen, including ones I'd taken myself, and asking me to single out which one had shaken me to the core. Not an easy thing to do when you've taken as many as I have and studied thousands more, many of them tragically gory. But really it was no contest.

"What else could it be?" I said. "The Tank Guy. Tiananmen Square." One guy, mentally preparing himself to be rolled over by thousands of pounds of moving metal.

"Because?"

"So okay, fine," I said, letting him know he'd made his point. Refusing to fight while refusing to back down—it was striking. "But if it works so well, why don't you advise the EZLN to try the same trick?"

"I am," he said. "Because even though their demand for justice is rock solid, the longer they stay on the path of war, the faster they lose their one and only advantage."

"Advantage? What advantage could they possibly have?" The poor little ski-masked bastards. This I could hardly wait to hear.

Which launched Stefan into yet another long speech, this time about the power of innocent suffering, which made me shudder, considering our history. I reminded him that we were the grandchildren of a murderous psycho. He reminded me that it was Djed and all his evil that had brought him to this conclusion. Followed by his decision to go find Mat in the jungle.

"And a lot of good that's done so far," I said pointedly, "since now you're an accessory to a kidnapping and pretty soon a torture and murder debacle. How's all that going to fly when the army finally catches up with this gang, and you a priest? If your noble bishop is already having PR problems, just think how this is going to help."

Stefan went quiet at this point. I knew I'd scored big, and filed that away. But he wasn't out of steam yet.

"I have a purpose here," he told me. "If I leave now, all the groundwork I've laid would go with me. Because most of my success or ultimate failure here depends on what I can model to the group. Not just my words, my actions. We are in the middle of a kind of play here, but nobody knows the script. We are writing it as we act it, and one false move on my part will change the whole trajectory."

"But Mat wants you out of here," I said. Somewhat cruelly, I know, but if that's what it took to burst Stefan's bubble, so be it. "He can hardly wait for you to be gone, can't you see it?"

He went quiet on me again, and I knew the shot had gone home. Then he rallied. "Of course I know it," he said. "When you're being tempted beyond your ability to resist, you don't want somebody watching that. You don't want to be reminded of who you really are or who you are meant to be. You just want to do what you want to do and be done with it. Without me here calling bullshit on his vengeance quest, he doesn't even have to question what he's doing. He's got a unanimous go-ahead from the group. But every time he sees my face, he's reminded that it's not unanimous after all. Somebody disagrees, somebody he respects. I'm the necessary dissenter, can't you see that? I don't have to say a word. All I've got to do is be here."

Dissenter. This time it was me who went quiet. Because I couldn't ignore that, could I, not after the great k'in quest. Not after all my help-ful attempts to flesh out Jan's big theory that there were some ancient Mayas who woke up to the fact that the only way to break the endless cycle of bloodletting was for someone to raise a hand and say, hey, take another look at what you're doing here. And my infuriating, rock-headed brat was maybe going to die putting that theory into action.

But there was something else he wanted to say.

"This is not just about Mat, Eva. It's about me too. And you. The three of us know what it is to come face-to-face with evil. We've been hurt by people who gave in to it. And now we have to figure out what we're supposed to do with that, how we're ever supposed to get past it." Stefan paused. "This may sound weird, but Mat is in some ways luckier than we are. He has the man who hurt him right here. He can go in there and take a look at him whenever he wants. We can't. Most people can't. But in the end, it all comes down to the same decision anyway: whether to keep raging against what can't be changed, or to figure out how to move on."

So this was the deal, I thought to myself, knowing I should have seen it coming. Stefan was here on a forgiveness mission. It wasn't just about not killing the guy. He actually wanted Mat to ignore the atroci-ties perpetrated by this Aguilar bastard, take him by the hand, and sing "We Are the World." I shook my head and glared down at the jungle floor, not yet ready to concede defeat, to admit that my quest to talk Stefan out of his lunatic mission was completely doomed.

But he still wasn't done with me. The next thing I know, he's bring-ing up Hana and her pious, thickheaded cruelties. He's bringing up Bruno and his endless wrath. He's bringing up Djed again. All people I would be glad to never think about, much less see, again. And I'm shaking my head and backing away and saying, flatly, "No way, Brat. No way. Don't even start down that road."

So he stops. And we stare at each other from fifty million miles across that damned gulf. His eyes looking, if possible, even sadder than they did two hours before. His hair a little grayer. And in the midst of all that anguished incomprehension, I hear something un-junglelike, something clear and quiet, yet questioning—not a voice but like a voice—and immediately I know who it must be. Anne. From her wheelchair in Palenque, not knowing where I am but worried to death about me. Doing her Quaker thing.

"Oh, *God*," I say, kicking the ground. "Will all you people just fucking *leave me alone?*"

Thus ends our sibling gabfest.

Chapter Twenty

Dolores-the-cook had not waited for us to serve dinner, but as soon as we got back to camp where the others, minus Jet and Mat, were still finishing up their grub, she dug into the pot over the fire and loaded up a couple of plates with beans and mountains of hot tortillas, then poured out more strong coffee. "Gracias," Stefan told her, and she gave him a grave smile. I wondered if she was part of the special forces unit or just the camp chef. If she confined herself to tortillas or blew things up too.

It had gotten dark. The only light came from the two small fires. Nobody looked at us; nobody spoke. Deep down, I was preparing for something—soldiers bursting from the trees with Uzis blazing, or the sudden raw noise of a Huey gunship equipped with high-powered floodlights. This group had kidnapped an important latifundista, after all. Cozy as this campfire was, we were completely vulnerable.

I kept my eyes open for Mat while we ate, half expecting him to materialize again, but he didn't appear, unless he was lurking out beyond the ring of light where I couldn't see him. So far—and in spite of his obvious fed-up-to-the-eyeballs love for my brother, a state of affairs to which I could totally relate—I didn't like Mat much. There was something strained about the guy, something that bordered on the fanatical, like what I'd seen among the fundamentalist crazies of Afghanistan. A holy zeal, though in Mat's case, not for religion.

Stefan and I did not talk during dinner. There were too many ears around us, and we were all talked out anyway. I could already guess what would happen next. The morning reappearance of my trusty roan, a final hug from my rueful but relieved brother, and a long, long ride back by myself to San Cristóbal.

But then Stefan surprised me. He used the last of his tortilla to clean his plate, handed our dishes to Dolores and said, "Eva, let's take a walk."

I looked out at the impenetrable blackness of the jungle. "Out where? There?"

"I have a light."

We both got up, and once again there didn't seem to be any problem with our going off alone together. Whatever else was in effect, my brother was not a prisoner. As for Jet and me, I doubted that we were either. I was pretty sure they'd rather have us gone than have to keep feeding us.

The jungle was so thick around us, the air so blank and lightless, that my breathing got tight. The great noises of the night had already begun. I could hear the lapping of the lake close by, which meant that under cover of darkness, a thousand thirsty animals were headed our way. I'd spent enough time in jungles to know that carnivores need water just as much as ruminants. But just as I was about to raise a protest, Stefan made a sharp turn away from the water, following another wisp of a footpath for what seemed like forever but was probably no more than a couple of hundred yards, and then stopped at what looked like a pile of brush but turned out to be the mouth of a cave.

I heard the click of a rifle safety, then Stefan muttering a password, something in Mayan. With that, the guard stepped forward, someone I did not recognize, pulling the paliacate up over his face when he saw me. There was a short conversation between the two of them. A mass of rock loomed over us in the dark, but the entrance was square and low, too low for us to enter without bending over. I could just see the fluted edges of a carved Witz monster's jaws around the sides. I'd been in too many of these with Jan and Rikki not to recognize it. This was no cave but a small, probably Preclassic temple with a burial chamber deep inside, no doubt ritually "killed" like the other ones we'd seen.

I wondered who had cleared the rubble from the passageway, whether it had been robbers or if this was yet another secret meeting place for Jan's ancient conspirators. Did he already know about this one? Maybe, especially considering his friendship with Trudi, who worked for so many years in the Lacandon jungle. But then again, maybe not. Too bad I didn't have my cameras with me. I had been missing them with an increasing pang, though I was glad I didn't have to worry about them here.

Stefan entered the low passageway first, with me following. The guard stayed behind to re-cover the entrance with brush. I'd already guessed where we were headed; the chamber where Aguilar languished, awaiting his fate. I didn't want to see him, and I didn't want to be a witness to what was going to happen sooner or later. Why had Stefan brought me? Did he hope my being there would slow everything down?

Bending low, we made our way around a sharp corner and right into the guy who'd taken my knife. He'd heard our footsteps and was brandishing that stupid weapon I'd bought in Flores. If Stefan hadn't spoken quickly to him, we might have been hurt. Aguilar's presence clearly had everybody on edge.

The chamber itself was roomy, large enough to hold a small crowd. But it was just the two of us, plus Mat and Aguilar, who was hunched over in one corner, blindfolded with a paliacate, his hands tied behind him and a rope around his neck in the way the old Mayas used to tie ropes around the necks of their war captives. His ankles were bound together with leather thongs so that he couldn't rise to his feet. He was sitting quietly with his head down, a short, bulky man with his scalp showing pink through his thin, dirty hair. He didn't look much like a butcher, but they never did. You don't have to look like a son of a bitch to be one. He was breathing hard, as though the position were getting to him, or as though he were afraid. By now, he'd been in this chamber for a few days at least.

Mat sat across from him, the ski mask still in place, though I didn't know if this was for Aguilar's sake or mine. He looked up when we came inside but did not react. I assumed that this little visit had been previously agreed upon, though I couldn't imagine why he'd allow me in. Was my actually seeing the kidnap victim in the same room with my priest brother supposed to cement my lips forever? Whatever was going on here, he had a very important prisoner, a rich man good for ransom or for trade. As Jorge had said, there were a number of Zapatistas being held in jail. Aguilar could be their ticket out. Or could be if Mat didn't work his will upon Aguilar first.

For it was clear to me now that Mat had likely not left his prisoner's side, except to oversee the first meeting between Stefan and me, since Aguilar was captured. This was a prisoner who was not escaping. And for Aguilar's solitary guard, hours and hours of nothing to do but study him. Hours of imagining, in slow, vivid detail, what had taken place during that other "trial": the burning cigarettes, the careful cutting, the brutal face smiling down, taking hits, maybe, from one of the cigarettes when it wasn't being used.

"Mat," said my brother. "Cómo estás?"

Mat shrugged.

"Have you eaten? Slept?"

Another shrug.

"How about him?" Stefan pointed at the sorry heap in the corner.

"No," said Mat.

"In four days? He has to eat."

"He's getting weaker. I want him weak."

"It's cruel, Mat. You know it's cruel."

The young comandante took off his glasses and rubbed his eyes. "Si," he said. "He is cruel also."

Stefan sank down on his haunches beside Mat, motioning me to do the same. The chamber was lit with homemade candles, which guttered and smoked. I automatically scanned the walls for k'in signs, and though nothing was immediately apparent, I did see faint red lines, not glyphs but the teddy bear-eared creatures we'd seen in the burial chamber at Tikal. No doubt others besides the soon-to-be-dispatched Aguilar had been sacrificed in here. I hoped not kids. I glanced again at the bound man in the corner, who gave a shuddering sigh with a faint squeak at the top of it like a newborn chick. He seemed far away somehow, beyond pain or fear.

"Has he had water?"

Mat nodded. "A little. Enough. I don't want him dying."

Whether this was good news in Stefan's view, I could not tell. But I knew what Mat meant: he wanted to make that happen himself.

"Have you done what I requested?" asked Stefan gently.

Mat turned his dark eyes, still without the glasses, on my brother's face. "I tried," he said, "but I could not." There was a finality to that, whatever they were talking about, that I didn't think anybody, even Stefan, could miss. This did not stop him. "Do you remember the garden?" he said. "And Peter cutting off the ear of the soldier?"

"Si," said Mat thickly. "How could I forget this? You have reminded me a hundred times."

Stefan leaned in close to him, as though he might draw Mat's head to his chest, though he didn't touch him. "Mat," he whispered, "it's you. It's not him over there, it's you."

"There is justice," said Mat, not looking at him, and I thought of Jan's Chilam Balam. Justice exists. O fools and children, why are you blind?

"And without justice, there is not mercy," said Stefan. "Of course not. But what about the woman caught in adultery, Mat? Nobody was pure enough to pick up a stone. Are you?"

"It is not just my father."

"I know."

"It is what they did to us in Guatemala. El genocidio."

"The genocide. I know. I know."

"It is all the years of them crushing us under their boots. Raping our women. Killing our babies. The pinche, bastards."

None of this was loud, but under his blindfold and in his stupor of hunger, Aguilar was listening. I could see the skin jumping around his mouth. He wasn't making any baby chick noises now, but I'd never seen a more pathetic sight. In a minute, he'd be peeing his pants, and for the first time ever, I wondered whether Djed had done that before he stepped off the stool beneath the tree in that Chicago park.

"Those babies," said Stefan, very low, "have the power to transform us."

Mat made a violent motion, as though to ward him off. "I am sick of this," he said harshly. "I have something to do."

"Sick of what? Tell me."

"Sick," he said, and his eyes were burning like the candles, "of your fucking Christ. Your god hanging there like a slave while they spit on him. What good does he do us? He cannot even save himself."

"*My* Christ?" said Stefan. "*My* Christ?"

"We had our own gods before they came and killed our ahauob and burned our books."

"Oh, Mat. I've never heard this out of you before."

"Before the white man brought his Christ to us to teach us to be better slaves."

"Mat. What's happening to you? Think. Don't let it carry you away."

"I know what is happening," said Mat fiercely. "I know. I am finally seeing things. I was blind as that bastard"—and he pointed toward Aguilar in the corner—"but now I see. We follow your Christ and what do they do? They shit on us, that is what they do. You want me to join Las Abejas, so . . . what? So I can watch them get slaughtered like sheep during one of their stupid demonstrations? Here in the jungle we are becoming men. You cannot stop us, Stefan."

"Your Christ, too, Mat. The same for all of us."

"So they can trample us."

"Then they trample us all, Mat. Not just you."

The young comandante gave a bitter smile—I could see it in his eyes—and said, cold as death, "You are a fool if you think that. A stupid, rich gringo."

I held my breath. I watched my brother shrink into himself for a moment. The man in the corner moved, stirred out of his daze by the tension rising in the chamber.

"I love you, Mat," said Stefan, and then there was a shout far down the passageway, a familiar voice that took me a moment to identify. Jet.

And right afterward, two shots.

"Oh, God," I said, and without thinking got to my feet to run out to him, and Stefan, trying to protect me, scrambled up and pushed me behind him as we stumbled toward the passageway, forgetting all about the guard, who was crouched, waiting with the knife for whatever might come bursting toward him. As Stefan slammed against him, putting out his hand in reassurance, the guard pivoted and struck, just an instinct, like anybody would do. Behind us from the chamber I heard Mat shout "No!" but it was already done, a sharp, whoofing sound coming from Stefan as my knife from Flores went into his belly, and me reaching for him from behind, his own arms cradling himself as he turned to me in surprise. Then his sagging body, me holding him up as best I could, calling for help, and the two of us buckling, locked together in some macabre sibling tango, till we went down onto the rough, cool floor of the passageway. I could feel his warm blood spreading over my chest and stomach. It felt like all the blood in his body, and I knew that he could bleed out in minutes if I didn't do something fast.

For just a second, holding my brother's weakening frame, I glanced into the face of the guard. I watched as he took in what he'd done, pushing his knife into the belly of a priest. If he lived a hundred years, he'd never forget it. I hoped he wouldn't, anyway. What he did to a good man. And then it clicked in again: Stefan was dying, would die, unless I did something fast. What had they taught us about stab wounds? Because I knew they'd trained us on that, they would have had to, people still used knives and machetes in some of the places photographers got assigned, and the AP was tired of losing war correspondents to incompetent first responders. They wanted us to be able to keep each other alive if we got shot or bombed or stabbed, at least for long enough to get help.

As gently as I could, despite the violent shaking of my fingers, I disentangled myself and struggled to my knees, then took as good a look as I could get in the dim light of the passageway. He was conscious, at least, if perplexed, and his eyes were locked on mine. I put a fake smile on my face and pushed back his thick hair. "Stefan," I said, "can you hear me?"

He nodded and tried to smile back at me. I put a hand on his forehead, then ordered Mat, who was huddled trembling on the floor beside me, to go get the candles. While he was gone, I put my ear down by Stefan's throat. He was breathing, and it was good and steady. No bubbling sounds. In a moment, we had light, albeit wavering, and the two of us—Mat calmer now because I was calmer, my preternatural focus kicking in—got Stefan uncurled from the fetal position he'd bunched into and carefully peeled away his shirt. We needed to see the wound. Thank God the guard had yanked out the blade as soon as he had realized what he'd done. If it had still been in him, we'd have had to leave it there, I remembered that much, because who knew how much blood would follow. At least this way we knew what kind of flow we were dealing with.

Which had to be staunched as quickly as possible. "Give me the knife," I said to the quaking guard. "Now." Which he did, and I cut a long swath from the bottom of my peasant skirt that I folded into a large pad and pressed hard over the wound. It looked like the blade had gone in beneath the stomach, which was bad. Other bits and pieces of the training were coming back to me—like how, weirdly enough, people often survive a direct stomach wound, but anything in the abdominal area below is another story. Sometimes the bleeding stops more quickly than you'd expect, and the person seems to recover, then dies a few days later of raging infection. Because it's pretty damn hard to miss the intestines when you stick your blade into someone's belly.

Stefan was trying to say something, but his teeth were now chattering so hard I couldn't understand him. Shock. He could die of it. "We've got to warm him up," I said sharply to Mat and the guard. "Whatever we can wrap him in." Mat turned without a word and headed back for the chamber, and in a moment was handing me a wool blanket, his own, no doubt, as I could not imagine him providing such a thing for Aguilar. Together, me using one hand while I kept the other firmly pressed against the peasant skirt compression, we lifted Stefan's torso off the floor long enough to tuck it around him. Without letting up on the pressure, I tried to gauge the volume of blood flow. It was slowing, or at least seemed to be. No artery, thank God. But he'd already lost so much.

Mat, who by now had pulled off his ski mask, had Stefan's feet in his lap and was chafing them and murmuring something I couldn't understand. Even though I wanted to kill him—if it weren't for him, Stefan wouldn't be here in the first place—I was absurdly grateful for the gesture. The young guard, way too young for all this, was crying and trying not to show it, crouching uselessly nearby. "Go get water," I said. "Now," and he raced off, glad for something to do. Stefan, I noticed, had stopped his violent trembling and was calmly, if silently, gazing up at me. "Talk to me," I said. "What's your pain level? Give me something between one and ten."

He pondered, everything seemingly in slow motion for him, and then said in a weak voice, "It's not that bad. You would think it would be, but it isn't. Kind of strange."

I vaguely recalled something they'd said about knife wounds to the gut. "Does it feel like you got your wind knocked out of you?"

"That's it," he said, sounding awed. "And my arms and legs are like wet spaghetti."

"Shock and blood loss," I said. "Neither of which will necessarily kill you. Stefan, you've got to concentrate now. Can you do that?" I was leaning over him, holding his eyes with my own, checking for those signs you learn to check for when death is close. But even though he looked exhausted, on the verge, in fact, of blacking out entirely, his eyes were clear and focused, and he was obviously still tracking.

"This is what you have to do, Stefan. You've got to be incredibly calm, incredibly relaxed. You've got to just focus on resting. You can go to sleep if you want, but before you do, you've got to drink as much water as you can. Do you understand? Lots of water."

He nodded obediently, while I calculated how long it would take the young guard to race to camp and get the water back here before Stefan passed out on me. I looked at Mat, who was kneeling beside me and looking remarkably youthful and unspoiled without the ominous pasamontaña over his face. So far, whether out of shock or guilt or incompetence, he hadn't issued a single order; in regard to Stefan, he'd handed over leadership to me. "We've got to get him into a larger space," I told him. "But he's got to be under shelter. And we can't move him far or we'll start up the bleeding again."

He thought this over, then said, "We must carry him into the chamber," which really was the only possible option, though I could not picture nursing my wounded brother right next door to the bound and gagged and slowly starving Aguilar. Just then the guard returned with the water and a tin cup, and Mat lifted Stefan's head so he could drink while I kept pressing on the wound. After a while, when we thought we might get away with it, the three of us eased him backward through the passageway to the torture chamber where Aguilar was cowering, fully awake, in the corner. "Can you get him out of here?" I said to Mat, jerking my head in Aguilar's direction, and for the first time since Stefan was stabbed, Mat's nakedly suffering face closed up and hardened. He didn't answer.

Once again, I felt like killing him—was I really going to have to watch my brother die in front of the asshole responsible for all this?—but then I felt my own self hardening too. That shield that came down on me when other people freaked out and started thinking with their emotions instead of their heads, and it was only a matter of time till they settled down and finally started listening to me. "Whatever," I said, shrugging. "Suit yourself, Mat. You're in charge, right?"

He winced at that, and for a moment I saw it from his side: a possibly dying priest, murdered under his watch, a kidnapped latifundista hog-tied in the corner, a gringa from who knows where witnessing the whole thing firsthand, and his own command of the situation slipping away fast. I might have felt a little pity if I hadn't been so exasperated with him.

But in the meantime, Stefan was starting to go groggy on me. I crouched down to listen to his airway: still clear. I laid my palm on his forehead: cool, but not cold, thank God, and his teeth were no longer chattering. I checked the bandage, which we had tied around his belly using more strips from my now considerably shorter peasant skirt. The blood was still leaking through, but much more slowly than before. He didn't look great, but he didn't look like he was in danger, either. More like he needed a good, long nap.

The question was, how to get him through the next few days without him developing infection. Because we couldn't know if the knife had pierced an intestine or something else. We couldn't know if he were bleeding internally. We had to get him to a hospital. But how? There was no way he could sit a horse for the long journey, and every other way out of this place involved military roadblocks and ongoing gun battles between the Zapatistas and the ejército. I had to think, I had to plan, but I also had to keep him alive. And how in the world was I going to do that?

Then something came to me. "Mat," I said. "I need to see Jet. The gringo. Can you tell your guards to find him and bring him in here? There might be a way he can help." If he hadn't been shot.

I could see him thinking this over. Yet another witness to the kidnapping, not to mention the attempted murder of a priest. He looked more than reluctant. "Mat," I said. "Please. Please. He's my brother. I'm trying to save him. Please."

"Si," he said then, and went out of the chamber and into the passageway, where he talked with the guard. Pretty soon I heard the guy moving off down the passageway and Mat coming back in. "The soldier at the entrance shot at him," he said, "and he ran away. We do not know where. But they will look."

"Thank you," I breathed. "Gracias. Muchas, muchas gracias."

He moved his hand then, a dismissive but shame-filled gesture, and I saw that the look of deep private pain was back on his face. Whatever else was going on with him, one thing was clear: if Stefan died, he'd be devastated. And this, no matter what else I thought of him right then, put him solidly on my team.

We waited for Jet, the walls around us flickering in the light of the homemade candles. My tired mind mused again over what else had gone on in here throughout the centuries. Who had been sacrificed, who had been buried with ritual pomp and circumstance, who might have met here to plot the overthrow of kings.

I wondered what Aguilar was thinking. If he had any idea what was going on, if he cared at this point about anything but himself and his own skin. If all this was a temporary reprieve to him, nothing more, if he was grasping at how to prolong whatever it was that was happening. Did it bother him that Stefan was lying wrapped in a bloody bandage? Stefan, who'd been trying to save him? I doubted it.

I gazed down at my brother, who had sunk into a deep sleep. Which was good, I hoped. Between the blood loss and the shock, he had to be completely bushed. Sleep was healing. Let him sleep.

Except that he looked dead. If it weren't for the slight rising and falling of his bare chest, he could easily be dead. He looked that peaceful, that disconnected from all the shit of the world. He might be dead soon, and then what was I going to do with that? How would I go on without my brother to back me up, without Stefan's unwavering devotion to me? It was the only piece of evidence, when it came right down to it, that I was worth a single damn thing.

I thought about those letters of his and how he'd always searched and sought and tried to figure things out in a way I never felt inclined to. No. "Felt inclined" made it sound like I'd actually considered putting my mind to work on life's big questions, which I had not. My excuse had always been that he was the smart one and I was the tough one, and never the twain did meet. But that was all bullshit. Self-deceiving bullshit that he saw right through, the thing that made him saddest but made him love me all the more, pathetic mess that I was. For the first time since the mayhem in the passageway, I felt my eyes filling and turned my face away so Mat could not see.

If Anne were here. Or Rikki or Jan or even Jonah. Maybe I could bear it then. I took a couple of shuddering breaths, fighting to save the dam from collapsing entirely, and then I felt it. A tentative hand on my shoulder, warm and sad, which in another moment or two I reached up and touched with two fingers, which helped. The priest in Mat that Stefan was trying to save, momentarily showing himself. And there we sat, waiting for the guards to come back with Jet until it crossed my mind that he'd never come back on his own. The guard had shot at him, and it was up to me to talk him out of wherever he was hiding.

"Mat," I said dully, "I've got to go myself. They'll never find him. Will you sit with Stefan till I get back?"

He looked at me for a moment, assessing my face for signs of weakness or strength, then nodded. "I will stay with him." Both of us glanced toward Aguilar in the corner, who had his face turned toward us.

"Thank you," I said, and struggled to my feet, amazed at how exhausted I was. Mat reached up and handed me his flashlight. "Gracias," I said again, then headed out of the chamber and through the passageway and into the jungle.

Chapter Twenty-One

As it turned out, Jet was not so difficult to locate. I had a feeling where he might be—as close to where they'd taken the horses as he could get—and so I made my way back to camp and followed the trail down which the roan and the bay had disappeared earlier that day. As soon as I began calling his name, he answered back from somewhere in the underbrush, scared-sounding but relieved at the same time. "Whoa, man," he said, clambering out to meet me on the path. "I thought they shot you in there. They sure as hell tried to shoot me. What did you do?"

I shone the light in his face, and he put up a hand to shield his eyes. "Hey!" His dreads, I took note, were covered in jungle-floor trash, and there was a major bug ambling down one side of his head, which of course he couldn't feel under all that stiff grime.

"Show me your arm. The one they cut with the machete."

"*Hey*," he said. "What the hell are you doing? Stop trying to blind me."

I lowered the beam, then played it over his wounded arm. "I need to see that. Right now."

"Okay, okay, don't go all Rambo on me." He was fumbling with his sleeve, then pulling it up to expose the forearm. I took his wrist and pulled it closer, holding the light right on it. It was still a fairly fresh wound, true, but it was long and could have easily gone nasty after all these hours in the heat under that filthy shirt of his. But it hadn't. It hadn't.

"Jet, I need your help," I said. "It's an emergency, do you get that?"

He was peering down at me with a querulous expression on his face, a skinny scarecrow in dreadlocks, but the word "emergency" seemed to put some metal in his spine. "What's happening?"

"I'll tell you later," I said, "but right now we need to get back to camp and grab whatever pot or kettle we can get our hands on, you got that?"

For a second, I thought he was going to snap me a salute. But then, "I can't go back to camp. They tried to shoot me."

"An accident, Jet. I swear. They won't shoot at you now. I promise."

And so we went, the two of us stumbling back down the thread of a trail by the bouncing light of the flashlight, and when we got there, I went straight up to Dolores, who handed me a couple of pots as soon as I asked, and then we were off to the lake where I hoped we would find what I was looking for, but who knew? And even if we did, would it be the same species? Because some of them, I'd heard, were toxic, and that's the last thing we needed to do to Stefan right now, poison him on top of everything else. Soon our light was bobbing around the marshy edge of the lake, the greenish water looking thick and maybe even salty, which would be a good thing, I guessed. I hoped. Then Jet spotted it, and we loaded up our pots and made our way to the temple and through the Witz monster entrance, the guard having long since given up on the password, and then we were down the passageway and into the chamber.

Mat looked up when we came in. I tried to tell by his expression whether Stefan was still alive, but I couldn't read a thing. Or on Aguilar's face either, whose head was now cocked fearfully and pathetically toward Jet, who for his own part was gaping around in childlike wonder. I set my pot on the floor and sank down on my knees beside my brother. Still breathing peacefully. No more blood leaking.

"Jet," I said without looking up. "Sit down. Don't ask any questions. In fact, don't say a single thing, okay? We don't want anybody shooting at you again, do we? I'll explain everything later."

Maybe it was the veiled threat, but he folded himself up without a word and sat by while I gingerly untied Stefan's bandage, thereby breaking Rule Number One regarding stab wounds to the belly, and lifted the blood-soaked pad from his abdomen. The hole immediately began to leak again. This was going to have to be fast, so without wasting another second on the should-I or shouldn't-I dance, I reached in the pot and scooped up a slimy handful of blue-green algae and trickled it into the wound, then spread more around the outside and pressed the pad back into place before the faucet turned fully on. Stefan did not stir. I retied the strip holding the pad in place and rocked back on my heels. Mat was looking at me.

"This might make him a whole lot worse," I said, "but what are we going to do? If it doesn't kill him, it might actually keep him from getting infected. It's called cyanobacteria, and some of it has antibiotic properties, or at least that's the theory. They're trying it out against certain plant diseases. I shot a story on it one time." It took me a minute to realize that I'd lost Mat. What English he had did not apparently extend to scientific terminology. But Jet was suddenly acting like a kindergartner who needed to go to the bathroom but had been told to sit quietly and not raise his hand. "What, Jet?"

"I know some of this shit! From living around the Lacandones. There are plants out here they use for stuff like stomach aches and snakebites and shit like that. They make teas out of bark and leaves."

"How about against fever?"

Jet put on his famous thinking cap. Mat, Aguilar, and I sat waiting. Then the light dawned with a radiance that was something to see. "Guatipil palm," he almost shouted, then looked around guiltily as if guns were about to go off in his direction. "Guatipil palm," he said again in a more normal voice. "You skin a piece of the stalk and chew it. Or make tea. I can't remember."

"Do you know what it looks like? Could you find me some?"

A confused look passed over his face. "Maybe," he said. "I mean I only saw it used once." There was a long silence while we all digested this sad fact.

Then, very quietly, as though it cost him more than he could ever say, Mat offered, "I know what it looks like. I know where to find some. I will get it for you." And without looking once at Aguilar, he took the flashlight from me and headed down the passageway.

As soon as he was gone, Jet said in a stagey whisper, "Who's that dude in the corner?"

"Never mind."

"Why's he tied up like that?"

I was leaning over Stefan, checking his skin color. If the cyanobacteria turned out to be the toxic kind, you would think something would be showing up by now. "I'll explain later."

"How long's he been here?"

I sighed and turned to look Jet in the face. "A few days," I said. "They kidnapped him when the war broke out. He's a hostage. Are you satisfied?"

"But the dude looks bad. Want me to feed him or something?"

"Oh, God, Jet, just leave it alone, would you? I've got enough on my hands here." I turned back to Stefan, who was still sleeping the sleep of the dead. What I was thinking was this: if he survived the night without any obvious negative effects from the cyanobacteria, I'd smear more into the wound, and if we could keep him from getting infected for the next, say, three days or so, then maybe he had a chance. Maybe he could make it through the critical period. After that, it became a question of when he could be moved and how to get him out of the Lacandon jungle and into a proper hospital.

First, however, Mat brought back the palm, plus handfuls of hierba santa leaves which he had blistered over an open flame back at the camp to use directly over the wound. Overnight and into the next day, we boiled teas from wild cloves and ginger and various kinds of bark the Lacandones used for inflammation and pain, and we lifted Stefan's head to sip them. We made him drink constantly. We wouldn't let him move, even when he began to hurt and get restless.

Meanwhile, Aguilar waited silently in his corner, gradually weakening from hunger and neglect until, two days after the knifing, Jet could not stand it anymore and brazenly arrived in the chamber with a plateful of beans and tortillas and a pot of hot coffee, announcing that he was taking over the prisoner. Mat, by now fully engrossed in keeping Stefan alive, did not so much as object, and I could see that he was sick to death of Aguilar, did not know what to do with him next, and only wanted him to vanish forever.

"Mat," I said in a low voice, "it's time to send Aguilar down to La Realidad, don't you think? They could use him there. I'll bet they could spring a bunch of people from jail with a big guy like that to trade."

A few days after that, with Stefan still touch and go, Mat finally gave it up. Whatever quest he'd been on and whatever he'd planned for Aguilar was over. The guard who'd shot at Jet, plus Jet himself, who by now had become inexplicably attached to his silent but grateful charge, were elected to transport the prisoner down to rebel headquarters. Three Zapatista horses were marshaled, presumably from the hidden corral in the jungle that was housing the bay and the roan.

Mat and I briefly left Stefan's side to bid the group adieu. Aguilar's hands were bound and tied to the saddle, and the guard who had stabbed Stefan was leading his horse. You could see Aguilar had lost some weight, but all in all he looked all right, considering. Throughout his long ordeal, he'd never said a word—never tried to cut a deal, never once begged for mercy. Maybe he knew from the start that none of that would help his cause. Maybe he knew without being told that it was all up to Mat, whether he would do to him what Aguilar deserved or do something else entirely, something illogical, like never lay a hand on him the entire time. In any case, Aguilar gave away nothing, not even as they left the camp and turned the horses south, and I thought to myself, still a bastard, you bastard, even though I had to admit I was glad it had turned out this way.

Jet, always another story, turned at the last, ripped his hat from his dreads, and waved it in the air like a rodeo king before settling back in the saddle for the long ride to La Realidad. Which I guess meant he'd miss Mat and me, or at least thought the two of us were worth a final gesture. His plans, he'd informed me, were to return afterward to his hut in the jungle where he intended to study up on Lacandon medicine.

As Stefan grew visibly stronger and, as best as we could tell, peritonitis failed to set in, we began talking seriously about how to get him out of there. It was then that I remembered the phony passports, still in one of the peasant bags I'd brought from San Cristóbal. The hard part was convincing Mat that Stefan and I could make use of the army without implicating his group in the process. "We are gringos," I kept insisting, "and when we show up at the closest roadblock we can find, we'll say we were visiting temples in the jungle with a tourist group from the States and our combi got filched by the Zapatistas, so we were lost and walking for what seemed like forever. And then we found some horses loose on the road, but my brother fell and hurt himself, so we've got to get to a hospital fast."

He finally agreed, though it wasn't until we were actually leaving the camp, Stefan looking terrible but able to crawl onto the back of a horse, that I understood what was really going on—Mat wanted to come with us. He was done with being a rebel comandante. He wanted to come back to whatever kind of life he'd been leading under Stefan's tutelage before all this began. I could see that as plain as day, but there was nothing we could do right then. My brother and I could not afford to present ourselves to the military accompanied by a Maya from the selva. But I could also see that Stefan, still out of it as he was, realized what had happened with Mat, and that when he was recovered, he would move heaven and earth to get his friend back where he belonged.

The day my brother and I finally left the jungle, we had no way of knowing that the ejército had signed a cease-fire with the EZLN twenty-four hours before, and the roadblocks we were counting on did not materialize as soon as I'd hoped. But eventually we came across a truck full of soldiers who never even asked to see our phony passports and who drove us back to San Cristóbal, where Stefan, after some blood work and a CAT scan that confirmed he did not need surgery after all, would spend the next couple of weeks in a hospital bed with multiple IVs in his arm. As soon as we got all that settled—my brother was healing, he would not die—I told him I had something I needed to do and that I'd be back in a few hours.

Then I left him there in the hospital and headed to Na Bolom to pick up the box and the letters I'd hidden in my room.

I spotted the old red jeep on the street before I saw anything else. And it was as though I'd been holding my breath for weeks and could finally let it go. They'd come for me. They did not hate me for abandoning them.

The taxi dropped me before the wooden courtyard doors, and I got out and walked inside, slowly, because I was suddenly as weak and shaky as Stefan. Jan must have been in the office and seen me through the glass, because before I was halfway to the veranda, he'd come hustling out, then stopped when he saw how bad I looked. How utterly and completely wiped out. When he began to move again, it was carefully, the way you'd come up on a wounded animal who'd been driven off and terrified and half killed and then, by a miracle, found her way back again.

I halted five feet away from him. He pushed back his red cap and gazed at me with those Dutch-blue eyes of his. I was too glad to see him to say anything. Maybe glad was not the right word. "Eva," he said, "what happened?"

I shook my head and walked into his arms. Not the arms of my brother or a lover but the steady embrace of a friend. "He made it," I told him, my voice muffled against the old blue work shirt. "We got him out and he's in the hospital and the doctors say he's going to be okay."

"Oh, that is wonderful," said Jan into my hair. "I am so glad to hear it. But who are you talking about, poor girl?"

"My brother," I said, and began to cry, the kind of weak, weepy, relieved sort of crying that comes when you've been trying to carry a burden way too big for you for way too long.

Later, when I had mopped myself up, he went inside to explain to people what had happened. I didn't want to see any of them, but instead went to my old room, which was unlocked, and over to the bed where I'd left Stefan's letters between the mattresses. For a moment, when I stuck my arm inside, I thought they were gone—and then I felt the edges of the packet and drew them out. They were all there, his letter about the goat in the pond and the wisdom of the French dude, the one about seeing the world through ecstatic eyes, the whole strange and wonderful universe of my aggravating, beloved brother. I had another little cry sitting there holding them.

And then I got down on my knees and reached under the bed, all the way to the back, and pulled out the box. As far as I was concerned, I never wanted to look inside it again, but I'd promised Stefan I would bring it back to him. His holy artifact. His own private crucifix.

When I had everything together, I went out and waited for Jan by the jeep. Together, we went to Iglesia de Guadalupe and told Jorge everything that had happened. Then we drove him to the hospital to see Stefan, a reunion that was something to behold. I told Jorge I had no idea what the Church was going to do with my brother, but that I hoped they would take him back, and Jorge said, almost crying, that he hoped they would too, and that he would also do his very best to help Mat return and to keep him from being prosecuted as a rebel and a kidnapper.

Then I talked to the doctor, who said that he thought Stefan would be ready to be discharged after the two weeks was up if there was a place he could go to keep recuperating for a month or so longer, which of course there was.

And thus, finally, the three of us—Jan, me, and my brother—returned to Palenque and the little yellow stucco house. And thus the two of them came face to face, she in her wheelchair, he still too thin and too pale, my friend and my brother. And as I suspected it would be, it was like watching two siblings who'd been separated at birth, meeting at long last.

Later that year, Stefan and I flew home to the States. Chiapas was still in turmoil when we left—the army violated the cease-fire only two days after signing it, and counterinsurgency groups, all pretending to be working for the cause of the indigenas, were proliferating like flies—but Bishop Ruiz's work on behalf of the poor went steadily on despite the confusing web of lies and counter-lies. The pacifist Las Abejas continued to stand firm. The Zapatistas, too, decided to put away their weapons—they'd made their point—and it was now a matter of garnering global support for their cause, which they handily did, thanks to the left-leaning Mexico City newspaper *La Jornada*, not to mention a brand-new phenomenon known as the World Wide Web. The handsome subcomandante, of whom I'd taken so many photos in the central plaza at San Cristóbal, was well on his way to becoming a rock star.

Stefan and I landed in California and drove up the coast to see Jonah, spending a few days walking and talking and sitting on redwood benches overlooking the sea. The monks were overjoyed to have my brother among them again, especially the few who'd known about his disappearance. Stefan went to daily Mass, and we had noon meals in the refectory and good wine in the moonlight with Jonah. And we got ourselves adjusted to the idea of what was coming next.

Chicago was easier with the two of us together. Bruno and Hana had visibly aged, which was no surprise considering how long it had been since either of us had seen them. Hana was ecstatic, crying and gripping Stefan as though to never let him go. Bruno was—understandably—more guarded, especially around my brat. But both of our parents were obviously blown away by our sudden reappearance in the middle of their lonely, bitter lives.

Stefan had been reinstated in the diocese before we left Chiapas, so he only had a week to spend in the bosom of the family. I, on the other hand, was now in between jobs, as in out of a job. Jan was spending the next months compiling his field notes with my photos in preparation for finally writing up his grand Maya Conspiracy Theory, so my services were no longer needed there. The k'in sign I'd hunted around for and found in Stefan's temple, faint but unmistakable, would have to wait till more peaceful times. I was done with war zones, but the next career move was anybody's guess. All I knew was that I needed something beautiful for a change. So the day before Stefan returned to

Chiapas, I rented an apartment near the Art Institute, thinking I'd give myself the rest of the year to reflect. Thinking I'd finally have some time to spend among the kind of photographs that had first inspired me.

Naturally, this meant I was completely available to Hana and Bruno, a thought which had at first filled me with horror. But Stefan was sure I would be okay. That a woman who'd been thinking clearly enough to smear blue-green algae into a knife wound could handle a couple of aging Croatians. So I decided I could.

What kept me going through those first long months without him, months filled with Croatian eating-fests at St. Silvan's and consultations with the doctors about Bruno's carotid artery and Hana's diabetes, was the knowledge that after Christmas, I'd be going back to Mexico. I was spending next year in Palenque with Anne. Because even though Jan and Rikki were both with her now, the two of them in shifts the way it should have been for a very long time, they were going to need more help soon. Maybe, between the three of us, not to mention Felice, we could keep her in the little yellow stucco house for a while longer than anyone expected.

Because that's the way it is, isn't it? Things are never what you'd planned on. They startle you into tears or knock you sideways with how beautiful they are, showing you you've never got it straight, no matter how many facts you string together. Persuading you, in the end, that the world is probably better off without you running the show.

Sometimes I find myself thinking of the jungle and its strange, underwater light, impossible to photograph and filled with a thousand mysterious implications. As though whatever is in there, screened off behind the green fronds and sudden floods of warm rain, is more real than anything you can see with the naked eye.

And then I raise a finger to my chest and touch the water lily.

Acknowledgments

This book was not an easy one to write. Though my research came from many sources, for information about the Preclassic and Classic Mayas, I relied heavily on Linda Schele and David Freidel's wonderful *A Forest of Kings: The Untold Story of the Ancient Maya* and Michael Coe's equally fascinating *Breaking the Maya Code*. René Girard's theory about the primeval roots of blood sacrifice came from several of his books, but mostly his *I See Satan Fall Like Lightening*. Stefan's descriptions of sacramental theology come in large part from Hans Boersma's amazing *Heavenly Participation: The Weaving of a Sacramental Tapestry*. The facts about the New Year's 1994 Zapatista uprising, which began the day after my husband, Mike, and I made a ten-hour bus ride from Palenque through the Lacandon jungle, came from microfiche newspaper accounts of the action as it unfolded during that week.

I am very grateful to Greg Wolfe, editor of Slant, who asked me to send him this novel and who spent a lot of time and energy asking me the kinds of questions that spurred a total rewrite. I am also grateful to Wipf and Stock for taking a chance on a new literary imprint like Slant. Words cannot express the depth of my gratitude to Julie Mullins, copy editor extraordinaire. Many thanks are also due to Caitlin Mackenzie, who has handled all the publicity for this book.

And finally, to my loving husband Mike—may God bless you and keep you forever for so cheerfully carrying both your load and mine during the long months I was locked away in my studio working on this novel.